The Mother Gene

For Karen,
My best to you!
Lynne

The Mother Gene

LYNNE BRYANT

atmosphere press

This book is dedicated to those who make the
messy,
complicated,
boring,
anxiety-provoking,
what-the-hell-was-I-thinking,
life-changing,
wouldn't-have-it-any-other-way
choice to mother.

CHAPTER 1

Miriam

CHARLOTTESVILLE, VIRGINIA
MAY 29, 2010

The University of Virginia Rotunda glowed in the buttery light of a balmy May evening. Dr. Miriam Stewart snagged a glass of white wine from a passing uniformed waiter and forced herself to sip it slowly. She pasted on her networking smile for members of the Preston Foundation Board of Trustees and honored guests. Charlottesville's elite were gathered to celebrate this landmark accomplishment in her decades-long career. *Chin up, Miriam. You're about to receive a multi-million-dollar grant. You can make a little small talk.*

Dr. Dennis Patterson had agreed to be her plus-one tonight, bless him. All these years of friendship, how could he refuse? Actually, he could have. But, thankfully, he didn't. He'd caught her deep-breathing earlier, when he opened the car door, handing his Mercedes keys to the eager parking valet.

"You okay?" Concern sparked in his brown eyes.

She stepped out of the car and grasped his hand. "I owe you big time. I know you hate these things as much as I do." She kept her voice low.

"Hm. Maybe I'll plan to attend a charity ball or two in the

fall. Bring you as my date." His lopsided grin said he was being sarcastic, but her eyes widened anyway. Dennis continued, "But we'll talk about that later. For now, I have to say, Walt did a fabulous job. You look beautiful." He gave her an appraising look. She smiled, feeling more relaxed. He could always boost her confidence.

Walt—Dennis's partner—had picked the dress from the classic standbys she kept stuffed in the back of her closet. She'd much rather be wearing her usual lab coat, button-down shirt, and slacks. She reached up to check the diamond-studded clip holding her wavy silver hair in place and quickly lowered her hand. Walt's voice rang in her head, "Stop fidgeting with your hair, Mimi."

When they'd entered the rotunda, Dennis had detached to circulate. He'd agreed to get her in the door, but she'd insisted she didn't need babysitting. Now, after several sips of wine, she cast her gaze about, trying to choose someone to start a conversation with. Ugh. She was beginning to rethink her position on Dennis staying by her side. He was so much better at these things. She nodded and smiled as she passed several well-wishers—fellow physicians, CEOs, philanthropists—all accompanied by their spouses. She hadn't meant to end up alone. But there had always been so much to do. And now? Now, she was facing retirement... old age... obsolescence.

The wine hit her empty stomach, and she wished she'd remembered to eat something. The mingled scents of expensive perfumes and colognes tended to make her nauseous. She glanced at her watch. Another hour until dinner. Her hunger was replaced by instant irritation when she realized she was still wearing her work watch—antique brass, wide face, leather band. She'd forgotten to change to the white gold one Hugh had given her for her sixtieth. Well, Hugh wasn't here, was he? The pinnacle of her career and he was gallivanting about somewhere in Africa. But—she reminded herself—*you didn't invite him.*

She searched the waiters' trays. Surely there were some kind of fancy canapes. This was Virginia, after all. Dennis, who had apparently made the rounds once, appeared at her side. Relief rushed through her, followed by gratitude. He held out a small china plate with three elegantly designed hors de oeuvres. "How's the mingling going?"

She bit into something that might have been caviar and shot him a look as she chewed.

"Mm hm. Just as I thought," he said.

"I'm getting there. Takes me a minute. You know that." She munched on a second delicate bite—this time something with olives on a crostini—while stepping slightly behind Dennis's tall frame. She surreptitiously removed her work watch, opened her evening bag, and dropped the watch beside the cell phone nestled inside. Out of habit, she glanced at the screen. Blank.

A nudge from Dennis snapped her back to the moment. "Incoming dignitaries."

Miriam brushed breadcrumbs from the corners of her mouth and tried to look poised as the Chairman of the Preston Foundation Board, Dr. Albert "Buddy" Preston, Jr., approached with his daughter, Rachel, her arm linked with her husband, Beau Howell.

"Why look, Daddy, here's our guest of honor," Rachel announced. Mindful of an unspoken protocol, Miriam reached to shake hands first with Buddy Preston.

Miriam still couldn't get past the irony. The grant she was about to receive was funded by a man she'd only ever known as Rachel's dad. Preston's medical career had moved well beyond the small Staunton practice of Albert Preston, Sr.—his father. Buddy had built a financial empire from investment in pharmaceuticals.

"Miriam, dear. Good to see you." Preston's smile was as

charming as she remembered. He wore the patrician features of an old-money Virginian. Early eighties, tanned skin, a full head of white hair. Even the gold-handled cane he used was stately. Miriam flashed back to her teenage years when Rachel's parents had seemed so elegant and refined compared to her own. Her father, a country carpenter; her mother, a mountain midwife. Both born and bred in the holler, as they called it. How Dr. Preston had intimidated her in those days with his pronouncement, "Now, listen to me, Miriam. Medicine is not a field for women."

She'd never forgotten Rachel's response, either. "Oh, Daddy, leave her alone. She's the smartest girl in our class." Rachel's choices might have completely flummoxed Miriam over the years, but somehow their friendship had remained an unbroken thread.

After high school, they'd gone on to Mary Baldwin College together. That was when things had started to change. Their first year, Miriam read *The Feminine Mystique* and her worldview had exploded. Rachel had joined a sorority and started planning her wedding. Rachel wanted marriage and babies. Miriam wanted a career and independence. Logic said they shouldn't be friends. Yet, here they were, decades later. Seeing Rachel again was always seeing the road not taken. She met Rachel's gaze and smiled. There it was. The old connection.

While Rachel and Beau looked on, smiling, Miriam clasped Buddy's oddly clammy hand. "Dr. Preston..." She sorted through what to say, suddenly conscious of the uncomfortable sense of obligation the pending award created. She pushed it aside. "Thank you so much. I—"

Preston raised his hand. Miriam noted the tremor. "Now, now. No need. Rachel has told us all about your stellar work. I'm sure you've earned this opportunity." Before she could say more, he patted her arm and turned to greet another ancient physician, who had rolled up in a wheelchair. Rachel remained attentive at her father's side; the perfect Princess as the King greeted his guests.

Dennis, who stood patiently at Miriam's elbow, whispered in her ear, "I think you've been dismissed."

Miriam smirked. "I think you're right." Annoyed by the old, too familiar feeling of being patronized, she forced herself to breathe. *Remember what you can do with five million dollars.* As Dennis chatted with Beau, she took the opportunity to study Rachel.

Buddy Preston beamed as he introduced her to his cronies, always so proud of his little girl. Rachel, like Miriam, was an only child. Her father and his now deceased wife, Sandra, had even moved to Charlottesville to spend their retirement years close to her and their grandchildren.

Impeccably dressed, as always, Rachel wore the latest fashion her favorite Charlottesville boutique had to offer. She looked lovely in an off-one-shoulder gown of slate blue silk charmeuse, tucked in all the right places to flatter her figure. Her persistently blond hair was swept into a French twist. It appeared she may have had more "work" done. Her wide smile seemed unusually tight. A pang of sadness gripped Miriam. Rachel was beautiful. Why did she try so hard to look younger? Olivia's voice chimed in her head. "Mom, it's a form of self-expression. A woman can choose how she wants to look." A Women's Studies doctoral student, Olivia believed herself to be an expert on modern feminism. But, in Miriam's day—*oh, god, did I just think that?* She winced. *In my day? Am I that old?* Maybe. Nevertheless—in her day—cosmetic surgery was an attempt for women to stay relevant—to men.

She scolded herself. If Dennis could hear what she was thinking, she knew what he'd say. "Miriam, give a little grace, my friend." *What is it tonight? All these nagging thoughts. Must be nerves over the award, being in the spotlight...*

measuring up. Dennis was right. She *so* needed to learn to be more gracious. Something else to work on in retirement.

Rachel stepped away from her father and focused her gaze on Miriam. Miriam braced herself. "It's so good to see you." Rachel's voice was warm and genuine. She reached for Miriam's shoulder, moved in for an air kiss, and said softly, "How are you, darling? I know how you hate a fuss, but we are so proud of your accomplishments."

Miriam gave Rachel a wry smile. "Thank you. I'm well." She chose not to respond to the comment about hating a fuss. It rankled a bit, but she had to admit Rachel was right. Being the center of attention was miserable. *Deep breath, Miriam.*

Rachel smiled demurely at Dennis and Beau. "Why, all I ever did was raise my three girls and follow Beau around." She laughed. The tinkling sound of Rachel's laugh had never changed. Miriam's jaw clenched. Why did her comment somehow seem like an insult to Miriam's choices? Rachel reached out to take her husband, Beau's, arm. He patted her hand, smiled indulgently.

The silence was only seconds. Miriam glanced at Dennis, but knew better than to make eye contact with him. He knew her too well. She might feel less annoyed if she didn't know that Rachel was every bit as intelligent as she was. Unlike Miriam, she'd never had to study. She could have done anything. Olivia's voice again, "Mom, you're devaluing the role of the woman who chooses to be a wife and mother." *Aargh,* she'd never get it right.

Rachel released Beau's arm and moved to pull Miriam aside. "I so appreciate you doing this dinner on such short notice. Daddy thinks he's in better health than he is. And..." she lowered her voice. "He got the news just two days ago. His sister died. You remember; the one who lived in France."

Miriam vaguely recalled Rachel's stories from their teenage years. The mysterious aunt who left Virginia and never returned. Miriam had always thought her life sounded grand... carefree. Part of her always envied that. *Carefree* wasn't exactly her bailiwick. "Oh, I'm so sorry. Was that the 'crazy' aunt you always talked about?"

Rachel produced a sad smile. "Yes. One and the same. She died in Paris. That's where she's been living all these years. Daddy's too old to travel there for the funeral. And, well, I never knew her. But, still, he's just heartbroken, you know?"

Miriam nodded and fished around for another conversation topic. "How are your girls?" she asked. No matter the number of months, sometimes years, that passed between seeing each other, asking about Rachel's girls was a sure topic. Rachel had her first baby within a year of her marriage to Beau—1968, right out of college. She'd already had two more before Miriam's daughter, Olivia, was born in 1980.

Rachel leaned closer and warmed instantly, tapping Miriam's arm with perfectly manicured nails. "Oh, they're all doing fabulously. My oldest, Madison, and her husband, Bradley, are seriously considering leaving Richmond. Beau and I have been doing our best to get them to Charlottesville. I'd be pleased as punch, of course, to have my grandbabies closer..."

Rachel paused to accept a glass of wine from a waiter. Rachel had graciousness down pat. So perfectly equipped for the roles she'd chosen—attorney's wife, doting mother—now grandmother, former PTA President, Junior League Social Chairwoman. Not for the first time, Miriam asked herself: what would it have been like to be Rachel? Rachel turned back, caught Miriam scrutinizing her. Miriam looked away and took a sip of her drink. Rachel chatted on. So good at it. "And how is your mother doing? And Olivia? Is she still out there in Boulder?"

Rachel looked past Miriam's shoulder as she spoke, scoping out the other guests. Miriam debated about how much to tell her. She remembered Dennis's gentle urging. "Maybe if you were a little more open with people. Let them know what's going on with you." Determined to *share*, she opened her mouth to speak, but Rachel was distracted when Beau approached and touched her elbow.

"Honey, I'm going to see if they've got something stronger at the bar." He held up a half-full wine glass. "Do you want anything?"

"No, I'm good. Thanks." Rachel waved Beau away and made eye contact with Miriam. Just as Miriam started again, Dennis joined them. Dr. Preston had ambled off and was deep in conversation with a group of older ladies. Rachel flashed her brilliant smile and grasped Dennis's hand. "So good to see you again. When was the last time...?"

He leaned in and grazed her cheek with his lips. "I believe it was the event for the horses?" Dennis's eyes widened.

Rachel laughed. "Yes, that's the one. Seems you always get roped into these things with Miriam." She winked. Charming. Always so damn charming.

She had to give it to Rachel. When it came to fundraising, she was a powerhouse. No one could say no to her. Most—no— *all* of the black-tie events Miriam had attended, up until now, were for Rachel's causes. Miriam figured she could at least show up for Rachel's events, even if she didn't have the skill set to participate in country club conversations in an intelligible way. When they were younger, Dennis had suggested Miriam try spending time at the Farmington Country Club with Rachel and her collection of professional wives. "Maybe you should go and... I don't know, be part of the group. Learn to do the girl-talk thing." Dennis had looked as in-the-know about girl talk as she was.

And she did try. But, inevitably, one of the women ended up complaining to her about painful periods, or how sex with her husband was not what it used to be. She had begun to feel like a cross between a gynecologist and a sex therapist. Being "one of the girls" did not turn out to be her forte.

She'd tried golf, but was terrible at it. Tennis? Exhausting. It seemed she only had one talent—her career. Conversations about decorators or the best preschools seemed so frivolous. The contrast between the haves and the have-nots jolted Miriam every single time she walked into an exam room at one of her rural clinics. Left her feeling at turns angry and hopeless. Her solution? Work harder. Her friendship with Rachel paid the price. It became event-based. Sustained mostly by the knowledge of who they'd been, by the secrets they'd shared.

Miriam and Dennis glanced at each other. She caught a tiny twinkle in his brown eyes when he said, "It's always a pleasure to see you again, Rachel. Miriam speaks so fondly of you."

Miriam shot a sideways look at Dennis. He was completely composed. Fondly? Yes, she loved Rachel. They were bonded in a way she'd never even shared with Dennis. But, really? Fondly? She grasped Dennis's arm, probably tighter than necessary. Time to change the subject. "Dennis has recently accepted the position of Medical Director for Biochemical Genetics."

"Isn't that impressive?" Rachel crowed. "Genetics is so fascinating, isn't it?" As Dennis began to tell Rachel about his new role, Miriam startled when her handbag vibrated. A silenced cell phone message. She excused herself and stepped aside, opened her bag, and looked at the screen. Her breath caught. The text was from her daughter, Olivia.

Need to see you before the award ceremony. Leaving home now. Be there in 15 minutes. Meet me on The Lawn?

She immediately edged toward the doors, avoided eye contact, and hoped not to appear rude. The guests spilled through the wide-open doors onto the expansive marble steps, mingling and sipping cocktails. Looking beyond the small gathering crowd, she tried to spot her daughter. Olivia had said to watch for her on The Lawn, the historic grassy expanse spread before the Rotunda in dappled verdant green. She had no idea what was so important that her daughter had to see her *before* the ceremony. Olivia should not even be out of bed right now; not after what happened. But the text message had not left room for Miriam's opinion. And she definitely had one. Infuriating sometimes, her daughter's stubbornness. Olivia might be thirty years old, but Miriam was the one with the medical degree. She tried to keep her face placid as she inched toward the door.

Dennis appeared at her side. "What's going on?" He kept his voice quiet. "I saw you looking at your phone." Worry tightened his voice.

"It was Olivia. She says she needs to see me before the ceremony." Miriam continued walking as she spoke. "Said she'd be on The Lawn."

"Wait." Dennis caught her arm. "Is she all right?"

"I don't know." She placed her hand over his. "Cover for me, okay? I'll be right back."

The evening air was sweet, scented from the nearby rose garden in full bloom with Lady Banksia roses. As Miriam worked her way down the steps, she scanned the wide expanse of lush green grass. Finally, she spotted her daughter's tall, solid frame. Her pulse quickened. Olivia paced restlessly across the quad, stopping frequently to rise up on her toes, crane her neck, and examine the crowd. She wore loose-fitting sweats and a baggy t-shirt; her curly black hair wild around a worried face. Frowning, she gripped something flat, the size of a large envelope.

Miriam swallowed hard and raised a hand to catch Olivia's attention. Olivia spotted her and returned the wave. Miriam allowed herself one look back at the festive crowd before walking to meet her daughter. As Olivia drew closer, Miriam saw that what she held was a file folder. The old-fashioned medical office type, brown manilla with lines on the outside to record visit dates. The kind used in doctor's offices before patients had medical record numbers. Her heart quickened and cold dread filled her chest. She ignored the feeling and focused on her daughter's stubborn expression.

Olivia stopped abruptly, breathing hard. Miriam charged forward. "You really shouldn't be out of bed—"

"Mom, I'm fine." Olivia's tone stopped her short.

"But couldn't this wait? What's so important that I have to see now?" Irritation crept in. "The dinner is about to start. And this award?" She forced Olivia to meet her gaze. "It's an opportunity of a lifetime."

"I *know*, Mom." Olivia's voice was edged with impatience. "But before you go in there and accept that grant, I need you to look at this file." Olivia's hand shook as she held out the worn file folder. "Just read it."

Miriam looked at the folder, but did not reach for it. In the fading evening light, she'd need her glasses to read the name—probably typed on the folder decades ago. She glanced once more toward the Rotunda. It seemed to glow with opportunity. Filled with her colleagues, supporters, and those with the money to make her dream—to offer Appalachian women contraceptive choices—possible. So close.

She turned back and stared at the object in her daughter's hands. A sinking feeling in the pit of her stomach let her know: this small, thin file would force some kind of choice. Her hand seemed locked at her side, her arm unable—or unwilling—to move. On the veranda of the Rotunda, a young man, dressed in a white waiter's jacket, black tie, and black pants rang a soft gong. Cocktail hour had ended. The guests moved toward the stately interior to locate their gilt-edged place cards for the pre-award dinner.

CHAPTER 2

Miriam

BIG STONE GAP, VIRGINIA
FIVE DAYS EARLIER, MAY 24, 2010

Miriam rested her hand on 20-year-old Annie Howard's bony shoulder and looked into her frightened blue eyes. "Ready?" Miriam kept her voice light. Annie had taken a long time to reach the decision; she certainly didn't want to scare her off now. Annie bit her bottom lip, wrinkled her freckled nose, and gave a quick nod. Miriam pulled on her gloves, moved to the other end of the exam table, and sat down. The nurse pushed the tray of instruments closer.

"Here we go. Deep breath," Miriam inserted the speculum, then deftly slipped in the IUD. She'd inserted so many of these, she could do it in her sleep. A sharp gasp, but by the time Miriam peered over the drape, Annie wore a weak smile. "Done," Miriam said, as she rose from her stool and patted Annie's knee.

Annie sat up, pushed the paper drape tight around her narrow hips and grinned. Crooked teeth were the only flaw in her fresh young face, pinkened now in a blush. "Thanks, Doc. That wasn't so bad."

"Not nearly as painful as labor." Miriam winked and pulled off her gloves, tossing them into the trash.

"Ain't that the truth," Annie's relieved reply.

"Now, if someday..." She turned to Annie and tried to make *someday* sound a long time away, "you decide you want another child. Remember, we can always take the IUD out." She watched Annie closely, hoping she comprehended the emphasis—*you decide.*

"Okay, Doc." Annie nodded once. Miriam prayed Annie's determination would last. Leaving her to dress, she left the exam room and walked down the hall to the empty clinic office—a space she currently shared with the new doctor she'd recently hired to take over the remote clinics.

Dr. Ramona Weir had left early today. She'd darted out of an exam room a couple of hours ago. "Dr. Stewart, I'm really sorry, but I gotta get home. Randy's school play is tonight and I still have to finish his costume."

Miriam had waved her away. "Yes, get out of here. I've got the last couple of patients." She remembered those frantic days of juggling a child and a medical practice. Compared to how tired she felt now, the single-mother life had been even *more* exhausting. She'd lived in a constant state of inadequacy over everything—medicine, motherhood, men. Wouldn't want to go back to those days. Yet...

Dr. Weir was young and passionate—just as she'd once been—ready to take over care of the ever-growing number of women visiting the clinic. Miriam's goal was met. This clinic was fully staffed—one of the few—with nurses, and now a new doctor. She'd assured herself Ramona was competent. Still, it had taken her six months to make the decision to retire. She was definitely retirement age—turned sixty-five in February this year. But she kept asking herself, *why now?*

The answer seemed simple enough. The sixty-plus hours a week she worked in women's clinics didn't allow her the time, or energy, to fulfill her dream: an all-inclusive women's health center. She'd base it in her adopted hometown of

Charlottesville and have satellite clinics all over the western part of Virginia. The Virginia Women's Contraceptive Center would be a place women could go without fear of judgment, a one-stop place that pulled everything together: from birth control to birthing classes, from mental health care and rehab to safe-house referrals.

She sank into the battered wooden desk chair, fatigued to the bone with another long morning of examining women struggling to navigate *the reproductive years*—the euphemism so imprecisely applied to a woman's experience.

Sometimes there were tears. "It was just that one time we didn't use protection."

Sometimes seething anger. "That son-of-a-bitch. I'll kill him."

Sometimes the flat tone of numbness. "I think I'm pregnant again."

Come on, Miriam. Remember the happy ones. Women who wanted nothing more than to have babies. Others excited to have lots of sex without the worry about getting pregnant. The last couple of years, the women's stories had all begun to blur together. Maybe it really *was* time to leave. Put out to pasture, like an old horse. Not quite how she wanted to see herself.

Probably why the opportunity, presented just last week, felt like a reprieve from her own self-imposed funk. The grant writing staff at UVA had contacted her; asked to float her project past several potential donors. She was dubious. How political would the whole process get? Politics had never been her forte. But the grant writing team had promised, "Lend us your name and experience and we'll do the rest." Quite a carrot they'd dangled before her. "Let's do it," she'd said. But she hadn't felt as confident as she'd tried to sound.

She sighed, pulled Annie's file toward her, and opened it. She reviewed the notes—five years of history. The first time Annie edged into the clinic waiting room, she'd been a sullen fifteen-year-old. Now, she was a success story—a win—finally choosing to take control after giving up three babies for adoption. She'd been off the oxy for three months now. Or so she said. Miriam nodded briskly and slapped the desk with her open palms, jolting herself out of her woolgathering. She picked up the pen, quickly made her final entry in the Annie Howard narrative, and flipped the file shut.

Hands splayed out on top of the file, she stared at the mosaic of wrinkles and age spots, tried to grasp the fact that she had just done her last pelvic exam. Ever. How surreal the whole idea of retirement felt. Thirty-five years of women, just like Annie, unraveling sex from pregnancy.

She finished her notes, packed her tote, and waved goodbye to Mary Lou, the receptionist. "Don't stay too late. Today's supposed to be a half-day for you."

"Oh, I won't, Doc. Bud's already got the grill lit."

"Oh, and Mary Lou?"

"Yes?"

"Please make sure Annie Howard's social worker gets the report about Annie getting an IUD today."

"I'm on it, Doc Stewart."

"Thanks."

Slipping out the back door of the hundred-year-old brick building, she tried to remember the date she'd established the satellite clinic. It took only a few seconds to recall—1977. Pre-Olivia—the way she marked time. Pre-Olivia and post-Olivia. Pre-motherhood and post-motherhood. Only there never really was a post-motherhood, was there.

The pre-Olivia years had been filled with a sense of unlimited possibility. A flash of the first day at the Big Stone Gap Women's Clinic. If she'd never met that particular patient, she might never have met Dennis. And without Dennis? She couldn't even imagine.

FEBRUARY 1977

Bonnie Ransom was her name. A bitterly cold morning. Bonnie shivered in a threadbare brown coat on the steps of the drafty brick building. "Good morning." Miriam shoved her keys into the lock with trembling hands. "Come on in."

Bonnie timidly signed her X on the line beside where the student nurse volunteer wrote out her name. The student ushered her into the exam room as Miriam pulled on her lab coat. A quick assessment, initial questions. Bonnie was only twenty-nine years old, but her emaciated frame and sallow sagging skin made her look closer to sixty.

"Something ain't right down there." Bonnie lowered her eyes and dipped her head toward her pelvis.

Bonnie's loss of appetite and the worthless food she consumed when she *did* eat had reduced her young body to a skeletal state. Miriam struggled to get a comprehensive history, pulling information from Bonnie like suture thread through thick skin. How could Bonnie endure so much pain and still manage to climb out of bed in the morning, much less feed and care for seven children? *Seven.* And to top it all off, Bonnie was worried that her lack of interest in sex might cause her to lose Buck, her husband of fifteen years.

"I ain't felt like doing my womanly duty," Bonnie refused to make eye contact. "And Buck don't like that. He wants us to have another young'un." Miriam boiled with anger at a man she would probably never meet.

Bonnie's test results came back. Cervical cancer. With no oncologists in Big Stone Gap, Miriam pursued a consultation with the Charlottesville Oncology Group. Their offices were located in the same building as her primary office. She was met with a look of disdain from the white-haired fossil, Dr. Miller, the managing physician. "Does she have insurance?"

"Um... I'm not sure. I don't think so." Miriam shoved her

sweaty hands into her lab coat pockets. The chance of Bonnie having medical insurance was about as probable as her having a hot tub installed on the side of the mountain behind her single-wide trailer.

Dr. Miller avoided eye contact. "You'll need to refer her to the state charity clinic in Richmond." He continued to read the medical file in his hands.

"But... what if she doesn't have that kind of time, Dr. Miller?" Her chest tightened and her heart rate quickened. Bonnie could die waiting the weeks it would take to get into the charity clinic.

Before she could say anything else, there was a knock at Miller's office door. "Come," Miller growled. A young man stepped around the door. Sandy brown hair, round black glasses, starched white shirt, paisley bow tie, perfectly creased pants, and shiny brown wingtips. Their eyes met, and he flashed a shy, lop-sided smile. "Oh, excuse me." He turned to leave. "I'll just come back..."

"Hold on there, Patterson," Dr. Miller waved the young man back into the office. Miller gestured toward Miriam. "Patterson, this is... um..."

"Miriam Stewart." She held out her hand and Patterson returned her shake. His hand was elegant, but solid and warm. There was something familiar about him. Then she remembered. Carrying box after box of books, he'd climbed the rickety back porch steps of Mrs. Pettiworth's house last weekend. He'd been dressed in faded jeans and a sweatshirt then. Very different from this polished look. "Did you just move into the downstairs apartment at Mrs. Pettiworth's?" Miriam asked.

"Sure did. I'm Dennis."

As much as her life was ruled by science and facts, she had a *coming home* kind of feeling about Dennis Patterson. Completely unexpected, but they would be friends. She was certain of it. "I live in the cottage out back. We're neighbors."

"Oh, so you know Mrs. Pettiworth pretty well, then?" His brown eyes were curious.

"Oh yes, she's quite a character. I'll have to—"

Dr. Miller cleared his throat loudly. "You all can visit about your landlady on your own nickel. I've got work to do." He leaned back. The complaint of the desk chair was so loud, Miriam worried it would tip backwards with his weight. Suddenly, Miller sat back up and brightened. "Dr. Patterson here could probably take your patient's case." Miller's smile was lazy as he chose a cigar from the carved box resting on the leather desk pad. He rolled it lovingly between his surprisingly delicate fingers. "He's the... youngest member of our oncology team. Looking for new patients. Right, Patterson?"

"Um, sure," Dennis said. She noticed a tiny twang of western Virginia in his accent. His hair fell across his glasses and he used them to push it back, propping them on top of his head. His eyes were warm; his expression open. "How can I help?"

They left the clinic and walked under the budding trees along the Main Street mall to Mo's coffee cart. Sitting across the table from Dennis, she was surprised at how easily her story poured out. Her passion for mountain women's healthcare. Her frustration with the system and frankly... with men. "Sorry, no offense."

"Hey." He held up his hands in surrender. "None taken. I'm just a boy from Black Tree Holler. Feel the same way about cancer care." For the first time she could remember, stretching all the way back to when she'd started med school, her heart thrilled at the sense of having found an ally. Especially with Dennis's next words. "Now, we need to talk about our shared landlady—not to mention our living conditions. But first things first. Tell me about Bonnie."

Miriam turned away from the building. Her chest felt heavy at the bittersweetness of the memories. She and Dennis hadn't been able to save Bonnie, but that experience had turned into decades of sharing the good stuff, the bad stuff, the accomplishments, the failures, the heartbreaks, the love affairs, all of it—personal, professional, family. Would it help to talk to Dennis about how this last official day of her medical practice felt? No, not yet. She'd spare him her emotional dithering. She stopped to gaze up at the faithful old redbud branching over the sidewalk, soaked in the soft light of the Blue Ridge Mountain spring. She took a last look around the familiar parking lot where once a month for her entire career, she had visited like a traveling salesman hawking his wares. Only instead of vacuum cleaners or life insurance, she had traded in contraception. She blew out slowly through whistled lips. Like a tired warrior leaving the battlefield, she trudged toward her elderly Volvo.

CHAPTER 3

Miriam

ON THE ROAD TO CHARLOTTESVILLE
MAY 24, 2010

Merging onto the highway for the five-hour trip back to her home in Charlottesville, Miriam couldn't stop thinking, *What now?* She watched her mind jump from one possible productive use of her time to another. Dennis's words flashed through her mind. "You and I are those people, Miriam. We need to be productive... all the time. It's a bit of a curse."

Dennis had talked her into teaching part-time at UVA. "Just think of all the knowledge you could share," he'd said.

"I'm not so sure I'd be that great with students," she'd worried.

"Oh, I don't know. Might do you good to be a little more in touch with the younger generation."

"I'm *in touch*," she'd spluttered. "Most of my patients are under thirty."

"Not patients," he'd persisted. "Students. Whole different world for them than it was for us." Thinking of his comment now, she let out a quick bark of laughter. After what happened last week on one of her first gynecology rounds, she might not be cut out for teaching.

Her knock on the hospital room door was more of a warning to the patient than a request to enter. She still wasn't accustomed to the gaggle of students trailing behind her. Unfortunately, teaching and patient privacy seemed an either/or proposition. The too-familiar feeling of defeat struck when she saw young Rosie Carter, a former clinic patient. Her weary eyes met Miriam's briefly before she dropped her gaze.

"I was just about to give her pain meds," the nurse at the bedside said.

"Please, go ahead." Miriam glanced at the chart and turned toward the students. "Mrs. Carter is a nineteen-year-old from Goshen Pass, admitted subsequent to blood loss from a first trimester miscarriage."

In her peripheral vision, she noted the students watching her as she approached Rosie's bedside. Rosie reached through the bedrails, her long fingers grasping for Miriam's hand. "Hey Doc Stewart. I's hoping you'd come."

Miriam took Rosie's work-roughened hand in her own and waited as the nurse finished injecting morphine into Rosie's IV. "How are you, Rosie?" She watched Rosie's pinched expression soften as the drug moved through her bloodstream.

"Better now."

Knowing her patient was drifting on a welcome cloud of relief, Miriam methodically relayed the medical facts to the bored-looking students gathered at the foot of the bed. "Para five—now para six—gravida three." Miriam continued to flip quickly through the chart, then raised her eyes. The medical students had quietly turned to look at each other in thinly veiled horror. A silent shared response to the calculus of a woman's uterus. Nineteen-year-old Rosie had been pregnant six times and only three of her children had lived.

Miriam palpated Rosie's abdomen, checked for pain, and

asked her about the amount of bleeding. "You should be able to go home this evening. Can Travis pick you up?"

"Yes, ma'am. He gets off shift at nine."

"Good, then we'll see you for follow up in the clinic next week." She'd led the students out of the hospital room before she remembered she wouldn't be there next week. The new doctor would take care of Rosie now. As Rosie's door closed behind them, she overheard a female student whisper, "*Omigod.* They should *so* tie her tubes." Miriam stopped and turned in time to see the young woman's equally disdainful male colleague widen his eyes and mutter something back to her. Their sniggering stopped abruptly when she stepped toward them. Standing within six inches, she glared from one to the other until they looked down sheepishly.

"I would suggest, Miss..." Miriam glanced at the young woman's nametag. It read: Conway. *Damn.* Same name as one of the major UVA benefactors. "...Conway..." Probably a granddaughter. For a split-second she considered holding her tongue. Silence had never been her strong suit. She continued in a subdued but steely tone. "...that before you pronounce judgment on a patient and decide she should be sterilized, you take into consideration you know *nothing* about this woman as a person, *or* her life, *or* why she is here today."

Miss Conway gazed steadily at her feet. "Yes, Dr. Stewart," she mumbled. The other students squirmed uncomfortably and avoided eye contact as well. Miriam looked around the bent heads of the group. One young woman, head up, eyes shining with righteous anger at her colleague's disrespect, dared to meet her gaze. She thought of her younger self. Then she turned and walked down the hall at a fast-paced clip to the next patient room, taking deep breaths to control the intense desire to wring the young Miss Conway's neck.

―――

She turned on the car radio, thought she'd listen to NPR. They were broadcasting the confirmation hearings for President Obama's new female nominee to the Supreme Court. No, she couldn't bear the rhetoric today. She turned it off. Back to contemplating the idea that retirement from practice gave her more time—especially if teaching or funding for her center didn't work out. But time for what? There *was* the problem of her mother, Lillian Stewart. Eighty-six years old and still determined to live out her days in the family farmhouse by the Maury River in Hazel Hollow. Lillian was still healthy, but Miriam had the sinking feeling it was just a matter of time before she'd have to step in and insist Lillian move in with her.

"I will leave here in a pine box and not before." Lillian's favorite thing to say if Miriam dared bring up the subject.

Reaching a dead-end with *that* particular dilemma, her mental list of projects flipped to her daughter. Olivia was so far away in Colorado. Understandable. Distance had been Olivia's way of making her own separate life. After all, Miriam had done the same thing as a young woman when she left Hazel Hollow. But for her, *distance* was the difference between Hazel Hollow and Charlottesville—less than two hours. Not thousands of miles away.

———

"When do you expect to finish your dissertation?" she had asked Olivia, during one of their catch-up calls last month.

Olivia had sighed. "Maybe about a year from now." Then, after several seconds of silence, "I... um... am actually thinking about having a baby." Her daughter slipped pregnancy into the conversation as casually as if she were mentioning taking up yoga.

"Now?" Miriam had asked. "What about your career?" Thinking back, Miriam chastised herself for overreacting. But had she not spent years watching women give themselves up in exchange for motherhood? Hadn't she earned the right to recommend caution—especially when it came to her only child?

She probably did come off a little overbearing. Why had she been so shocked? Olivia was, after all, thirty years old. Miriam must have assumed... What *had* she assumed? That her daughter wouldn't want children because she was a lesbian? Or worse, did she have some latent homophobia, making her believe Olivia *shouldn't* be a mother? *Oh god.* This was all too complicated. "What does Amy think of this idea?" she'd persisted when Olivia didn't respond.

"Um... she's coming around."

Miriam could always tell when Olivia was hedging. "Coming around? Sounds vague. Does she want a baby? I mean... how did you decide it would be you to... carry it?"

"Um... I guess Amy's never really thought about actually being pregnant. She's a career lawyer. Hasn't really even considered kids. And, well... I have. A lot. *If* she decides she wants to do this together, then I'll be the birth mom."

Miriam rolled the term *birth mom* over in her thoughts. How did you separate the biology part from the nurturing, parenting part? She was conscious of an uncomfortable truth. She could relate to Amy more than her own daughter, strangely. Still, after thirty years, a twinge of guilt knowing she'd never intended to have a child. Always followed by the awe at this person she and Hugh had made together.

"What about a donor?" Miriam asked.

"Oh. I'm going to use a sperm bank." Olivia was maddeningly nonchalant.

Now, here was a way for her to help. "No, no," Miriam said before she could stop herself. She had to be more reserved, or she was going to push Olivia away.

"Mom, I..."

Miriam jumped in and tried to redeem herself. "You can't

trust some anonymous retail business for a father for your child."

"I'm not looking for a 'father for my child,' Mom."

Miriam sputtered. "You know I meant donor. Don't split hairs." The protectiveness toward her daughter was visceral. She had actually felt her gut tighten. Stories of male doctors impregnating women with their own sperm rattled through her mind. "Don't you know anyone? Let me help you find someone," she coaxed. "I have medical students. We could vet them, have them tested." Surely, Olivia could see the logic in this?

"Um..." Background noise and voices. "Mom, I'm sorry, I have to go. Amy's home. I'll call you next week."

———

Miriam shook her head and stared at the approaching exit for the business district of Wise, Virginia. Stubbornness must be a genetic trait among the Stewart women. She turned off the highway toward the tiny town just east of Big Stone Gap. The home of Mountain Brew Coffee where she always grabbed a sandwich and coffee for the drive.

She shivered a bit with the chilly spring air and pulled her sweater closer as she got out of the car and stepped into the shop. Pine floors, rustic furniture, and the rich aroma of coffee greeted her, along with TJ, the young woman who seemed to be there no matter what the hour of her visit to the coffeeshop.

"Hi, Doc." TJ's grin wrinkled her pierced nose. "The usual?"

She chatted with TJ for a moment, then sat down at a table near the window to wait. She stared at the Victorian-era brick store fronts across the street. Buildings erected when Wise was in its heyday as a mining town. Just down the street was the building where, for so many years, she had held a cancer screening clinic, another of her monthly mountain rounds.

"Here you go, Doc." TJ startled her out of her reverie.

She thanked TJ and returned to her car, coffee and turkey-Swiss sandwich in hand. Sighing, she slipped an Emmylou Harris CD into the player and settled into the ride. Her thoughts drifted out over the lush green valleys and velvet-soft mountains mirrored in Emmylou's voice. Her throat tightened, and she punched the eject button a little harder than necessary. Emmylou mixed best with a self-indulgent case of longing and sloppy emotion. Nope, not today. She switched to light jazz.

It was strange to think of not having the daily rhythm of work. She prided herself in the changes her practice had brought. All kinds of women in all kinds of circumstances knew they could count on her to give them control over their lives. She'd found fulfillment in her work. The feeling of being useful, of producing something, was as familiar as the landscape surrounding her.

Her thoughts turned again to Dennis. Unlike hers, his work in cancer care—his patients' daily struggles against death—had caused him to spiral into depression three years ago.

"Do something different," she'd suggested.

He'd argued emphatically—how could he possibly abandon his patients? He'd gone over all of the reasons to push on—it's just a phase, he'd get past it. In the end, she and Walt had to do a sort of intervention, force him to see how much of himself he'd lost, *they* had lost. Thankfully, he'd given in and agreed to take a leave of absence from his practice. To occupy his time, he'd pursued more education in one of his long-term interests—genetics. He'd completed a PhD a couple of years ago. And, in the process, found his passion and his sense of purpose again. And now, true to form, he'd been put in charge of the department at UVA. They'd weathered that storm of his. They'd weather this one of hers—maybe. She reflected on her conversation with Dennis last week.

He'd agreed to help her pack up her primary office. She'd felt a bit lost letting go of the coveted third story space in one of the old brick buildings just across from the campus. The packing had brought on an unexpected melancholy. What had she really accomplished? She'd stopped to make a pot of coffee. As she poured a cup for each of them, she said, "I just always wished there was a blood test, you know?" She handed the mug to Dennis.

Dennis frowned. "A blood test for what?" He took the coffee and dumped in two packets of sugar. Always two. Unless he hadn't slept much the night before. Then it was three or four.

Miriam stared out her office window. Students lounged in clumps in the spring-green grass. "I think I'd call it the Mother Gene," she murmured.

Dennis stopped stirring and dropped into the side chair, setting his untouched coffee on the edge of her desk. "Good Lord, Miriam. Have you lost your mind?"

She turned and met his wide, incredulous eyes. *Had she said that out loud?* Stuffing the defensive feeling, she rallied. "Wait. Let me finish. I think this is a good idea."

Dennis clasped his hands together, elbows on his knees, head down, staring at the floor while she talked. This was his listening pose—the one he used when he was trying very hard not to interrupt her.

"So, the results of the test would tell me: this woman has the Mother Gene, this woman does not." Miriam stared at the top of his bald head.

Dennis raised his eyes to hers. He looked skeptical. "And if the woman doesn't? What then?"

She warmed to her own idea. "Well... then we're back to informed choice, right? I could tell her that, according to this test, there's a strong probability you should not have children." She paced and held up a finger to emphasize her point.

Dennis's face pinched into incredulity. "And who the hell gets to decide what the Mother Gene is?"

She threw up her hands. "I don't know." She dropped her arms and picked up her cup. "I don't have all that worked out yet. Maybe psychology and sociology researchers could partner with geneticists, like you." She motioned toward him with her coffee cup.

Dennis cocked his head to the side, his mouth open. He was processing, but she pushed on. "Anyway, this test would empower women even more. They could know if they have what it takes to be a mother."

"And you honestly think women would believe the test results and choose *not* to have children?" Dennis sat back in his chair and crossed his arms. From the look on his face, she wished she'd kept the idea to herself.

"I think some might, yes." A twinge of uncertainty—more than she was willing to admit. She had always wanted something scientific and logical to hang on to. Pretty much a pipe dream. "I heard they've isolated a gene for violence."

"Yes... the infamous Warrior Gene." Dennis rolled his eyes and pushed his black glasses up farther on the bridge of his narrow nose.

"So why not one for motherhood?" She couldn't stop re-engaging.

"It's an ethical minefield, is why." He shook his head and reached for the cooling coffee.

"And the Warrior Gene isn't?" She stepped closer. "Listen." She glared at him until he returned her gaze. "Ever since we started practicing medicine—you in oncology, me in gynecology—you've always said that our jobs were to offer options, right?"

"Right."

"So, this would be another credible, scientific option."

Dennis nodded, remaining silent. Finally, he spoke."I gotta tell you, Miriam, this all sounds a bit dystopian. Things don't work out well when we try to control who has children."

Dennis stared at her until she began to squirm under his scrutiny. She looked away and out the window again. How many of the young women down there on the grass, laughing and chatting with each other—some studiously rushing to class, some lazing under a tree wrapped around some young stud—would end up pregnant before they had a chance to take control of their lives?

"Let's take you..." Dennis sat back and crossed his legs.

She sat down heavily in her desk chair. *Uh-oh.* He looked intrigued by this line of thought, but her stomach clenched.

"Do you think you have this Mother Gene?"

"Oh, hell no," she answered without hesitation. Dennis let out a short guffaw of laughter, and she grinned at him. "Maybe it skips a generation," she said. Olivia's intense desire to have a baby popped into her thoughts. "But I compensated," she continued. "With you and Walt." Would he get her meaning? She couldn't have raised Olivia without Dennis and his partner, Walt.

Dennis's expression warmed. "That's true." He tilted his head, the corners of his mouth drawn down. "Walt has always been quite the mother hen. Maybe he has the Mother Gene."

"Maybe." She chuckled. "He's more maternal than I ever could be."

Dennis held out his hand, his long index finger pointed at her. "And that's my point. Olivia turned out great." Miriam couldn't disagree with him. She thought of her earnest daughter whose passions were so different from her own.

Dennis continued. "Back to this idea of a Mother Gene..." He laid a hand on his chest. "You're dabbling in my world now." He referred, she was sure, to his recent promotion to

Director of Biochemistry and Molecular Genetics for UVA. "Having, or *not* having, the gene for something doesn't automatically mean you'll have whatever outcome it is you expect."

"That's true." Miriam frowned. *So* deflating when Dennis shot holes in her theories. Damn him. If only he were an intellectual snob, she could hate him. But he was the furthest from a snob that a person could be.

"I mean, look at you." Dennis gestured toward her. She glared at him. *Where is this going?* He pushed on. "You're different from all of the women you went to high school with. Same background, raised the same way. Take your friend Rachel, for example. Instead of marrying young and cranking out babies, like she did, you chose a career and no marriage—and, well...one baby." He smiled and picked up the photograph of Miriam, Olivia, and Hugh. The one taken at Olivia's UVA graduation—a rare shot of them all together. He set the photograph down. "It's the old *nature versus nurture* question. Who's to say if mothering is in the DNA, a random set of circumstances, or some combination?"

Miriam thought about this idea for a few seconds. Nature *and* nurture. Lillian's loving blue eyes—sharp, watchful—floated into her consciousness. She mused, "If anyone *ever* had the Mother Gene in her DNA, Lillian Stewart does." Her thoughts drifted back to Rachel. She probably believed she had the Mother Gene in spades. Miriam was transported to the early days of Olivia's life. After Rachel finally got past the fact that Miriam was not going to marry Hugh, she had set her sights on Miriam being a card-carrying member of the *mommy club*. Miriam remembered the conversation as if it were yesterday. Rachel had tip-toed into the living room—probably shushed by Dennis or Lillian. Miriam had just finished breastfeeding Olivia. As her daughter slept peacefully in her arms, she'd pondered how the hell she was going to keep the breastfeeding up when she went back to work.

Rachel had gushed, "I want you to join Mommy and Me. It's so fun. We take the kids to the park. We share parenting tips. During the summer, we hang out at the pool at the Club. You'll love it."

Miriam's mouth had dropped open. "Rachel, really? Can you see me sitting around chatting about the best brand of diaper cream?" In retrospect, she'd probably sounded a bit condescending.

Rachel had looked crestfallen. "Um... maybe not."

Somewhere in her post-partum brain, Miriam had realized her filter was down. But it had been too late. She'd pushed on. "And when am I going to have time to go to the park? You know the hours I keep."

Rachel's voice rose as her neck gradually turned pink—that thing that happened when she was angry. "Fine, Miriam. I'm just trying to help you out here. Get you connected to other mothers. Someone besides your precious patients."

Miriam had fought down anger. Couldn't Rachel see she was torn, part of her wanting to fit in, all the while knowing she never would? She stuffed the conflict. Rachel wouldn't get it. "I'm sorry, Rach. I know you're trying to help."

"I am." Rachel poked out her lower lip. "I never see you anymore. You spend all your time with your gay friends. I swear, Miriam. You'd think they were your *only* friends."

Miriam had clamped her mouth shut and hadn't argued further. She had done what she did best: she'd changed the subject to something about Rachel. Dennis and Walt were not only her closest friends, they were her family. No arguing there.

She jerked her head up when Dennis spoke. She'd been lost in her thoughts. "You speak the truth," he said. She looked at him, trying to discern what he was talking about.

Dennis's face softened. "Hello. Earth to Miriam." He grinned. "I was talking about Lillian. She's been a mother to all of us." Miriam always warmed at how he and Walt treasured Lillian. He continued as he rose, picked up a marker, and began to label one of the stuffed cardboard boxes. "Speaking of DNA..." He tapped the marker against the side of his head. "Walt told me to remind you about the genealogy project you two are doing."

"Yes, I've registered with the website." Miriam looked down into her coffee cup. "I even sent off my sputum sample for their DNA test." She glanced up at him. He raised his eyebrows, but didn't comment. Probably couldn't believe she'd trust the test quality of a commercial venture. But this DNA test was no big deal. The family tree project was something she and Walt would enjoy doing together... at least that's what Walt said.

"Walt will be glad to hear that. He is *so* excited." Dennis gestured with the marker. "He's been binge-watching that show on PBS... what's it called?... something about roots..."

"I hope he's not counting on me to know anything about genealogy." Miriam tensed. "Not to mention, my knowledge of genetics is limited to inheritable birth defects." Dennis had an opening to agree with her, but was kind enough not to. She reached for the tape to close up another box.

"Miriam?"

"Yes?" She didn't look up.

"This is for fun, remember? This is something *interesting* for you to do now you're retired."

She sighed, wishing once again she was less intense. "Who knows?" She peeked at her watch, surprised at how late it had gotten. "Maybe it *will* be fun."

Dennis walked over and pulled her into one of his reassuring hugs. "Miriam, you are exhausting, but I love you." He sighed. "You can give yourself permission not to make everything so difficult."

CHAPTER 4

Miriam

CHARLOTTESVILLE, VIRGINIA
MAY 24, 2010

Thankfully, the long drive home was almost over. Too much rumination. She was about to take the Charlottesville exit when her cell phone rang.

"Miriam, is that you?" Aunt Jo asked in the way people who rarely talk on the phone verify they are speaking to a real person.

"Yes, Jo." Her pulse quickened at Jo's panicked tone. "What's wrong?"

"Your mama has done fallen down the river bank and broke her wrist. I had to call the 911, just like you told me to."

She thanked Jo, reassured her that she would take it from here, hung up, and immediately called the Staunton Hospital Emergency Room. Lillian was no longer there. She had been admitted to the main hospital. Fear quickened Miriam's heart as she waited to be transferred to the physician. A brief conversation reassured her. No stroke or cardiac episode. "We just thought a few hours of observation might be a good idea," the doctor said.

Next call, the hospital floor. As the operator made the

connection, she tapped the steering wheel impatiently. A nurse answered. "Lillian Stewart's room."

Miriam swallowed her fear and shifted into professional mode. "Dr. Stewart calling. Mrs. Stewart is my mother. Can you put her on, please?"

"Just a moment." After what seemed like an eternity, the clearing of a throat scraped in her ear.

"Hello, Miriam darlin'."

Lillian's voice was fragile. Miriam pressed harder on the accelerator. The wave of emotion was unexpected. She should be feeling relieved, not more worried. This was all her fault. She'd delayed doing anything with Lillian for too long. "Aunt Jo called me about your accident."

"Mm hm."

"So, listen, okay?" Miriam went straight to the solution.

"I'm listening," the scratchy reply.

"I'm going by my house to pack a few things and then I'll come and pick you up. They're going to discharge you later." She mentally calculated the time: ten minutes to her house, fifteen to pack, forty-five to Staunton, another half hour for the drive to the farmhouse. "We should have you home in time for bed."

"That's good. I'll be ready for you."

"And Mother?" Miriam didn't stop to second-guess the plan she'd quickly formulated.

"Yes?"

"I'm going to have Olivia come out and the two of us will stay with you for a while." She kept her voice firm. No room for argument.

"Well, now, I don't know as that's necessary..."

Lillian's response was no surprise. Miriam ignored it. It dawned on her that in her haste to reassure Lillian with her plan, she'd forgotten to ask... "How are you? Are you in pain?"

"Oh, I'm fine. Just a little tired is all. The nurse says that medicine she gave me might make me sleepy."

Miriam was momentarily relieved to know Lillian wasn't in pain. Then, the relentless knowledge after years of experience with women of all ages kicked in. "You know this could have been your hip, don't you?" Now was *not* the time, but she felt incapable of passing up the opportunity.

"Oh, now, Miriam. Don't fuss." Lillian had a maddening way of equating Miriam's scientific expertise with nagging. "The river bank was slick after the rain is all... You should see the rhododendrons right now..." Her voice faded.

"Do I have to remind you again of the mortality rate of women your age who fall and break their hips?" Annoyed with herself for not being more in control, she took deep breaths. *Just. Shut. Up.*

"I'm sorry, Dr. Stewart." The nurse's voice was gentle. "Your mother says she's too sleepy to talk anymore."

"Oh. All right..." *Phone number.* She hurried on, "Let me give you my cell phone number. Please, call me immediately if anything changes."

"Don't worry, Dr. Stewart, we'll take good care of her."

She hung up, awash with guilt for haranguing Lillian while she lay injured in a hospital bed. But the woman was an expert at dodging not-so-subtle pressure. Wasn't this the perfect opportunity? Couldn't this injury be the thing to shake her out of her crazy ideas about continuing to live in that isolated farmhouse so close to the river?

She turned on Locust Avenue and into the alley behind her home. Work bag, empty food bag, and coffee cup balanced in her arms, she stepped through the back gate into the deep shade of the towering white oak in her back garden. A large wheelbarrow full of branches blocked the brick path leading from the small rental cottage at the back of her property to the back door of her house.

She frowned, but then remembered. The wheelbarrow

meant her tenant, Nate, had been doing the yard cleaning they'd agreed would lower his rent this month. She still couldn't believe Nate was already a senior, double majoring in sociology and engineering, with a passion for international relief work. Another young man trying to save the world. Just like Hugh had been all those years ago. She supposed she still had a weakness for them.

Nate emerged from the open front door of the cottage. He wore baggy khaki shorts and nothing else. His wiry, muscular young body glowed with health. There was something about the way the sun caught his brown eyes that made her feel the same frisson of excitement she'd felt the first time she'd met Hugh. Embarrassed by such feelings, she hoped Nate didn't notice her flushing. After all, she was old enough to be his... dear god... his grandmother. Must be the season change—spring always made her feel strange.

"Yo, Dr. Stewart," Nate called. "I've been picking up tree limbs like you asked, but what should I do with them?"

After instructing Nate to bundle the branches and leave them in the alley for the trash pick-up, she turned toward the house. She stopped short, a thought that had been simmering at the edge of her mind now fully formed. "Nate, how long before you leave for your summer internship?"

"This Friday, as a matter of fact." He scooped up an armful of branches. "Why Doc? What's up?"

"Would you be willing to do a little extra work for me this week? I'd like to have the cottage and the garden ready... it's my mother. She's had an accident..."

"Oh man, not Miss Lillian." He dropped the branches and stepped toward her. His handsome face creased in worry. "Is she all right?"

Nate had shared with her that he had no living grandparents. During one of Lillian's rare visits to Charlottesville, she and Nate had taken quite a liking to each other. Miriam had initially been surprised by their connection. But her mother had this mysterious way with people—young, old, didn't matter. People opened up to her. So often, she'd envied Lillian's gift. She warmed toward Nate now, seeing the genuine concern in his eyes. "Yes, she's going to be okay. It's a broken wrist. Thanks for asking." She sighed, the weight of the day catching up to her. "I worry about her living up there in the hollow alone."

"I'll do whatever you need, Doc." Nate's brown eyes were earnest. "Finished with classes. Just hanging out until time to leave for DC."

She reviewed a list of projects to make the cottage more appealing to Mother—paint, furnishings, a repair of the broken porch rail. "I especially want to be sure the pond is up and running." She looked across the garden at the neglected koi pond that had seemed such a great idea at the time. "Mother loves looking at water."

Nate looked at the pond and scratched his head. "Sure, no problem."

"I'll check in with you later in the week." *Was she doing the right thing?* She dismissed the thought. No time now for doubts.

She walked toward the screened-in back porch of her home and familiarity wrapped comforting arms around her. She caught hold of the same, still loose, railing her hand had gripped for thirty years. Climbed the same rickety steps she'd watched Dennis climb so long ago when he too had become Miss Pettiworth's tenant.

Today the rush of bittersweet memories felt almost unbearable. Back in the day, the whole street had been turn-of-the-century era houses chopped up into apartments catering to medical or law students. Some, like Miss Pettiworth's, boasted cottages that had been kitchens or coach houses when the homes were first built. The bohemian spinster—Jane

Pettiworth—had ruled over the comings and goings of the tenants of 201 Locust Avenue. During the early impoverished years of Miriam's medical practice, *she* had been the tenant in the tiny cottage Nate now occupied. She'd lived in the cottage when she met Dennis. She'd still been there when she met Hugh. Olivia had slept in a tiny bassinet by the bed. Had taken her first steps from her arms to Walt's in this weedy garden. Would Mother grow to love the cottage as she had all those years ago?

In 1980, five years into her medical practice, life took a sudden turn, rooting her further into this particular place. Miss Pettiworth's low Southern drawl filled her mind. "Miriam, you're my only family now, and I want you to have the house when I pass." Six months later, Miss Pettiworth was gone.

Over the years, the big houses on her street had been purchased and restored to their former glory. *Her* house was... not quite glorious, but home. From the top of the steps, she stopped to look over the fence at the tall windows overlooking the garden of the house next door. She didn't see Walt or Dennis. The solar garden lights in their *glorious* garden were starting to pop on.

She smiled wistfully, remembering Dennis and Walt's love affair. It had all started with that house. Walt had been in charge of the restoration. Dennis had been smitten from the first time Walt brandished a blueprint. They'd ended up buying it together. Walt had made it perfect. He'd nagged her for years to update her house. But she loved it as it was. Of course, she'd taken out the flimsy walls separating the high-ceilinged rooms into apartments, refinished the floors, updated the bathrooms. But she'd mostly kept the finishes the same as when Miss Pettiworth sat at the kitchen table, smoke curling from the Virginia Slim in an ivory cigarette holder between her fingers, long silver braid trailing over her shoulder, psychedelic caftan sweeping the floor.

Upstairs in her study, Miriam opened the blinds and peered down to the alley. She watched the ripple of Nate's sinewy muscles in the dusky light as he piled the bundles of tree limbs into neat stacks. Her thoughts turned again to Hugh and those long-ago summer nights when they made love on the narrow twin bed in the cottage, laughing and shushing each other, lest Miss Pettiworth hear them. Afterward, Hugh was always in the mood to talk about his plans for international relief work.

"It will be so great. You'll see, Miriam." His arm would be around her, holding her close, her head tucked into his shoulder. "I can organize everything for the clinics, order the supplies, bring in transportation. And you... you can run the medical side. I'll manage the staff. We can make such a difference..."

The next day she'd return to the mountain gynecology practice she'd begun to carve out from her home-base in Charlottesville. Her anxiety level would begin to rise. *Was life always to be about choosing?*

She'd let him go. At the time, she'd had no idea their two weeks together had given her Olivia. "If you ever change your mind..." He'd kissed her then and walked away. In all the years Hugh had come and gone, she could still remember the way he looked as he boarded that plane for Africa.

She shook away the thoughts and tapped Olivia's number on her cell phone screen. After only two rings, "Hi, Mom." Olivia instantly sounded suspicious of her call. This time she has reason to be, Miriam mused.

Deep breath. "Hi, Liv. I have some bad news. Your grandmother has had a fall."

"Oh, no," Olivia gasped. "What's happened? Is she hurt?" Olivia listened quietly, uttering an occasional murmur of understanding as Miriam relayed the limited details.

"So, it's time," Miriam concluded.

"What do you mean, Mom?"

"It's time to bring her to Charlottesville to live with me."

"Oh."

A million questions, a thousand disapprovals, a hundred reasons why *not* to move Mother were carried in that one little "Oh." Maybe she was being defensive. She pushed on to the harder part. "And I need your help."

"Me? Why me?"

"To tell you the truth"—she took a deep breath and got it all out at once— "I do *not* want to face your grandmother alone. We both know she's going to refuse to move. And, well... I need your support." She let out her breath, annoyed by this uncomfortable feeling of vulnerability.

"Okay, Mom, you have it."

That was too easy. A little guilty that her next thought was to wonder why Olivia was being so accommodating, she ignored her reservations and pushed on. "I've had an idea. My tenant, Nate—you remember Nate, don't you?"

"Yes, of course." Olivia sounded annoyed.

How am I to know if you remember Nate? "He's graduated and he's moving out, headed to DC for an internship. I thought I'd convince Mother to come to Charlottesville for a visit." She set her cell phone on the desk and pressed the button for speaker phone. She picked up her mail and sorted through it, stopping abruptly when a letter from Hugh reached the top of the pile. The letter held the international stamp of Ghana with the elephant theme he loved so much.

"Okay... And?"

What was that in Olivia's voice? She dropped the letter into her tote and pulled her attention back to the conversation. "Well, it's not as if she can continue to live up in the mountains, right?" Prickling, she laid the remaining mail on the desk and held her hands up in frustration, glad Olivia could not see her right now. She didn't wait for her to answer. "Anyway, I could fix up the cottage for Mother—I think she'd prefer her own space. I'm hoping..." She paused and stared at the phone.

"You're hoping...?" Olivia's voice was quiet.

"...that she'll begin to see it as a comfortable place to maybe stay... permanently." Miriam ended in a rush. Silence followed. "Hello?" Miriam's voice rose. "Are you there?" Muffled voices filled the background.

"Yeah, I'm here... sorry, had to say goodbye to Amy." Olivia sounded flustered. "Okay, so I'll need to see about flights..."

After they made a plan to check in with each other, Miriam tapped to end the call, relieved—and surprised—Olivia had agreed to come to Virginia at a moment's notice. She was certain Olivia disapproved of her plan, but this was not the time to quibble. As she pulled her laptop from its case and set it on the desk, her thoughts returned to Lillian. Was she in more pain than she admitted? Had the fall frightened her? So nonchalant about the whole thing. Another Lillian Stewart tactic—the Queen of *I'm-Fine*.

Squelching her frustration, she forced herself to focus on a mental list of what she needed to bring to the farmhouse. Her mother lived *so very simply*. Any visit longer than a day required bringing a little civilization along—wine, good coffee, a trip to the bakery for something besides that damn grocery store bread Lillian loved.

Realizing the login screen was ready, she signed in and clicked on her email for a last check before leaving. A tickle of excitement raised the little hairs at the back of her neck as she clicked on an email from *Ancestry.com* and found her DNA test results had arrived. *I suppose that project will have to wait awhile.* Certain the results would be too complex to review right now, she quickly skimmed her other emails, deleted a few, shut down her laptop, and shoved it into her tote. Out of habit, she dropped in the most recent copy of *Obstetrics & Gynecology* and proceeded to her bedroom to pack a few things for the week.

Packing done, she left her house, waving at Nate as she pulled out of the driveway. She reached to tune Sirius radio to her favorite seventies rock station. *Ah, the seventies,* she sighed, *when all of my dreams were coming true.* The recent, and lately, familiar ache for her younger self surfaced. How lucky she had been to be part of a generation of women who had more choices than ever before. Germaine Greer and Betty Friedan had been her idols. Birth control was legal and available. Sex wasn't as laden with the possibility of some scary disease as it was now.

Even so, with all of her *liberation,* she'd ended up accidentally pregnant. Hadn't even considered—well, maybe for a moment—marrying Hugh. She'd tried to do it all. By the time Olivia reached elementary school age, she'd settled into being *that* mom. Single, reasonably attractive. The one the other mothers either envied or hated—sometimes depending on how flirtatious their husbands were. She admitted to herself, she had kept the other women at arm's length. And each time the nagging little prick of longing surfaced—for her own soulmate, or partner, or for god's sake, someone else to do the laundry—she'd squashed it.

Her thoughts flipped to Lillian. *Had her dreams come true? Had she even had any dreams in her narrowly confined world?* Once again, the deep longing she always experienced in her relationship with her mother surfaced. As intensely as they butted heads at times, she could not bear the thought of losing Lillian. Each of their well-ordered lives was on the brink. Lillian had to leave her beloved farmhouse—there simply was no other way. Olivia—planning to have a baby with Amy—huge decision. And her. Newly retired and not sure who she was if she wasn't someone's doctor. The tangled knot in her stomach tightened as she forced herself to sing along with Stevie Nicks. Was this simply a new season of her life?

CHAPTER 5

Lillian

STAUNTON, VIRGINIA
MAY 24, 2010

Lillian thanked the nurse and turned on her side to look out the window. She could see a small section of green grass edging the parking lot. Not much else. Eighty-six years she'd managed to avoid hospitals. Doctor's appointments here and there—nothing serious. But, now, here she was, people fussing and poking, doing tests with big machines—all over a little break in her wrist.

This morning had started out like any other day. Cup of coffee at the kitchen table. She'd worked the crossword in the newspaper while her oatmeal cooked. Washed up her breakfast dishes. Puttered out to the henhouse to see if Fanny had laid anything. She'd been pleased to find an egg in the nest. Decided she might have that later. Poked around the barn a bit, checked the tools. Planting season was coming up soon. Back to the house for a second cup, then out to the mailbox just as Rosie, the mail carrier, pulled up in her little red truck. Rosie was one of Miriam's patients. She'd recently gotten out of the hospital after a miscarriage. Back to work too soon, if you'd asked Lillian.

"How you getting on, Rosie?" she'd asked. Rosie looked pale and tired. A miscarriage was no small thing. Took a toll on a woman's body. And her heart.

"Doing all right. A little bit weak, if I'm honest. But... mouths to feed and all."

"You sure you don't need to take a little time off?"

"Oh no, I'll be fine." Rosie gripped the steering wheel of the mail truck and shifted in the seat. Lillian caught the flash of pain in her grimace. "Saw Doc Stewart when I was in the hospital."

"That right?"

"Yep. Strange it was. Had a whole bunch of young'uns in white coats tagging behind her. I reckon she was their teacher. Had no idea she was a doctor teacher too."

Lillian kept her expression interested, but hid the surprise. This was news to her. "Suppose she's got a lot to offer young doctors." She didn't mention Miriam's retirement. Wasn't sure if she'd told her patients yet. The child had agonized over the decision of whether or not to end her career.

Rosie smiled and handed Lillian her mail. "Well, I'd better get going. You have a good day, Miz Lillian."

"You too, Rosie. Hello to the family." Lillian waved and turned back toward the farmhouse. She sorted through the stack of mail. Bills, circulars, and a letter. Postmarked Paris, France. She smiled with the pleasure a letter from Evelyn always brought. But when she looked again, she noticed the handwriting on the envelope was not Evelyn's usual loopy scrawl. It was neater, smaller. Strange. She made her way up the porch steps, dropped the other mail on the table beside her rocker, and slid her thumb under the envelope flap.

Dear Lily,
I'm writing to let you know, we've lost our darling Evelyn. She would never let me tell you about her fight with breast cancer. Please take comfort in knowing she

had excellent hospice care. At the end, she was sur-rounded by loved ones and her pain was managed quite well. One of her greatest pleasures over the years was your stories of Hazel Hollow and Jo, Elijah, Miriam, and your granddaughter, Olivia. You were such an im-portant part of Evelyn's life. She always believed you were the only person in Staunton who truly under-stood her. I know she would want you to smile when your memories take you back to those days.
With affection,
Charles

She wondered now, as she stared out the hospital window, if the letter was still in the pocket of the jacket she'd been wearing this morning. After reading the letter, her first thought had been to go to the river. She needed its comfort. Problem was, she paid no mind to the roots on the riverbank like she usually did. Tears had blurred her vision. If Jo hadn't come looking for her... But, even with the pain, all she could think as she lay there was: *Evelyn is gone.* She still couldn't take it in. She remembered the day she met Evelyn. Lillian and her mother, who was the midwife for Hazel Holler, had ridden their horse, Pearl, into Staunton. Mama had to visit the phar-macy for the medicines she needed for her delivering mothers.

STAUNTON, VIRGINIA
SPRING, 1938

Mary O'Toole yanked open the screen door of Duggins Phar-macy. Lillian trailed behind, looking around at the fascinating things Mr. Duggins had for sale. There were jars, bottles, and boxes with colorful labels for just about any ailment a person could imagine. She peeked through the dividing wall of shelves to the soda fountain side of the shop, but jolted to attention when Mr. Duggins peered over his high counter and said to Mama, "And this one is for you, Mary."

Mama glanced around and drew closer to the counter. Lillian pretended to be examining a display of Ivory soap, but looked when Mama turned her back. Mr. Duggins spoke softly and pointed to the small brown bottle he held up for her inspection. Mama nodded, taking in his instructions. When she turned, wearing her no-nonsense expression, Lillian quickly looked away.

"All done." Her tone was brisk. "We best get over to Mrs. McDonald's." Over her shoulder she threw, "Good day, Mr. Duggins." She frowned at the line of customers behind them, stepped around the dividing shelves, and started down the aisle past the soda fountain. Lillian was thrilled. But Mama didn't stop. Didn't even slow down.

Lillian struggled to contain her disappointment. There would be no ice cream today. She tried to keep her eyes straight ahead as they passed the soda fountain counter, but couldn't help glancing at the shelves lined with jars of mouth-watering candy and fancy crystal glasses. She was especially curious about three girls who sat on tall stools. *What kind of girls are happy in fancy dresses and those perfectly rolled curls in their hair?* Two of them giggled and sipped frothy white sodas through red and white striped straws.

The third girl sat a little apart from the others. Her dress was loose and comfortable-looking and she wore saddle shoes instead of those shiny black ones with straps. Her short dark hair was wavy and loose. Lillian allowed herself one quick peek at the girl's face as she passed, surprised to catch bright green eyes and a wide grin. Lillian paid her back with a hint of a smile.

"Country come to town," one of the fancy girls whispered loudly to another, after Lillian and Mama passed by. A hot flush traveled up Lillian's neck to her cheeks. Hugging the library book closer to her chest, she clinched her fists and held her head high. She traded her embarrassment for knowing, in a few minutes, she'd check out a new book.

Mama patted her arm when she left her at the book truck. "I'll see you at Mrs. McDonald's as soon as you're done."

"Yes, ma'am." Lillian was already preoccupied with the rows of books before her. Six years ago, she'd fallen in love with the stories about a girl named Laura Ingalls. Laura's adventures out on the prairie were exciting and so different from the holler. The book she finally held in her hands today, after waiting for weeks for it to be returned, was called *On the Banks of Plum Creek*. In this one, the family had moved all the way to Minnesota.

Absorbed in the first pages of the story, she walked in the general direction of Mrs. McDonald's house and munched on an apple she'd tucked into her pocket. She almost dropped the book when someone touched her arm. She turned with a backward step to find the girl from the soda fountain with the short dark hair and plain clothes standing before her. Pretty heart-shaped face with sparkling green eyes. Looked about her same age. Under her simple cotton dress, she already had visible breasts, unlike Lillian's still almost flat chest.

"Hi." She stuck out her hand. Lillian's mouth dropped open, and she fumbled to catch her book before clasping the girl's hand. "My name is Evelyn Preston, and I believe that you and I should be friends."

Lillian was so taken aback by the girl's abrupt announcement she couldn't come up with a reply. Before she could think of something to say, Evelyn had linked an arm through hers and steered them toward the shade of a wide crabapple tree hovering over the sidewalk. Evelyn plopped onto the ground, careless of her dress and shoes, and patted the grass beside her. Lillian was now more curious than dumbfounded, so she lowered herself to the grass, holding her book in one hand and the half-eaten apple in the other.

"I saw you in the drugstore today and I heard what those nasty girls said," Evelyn announced. "I'm not like those girls, you see. And you're not like those girls." Her eyes raked over Lillian's mousy brown braids, her freckled nose, bony shoulders, worn overalls, and scuffed boots. "So, the natural conclusion is that we should be friends. What are you reading?"

Lillian looked down at the book in her hands, completely forgotten when Evelyn appeared. She felt again the quiver of excitement at the prospect of a new story. She'd never had a friend to talk with about books before. Reading was a special pleasure; she didn't even share it with Mama. Her only other friend was Josephine—Jo—Stewart. But Jo couldn't read much more than three-letter words, even though she was twelve. Jo was her fishing buddy, had been her doll-playing buddy— when she was younger.

"Well?" Evelyn reached for the book.

Lillian pulled the book back toward her chest. "It's the new one by Laura Ingalls Wilder. I've been waiting on it for five weeks."

"Oh yeah, *On the Banks of Plum Creek*," Evelyn nodded. "I have that one."

"You own it?" Lillian asked without thinking. She didn't know anyone who owned books other than Mama, but her books were all about delivering babies.

"I do. Daddy bought it for me. I have lots of books." It didn't sound like bragging when Evelyn said it. Matter-of-fact, like stating her name or address. "But I would much rather read Agatha Christie. I just finished *Death on the Nile*. Maybe you could come over to my house sometime and I would lend you any book you wanted to borrow."

Lillian didn't know what to think. Evelyn already had two things she didn't have—a daddy and lots of money. She pushed herself up off the ground. "Um... I'd better go. My mama will be expecting me."

Evelyn didn't take to being put off. "Where's your mother? Can I walk with you?"

Not wanting to be rude, Lillian nodded. They fell into step beside each other on the shady street toward Mrs. McDonald's house. Evelyn asked, "Who *is* your mother? I loved her clothes. She looked so...strong."

This was a comfortable subject. Lillian was proud telling Evelyn about Mama being a midwife in the holler. "She visits old Mrs. McDonald when we're in town," she finished. "Mrs. McDonald was a midwife until she went blind and got afflicted with the arthritis. Had to move to town to live with her daughter when it got so bad she couldn't even get to the barn to feed the stock."

Evelyn stopped in her tracks, reached out, and placed her hand on Lillian's arm, holding her in place. "Wait." She looked at Lillian with a knowing grin. "Does Mrs. McDonald have a daughter named Mavis?"

"Yep. Mavis is a housekeeper for the doctor here in town."

Evelyn laid her hand on her chest and said, all excited, "That's us."

Lillian frowned. "Who is us?"

"My daddy is Dr. Preston, and Mavis has been our house-keeper for years."

"Oh," was all Lillian could think to say. Now, she was *certain* a friendship with this girl was not for her. Evelyn was one of those rich town people who thought they were above people from the holler. But Evelyn didn't seem to be put off.

"See, Lillian, we're practically family already. How old are you?"

"Fourteen." Lillian twitched nervously. Maybe she *was* "country-come-to-town" like that girl in the drugstore had said.

"I'm fifteen, but I've always wanted a younger sister,"

Evelyn stated matter-of-factly. Lillian could tell from her open-face and friendly eyes that Evelyn was sure she'd feel the same way. She tried to sort out what to make of Evelyn. She hadn't even known she wanted a friend. Why, all of a sudden, did it feel important? "Tell me about where you live," Evelyn said, her eyes bright.

Lillian couldn't help warming to her. Evelyn listened real interested-like to her description of the holler, the river, and hers and Mama's cabin. She told her about Jo and the rest of the neighboring Stewart family, who lived just across the ridge. She even surprised herself by telling Evelyn about Jo's brother, Elijah—also fourteen—and how annoying he could be.

"Sounds like you like him." Evelyn gave her a knowing smile.

Lillian's cheeks burned. She didn't deny it, but she did change the subject. "Do you have a fellow?"

"Not anymore. I thought I might, but it was a doomed love affair." Evelyn put on a face like a tragic movie star and held her hand to her heart. Lillian laughed and then caught herself when she realized Evelyn was serious.

"Why was it doomed?"

Evelyn leaned in close. "He's a Monacan Indian." She must have seen Lillian's eyes go wide. "Shocking, isn't it? Mother and Daddy would have a fit if they knew. Probably lock me in the house until I married some white boy they chose." They walked in silence for a short distance, Lillian uncertain what to say.

Lillian had a sneaking suspicion that Evelyn's interest in the Indian fellow had more to do with the forbidden than with love. Was that what hers and Evelyn's friendship was—just another interest in the forbidden? She felt a little guilty for being so suspicious of Evelyn.

Lillian knew of the small Monacan Indian community and the Indian Mission School on Bear Mountain. Twice, when the

Indian midwife wasn't available, she'd gone with Mama to deliveries there. Her thoughts drifted to the confusing conversation she'd overheard between Mama and the white-haired Indian grandmother after the delivery of her grandson. Mama said, "Now, you know the situation with the birth certificates." The grandmother had nodded. "What do you want me to record?" Mama asked.

The old woman had lifted her chin and quietly, proudly said, "Indian."

Mama had dutifully filled out the record just as the woman had asked. "I have to tell you, I've heard rumors they're changing any birth certificates that say Indian to Colored."

"No colored."

"Yes, ma'am," was all Mama said.

She'd never seen Mama so mad as she was the day she came back from the mailbox with an official-looking letter. Lillian had read the return address: The Virginia State Registrar of Vital Statistics. Mama had ripped that letter in two and thrown it in the fireplace.

"I'm not doing it," she'd said. "Let them throw me in the penitentiary." She'd slammed her hand down on the table. "There are hardly any Indian families left in this holler after all that Dr. Plecker fellow has done. Evil man. If he has his way, he will force every Indian in Virginia out. If they want to be registered as Indian, then that's how I'll record them." Lillian hadn't fully understood what Mama was talking about at the time, but she did know folks in town treated Indians the same way they did Colored. Mama said it was ridiculous—two different water fountains, two different entrances. Signs saying Whites Only.

Was Evelyn just being rebellious or was it dangerous? She returned her attention to Evelyn. "How did you come to get sweet on an Indian boy?"

"Last April, I went with Mother to the Indian Mission

School to deliver clothes and toys for the children after the spring charity drive." Evelyn stuck her chin in the air and mimicked her mother. "'Now, Evelyn, we are here to help these poor people, but we are *not* here to make friends. Do not talk to the Indians. Stay close to me and do not go wandering off.'"

Evelyn grinned and her green eyes shone. "But there was this boy. So handsome. Thick black hair and dreamy brown eyes. He was helping unload the boxes. I smiled at him when Mother wasn't looking. But he wouldn't smile back and he kept looking toward the building where the teachers were. Kind of nervous-like, you know?"

Lillian nodded. She could guess why he was nervous. Especially after what Evelyn's mother said.

"Finally, when Mother and her ladies and the teachers went to get lunch ready, he sat down by himself under one of the trees. I brought him a cup of water and introduced myself. He wasn't very friendly at first. But, when I asked about the mission, he opened up a little bit. Told me about the school and his family. I found out he and his brother picked apples at the State Hospital orchards during the harvest season. I was just about to tell him my daddy worked at the State Hospital when Mother hollered my name and I had to run back."

"Did you see him again?" Lillian couldn't help but feel a thrill at her audacity. There was mischief in Evelyn's eyes when she answered.

"I rode my bicycle over to Western State last fall during apple picking. I tried not to be conspicuous. I looked and looked." Evelyn pantomimed sneaking around, her hand shading her eyes, peering into the distance. Lillian burst out with laughter and Evelyn grinned, enjoying the drama. "And then I spotted him. At the very same time, Lily, he looked up and saw me." Evelyn stopped and collapsed against an old oak tree so big it pushed up the sidewalk. "It was like Romeo and Juliet.

Our eyes met. He smiled..." Evelyn let out a long, wistful sigh. "I waited for him at the bottom of the orchard behind one of the bigger apple trees. He sneaked away when they stopped for lunch."

"What did you do?" Lillian imagined all sorts of things, but Evelyn's answer was a surprise.

"We talked and talked about our dreams, Lily. He wanted to leave Staunton as much as I did. There's a war brewing over in Europe right now. I didn't even know until he told me."

Lillian remembered Mama reading in the newspaper about war coming over in Europe. Mama had said, "*Surely* Mr. Roosevelt won't get us into another war."

Evelyn continued, "Anyway, he and his brothers want to register for military service, but as Indian, not colored. He says they'll fight for their rights all the way to the Supreme Court if they have to."

Lillian listened quietly, remembering her mother's angry outburst over the birth certificates, thinking of what Mama would say if she told her about Evelyn. Maybe she'd just keep Evelyn to herself for now.

They walked on and Evelyn's voice tightened in frustration. "My mother must have suspected something because ever since last fall, she's kept such a tight rein on me, I can scarcely breathe." She stopped again and planted her hands on her hips, her eyes blazing. "She can send me to all the church socials and Junior Women's Club meetings she wants. I am not giving my heart to some boring boy planning to follow in his daddy's footsteps and stay in boring old Staunton, Virginia. Boring, boring, boring." She shook her head from side to side with each word.

Lillian stopped to listen, but now stepped forward, hoping to coax Evelyn forward. Mama would be wondering where she was. "And did you give your heart to the Indian boy?"

"No." Another long sigh. "It really *was* a doomed affair.

The Indian Mission School only goes through seventh grade. When I saw him at apple harvest, his family was fixing to send him off to Hampton for more schooling. I'll probably never see him again."

Lillian was about to ask more questions when the clock on the Presbyterian church struck twelve. "Jeepers," Evelyn exclaimed. "I gotta go. My mother will be madder than a wet hen if I'm late." Evelyn surprised her with a tight hug. "Let's meet at the book truck next Saturday." Evelyn held Lillian's arms, her green eyes pleading.

"We won't be back for two weeks," Lillian said. Evelyn would forget all about her by then.

"Two weeks then," Evelyn said.

"All right." She was confused at the prospect of being friends with this strange and insistent girl. She raised a hand goodbye as Evelyn rushed off toward the center of town. Just before Evelyn turned the corner, she stopped and called out, "Saturday, ten o'clock?"

A little quiver stirred inside Lillian as she nodded and waved. Feeling a little let-down after the excitement of meeting Evelyn, Lillian made her way onto the side street, away from the hubbub of the main street, and knocked on the wooden door of Mrs. McDonald's small house. Mrs. McDonald threw open the door, her blind eyes crinkled at the corners in a smile. "Is that you, Lillian?" She reached with a cool, wrinkled hand to touch Lillian's cheek.

"Hello, Mrs. McDonald." Lillian gently grasped the old woman's hand.

"Your mama has been wondering where you were." She backed up for Lillian to enter and called, "Mary, Lillian's here."

"About time," Mama sounded from the sitting room. "I was about to send out the hounds."

Lillian pinched her mouth in rebellion, knowing Mrs. McDonald couldn't see her being rude.

"You just go on into the kitchen and help yourself to some of those cookies." Mrs. McDonald patted her shoulder as she stepped into the small entryway. The house, as always, smelled of cinnamon.

As Mama and Mrs. McDonald settled back into their chairs in the sitting room with their cups of strong Irish tea, Lillian sought out the familiarity of Mrs. McDonald's kitchen. She helped herself to a plate of ginger cookies, poured a glass of milk, and set it on the kitchen table. She was as contented as a fat yellow tabby cat in the sun when she dropped into a chair and finally opened the book she'd been longing to read. She smiled as she thought of Evelyn Preston. It had never occurred to her that she might make friends with a town girl.

She reached for another cookie and looked up from her book when Mama began talking much louder than usual. "What? Rounding them up? What do you mean *rounding them up?*"

Mrs. McDonald's loud shush caused Mama's voice to drop low enough Lillian could no longer hear them. She returned to her book. They must be talking about cattle or horses.

Mama was quieter than usual on the ride back up the mountain to the holler. Lillian was sleepy and contented with her arms wrapped around Mama's solid waist, her new library book stowed safely in the saddle bag, swaying gently to the back-and-forth lurching of Pearl's hips. They stopped for lunch, settled on the river bank, their legs stretched out in front of them. Pearl grazed on a nearby patch of new green grass. Lillian told Mama about the girls at the soda fountain. Mama had been too far ahead to hear the nasty comment.

"Ignore them, Lil." Mama had an exasperated tone in her voice. "They're right. We *are* country." She turned toward Lillian, the familiar wide gap-toothed smile filled her face and crinkled the edges of her blue eyes. "I wouldn't trade the holler for any other place on earth." She motioned toward the river and the green hillside covered with bluebells.

Feeling a surge of love for her mother, who didn't let what other people thought bother her one bit, Lillian decided, once again, she wanted nothing more than to be like Mama. But she also decided to stick with her earlier thought and not tell her about the strange girl named Evelyn Preston. She wasn't quite sure why she kept Evelyn to herself. Maybe it was because Mama had never trusted "that town doctor," which is what she called Dr. Preston, the man Lillian now knew was Evelyn's daddy. No, for the time being, her new friend would be a special secret all her own.

There was a mysterious touch of sadness in Mama's smile today and her next words filled Lillian with a sense of danger. "Stay in these mountains, Lillian," she said, an urgency to her voice. "I've taught you every hill and holler, how to read the signs for when to plant the garden, how to fish and hunt. You'll have everything you'll need for a good life. There will be times when you need to go down into town, but don't stay long. You're safer up here."

Mama didn't say why town wasn't safe, so Lillian was left not knowing what to think. She understood that town, with its brick houses so close together and its tall mansions near the park, was different. In the holler, reaching another cabin meant a walk over the mountain ridge or through the woods. It was true, she didn't like the noisiness of Staunton. And she especially didn't like the stares from town girls like the ones at the soda fountain. But now? Now there was Evelyn. And she couldn't stop wondering what it would be like to be her friend.

Mama looked so worried as she gazed out over the river that Lillian felt an unfamiliar ripple of fear. "And you, Mama," she said. "I have you."

Mama didn't answer. Lillian was puzzled by her silence, but knew Mama didn't talk much, so she didn't think more about it. She lay back on the soft grass and cupped her hands behind her head. Sighing with contentment, she looked up through the thick branches of the sycamore trees filling out with delicate new leaves. A tingling feeling of life opening up rippled through her. Same one she'd gotten on the day her first monthly started, knowing she'd have her own babies someday. Possibility. Right behind that feeling was a quiver of excitement about her next trip to the traveling library. More than the books she always looked forward to, she couldn't wait to see Evelyn again.

STAUNTON HOSPITAL
MAY 24, 2010

Lillian turned onto her back. The tube connected to her arm, dripping something from a plastic bag, caught on the covers, and she wriggled her arm around to free it. All these years, keeping Evelyn's secret. So many times, she'd wondered if she'd done the right thing. Evelyn had never wavered from her vow. They were sisters. Across thousands of miles, an ocean, and lives that couldn't have been any more different, they'd loved each other through their letters and Evelyn's postcards. Lillian had gotten to experience a whole other life without ever leaving Virginia. There'd always been that nagging touch of guilt. Should she share *her* Evelyn—because that's how she thought of her—with her family? Lillian's simple existence couldn't possibly measure up to the fascinating life Evelyn had lived.

The pain medicine started to work, and she closed her eyes. No, even with Evelyn gone, she'd keep her promise.

CHAPTER 6

Miriam

Miriam had gotten Lillian home from the hospital and settled into bed last night. And she had managed to keep her there most of the day today. But as the afternoon waned, the determination was crystal clear in the way Lillian held her head and the set of her wrinkled mouth when she announced, "I'm going to the porch." Fatigue softened Lillian's usually resonant voice, but better not to argue. With a quiet sigh of frustration, Miriam reminded herself: *choose your battles.*

She followed Lillian out onto the wide front porch, remaining close enough to catch her if dizziness struck. She jerked to a standstill when Lillian stopped abruptly to gaze out over the wide front lawn sloping down to the river. Scrap, her elderly beagle, sauntered over from his favorite spot on the porch steps and nuzzled her leg for attention. Distractedly, she reached toward him with the hand partially covered by a cast. He jerked his head back to sniff the strange blue object coming toward him. Lillian laughed. "Sorry about that, old boy." She reached across with her other hand and scratched his head.

Miriam breathed in the balmy May air. The sky was a

cloudless azure blue. She indulged in a moment of nostalgia for her childhood home and these mountains. When Lillian began to move again, she grasped her elbow and guided her to her favorite hickory rocking chair. When Lillian shivered, Miriam hurried back to the front room for a quilt from the blanket chest and placed it over her frail legs. Lillian rested her cast on the arm of the chair and seemed to relax her shoulders. When she glanced up, Miriam averted her eyes.

"Good to be home," Lillian said softly. "Thank you, honey." She met Miriam's gaze with those familiar sky-blue eyes. She reached for Miriam's hand and squeezed it. Her frail, cool fingers were knobby with arthritis.

Miriam tried to be still, but after a second or two, she carefully withdrew her hand, biting her lip. "I'll see if the coffee's ready." In the kitchen, she gripped the countertop and took deep breaths. *What is wrong with me today?* The realization wrenched her heart. She hadn't been able to do a thing for her father when he had his accident. Not a damn thing. The last time she'd looked into his gray eyes had been... She shook her head slowly, shocked at how long it had been.

AUGUST, 1972

She'd gotten her dream residency. Of course, the men in her graduating class from UVA Medical School scoffed. "Why do you want to go to some charity hospital in Boston?" They knew how hard she'd worked to be in the top of the class. She could have chosen any of the prestigious locations—NYU, Johns Hopkins. She chose Boston Hospital for Women. Tomorrow, Mother and Daddy would drop her off at the Greyhound station—two long days on the bus, 600 miles away—she didn't know when she'd see them again.

She sat in her usual place—the top porch step—her back against the post. Elijah was in his rocker, smoking his pipe.

The hot August sun faded behind the mountain. She turned her face to catch the tiny bit of breeze coming off the river and sipped her iced tea. Through the screen door, sounds of Lillian in the kitchen. She'd insisted on making Miriam's favorite meal, chicken and dumplings, for supper.

"I just hope there are other women," she sighed. She turned to look at her father. He met her gaze, looking thoughtful. Her parents knew what she'd been up against the past four years as only one of two women in her class. The condescension, the sexist jokes, the outright sabotage. Their constant encouragement had been the reason she'd kept her head down and plowed through, determined not to let her male classmates get to her.

Elijah set his pipe down, picked up his tea glass, and sipped as he looked out across the lawn. "I reckon some men ain't comfortable with strong women." He was silent for a long time.

Miriam thought of Rachel's comment back in their undergrad days. "You have to let the man think he's stronger than you. They need that, Miriam. It's just how they are." She wanted to scream in frustration. *What is Daddy trying to say?*

He turned to her, his gray eyes shining. "Don't mean you should change a thing, baby girl. Don't ever make yourself less to make a man feel better." He set down his tea and picked up his pipe. "Your mama has taught me that much about strong women. And you come from a long line of them."

Lillian pushed open the screen door. "A long line of what?"

Miriam smiled. "Daddy says I come from a long line of strong women."

Lillian nodded. "I reckon that's right." She leaned against the door frame. "You remind me so much of your grandmother, Mary. She believed a woman should have a mind of her own, do what she loved." Lillian sighed then. "Not easy is all. Making your way in this world, doing things your own way, is damn hard. But if anyone can do it, you can." She walked over and kissed the top of Elijah's head. "Now y'all come on in and eat before it gets cold." She turned and headed back toward the kitchen.

Elijah and Miriam rose from their seats. She leaned in close as he encircled her shoulders with his arm. "You go be a doctor. Don't you let anybody stop you."

"I'll do my best, Daddy."

So much love, she had felt bathed in it, like cool lake water on a scorching summer day. Eight months later, she was exhausted, just off a twenty-hour shift. She'd delivered six babies—two of them stillborn, one so small she feared he wouldn't make it through the night. She didn't even take off her clothes before she collapsed onto her bed in the drafty dorm room of the women's residence.

The jangling of the telephone in the hall woke her. She stumbled out of her room to answer it, her mind fogged with fatigue. Surreal, hearing her mother's voice. She never called. Rarely used the telephone.

"Miriam, honey..." Lillian's voice caught. A cold chill gripped Miriam.

"What's wrong?" Miriam's heart beat wildly. "What's happened?"

"Your daddy... there was an accident with the tractor..."

And just like that, he was gone. She took a leave of absence to make the long bus ride home for the funeral. Elijah was buried in the family cemetery next to the grandparents she had no memory of, Jack and Jane Stewart. After the burial, their farmhouse filled with family, neighbors, and food. She was surrounded by people she didn't know whose houses Elijah had built, whose babies Lillian had delivered.

Finally, when it was over, Aunt Jo, the last to leave, squeezed her into one of her bosomy hugs. "Don't you worry 'bout your mama, now. I'll watch out for her."

After Aunt Jo left, she sank into a chair at the kitchen table. The quiet surrounded her like a blanket. If only she'd told her father how his love had made her feel safe... safe to be strong. She reflected on the men in her life over the years since high school. She'd always compared them to him. Today, she had an inkling none of them would ever measure up.

Lillian came into the kitchen. "Should I make us some coffee?"

"Got anything stronger?"

"Sure do."

They took a bottle of Elijah's favorite whiskey and two enamelware cups down to Lillian's thinking spot on the river. Miriam leaned back against the old hemlock tree and sighed. "I can't wrap my head around it."

Lillian shook her head. "No, me either," she sighed. Silent tears streamed from her eyes. "I reckon death comes for all of us."

———

Now, once again in Lillian's kitchen, Miriam swallowed all of her what ifs, poured two cups of coffee, black, the way they both preferred it, and rejoined her mother. She sat in Elijah's nearby chair and rocked distractedly, tapping her foot with each rhythmic movement of the chair.

"We all have to go sometime, you know," Lillian said.

Eerie, how Lillian seemed to read her mind. Gripping the arms of the chair, she sputtered, "Motherrr." Her chest tightened and she looked away. They both stared out across the bright green grass, fading into the late afternoon shadow at the river's edge.

On some level, Miriam knew Lillian was at peace with this last portion of her life. Other people—Rachel, for example—seemed to deal gracefully with losing their mothers. But try as she might, she could not come to terms with any harm coming to her mother because of some preventable cause. After all, prevention had been Miriam's métier, had it not? *And I'm good at it, dammit.* Maddening not to be able to apply that skill to her own mother.

Out of nowhere, Scrap launched himself off the porch, baying as he crossed the lawn. Miriam jumped and spilled her coffee onto the front of her cashmere sweater. She dabbed at the stain, annoyed. A Toyota sedan with an *Uber* sticker on the windshield pulled into the driveway. Olivia emerged from the rear passenger seat and waved toward them. She turned back to take her bag from the driver and thanked him before he drove away.

As Olivia approached, Miriam looked over at Lillian, who smiled and waved with her good hand. Miriam breathed a sigh of relief, mentally patting herself on the back for asking her daughter to come. Olivia charged toward them, all legs in rumpled khaki shorts and t-shirt, her young face shiny with oil, her hair yanked into a messy ponytail. A cocktail of envy, joy, and a dash of anxiety at Olivia's presence rippled through Miriam. Olivia rushed up the porch steps and dropped her duffle bag.

Miriam rose and opened her arms. Olivia towered over her by several inches. "Hi, Mom. How are you?" She bent and gave Miriam a cursory hug, then shrugged out of her backpack and turned to Lillian. Miriam folded her arms and sat back down.

"Hi, Gran." Olivia dropped to her knees in front of Lillian's rocker. Miriam was a little awed at the way Olivia deliberately contained her kinetic energy and looked into her grandmother's eyes. So tender, the way Olivia took Lillian's hand, how they laughed quietly together about the blue cast on her wrist and hand. The easiness as Olivia turned and plopped down on the porch, sitting at Lillian's feet. "It's great to be back." Her voice caught as she clasped her knees in front of her and looked out toward the river and the mountain ridge beyond. "I've really missed you *and* your mountains, Gran."

Miriam couldn't stop her first thought: *That's certainly not going to help my case.* She also couldn't prevent herself from interjecting, "And your grandmother is lucky the ambulance could find her up here on *her* mountain. I'm thankful it's only her wrist."

"Now, Miriam." Lillian used the frustratingly calm voice that implied Miriam was over-inflating whatever she was feeling. Olivia simply looked from one to the other of them and smiled. They chatted quietly for a while—Olivia's flight, Lillian's injury, Scrap's aging hips. The evening light turned golden, and the sun started to drop behind Brush Mountain.

Miriam stood, picked up the empty cups, and balanced them together in one hand. "I'll go get some dinner started."

"Need help?" Olivia asked.

"No, I've got it."

In the kitchen, she reached into the refrigerator for the spicy chicken tortilla soup from her go-to spot in Charlottesville, Revolutionary Soup. She poured it into a saucepan and stirred, contemplating the events of the last two days. Last night's dinner with Walt and Dennis to celebrate her retirement had been canceled. Here she was in Hazel Hollow with her injured mother and worried daughter, trying to figure out what to do. So much for the *fun* Dennis mentioned she should have doing the genealogy project with Walt.

A sudden realization that, with all of her dithering over Lillian, she had completely forgotten the email with her DNA results. She put a lid on the soup, retrieved her laptop from the front bedroom, returned to the kitchen, and sat at the table. She turned on her laptop and stared into space, waiting for the achingly slow internet to connect. Finally, she was able to sign into her *Ancestry* account.

She clicked on the results link for her DNA profile. While the results were loading, she rose from her chair to stir the soup. She decided to pour herself a glass of the wine she'd brought from home. By the time she returned to her laptop, the screen had done that annoying thing of turning black. She tapped the space bar and re-entered her passcode. The DNA results screen opened before her. She reached up and pulled her glasses from the top of her head to peer at the detailed report. She was so absorbed in the information, so dumbfounded by the graphics before her, she did not notice Olivia and Lillian walk into the kitchen.

"Mom, you're sitting in the dark." Olivia flipped the light switch, flooding the kitchen with the warm glow of the schoolhouse fixture over the table. Miriam squinted and stared blankly as Olivia rushed to the stove. The plopping of the soup's rapid boil sounded somewhere in the distance. "And the soup is sticking." Olivia turned down the gas flame. "Mom, are you okay?"

Lillian took a seat in the chair across the table. As if from very far away, her face creased in a frown of concern. She sat in the same chair where she'd sat for Miriam's entire life. But instead of the familiar wrinkled face, Miriam saw a stranger. She looked at Olivia, opened her mouth, and closed it again. Her heart began to beat rapidly. The room felt hot and close. She finally managed to say, "I need some air." She slammed the laptop closed and headed for the front door.

"Mom?"

When Olivia followed her, she tossed over her shoulder, "Stay with your grandmother."

She threw open the screen door and walked out into the cool night air. The stars were just starting to come out. She blindly walked toward the river, craving its solace, anything to quiet her racing mind. What she had seen on the laptop screen had changed everything.

CHAPTER 7

Olivia

HAZEL HOLLOW
MAY 25, 2010

Olivia knocked lightly and poked her head in the door of Lillian's room to make sure she was settled for the night. "Hey, Gran." Similar to Colorado, early summer evenings in the mountains of Virginia were still cool. She smiled at the sight of Lillian sitting up in bed under one of her homemade quilts. A blue knitted cap covered her head and her long gray braid draped over one shoulder.

"Hi there, darlin'." Lillian twisted off her glasses, struggling to use the gnarled fingers protruding from the cast.

Olivia moved quickly across the creaky heart pine wood floor and reached to take the glasses and set them on the table. "Just coming in to say goodnight. Can I get you anything?"

Scrap raised his head from where he was curled on the braided rug beside Lillian's four-poster bed. Olivia scratched behind his ears and stepped over him to sit on the side of the bed. She snuggled into Lillian's bony hip. Memories of her little-girl-self flowed unbidden: curled up beside her grandmother, strong arms holding her close, the gentle mountain voice telling stories about Hazel Hollow. She swallowed a lump in her throat. How good would it feel to be that little carefree girl again, wrapped in Lillian's safe embrace?

Lillian smiled and reached up to smooth the curly black hair away from Olivia's face in that comforting way she always had. "I'm glad you're here, my sweet Livy." Lillian's blue eyes were still bright, her mind still sharp, even at eighty-six years old.

"Me too." Olivia reached to rest her hand on Lillian's shoulder. "We're going to take good care of you."

"I suspect you will." Lillian covered Olivia's warm hand with her cool one. "Livy?"

"Yes?"

"You'll need to take good care of your mother this summer, too, you hear?" Lillian squeezed her hand.

A small snort of bitter laughter escaped. *Her? Take care of Miriam Stewart? That would be a first.* But Lillian looked entirely serious. Strange. As always, when her grandmother's eyes fixed on her, she felt naked. Known. She bent to kiss Lillian's forehead. "Sure. I can do that." At the moment, she was unwilling to guess what Lillian might mean. She was exhausted and just wanted to sleep. She had her own issues to deal with, after all.

"Goodnight, Gran."

"Goodnight, Livy."

———

Olivia made her way back through the kitchen, and past the front sitting room, with the same old blue brocade settee and uncomfortable floral fabric armchair that had been there all of her life. Lillian always said, "That room is for company. I don't have much use for it otherwise."

Visiting Lillian's house meant she had to share the large front bedroom across the hall from the sitting room with Miriam. Typically, this was only for a few days during her annual visit to Virginia. This particular visit, however, was different. Because of Lillian's injury, this visit might be a lot longer. She vacillated between wanting to help her grandmother and dread at an entire summer with her mother.

Opening the door quietly, she remembered her phone was on the bedside table. She hadn't talked to Amy since leaving Colorado before dawn this morning. Already, Colorado, this morning, and Amy seemed a world away.

Except for moonlight pouring through the large wooden mullioned window that overlooked the front porch, the room was dark. The high-ceilinged space was long enough to hold two double beds—always a bit strange to share such intimate space with her mother—Miriam Stewart had a way of filling up a room. As her eyes adjusted, she cringed to see Miriam was not in bed as she'd hoped. Instead, her mother stepped from the dark corner and stood in front of the window, chewing on her bottom lip.

"Mom, you okay?" Olivia plopped down on the bed and reached for her phone, glancing to see if Amy had called. When Miriam didn't respond, she dropped the cell phone on the bedside table and inspected her mother closer. Olivia frowned. Miriam had obviously been running her hands through her silver hair, and wisps of it stuck out wildly from the clip that usually held it smoothly in place.

"Is she asleep?" Miriam's voice sounded scratchy, ragged.

"I think so." Olivia sank back against the headboard, pulled a pillow into her lap, and hugged it to her chest. Something was happening here. Her mother was always the same: level-headed and predictable. *Do I really want to know what's up? Of course you do, idgit. Grow up.* "Mom, what's wrong? Is it something about Gran?"

Miriam finally stopped pacing and dropped into the frayed wingback chair near the window. The moonlight added a ghostly glow to her silver hair. Her mother's solid self faded into someone Olivia didn't recognize.

"It's the DNA test I did." Miriam gripped the chair's arms and pushed her thin body erect. "You know the one I suggested we both do?"

Olivia felt the intensity of her mother's gaze. *Another of Mom's plans dodged.* But she nodded, frowning. "What about it?"

"It's... it's..."

"It's what?" Olivia's voice came off a bit sharper than she intended.

Miriam jerked her head up, eyes glazed. "Not what I expected. I think they must have gotten my results confused with someone else's."

Now, this sounded like her mother's usual—distrusting of any laboratory or clinical findings but her own. "What do you mean?"

Miriam stood and walked over to her bed, picked up her laptop, and opened it. She thrust it into Olivia's hands. "Look at this."

It took a moment for Olivia to orient herself to the way the results were organized on the screen, but then... At first, she felt oddly numb. She stifled an unexpected smile at the irony. Miriam, deflated like a whirling balloon, sat limply on the bed, staring into space. Olivia ventured, "How could this be? I thought your whole side of the family was Scottish and Irish?"

"So, did I." Her mother's expression was blank, unreadable. She turned to look out the window.

"What are you thinking?" Olivia ventured tentatively.

"I don't know what to think." She shook her head. "I'm unmoored."

"It's just a silly DNA test, Mom. Maybe there were ancestors that Gran and Grandpa didn't know about." Even as she made light of it, Olivia fought a crazy desperation to recapture her in-charge, competent mother. *Doesn't she know I need her to have her shit together right now?* Miriam turned to look at her and Olivia recognized the set of her mother's jaw. The cold-hard-facts woman was back again.

A flutter of relief at Miriam's flat, unyielding voice. "Your grandparents told me about *each and every* one of my ancestors, Olivia." Miriam pulled off her glasses and rubbed her nose. "And each of every one of them was Scottish or Irish."

Olivia couldn't think of a single thing to say. Her mind drifted to the recent, seemingly endless, hours she'd spent online, pouring over sperm donor attributes. She'd been desperate to choose correctly. Would the child she planned to bring into the world have a sense of history, of belonging to a family? She *got* what her mother meant about feeling unmoored. Her grandmother's long history in these mountains had always been a tether, one of the few things she and her mother shared. Olivia took a deep breath. This shifting sand was *not* an option right now.

"You have to ask her." Olivia surprised herself with her own forceful tone.

Miriam dropped her head into her hands, rubbing her face. When she looked up, she held her cheeks in her hands, pulling them and her mouth down. "How can I do that? Your grandmother is not going to understand a DNA test. She's not going to put any credence in... modern technology." She motioned toward the laptop.

Her grandmother's words rang in Olivia's mind. *You'll need to take good care of your mother this summer.* Lillian wouldn't have known Miriam was going to test her DNA. Did she simply sense, as she always seemed to do, that Miriam would be struggling with something?

In the uncomfortable silence, Olivia's mind whirled through options. She could run away from this whole nightmare. Plead a non-existent academic emergency. She *was* getting ready to write a dissertation after all. Go back home to her comfortable Boulder life with Amy and their dog. Relief relaxed her shoulders. She could avoid dealing with the certain conflict when her mother confronted her grandmother about this DNA thing. Not to mention that she could avoid disclosing hers and Amy's little genetic experiment.

But... For the first time Olivia could remember, it seemed as if her mother needed *her* to be the objective, logical one. She rose and moved to sit on the bed beside Miriam. There didn't seem to be any other way than through the middle of this. She took in a deep breath and tentatively placed an arm around her mother's thin shoulders. "You have to ask her." She tried to be gentler this time. "You need to know, and that's okay. Gran has a choice. She will either tell you, or she won't even know what the results mean." Olivia blinked back the tears stinging her eyes. *I might be getting the hang of this adulting thing.*

But, nope. Her mother stood abruptly and began pacing the room again. Olivia watched her, feeling useless. She recognized the usual movement that said her mother was thinking... or, more likely, scheming. "Maybe it doesn't matter." She flung her arm out, her voice rising in pitch. It seemed she was talking to herself, forgetting Olivia was there. "But... But what if this dredges up some story I'd rather not hear?" She looked so lost.

Confusion crept into Olivia like the early morning mist settling onto the Shenandoah Valley. Her mother might actually need her and she was terrified of making a false step. Miriam gazed out the window at the moon. Even though the room was dark, Olivia hesitated to turn on the lamp. The moon was bright enough to see her mother's outline. Her shape was somehow more approachable than the brightly lit details of her.

"Mom." Olivia mustered her strength and spoke softly to her mother's thin, straight back. "How about we ask her together?" Her mother turned and looked at her blankly for several seconds, then nodded silently. For once, no argument.

CHAPTER 8

Olivia

The morning after Miriam's DNA discovery, Olivia woke to the smell of coffee. She opened her eyes enough to notice her mother's bed was empty. Miriam always woke up ridiculously early. Olivia pulled her hair up, knotted it on top of her head, and tucked the quilt up around her ears. She tried to will away her worry in exchange for a few more moments of sleep; hoping to drift back into a pleasant dream about a baby with her dark, curly hair and Amy's green eyes.

Instead, her thoughts fixed on a few weeks ago. Amy had still not been entirely clear on her thoughts about *Project Motherhood,* as Olivia liked to refer to their big decision. Olivia walked on eggshells; anxious she would talk Amy out of parenting because of her own fears. In the end, they'd had a very grown-up, but somewhat terrifying, conversation. Now, sixteen hundred miles away from Amy and their familiar life, Olivia wondered if they had made the right decision.

The curtains across the open window moved with the soft morning breeze. The scent of the blossoms of the ancient pink crabapple drifted in. She wondered what today would bring between her mother and grandmother. The slam of a car door outside and she was wide awake. She hadn't heard a car in the driveway.

She rolled out of bed, reached for the CU sweatshirt on top of her suitcase, pulled it over her head, and peeked out the curtain. Miriam walked from her car back toward the house. She was dressed in a white linen shirt, jeans, and short boots. Her silver hair was smooth and clipped back as usual. She wore her signature red glasses. Her lean figure always struck Olivia as such a contrast to her own full breasts and rounded hips.

Olivia hurried into the front hall and met Miriam as she was coming in the front door. "Good morning?" No response. "What's up? Have you been out already?"

"No." Her mother seemed pricklier than usual. "I was just putting my things in the car."

She followed Miriam's gaze down the hallway to the open kitchen door. In the bright morning sun pouring across the room, Lillian's hands were all that was visible of her as she sat at the table. The one with the blue cast rested on the table. The other, browned from the sun, battered and spotted with age, balanced a cup of coffee and brought it to her lips. Olivia turned back to her mother and, just for a moment, caught an unfamiliar look in her eyes. Then Miriam flattened her mouth into a line and motioned toward the bedroom.

Olivia did as she was instructed and stepped back into the bedroom. Her mother followed her and stood with her back against the closed bedroom door. Miriam was cool and unemotional, as if she were seeing one of her patients. "Listen." She pulled her glasses from her face and cleaned the lenses with the edge of the sheet. "I need a little time to take care of some things today." She raised her eyes briefly to Olivia's. She walked over to pick up a tote from beside the bed. "I've told your grandmother that the hospital called and I need to make rounds for one of the professors who is ill."

"But I thought we were going to talk to—"

Miriam held up her hand, in the no-arguments way she had of stopping Olivia mid-sentence. "I've decided I'm not going to bring this up with your grandmother until I have a chance to validate the DNA results. Frankly, I don't believe the test results are correct. I've decided to have them redone. I'm going to talk to Dennis, see what his lab can do..." She rifled through her bag.

"Oh, okay." There would be no changing her mother's mind. *So, I'm supposed to be here with Gran alone? What happened to the whole mother-daughter togetherness thing?* "When are you coming back?" She reached for her sweatpants and pulled them on.

"Tonight." Miriam pecked her cheek, her cool lips barely touching. "I won't be late. I'll call you when I'm on the way back. I'll bring some dinner from Charlottesville."

The sudden rumble of her stomach reminded Olivia of more practical things. "Is there any food in the house?"

"Some. Your grandmother tends to open a can of soup pretty often these days." Miriam turned toward the mirror over the dresser and smoothed her hair. "I'm off then." She yanked open the bedroom door. In the hallway, she stood by the front door and called toward the kitchen, "Bye, Mother. I'll see you this evening." Olivia picked up on something vulnerable sort of radiating from Miriam like the scent of the ginger-scented lotion she always wore. It made her want to put her arms around her petite, prickly mother and hold her close. *Like that would ever happen.*

Olivia stood frozen as her mother hurried out the door, down the steps, and got into the car. She stepped onto the porch, following. "Love you, Mom." She raised her hand in a tentative wave.

Miriam held up one hand. "Love you too." She waved

distractedly as she adjusted her rearview mirror with the other hand.

An unidentifiable intensity gripped Olivia. She hurried down the steps and, just as her mother turned to look behind her in preparation to back the car out, she knocked on the car window. Miriam jumped, turned toward her, frowned, and pressed the button to roll down the window. "What's wrong?"

Olivia found she couldn't speak. The strange feeling erased by her mother's *doctor gaze*. "Nothing's wrong..." she blurted. "Just wanted to say, um, call me if you need to?"

"Sure thing, dear."

Olivia stepped away from the car and watched Miriam pull away. The determined set of her mother's jaw made it very clear—Miriam Stewart had a problem to solve.

CHAPTER 9

Lillian

HAZEL HOLLOW
MAY 26, 2010

Lillian sat in the same chair at the same kitchen table where she had sat for most of her eighty-six years. She marveled at the cast on her wrist, a lovely shade of blue. She'd been a bit taken back when the young man at the hospital, who was dressed in what looked like pajamas, asked her to choose a color. She propped her elbow on the table and turned her arm this way and that. She rapped the knuckles of her other hand on the cast. Solid yet light.

She took in a deep breath. *Does hurt like the devil.* With the ache in her wrist and the idea of brokenness, her thoughts drifted, as they so often did these days, to her girlhood. She remembered watching her mother set a particular broken arm. She was ten-years-old and Jo was eight.

AUGUST, 1934

Lillian and Jo sat, cross-legged, under the cool shade of a hemlock tree in the clean-swept dirt out in front of the Stewart's cabin. "Pay attention, Jo," she growled in frustration, as she tried in vain to teach Jo how to play Fox and Hens. Jo kept laughing and moving her pieces of corn off the board.

She craned her neck, looking over Jo's shoulder to make sure she could still see Jo's two younger brothers playing in the meadow south of the cabin. The responsibility to watch out for Jo *and* the boys weighed heavy. At the sound of another long scream from inside the cabin, Jo stiffened and winced. The cry from Jo's mother crept under Lillian's skin. Miz Jane was in labor with her sixth child.

"You think Mama is all right, Lil?" Jo's plain round race squeezed in worry.

She reached for Jo's grubby hands with their short, stubby fingers and dirt-lined fingernails. "She's going to be fine, Jo. My mama will help her through. And you're going to have a new baby brother or sister." Jo smiled at this and bobbed her head.

Lillian's gaze traveled down the side of the cabin toward the back. Jack Stewart, Jo's daddy, paced beside his wagon and muttered to his mule, Daisy. He sneaked a sip of moonshine from the jar he kept hidden behind the seat. She punched Jo gently with her elbow. "Look." She pointed toward where Mr. Jack stood. Jo turned, saw her daddy, and giggled. Lillian had hoped he would distract Jo. It worked. "Your daddy still gets so nervous, even after five babies," she said. Jo threw her arm up and swept it in a wide wave to her daddy, who smiled sheepishly and raised his hand.

Shouts from beyond the meadow brought Lillian to her feet. With Jo at her heels, she ran toward the voices. Mr. Stewart turned to look toward the commotion. At the edge of the meadow, Lillian stopped. She held up her hand to shield her eyes as she squinted into the bright sun. Elijah Stewart and Jed, their cousin, burst out of the woods and started up the path toward her. Elijah was one of Jo's older brothers, same age as Lillian. Elijah's face was as gray as ashes. He held his left arm with his right hand. Blood seeped between his fingers.

"He done fell out of that old chestnut down by the river," yelled Jed, who flailed his arms around and trailed behind Elijah like a scared puppy.

Elijah grimaced as he stopped in front of her and said through a tightly clenched jaw, "Lillian, can you go get your mama, please?"

For a split second, she wondered what to do. There was no interrupting Mama during the last stage of a delivery. But blood dripped down Elijah's arm. His dove-gray eyes were shiny with pain. She made up her mind. Mr. Jack had walked round to the front of the cabin. When she looked at him, he nodded.

Slowly, she opened the cabin door. Silence. The particular silence before the baby's cry. A tiny wail. Then, Mama's soft murmurings to the new baby. Lillian stopped at the bedroom door to watch for a moment. Mama wiped the baby clean and wrapped it tightly in a soft blanket. She gently handed the swaddled baby to an exhausted-looking Jane Stewart. Lillian slipped in the door.

"Lillian?" Mama caught sight of her waiting. Surprise raised her auburn brows.

Lillian tip-toed past the sleeping pair in the delivery bed and whispered to Mama. With a humph, Mama stomped out of the bedroom to the front door. "What in the devil's hell do you think you were doing, Elijah Stewart?" Mama wiped her blood-covered hands on her apron. Her red hair stood out wildly around her pink, flushed face. "Lillian, go to the woods and cut me two thick straight sticks. Josephine, bring some hot water and tear strips from those rags in the kitchen. Elijah come in here to the kitchen table. Jed, make yourself useful and go find your cousins."

As the other children jumped to obey Mama's commands,

Lillian and Elijah stood frozen on the porch steps. Mama passed them and strode quickly over to Jack Stewart and reached up to clasp his shoulder. "Well, Jack," she grinned. "You got yourself another girl."

Lillian turned to Elijah. She looked into his eyes, noticed the stubborn set of his strong angled jaw. A strange spark ignited in her belly. Something she didn't recognize. "Elijah Stewart, you're a dumbass, falling out of a tree." She gave him a half-grin and flounced off toward the woods to find the strongest, straightest sticks for Elijah's broken arm.

———

This contraption on her wrist was nothing like the heavy wooden splint her mama had fashioned for Elijah. But that had been 1934, not 2010. Elijah's arm had healed just fine. Wouldn't he laugh to see her sitting here at the same kitchen table that used to be in his mother's kitchen? Almost eight decades later, whining over a little break in her wrist.

Miriam had brought home a bottle of little white pills and told her to take one every four hours, but she wasn't much on taking pills. Back when Elijah broke his arm, his daddy had offered him a swig of moonshine. *Now that might be nice.* Lillian smiled.

Olivia shuffled into the kitchen, wiping her eyes with the back of her sleeve. Her cheeks were blotchy, as if she'd been crying. Maybe it had to do with Miriam. She'd taken off in a rush and a huff this morning. Something about helping out at the hospital. Lillian felt a touch guilty for savoring the little break from Miriam's reminders about her nearness to death. They were as constant these days as the tick of the old clock on her bedroom mantel.

"Good morning," Olivia mumbled, dropping a kiss on the top of Lillian's head. She padded over in her sock feet and poured coffee. "How's your wrist feel this morning?" she asked over her shoulder.

"Oh, I reckon it's fine." Lillian didn't see much use in complaining. "I'm a tough old nut, you know." She smiled across the table as Olivia sat down and cupped her hands around her coffee cup. Dipped her head down over it like she was praying. "Did you sleep well, Sugar?"

Olivia raised her eyes. Hickory-nut brown with long black eyelashes. Lillian couldn't see much of Miriam in Olivia. Miriam had beautiful dark green eyes, and she'd had wavy dark brown hair as a younger woman—before it turned silver. She'd always thought Olivia favored her father. He was a handsome man—dark eyes and curly hair, tall and muscular.

Thinking about Hugh, she surmised she'd last seen him at Olivia's college graduation. Must have been more than ten years ago now. He showed up for such occasions, then away he went—off to travel to some new place, somewhere foreign usually, with some kind of natural disaster. She didn't understand why there weren't enough people in need right around here to keep him busy. Miriam had certainly found them. She'd spent over thirty years taking care of women in the entire western part of the state. Hugh had pert-near missed Olivia's whole life. But... she reckoned that was his calling. And you can't ignore your calling.

"Yep, slept pretty well." Olivia sipped her coffee. "It's so quiet here. Almost too quiet, you know? I miss the backdrop of noise you get in the city."

Lillian nodded. But she had no idea about living with city noise. "One of the things I love the most..." Lillian turned to look out the open back door, through the screen-door, to the dew-covered grass sparkling in the morning light. "The quiet. I can't imagine not waking up to the birds singing or the sound of the river." Lillian maneuvered her coffee to her mouth. Olivia was studying her. There was something the child wanted to ask. *Reckon she'll ask in her own time.*

"How about I make us some breakfast?" Olivia popped up, walked to the refrigerator, and yanked it open. "Want some eggs?"

"That sounds good. I think there are a few in there. Fanny hasn't been laying the way she used to lately. I reckon we're both getting old."

"Oh, Gran." Olivia drew out the words, gently scolding. Probably didn't want to hear about her grandmother getting old. The child pulled out eggs and butter from the icebox and started rattling around in the cabinets searching.

"Iron skillet's on the back of the stove."

"Oh, yeah. Why do I always forget that?" She tapped her forehead with the heel of her hand and laughed.

Lillian pondered this drawn-out process of growing old. How must it feel to her daughter and granddaughter to watch her fade away like a weathered old corn stalk? She hadn't had the chance to watch her own mother grow old. Another wave of sadness caught her unexpectedly, thinking of the horrible day Mama died. And now Evelyn was gone, too.

CHAPTER 10

Lillian

HAZEL HOLLOW
SUMMER, 1938

A knot of fear formed in Lillian's stomach when Mama moved around the kitchen, as if each step was excruciating. She dropped heavily into a kitchen chair, bending at the waist. She was spooky pale. "Can you saddle up Pearl, Lil?" Mama asked in a tight whisper. "We need to get to town right quick-like."

Running for the barn, the cold heavy feeling in her belly told her things were about to change. Mama never complained about anything. She was always busy taking care of everyone else.

They climbed onto Pearl's back and plodded slowly into town. Down along the path by the river, up through the pasture of the Johnson's dairy farm. Lillian had the crazy thought that the Johnson's cows looked at them as if they were saying goodbye. She could feel Mama's short, shallow breathing as she pressed against her back. Her own breathing changed to match Mama's. The rapid breaths left her so dizzy she worried she might slip off Pearl's backside. She gripped Mama tighter and felt a pang of fear when Mama groaned in response to the tightened hold.

"Mama, what's wrong?" She was desperate to help. Anything to stop the hurting.

Mama patted her hand as she pulled the reins to turn Pearl onto the main road. "Don't you worry. It's just a bad stomachache. I'll be right again in no time." The way Mama's words came tight and short, it was like she was holding something in; the same way the laboring mothers breathed in little puffs when it was too early to push their babies out.

The sky clouded over and got grayer the closer they got to town. Lillian wondered if she'd see Evelyn, and then felt guilty for even thinking about anyone besides Mama. Her friendship with Evelyn was still something she kept to herself. Mama didn't have much good to say about the way Dr. Preston treated the mountain women.

Lillian thought about the Saturday a few weeks ago when the newspaper photographer had snapped a picture of her and Evelyn as they turned to leave the book truck. The town of Staunton was moving the library into a permanent building and the story had made the news, including Lillian and Evelyn's photograph. Lillian and Mama had been visiting Mrs. McDonald when her daughter Mavis came home with a copy of the newspaper.

"What a lovely photograph of you." Mama smiled, looking proud as they all stood around Mrs. McDonald's kitchen table looking at the newspaper spread out before them. "Who's the other girl?"

"That's Evelyn Preston," Mavis answered, throwing a look toward Lillian. Since Mavis was the Preston's housekeeper, had Evelyn told her about their friendship? Lillian kept her mouth shut as Mavis continued, sounding know-it-all. "She's the youngest. The Prestons also have a son, Buddy. He's two years older. I'm telling you, was Mrs. Preston ever upset when she saw that picture."

"Why was that?" Mama asked, an edge to her voice.

"Oh, you know how those society people are." Mavis flicked her wrist away from the paper. "They don't want their darlings associating with us hillbillies."

Lillian's heart sank. Evelyn had never extended another invitation for Lillian to visit her. Now Lillian thought she understood why.

"Damn puritanical snobs." Mama turned toward her and frowned. "Lil, do you know this girl?"

"No, ma'am." Lillian looked away, jittery with her lie. "We were checking out books at the same time and the photographer asked to take our picture."

Lillian kept a smile on her face and laughed along, as Mavis entertained Mama and Mrs. McDonald with stories of the snobbish Alva Preston, Evelyn's mother. But inside she felt shamed. Could she trust Evelyn? Evelyn was full of dreams and ambitions. She went to picture shows and read everything from John Steinbeck to movie magazines. Lillian even knew Evelyn's favorite movie star—Myrna Loy.

"You just watch, Lily," she'd say, as they sat on the grass under the same tree where they'd sat the first day they met. Evelyn was the only person who had ever called her Lily. It felt exotic and modern all at the same time. "I'm going to leave this little town. I'm going to see the world and break men's hearts." Evelyn motioned in the air like she was one of the actresses she talked about so much.

By the third Saturday of their meetings at the book truck, Evelyn had finally coaxed Lillian into saying what *she* wanted in her grown-up life. "I want to be a midwife like my mother someday and have a husband and babies." She had been embarrassed because, in comparison to Evelyn, her dreams seemed small. She hadn't looked at Evelyn when she spoke, but she heard her huff.

"I don't know why you'd want to saddle yourself with a husband and a bunch of kids." Evelyn smiled as she rose, held out her arms, and twirled around, her short hair rippling in the breeze. "But I promise to send you postcards from far-away places." She'd taken Lillian's hands, and they'd spun to-gether, laughing. Lillian had thought she'd love to get post-cards in the mailbox.

When they reached the Staunton Infirmary, Mama tied Pearl under a tall oak tree near the sidewalk and put a hand on Lillian's shoulder. Mama's hand was hot and heavy through Lillian's thin shirt. "You wait here with Pearl. I'm going inside here to see the doctor. He will give me some medicine for the pain, and before you know it, we'll be on our way." Mama must have seen the fear in Lillian's face because she touched her cheek and said, "My fierce mountain girl. Don't be afraid."

Lillian didn't feel very fierce as she watched Mama mount the wide steps. How bad must the pain be if Mama was willing to see the town doctor she hated so? Mama winced every time she picked up a foot to climb toward the infirmary door. Lillian felt each of Mama's agonizing steps in her own belly.

A nurse in a starched white uniform and cap appeared at the open door. As Mama gained the top of the steps, the nurse reached out and took her arm. Another stab of fear. *What would they do to her?* Mama must have said something, be-cause the nurse glanced back at Lillian and nodded. The nurse had kindness in her eyes. Lillian breathed a little easier, think-ing this woman might have special ways of making people bet-ter that maybe Mama didn't know about.

Lillian had never known Mama not to be able to help someone if they were ailing. And if Mama couldn't help them, then death took them. This thought terrified her, and she pushed it aside, forcing herself to settle on a large root that protruded from the patchy grass underneath the tree. Pearl stood very still as if she were waiting for Mama as well; her ears twitched at the sounds around her.

Mama went into the infirmary at eight o'clock in the

morning. Lillian's bones vibrated at the sound of the bell on top of the Presbyterian church when it rang eight times.

She waited for hours. Mama had slipped an apple and a piece of cornbread into her pocket. When the clouds burned off and the sun was high in the sky, she couldn't stand the gnawing in her stomach any longer. She ate the apple, nibbling it slowly and telling herself one more bite and the white-uniformed nurse and Mama would reappear at the wide doors. Mama would be smiling and feeling better and the nurse would approve of her for being such a faithful daughter, waiting patiently and tending Pearl.

When the apple was down to the seeds, she fed the core to Pearl and looked around for some water. Up in the holler, Pearl drank from a trough in the barn or simply walked down to the river. Lillian didn't see a water pump anywhere around. But Mama would come out any minute and they could stop by the creek and give Pearl a good long drink.

She sat down under the tree. The rhythmic sound of Pearl's soft breathing brought on an unexpected sleepiness. She leaned her head against the tree trunk and was about to doze off when she heard a soft voice. "Lily?"

Evelyn stood before her, a puzzled look on her face. She wore a pair of wide-leg pants and a blue plaid cotton shirt and clutched a composition book in her hands. A pencil rested behind her ear.

"Hi." Lillian rose from the ground and dusted off her backside.

"What are you doing here?"

"Mama's feeling poorly. She's gone into the Infirmary to see your daddy." Lillian tried to sound casual and not as terrified as she felt.

"Oh my." Evelyn reached out to take Lillian's hand. "I was just on my way home for lunch, but I'll sit with you and wait."

"You don't have to do that."

"I want to, and don't you argue." Evelyn's tone, Lillian had already learned, meant she was determined to get her way. "Besides, I can tell you all about the new story I'm writing." She plopped onto the ground under the tree, heedless of the dirt on her new pants, and pulled Lillian down beside her.

"I like your pants," Lillian said.

"Do you? I do too. I found a pattern and Mavis made them for me. Mother is beside herself with worry about what the ladies in her club will think. But I told her I don't care. Katharine Hepburn wears pants. So can I."

Lillian smiled for the first time that day, enjoying Evelyn's spunk.

As the long hours of the afternoon passed, Evelyn shared her new story—her stories were always about young women traveling the world and meeting dashing men. She talked of books and movie stars and how Margaret Mitchell's book was going to be made into a movie.

"I can't wait to have adventures." Evelyn turned curious eyes on her. "Don't you want adventures, Lily?" Then, her face fell into sadness and she looked down. "Of course, you're not thinking about adventure when you're worried about your Mama. I'm sorry."

Lillian thought about Mama. No. Adventure wasn't high on her list today—any day, really. Evelyn didn't seem to understand that. What it would be like to be Evelyn? "I suppose I like things the way they are," she admitted, her stubborn pride mixed with fear of losing Evelyn's interest.

Evelyn sighed. "I wish I could be that way."

This surprised Lillian. But then Evelyn began rambling again, this time about Scarlett O'Hara and how sassy she was and how Vivien Leigh was going to make the perfect Scarlett. Lillian listened. She liked talking about books and stories, but didn't have much interest in picture shows. She'd never been to one and knew that Mama would think it was a waste of a good nickel to spend it on something so frivolous.

The sun dipped toward the horizon. It would soon disappear. If Mama didn't come out soon, they would be doing all the evening chores in the dark. The growling in her belly made her reach for the cornbread in her pocket, but the worry that Mama might be hungry stopped her from eating it. She agonized over what to do.

"Why don't you come home with me for dinner?" Evelyn asked.

"No, I can't leave." Showing up at Evelyn's house was the last thing she wanted to do. "Mama might need me."

Evelyn leaned back against the tree with a long sigh, just as a group of ladies approached on the sidewalk, clucking like hens in conversation with each other. Each of the ladies wore some kind of fancy hat, a shirtwaist dress, stockings, and black leather shoes. They carried handbags over their arms. Absorbed in their conversations, they did not notice the girls until they were upon them. Evelyn had gone silent and watched the approaching ladies with a wary eye.

A tall, stern-looking woman with piercing eyes stopped and glowered at them. She had wavy dark brown hair circling her face under a hat trimmed with a red feather. Lillian wondered if it came from a redbird. The other two ladies stood a short-way apart, waiting and whispering behind their hands.

"Evelyn Preston, what in heaven's name are you doing here?" the woman asked.

Evelyn stood up abruptly, dropped her composition book behind her, and moved to stand in front of it. "Hello, Mother." She raised her chin and set her shoulders back. So, this was Evelyn's mama. She looked down her nose at Lillian who wanted to crawl behind the tree. "I'm keeping my friend Lillian company." Evelyn motioned toward her. Lillian nodded toward Mrs. Preston, forced a polite smile. "Lillian's mother is feeling poorly, and she's gone into the Infirmary to see

Daddy." Lillian was caught by a sudden sick feeling, reminded that Dr. Preston was Evelyn's daddy and how much Mama detested him. She'd never really understood why.

Mrs. Preston glanced over at her friends, who had started another round of whispering when Evelyn referred to Lillian as her friend. "That's very kind of you, dear." Lillian didn't really believe she felt that way. "But, it's time to come home now. Your father will be home soon and I'm sure Mavis will have supper ready."

"But, Mother, I..."

"No arguments, dear." Mrs. Preston put her arm around Evelyn's shoulders. "This girl..." She stopped, motioning toward Lillian.

"Lillian. Her name is Lillian." Evelyn pulled out of her mother's hold and crossed her arms over her chest.

"Yes, well...Lillian should go inside the Infirmary and wait." Mrs. Preston didn't even look at her. The other two ladies abruptly said they best be getting home and hurried away, leaving the three of them standing together.

Evelyn reached for Lillian's hand and looked into her eyes. "Lily, I'm sorry. Are you gonna be okay?"

"She'll be fine dear." Mrs. Preston pulled Evelyn toward her again and turned to glare at Lillian. "Run along inside." She waved her hand toward the building, shooing Lillian away as if she were a stray dog. "The nurses will help you."

Lillian watched as Mrs. Preston marched Evelyn away, remembering Mama's words, "Damn puritanical snob." She tried to rouse up some of Mama's anger, but right now all she could feel was lonesomeness. Before she got very far away, Evelyn turned, waved, and nodded toward the composition book she'd left under the tree and winked. Lillian smiled weakly and held up her hand. After Evelyn and her mother disappeared into the gathering darkness, Lillian stooped and picked up Evelyn's composition book. She stuffed it into

Pearl's saddlebag.

She stared at the Infirmary building for a long time. Finally, when the electric light on the front of the hospital came on and the lights inside did too, she made a decision. She looped Pearl's reins another time around the tree. "You wait here, Pearl," she said, patting her. Gathering her courage, she set one foot in front of another up the steps to the big double door. A sign on the door read, "Whites Only." A sign below it with an arrow pointing to the side of the building read, "Colored Waiting Room."

Pushing open the heavy door, she stopped just inside to look around. The first thing she noticed was the smell. The other place in Staunton she'd been in—besides Duggins Pharmacy—was the mercantile. It smelled of spices, nails, pickles, and new fabric all mixed together. They had each of those things at home. Familiar smells. But this was a sharp and unnatural smell. Not like dead things, but not like anything alive either.

The floor was hard and had a glow to it. The windows were ceiling high. There were doors everywhere. From somewhere behind one of the doors, came a soft moan. Two nurses at the end of the hall passed back and forth between the rooms, carrying strange objects, their footsteps short and clipped, like a woodpecker on a hollow tree. They looked neither right nor left. It was like she wasn't even there. She pulled on her braids to straighten them and shoved her hands into the pockets of her overalls.

She inched forward, not wanting to get caught between one of the nurses and one of the doors. After a few minutes of standing and waiting, she turned to look out the front window at Pearl. Somehow seeing their horse, patiently waiting to take her and Mama home, made Lillian braver. Something had to be done. The next time one of the nurses came out of a door she stepped forward, trembling a bit, but making sure to get herself noticed.

The nurse closed the door behind her and stared at Lillian. Frowning, she slid a hand holding something that looked very pointed and scary into her pocket. This was the same nurse who had taken Mama into the hospital. Lillian searched for what to say, but couldn't get any words out. Before she could speak, the nurse's expression changed from a frown to a sad, pitiful look that reminded Lillian of the way Mama had looked when she told Lillian her favorite dog had died.

Her heart pounded in her chest. Something was terribly, terribly wrong.

"Oh, good heavens, I forgot," the nurse said breathlessly. She clamped her hand over her mouth as if to keep any more words from coming out.

Lillian's mind raced, and she tried desperately to tell herself that this was good. Mama had gotten better, and the nurse had simply forgotten to tell her. Mama was probably resting behind one of those doors, waiting for Lillian to come and fetch her.

She flinched as the nurse reached for her arm and gently guided her over to a bench. Lillian hadn't noticed the cushioned wooden bench before. It was soft when she sat down. The nurse bent over in front of her and took both of her hands. The nurse's hands were cold and bone dry.

"I'm so sorry, child," she said. "Your Mama was very sick..."

Lillian heard only fragments of what the nurse said.

"Mary should have come sooner... Nothing the doctor could do..."

She pulled her hands out of the nurse's grasp and stood up. "Where is Mama?" Her own voice was shrill in her ears and an icy chill of fear stiffened her spine.

"She's gone, child."

"Gone where? Can I go with her?" Panic rose in her throat.

She swallowed hard and stepped back.

"She's passed." As if from very far away, Lillian watched the nurse move toward her, arms outstretched.

She stood very still trying to organize her thoughts, but she found none. She had to get out of that place. The nurse tried to grab for her as she turned and ran for the door. Lillian was too quick. She tore down the sidewalk, loosened the reins from the tree, and threw herself onto Pearl's back.

"Wait, child," the nurse called from the Infirmary steps.

Lillian kicked Pearl's side and set her at a gallop, headed toward the end of town. They flew past businesses, houses, a few people who stopped to gawk as she and Pearl hurtled through the streets. She didn't stop until she reached the creek outside of town, where Pearl would go no farther without a drink.

Lillian collapsed over Pearl's neck, feeling the animal's warmth against her body and insisting to herself that Mama could *not* be gone. Any minute, she would walk up, chastise Lillian for leaving in such a hurry, laugh, and whisper behind her hand so that Pearl couldn't hear, "I'm so hungry, I could eat a horse." One of their favorite jokes.

Lillian couldn't cry. She could scarcely breathe. All she could think about were Mama's words, "You're safe in the holler."

Sobs caught in her throat and she swallowed them down. Grabbing Pearl's reins, she pulled the horse away from the water and nudged her back toward the road. Darkness fell and the mist gathered around her as it settled into the floor of the valley. She slumped over the saddle and loosened her grip on the reins as Pearl made her way along the familiar track toward home.

Pearl turned onto the path through the woods. Lillian squinted to see through the fog. The trees cast long eerie shadows across the forest floor and she heard the howl of a timber wolf in the distance. She felt no fear. Her heart was numb. There was only one thing for certain. She'd never leave the holler again.

MAY 26, 2010

Lillian often thought of her mother these days—the fiery woman who had emigrated from Ireland as a child and had taken up the midwifery calling at sixteen. Mary O'Toole had been the center of her world. Lillian had never known her father. When she'd asked about him, all Mama would say was he'd been a traveler. "You were his gift to me."

And now, as she watched her baby's baby sip coffee and stir eggs, she had a strong knowing. There was something different about Olivia. She'd swear the child was pregnant.

CHAPTER 11

Miriam

CHARLOTTESVILLE
MAY 26, 2010

Dennis rolled his short metal stool closer, ducked to look inside her mouth, and inserted a swab into her cheek. The fluorescent office light bounced off his shiny bald head. "Why didn't you come to me in the first place?" Annoyed with him for asking her a question when he had just put something in her mouth, Miriam frowned and jabbed a finger toward her cheek. Dennis chuckled.

As irritating as he could be sometimes, her old friend's presence always calmed her. She took in the perfect knot of his tie, his chambray blue button-down shirt, crisp white lab coat, breathed in his reassuring clean spicy scent.

"For one thing, it's personal," Miriam replied the moment Dennis removed the swab from her mouth. He inserted the swab into a plastic container. Good. Done. These new results would discredit her previous DNA test and all this nonsense would be sorted. "And, secondly." She wiped the corners of her mouth with her thumb and first finger, then reached into her tote for the only cosmetic she used. She pulled out a mirror and reapplied her lipstick. Snapping the compact shut, she looked at him over the top of her glasses. "I keep my personal files out of the UVA data base."

"I see." Dennis's mouth creased into the lopsided smile she cherished... most of the time.

"Just your usual paranoia."

She crossed her legs and waggled her foot as she watched him label the DNA sample with her name and date of birth. "I don't want my private information in the hands of some curious medical student—or even one of your pathologists. Promise me you'll handle this yourself?" She caught his eyes to let him know this was one of *those* times. She didn't plead often. Never really.

"I promise." Dennis peered back over his own round black glasses. "Haven't I always kept your secrets?"

She frowned; her mouth formed into an o. "Wha..." Then she smiled sheepishly. It was true. He had, over the years, been her confidante. Everything from her own surprise pregnancy to her sometimes not entirely above-board schemes to get supplies for the mountain family planning clinics. All of it. She sighed. "This DNA test was supposed to be a lark. A jumpstart to a retirement project."

"And now?" Dennis asked.

"Now, self-indulgent or not, I *have* to know." An image of her mother's familiar wrinkled face and bright blue eyes came into focus, followed closely by her father's strong, angular features, gray eyes, and sandy hair. The parents she had always known. The people who shaped who she had become. She could not lose that solid ground.

"Be right back. Sit tight," he said over his shoulder. Dennis left the exam room with her sputum sample in his coat pocket.

Miriam pulled out her cell phone to check email, but couldn't concentrate. She let out an exasperated sigh and pushed herself out of the uncomfortable patient chair. She paced the tile floor of the exam room as her thoughts turned to earlier this morning. She had returned to Charlottesville early enough to stop by Mudhouse Coffee at the downtown mall before her visit with Dennis. Outdoor table, balmy spring morning, the background buzz of students' hushed early morning voices. She had tried to relax. Then she'd remembered the letter from Hugh, still buried in the bottom of her tote. She fished it out and read it slowly. The spring breeze rippled the paper in her hands. *I'll be back in the states in a couple weeks... I need to talk to you right away.* The unexpected urgency in his words with no explanation had caused her heart to quicken. She had crumpled the letter and stuffed it back into her tote. *Now, Hugh? Really?*

"So, if I can ask..." Dennis walked into the exam room and interrupted her thoughts. "Why don't you trust the other results? That particular company you mentioned has a pretty good reputation for accuracy."

"Let me put it this way..." She dodged his curiosity. "The results were not what I expected." Dennis frowned, a question in his eyes. She looked down. "I'd prefer to have a second analysis run...I'm pretty sure the results will be very different." She held up her hand. "I don't want to talk about it. How long before the results are back?"

Dennis stared at her for several seconds. Most likely trying to decide if it was worth the argument. Finally, he arranged his face into a resigned expression. "At least a couple of weeks. It could be as long as a month." He paused. "You okay?"

"Of course," she lied. She felt his eyes on her as she reached into her tote for her car keys. "It's just... I have a lot going on with Mother breaking her wrist and all. I suppose she'll be coming to live with me."

"Oh, really?" Dennis sounded more than a little incredulous. He'd earned the right to be surprised given his years of listening to her alternately complain about and admire her mother's independence.

She told him about her plan to move Lillian into the cottage. The dubious expression in Dennis's eyes pushed her on. "It will be *great*. She'll be right there where I can look out for her, but she'll have her own space." She collapsed into the patient chair again. Heaviness gripped her. "You don't think it's going to work, do you?"

Dennis met her gaze thoughtfully. He sat on the stool, ran his hand over his bald head, adjusted his glasses, and rubbed his chin. All the particular gestures she had seen him make so many times over the years—usually when he was struggling to convey bad news. Finally, he spoke. "Now, granted..." He held up his hands in a gesture of stopping her arguments before they started. "I've only spent time with Lillian over the years on holidays and special occasions, but from what I know of your mother, you're in for an uphill battle on this one." He sat back and crossed his arms over his small belly pooch. "Why not just leave her be?"

"I can't let my mother die up there in that farmhouse all alone." Her voice rose. "What if I can't reach her in time? She won't use a cell phone. She refuses to have live-in help." She jolted out of the chair and paced the office floor. "I have no idea when the timing is right. All I know is that she fell and broke her wrist. What if it's her hip next time?" She stopped briefly to scrutinize his reaction. His face was parked in neutral. "I can't stand the stress anymore. And I certainly don't want to live up there with her in that isolated place. I did that for the first eighteen years of my life."

Dennis nodded and remained silent. In a surge of gratitude, she wanted to hug him for always knowing when she needed to vent. Exhausted, she plopped down in the chair again and sighed. "Nothing makes sense right now, to tell you the truth. I don't know what to do about Mother. And Olivia is on a quest to get herself pregnant." She stared at the floor, her thoughts tumbling in a disturbingly unordered way.

"Excuse me?" As if he hadn't heard her correctly.

She ignored his question, not finished with her litany of issues. "And to top it all off, I checked the mail yesterday and..." She glanced at Dennis and then lowered her eyes.

"And?"

"I've had a strange letter from Hugh."

"That's it." Dennis stood up with purpose. "Call Lillian and Olivia and tell them you won't be back tonight." Dennis's tone brooked no arguments. He pulled his cell phone from his lab coat pocket and tapped the screen.

She lifted her leaden body. What was this heaviness she felt? "Wait, Dennis... I should go back. They're expecting me."

"Olivia can manage Lillian for one night. I'm calling Walt." He placed the phone against his ear.

Walt's voice sounded through Dennis's phone. "Hi, hon."

Dennis eyed her as he spoke to Walt. "Miriam is in need of some porch time." She sighed and dropped her chin. "Mm hm," Dennis murmured. She raised her head. He nodded as he listened to Walt, gaze still locked on her. After the short exchange, he returned the phone to his pocket. "Cocktails at four. And Walt's making dinner." She didn't argue.

CHAPTER 12

Olivia

HAZEL HOLLOW
MAY 26, 2010

Olivia anticipated the familiar feeling. The dull ache in the floor of her pelvis, the sensation of heaviness followed by the streaks of blood on the tissue. Her breasts were tender and swollen, her belly full and bloated. All the signs were there. Her period should have started by now. But nothing.

She flushed the toilet and sat down on the edge of Gran's long white clawfoot tub. Could the insemination have worked the *first time?* It had been around five weeks, but she hadn't expected to come up pregnant on the first try. She considered her friends, many of whom had tried for months. "Hang in there. It will probably take several tries," they had said.

Everything right now felt surreal. The possibility of pregnancy so quickly, being at Gran's, so far away from her real life. Her mother's freak-out over her DNA and her unrelenting intention to move Lillian to Charlottesville. It all swirled around in her mind, refusing to coalesce into anything that made sense. She longed for Amy's solid, grounded presence. Just the thought of Amy made her feel calmer.

Olivia rose from her perch on Gran's tub and examined

herself in the wavy old mirror over the sink. Would she look any different if she *was* pregnant? Lowering her hand to her full breast, she noticed again the tenderness and shivered with excitement at the possibility her body could already be making a baby.

She brushed her teeth and tried to slow down—her thoughts, her fears, her pace. She'd planned to skip her summer visit to Virginia, dissertation work as an excuse. She'd avoid any further conversation with her mother about possible sperm donors. Then, after the first trimester—which would hopefully be in the fall—they'd visit Charlottesville and announce the news to Mom, Gran, Uncle Dennis, and Uncle Walt.

So much for planning. Who knew Gran would break her wrist? And even more surprising: that her mother would call begging—well, as close as she *came* to begging—Olivia to stay at Lillian's for the summer. She was not in *any* way prepared to tell Miriam she might be pregnant *already*. Nor to admit she was *not* going to interview the men her mother had identified as highly desirable donors. Her commitment to Amy was solid. The donor would be anonymous.

She finished brushing her teeth, then glanced at her phone, considered calling Amy. She should probably check on Lillian. But when she opened the bathroom door and peered down the hall, her grandmother was no longer in the kitchen. "Gran?" She looked in her room. Not there. As she walked into the kitchen, she heard Lillian's old truck roar to life, then shudder to a stop. Quickly, she headed for the back door.

———

Lillian and Aunt Jo had their heads under the hood of Lillian's 1964 turquoise and white Ford pickup. Aunt Jo wore heavy work boots and coveralls smeared with grease. Her stubby iron-gray hair was hidden by a backwards John Deere cap.

Lillian—dressed in a bright yellow cotton shirt, jeans, and clunky sandals—held her casted arm out from her body and, with the other hand, fiddled with some part of the truck's engine. Aunt Jo pulled a container of something from a wooden crate at her feet. Scrap, who was stretched out in the cool dirt under the truck, created a small cloud of dust with his thumping tail when he spotted Olivia.

"Hey guys, what ya doing?" She crossed the short distance from the steps to the truck. Scrap wiggled out from under the truck and ambled over to greet her.

Aunt Jo turned to her and grinned. Aunt Jo's toothless pink gums were kind of disturbing. According to the family story, Aunt Jo had all her teeth pulled when she was twenty-five. When it came time to be fitted for dentures, she had refused, saying she could chew perfectly well without them.

"Need to add more oil to the old girl." Aunt Jo's voice filled with excitement. "Have to keep her running good, ain't that right, Lil?" She looked for Lillian's approval, her face wide open. When Lillian nodded, Aunt Jo looked earnestly at Olivia. "Lil opens the cap and I pour in the oil. I have a funnel." Jo proudly held up the greasy red funnel clutched in her left hand.

"That's right, Jo." Lillian smiled. "And you do a good job of that." She turned to Olivia. "Livy, hon, could you loosen that oil cap? I can't seem to make my old hand work this morning." She waved her casted wrist and added, "And I can't do anything with this dang arm."

Olivia approached the truck tentatively. "Sure." She stared into the maze of hoses, caps, and engine parts. "Um... which one is the oil cap?"

This brought a hoot of laughter from Aunt Jo. "She don't know where the oil cap is."

"Now, Jo." Lillian clucked like a hen. "Not everyone's been working on cars their whole life. Behave yourself."

"My job is to pour in the oil," Jo repeated, ignoring Lillian. Olivia followed her grandmother's bony finger to the oil cap and gingerly twisted it off. Aunt Jo funneled in the oil, whisked out the dipstick, wiped it clean with an oily cloth from her pocket, inserted it again, removed it with a flourish, squinted at it, and pronounced the truck ready to go.

Olivia screwed the cap back on, realization dawning. "Hang on a minute..." She frowned and glared at the pair. Jo bustled around the truck, closed the hood, and dusted off her hands. Lillian examined a spot on her cast, then opened the door of the truck and peered inside. Neither of them looked at her. "You're not planning to drive, are you, Gran?" Lillian was always the one to drive when they went to town. Aunt Jo didn't have a license.

"I reckon so." Lillian lifted her chin. "I can steer with my other hand, you know, and it *is* grocery day."

Aunt Jo stood beside Lillian and nodded enthusiastically. "Yep, grocery day." She held her hand up to her mouth as if sharing a secret. "And I'm going to buy me some chocolate ice cream today." She hurried over to sit on the porch step and remove her boots. She stood and began peeling off her coveralls, revealing a startlingly bright, baggy floral-print dress. She folded her coveralls neatly, set them on the steps, and reached for a pair of red sneakers. She pulled them on to her knotty old feet.

Olivia sensed she should tread lightly. The last thing she wanted was to offend her grandmother, but she was also horrified at the thought of the two of them driving into Staunton alone. If something happened, her mother would never forgive her. "How about I drive you?" she asked. This could actually work well. Maybe she'd purchase a pregnancy test without Gran or Aunt Jo noticing. "I can help with the groceries, and we could drive around Staunton a bit. I was hoping to check out the Mary Baldwin University library while I'm here. I need to get started on my dissertation research, you know."

Lillian and Aunt Jo looked at each other. She was uncertain how to interpret the unspoken message that passed between them. Seemed more like resignation than interest. Her grandmother seldom went into town and preferred to stay at home, but wouldn't a short outing beyond the grocery store give them something to do? After all, her mother had left her stranded here with two old women and no car. She might as well make the best of it.

"All right then." Lillian settled the question. "Jo, put that crate back in the barn, and I'll fetch my list."

Olivia looked down at her clothes. She still wore her baggy sweats. Her hair was wild. "I'll quick change and be right out." She headed up the steps. A wave of nausea lurched through her stomach. She gripped the porch rail.

"You all right, child?" Lillian hurried to stand behind her and placed a hand lightly on her back.

In that moment, all she wanted was to drop onto the porch steps and pour her heart out to her grandmother. *I might be pregnant. I'm not sure I'm doing the right thing. I don't know how to tell Mom that I won't be choosing a donor the Miriam Stewart way. Oh, god, I miss Amy. And... And... if I am pregnant, I'm terrified and excited all at once.*

She didn't. She couldn't. All of it remained bottled up inside. She ignored Lillian's probing eyes. "Just a little queasy. Probably still dehydrated from traveling." She opened the back door and held it for Lillian. "You grab your list and I'll be ready in a flash."

"Don't rush," Lillian called after her. "I don't do anything in a flash anymore."

CHAPTER 13

Lillian

STAUNTON
MAY 26, 2010

Jo, smelling of equal parts engine oil and talcum powder, sat between Lillian and Olivia for the trip to Staunton. Jo had a habit of naming everything she saw, starting when they reached the highway, all the way into town. Lillian gazed out the window, while Olivia acknowledged Jo's every comment, "Oh, yes... mm hm... look at that."

When they left the holler to drive into Staunton, Lillian always recalled the years of making the trip by horseback or wagon. Elijah had bought their first truck just before he left for the War. Insisted she learn to drive. She'd discovered she enjoyed driving. But no matter how often she traveled to Staunton, the feeling was always the same—an inkling of dread.

Folks bragged about Staunton being a pretty little town. Maybe, if she had lived someone else's life, she might feel affection for it. But even with the good memories—the year she met Evelyn, the book truck, hers and Elijah's honeymoon, Miriam graduating high school, then college—try as she might, she felt no love for the town. Discomfort gnawed at her whenever the familiar places appeared; the ones she couldn't help but associate with pain of one sort or another.

Furthermore, she did not care for being a passenger instead of the driver. Brought up a helpless feeling she could scarcely tolerate. Always needed to be sure she had a way out of Staunton—whether it had been Mama's old horse, Pearl, her own truck, or her own two feet. She focused on the honeysuckle blooming along the highway. Olivia simply wanted to explore a bit. The child didn't have the same memories. She'd not taken much interest in the town before now. Her visits over the years had focused on the farm. Staunton must feel new for her. Seemed to have a whole new set of questions. Like now. "What was that big building up there on the hill again? I know you've told me before, but I've forgotten," Olivia asked.

Before Lillian could answer, Jo blurted, "That's the loony bin. Where they'll lock you up and keep you for your *whole life.*"

"Now, Jo, you be quiet." Lillian patted Jo's bony knee. "That's Western State Hospital." The old familiar knife of pain stabbed her stomach just from saying the name.

"Is it a mental institution?" Olivia asked.

"Yes, for a long time it was. Closed now. It's on the National Register of Historic Places. I read in the newspaper that the city spent fifteen million dollars to fix it up after it fell into disrepair. Made parts of it into a hotel and a fancy restaurant." Lillian worked to keep her tone informative and not disgusted. If those people eating at that fancy restaurant, sleeping on king-size luxury beds knew what had gone on there, she suspected they might lose their appetites.

"Humph," Jo snorted. "Bad place. But we got away didn't we, Lil?"

"What do you mean?" Olivia turned to glance at Jo, sharp curiosity in her eyes.

"Hush now, Jo." Lillian squeezed Jo's arm.

"Ow." Jo poked her lip out and pulled her arm away.

"Ignore her, Livy." Lillian smiled and forced a chuckle. "Jo's probably remembering silly children's talk." Olivia turned her gaze back to the road. Lillian met Jo's eyes and shook her head ever-so-slightly.

"That's the feed store." Jo pointed at the Augusta County Farm Co-Op. "Daddy bought horse feed there when I was a girl. He let me come with him."

Lillian smiled with relief that Jo had moved on to a better memory. Jo had worshiped her daddy. Jack Stewart's only living girl out of six children. Even after it became clear Jo was simple-minded, he'd treated her with tenderness, encouraged her every interest, and taught his four sons to do the same.

As Olivia and Jo chatted about the Co-Op, how it had changed over the years, was now a True Value Hardware, Lillian thought about all the years of friendship she'd shared with Jo. She remembered the night she eavesdropped on a late-night conversation between Mama and Miz Jane. They sat by the Stewart's fire. Mama had sighed and stretched her feet toward the fire, worn out from a particularly hard delivery. "The cord was wrapped around the baby's neck,"

"Like my Jo," Jane mused quietly as she stared into the fire. "Do you think it will affect her baby's mind?"

"Hard to tell yet," Mama said. They'd both grown quiet. But that snippet of conversation was enough for Lillian to finally understand.

"So, which grocery store do you use?" Olivia interrupted Lillian's musing.

"Piggly Wiggly closed. We don't like that," Jo said.

"The Kroger on Statler," Lillian answered.

"The Piggly Wiggly was right there." Jo pointed to a deserted-looking building in an older neighborhood made up of small worn-down houses.

"You'll turn right at the next light," Lillian directed.

Jo pointed at another building as they drove through the narrow, tree-lined streets of Staunton. "That was Dr. Preston's Infirmary back in the day. My daddy died there, and your great-grandma did too."

"I remember you telling me she died young." Olivia's voice was quiet. She didn't ask any more questions. Maybe she somehow sensed Lillian's discomfort.

Lillian winced. There was a much more direct route to the Kroger without going through this part of town. She wished Olivia had taken it. Too late now. And too late to stop the memories. She hoped Olivia and Jo would not notice her swipe away the unbidden tear on her wrinkled cheek. Because of her mother's untimely death, the Stewart family insisted she stay with them for a while. If only she hadn't agreed.

CHAPTER 14

Lillian

HAZEL HOLLOW
SUMMER, 1938

Jo's daddy, Jack Stewart, hitched Pearl to the wagon and went to Staunton to fetch Mama's body. Lillian still couldn't take in that Mama was gone even when Miz Jane, Jo's mama, looked at her with those sad, sloping eyes and said, "We'll bury your mama in the cemetery up on the ridge behind the cabin."

Standing by the freshly dug grave, lonesomeness gripped Lillian. Felt as if her feet shot out roots so deep they wound around the pine coffin, planting her alongside Mama and Jo's baby sister, who had died of the pneumonia a few months earlier. The preacher said, "Amen," and Miz Jane put her scrawny arm around Lillian's shoulders. "Come now, child," she said softly. "Say your goodbyes to your mama, and let's get home."

Home. The word was wrong in Lillian's ears. For Miz Jane, home meant the Stewart's cabin, along with Mr. Stewart, Jo, and their four sons. They had done her a kindness by taking her in, insisting she stay with them, saying she was too young to be on her own. She'd been too sick with sadness to argue. But the Stewart cabin wasn't home. She'd bide her time there for now. But it was *not* home.

———

A month after Mama's burial, Lillian sat with Jo on the front porch of the Stewart's cabin, their legs swinging over the side above the dirt yard. Jo lined up her rag dolls on the wooden planks between them. "How many babies do you want, Lil?" To anyone else, the question might have come out of nowhere. But Jo knew how Lillian loved babies. Missing her mama meant missing new babies too. Lillian wondered if the midwife from over in the next holler was doing Mama's deliveries.

"I don't know, Jo." Lillian was irritable with Jo—more than she meant to be. Evelyn's smiling face came to mind. The new friendship they'd begun had been cut short by Mama's sudden death. Evelyn didn't ask questions like Jo's. Lillian remembered one of their last conversations.

"Lily, don't you think it would be better to be free than to be beholding to a husband and children?" They had climbed into an old oak, its branches spread over a meadow on the edge of town, each taking a wide limb for a seat. Evelyn leaned against the trunk, twirling a strand of her hair around a finger and writing in her composition book.

"I don't think it would be so bad," Lillian had said. She hadn't admitted to Evelyn how she wanted nothing more than to get married and have babies. She'd smiled secretly as Elijah Stewart swaggered into her thoughts. Just last year, right before she died, Mama had told her exactly how it all worked between men and women and how babies got made. Mama had made it sound special. Why wouldn't Evelyn want that? She and Elijah would make beautiful babies. They would have her blue eyes and his shiny brown hair.

Now, watching Jo play with her dolls, Lillian grew sad. Mama was gone and would never see her babies. "I want four," Lillian answered Jo's question, frowning as she figured how she might space out her babies. Mama hadn't gotten to the part about how you only have babies when you want to. Maybe one every other year. "Two boys and two girls."

Evelyn would probably roll her eyes at this, but she needn't worry about Evelyn anymore. Their friendship was over before it got started good. Lillian had no desire to go into town now. It was safer to stay in the holler—just like Mama had said. And Evelyn would never come up here.

"What about you?" Lillian asked Jo to be polite, even though she was pretty sure Jo couldn't manage real babies. She was too much of a child herself.

But Jo had stopped listening and was looking toward the road. Lillian followed Jo's gaze and saw two women in the distance. They were red-faced and breathing hard as they walked up the steep path to the Stewart's cabin. Looking past them, Lillian could see a large black automobile parked on the narrow mountain road below.

"Ma, somebody's coming up from the road," Jo yelled toward the open front door.

Lillian sensed danger the way a squirrel senses a shotgun nearby. She jumped up and yanked open the screen door. It slammed behind her as she crossed the rag rug in front of the wide stone fireplace, almost tripping on Miz Jane's rocking chair. She slammed through the door into the small lean-to kitchen, where Miz Jane stood at the washing tub finishing the dinner dishes.

"Why, Lil," Miz Jane said, grasping Lillian's thin shoulders, "What's the matter with you, child? You look like you've seen a ghost."

Before Lillian could reply, Jo came barreling in. "Ma, there's two ladies from town in the front yard and they said they want to see my folks."

"Stay here." Miz Jane pulled off her apron and threw it on the Hoosier.

Lillian and Jo peeked through a crack in the kitchen door.

How calm Miz Jane was as she ushered the two women into the front room. How could she treat this as so ordinary? People from town meant only one thing. Death.

One of the women wore a blue hat with a yellow feather. Her matching blue dress stretched over a broad bosom, against which she clutched a clipboard. The other woman, skinnier and younger, wore a yellow-flowered dress and wire-rimmed spectacles. She nodded as blue-hat woman said, "We are members of the local *Fit Families Society,* and we are here on behalf of the Augusta County Health Department."

"You all have a seat." Miz Jane was polite, even kindly. "I'll go fetch my husband. Would y'all like some coffee?" She backed toward the kitchen. Both ladies, who took seats on the edge of the two straight-back sitting room chairs, murmured "yes." As soon as Miz Jane turned her back, they peered all around the room as if they were sizing up the Stewarts' plain furniture. There was nothing wrong with the Stewart's house. Maybe not as clean as hers and Mama's, but still, nothing wrong. The women looked at each other and pursed up their lips.

Miz Jane's whisper was urgent as she came into the kitchen and closed the door behind her. "Where's your daddy, Josephine?"

Lillian guessed Miz Jane was afraid Mr. Stewart was down at his still and if he was, there would be no sending Jo after him. Miz Jane did not allow Jo and Lillian anywhere near the still, under *any* circumstances. What Miz Jane didn't know was she and Jo had explored that part of the woods plenty of times; sneaking to watch Jo's daddy load the sour-smelling mash and stoke the fire. What Jo's mama didn't know wouldn't hurt her.

"I think he's at the barn, Ma," Jo said. She stood up straight and got all serious. Her mama needed her and she would not fail. Before Lillian could protest, Jo had her by the arm and they were out the back door, Jo dragging her toward the barn.

How she wished she was safe at home in her own cabin a few minutes away over the ridge and not at the Stewart's place. Her stomach twisted at the prospect of anything to do with town people.

"And when you get back, check on the coffee," Miz Jane called as they started down the back path. "And there's some tea cakes in the Hoosier."

"Yes'm," Lillian nodded.

"Hurry, Lil," Jo said over her shoulder as they approached the weathered barn. Chickens clucked and scattered with a ruffle of feathers in the dusty air. Jo shooed them away from the barn door with her boot.

They found Mr. Stewart and his two oldest sons with their heads under the hood of the broken-down truck that, according to Jo, her daddy had traded a case of moonshine for.

"Daddy, there's some ladies from town here to see you and Mama." Jo breathed hard after her sprint from the cabin. Lillian stood back, her hands shoved into the pockets of her cotton dress, waiting to see what Mr. Stewart would do. Jo's older brothers raised their heads and watched their daddy.

Mr. Stewart pulled a rag from the back pocket of his overalls and wiped grease from his hands. His puzzled frown confirmed Lillian's suspicion. It was somehow not right for those two women to be up in the holler in the middle of the day. But his response was as confusing as Miz Jane's. Why weren't they worried?

"Is that right?" He smiled broadly at Jo with his handsome grin. "You boys stay here." He nodded toward the truck. "Work on that radiator. I'll see what this is all about."

"Come on, Lil." Jo pulled on her again.

"I think I'll stay here." Lillian would rather be anywhere right now than up at that cabin.

But Jo was relentless. "Please, Lil. You know Mama said for us to watch the coffee."

Lillian dragged herself behind Jo as they kept pace with Mr. Stewart's long stride. Every step taking her back toward strangers. Back in the kitchen, Lillian and Jo tip-toed around like mice, making coffee, straining to hear the conversation.

"We are concerned about your children's health," the older, blue-hat lady said. "Mrs. Stewart, you look quite poorly yourself." Her tone dripped with worry.

"Why yes, you're thin as a rail. How long have you been losing weight?" This question came from the pretty one in the yellow dress.

Lillian and Jo leaned toward the door, but couldn't hear Miz Jane's murmured reply.

"She's been poorly ever since our last child was born." Mr. Stewart's boots clumped across the plank floor as he walked over and stood behind Jo's mama.

"Oh dear, I'm so sorry," said blue-hat woman. "And how long has that been?"

"My youngest died of the pneumonia eight months ago. She was nigh on to four years old." Miz Jane's voice was choked and sad. "I reckon I'm still grieving. Ain't much hungry."

Jo reached out and put her hand on the door as if she could send comfort through the cracked wood. They stood close by the door. Jo's cropped head only came to Lillian's shoulder.

"So, in addition to the girl and boy who are in the kitchen, how many children do you have?" asked yellow-dress woman.

Jo looked at Lillian and screwed her face into a such a ferocious frown that Lillian had to stifle a laugh.

"That ain't no boy." Mr. Stewart's laugh rumbled through the door crack. "That's my girl Josephine. She likes to dress like her brothers."

At hearing her daddy's deep-voiced response, Jo grinned proudly.

"Oh, I see." When Lillian peeked through the crack of the

door, she saw blue-hat woman was writing something on a paper attached to the clipboard she held on her lap.

"The other girl is not ours," Miz Jane said. "But we've taken her in. She lost her mama a month ago, and she has no one else."

"Poor child," said flowered dress.

Anger rose in Lillian's chest. She wasn't some "poor child" for them to pity. She'd be able to live on her own soon. She looked over at Jo and made a prissy face, mocking the woman. Jo snorted and clamped her hand over her mouth.

"We've also got ourselves four sons." Mr. Stewart sounded proud.

"My, you *do* have a large brood." After a pause, during which blue-hat continued to write, flowered dress cleared her throat and said, "Our orders from the County Health Department are for all of your children to check into the State Hospital in Staunton for health testing."

"And the orphaned girl, of course, should come along too," blue-hat added.

Lillian's stomach tightened. She wasn't going *anywhere* for *any* tests.

"What kind of health testing?" Mr. Stewart asked. The wariness in his voice gave Lillian goosebumps. Jack Stewart felt the same way about town people as she did.

"Oh, they are simple tests that are required by Augusta County," blue-hat said. She fluttered her puffy hand as if it was all nothing. Lillian held her breath. She didn't want to miss blue-hat's answer. "The tests are a general assessment of the physical and mental health of the residents of the county."

Yellow dress chimed in. "You *do* want your children to be the healthiest they can be, don't you?"

"Of course," Miz Jane said. Miz Jane focused on her hands, folded in her lap, real humble-like. Then she looked up at Jo's daddy and they both nodded. But they didn't look very sure.

Lillian wondered what having these so-called tests had to do with being healthy. Mama would have put a stop to all of this.

Lillian thought of Mama going to see Dr. Preston and never coming out again. She remembered to breathe when Jo poked her. "The coffee's ready."

Lillian and Jo poured coffee into the two cups they had washed. They placed the cups on the special tray Miz Jane used when the preacher visited and added a small jar of sugar, two spoons, and some milk in a small fruit jar. Lillian carried the tray and Jo came behind with a plate of the tea cakes they'd found in the Hoosier. They set the offerings on a small spindle-legged table between the two ladies.

"Thank you, girls," Miz Jane said. "Y'all can go back to your game now." She looked at Lillian with eyes pleading for her to keep Jo occupied.

Back in the kitchen, Lillian whispered to Jo, "Be real quiet now, and we can stay here and listen. You make one peep and you're going to the barn." Jo nodded so hard her short hair bobbed up and down. They took up their positions by the door again.

When the ladies started to take down the names and ages of everybody in the Stewart family, plus Lillian, Mr. Stewart started tapping his foot and his right hand twitched. "I reckon I'll leave y'all to it then. I best get back to work." Mr. Stewart slammed open the kitchen door so hard that it sent Lillian and Jo scurrying across the linoleum. They quickly busied themselves at the sink.

Mr. Stewart gave them a wide smile. "Town folks." He winked and shook his head. "Putting on airs and writing down things." Neither of Jo's folks could read or write, and Lillian wondered for a minute if she should offer to go in and sit with Miz Jane. Mama's voice rang in her memory.

"Lillian, don't ever let anyone in the holler tell you that reading and writing are not important." Mama had said those words to her ever since she'd started learning her letters—as far back as she could remember. Mama had believed in a lot of things different from most mountain folk. The importance of book-learning being one of them.

But Lillian could not bring herself to go into that room. No, best to stay here, out of sight. Besides, she had to watch Jo.

Mr. Stewart reached for the leftover cornbread resting under a feed sack napkin on the table. Tearing off a chunk, he stuffed it into his mouth and stood for a few minutes by the sink, chewing and looking thoughtful. After he washed the cornbread down with a drink of water from the sink, he lifted his hat from its hook by the back door. "You girls behave yourselves," he whispered. "Don't let them uppity women stay too long." He grasped Jo around the shoulders, hugged her to him, and chuckled as she squirmed in his arms. He kissed the top of her head and closed the back door behind him.

When they went back to listening at the door, the ladies were saying their goodbyes. Miz Jane called from the sitting room, "I know y'all are in there listening." Her voice was weary. "You can come in here now. They're gone."

"What did they want, Mama?" Jo plopped into a sitting room chair. Had Jo not understood any of it?

"Nothing for you to worry yourself about." Miz Jane got up and looked out the front window. Lillian looked too and saw the women kicking up dust behind them as they walked toward their big black automobile. Miz Jane had a strange, distant look in her eyes. "The County is doing some tests to make sure all the children up here in the holler are healthy."

"What were those papers they had?" Lillian asked. She'd seen one of the women handing her clipboard to Miz Jane, just before she'd had to stop listening and get the coffee.

"Nothing important, I reckon." Miz Jane sighed, collapsing into a chair. "Just wanted my X on the line giving my permission." Miz Jane pulled a handkerchief from her pocket and mopped at her face, which all of a sudden was dripping with sweat. Her face and neck were as red as a ripe tomato.

Lillian remembered Mama saying these flashes of hot sweatiness happened to women when they got older. "Nature's way of making a woman glad for old age."

Miz Jane looked so weary; Lillian was surprised she didn't take to her bed. Jo dropped down at her mama's feet and put her head in her lap. Lillian wasn't sure which one needed comforting the most. Jo was what the mountain people called simple, but she was her mama's only girl-child. "Jo..." Miz Jane struggled to control a sudden fit of coughing, "...fetch me a glass of cold water, will you?"

"I got it," Lillian said. As she cranked the pump handle, sending cold water gushing into a tin cup, she couldn't shake the feeling something was fixing to change.

MAY 26, 2010

Olivia took the street through the Mary Baldwin University campus. "Oh, I see the science building is named Preston Hall." She stopped for students at the crosswalk. "Is that named after the same guy? The doctor who ran the infirmary?"

"We don't talk about him." Jo muttered under her breath, nervously looking down. Lillian reached over and placed her hand over Jo's.

"Pardon?" Olivia asked.

Lillian was pleased Olivia had not heard Jo. "Yes, he was quite well known in these parts," Lillian managed to say, as she held Jo's hand, now balled into a fist.

There were very few times Dr. Preston's name came up, but when it did, Jo's temper was triggered. Lillian was relieved when they pulled into the Kroger parking lot and Jo was distracted with selecting the perfect grocery cart from the rack near their parking place. "I push the cart and Lil puts the groceries in," she announced.

"Yes, ma'am." Olivia smiled as she followed them into the chilly grocery store produce section.

Lillian pinched tomatoes and shook her head at their pallor. Olivia seemed as jittery as a long-tailed cat in a room full of rockers. All-of-a-sudden, her granddaughter announced she needed to run over to the drugstore next door for a couple things. "I'll be back in a few minutes. In plenty of time to help at check out."

Unsure why the child looked so nervous and flushed, Lillian nodded and waved her on. "You go ahead. We're doing all right here." Lillian laid her hand on the end of the cart so an enthusiastic Jo wouldn't run into her ankles. *Strange how secretive that child seemed sometimes.*

CHAPTER 15

Olivia

HAZEL HOLLOW
MAY 26, 2010

Olivia unloaded the bags of groceries and put on a pot of coffee. Lillian settled into her usual chair at the kitchen table while Jo lumbered about putting the groceries away. Closing the cabinet after the last item, Jo announced, "I got to go home now. I have chores to do and chickens to feed."

"Oh my gosh, Gran," Olivia wailed. "I forgot to feed Fanny."

"Don't you worry, young'un." Aunt Jo patted her shoulder. "I'll take care of Fanny." She rolled up the coveralls from earlier and stuffed them into one of the grocery bags, along with the chocolate ice cream. "You just look out for Lil, here." Lillian patted Jo's shoulder as she bent down and kissed her on the cheek.

Olivia smiled wistfully. Faithful friends, sisters-in-law, for decades. Thoughts of how it might have been to have a sister spiraled to whether she and Amy should have more than one child. This was followed by the prospect of going through this whole process of getting pregnant more than once. Maybe better not to think about sisters right now.

She jerked her attention back to the moment and clasped Jo in a hug. The chocolate ice cream Aunt Jo clutched chilled her tender breasts. Over Jo's shoulder, she spotted her backpack carelessly thrown on the kitchen table. The pregnancy test she'd managed to purchase without Gran and Aunt Jo's notice rested inside. She needed to figure out how to sneak away for a few minutes.

She followed Aunt Jo to the back-porch steps and watched her toddle down the driveway in her bow-legged walk. Right before Aunt Jo disappeared among the trees lining the road from Lillian's house to her cabin, she turned to wave. "See y'all tomorrow."

Olivia waved and turned back into the kitchen. Lillian had gotten up to choose a coffee cup from the cabinet. "Here, let me get that for you." She rushed to reach for the cup.

"I only broke the one arm, you know." A smile sparkled in Lillian's blue eyes.

"I know, but let me take care of you. It's okay to relax."

Lillian furrowed her brow with an audible harrumph. "Seems all I do these days is relax." And under her breath, she added, "At least I'm still getting to do it in my own house."

"I heard that, Gran." Olivia smiled as they exchanged knowing looks. Her grandmother would definitely go out kicking. Admiration for her independence buoyed Olivia, followed by a sharp stab of sadness. She couldn't imagine the loss Lillian would feel having to leave her home.

"I believe I'll take my coffee out on the front porch." Lillian moved toward the front of the house.

"I'm on it." Relieved to have a task to focus on, Olivia followed with her grandmother's coffee and settled her into the rocking chair, pulling a small table close for the coffee. Scrap dumped his rounded, creaky old body at Lillian's feet. Snoring within seconds. Time for *the test*. Olivia covered her mouth and fake-stifled a yawn. "I think I'll take a nap. That okay?" A little guilt. She wasn't sleepy at all. As a matter of fact, her anxiety level right now was through the roof.

"You go ahead," Lillian said. "Scrap and I might doze a little ourselves."

She retrieved her backpack from the kitchen and carried it to the bedroom, where she pulled out the pregnancy test. She brought the test and her cell phone into the bathroom and locked the door. Her hands shook as she opened the box and removed the instructions. She jumped in surprise when the clattering jangle of the land-line telephone sounded in the hallway. The instruction sheet slipped from her hands, slid across the black and white tiled floor, and disappeared underneath the claw foot tub.

"I'm coming. Hold your horses," Lillian called from the porch.

Olivia cracked open the bathroom door and stuck her head out. "Want me to answer that, Gran?"

The screen door opened and closed. Lillian's footsteps came toward her. "No, I have it. You go on ahead and do your business."

Olivia pulled her head back into the bathroom, closed the door, and relocked it. *My business? Does Gran know what I'm doing?* She scoffed at her silliness and dove under the tub. She sneezed at the dust and cobwebs as she laid her face on the cool tile and reached for the instructions, frustratingly just out of her reach. In the hallway, Lillian picked up the phone. Olivia lay quietly on the floor, listening to her grandmother's side of the conversation.

"Hello?"

"I'm doing fine."

"Mm hm. Olivia drove us to the Kroger, and we bought groceries."

After a long pause, Lillian said, "I'm sure Olivia can find something to fix. You do what you need to do, and we will see you tomorrow."

Another long silence. Must be her mother calling. But why was Miriam staying in Charlottesville tonight? Loneliness grabbed at her heart. So strange. Her emotions were all over the place. Maybe this was a good thing. After all, if she *was* pregnant, it would give her time to figure out how to tell her mother. Or not. Yet... She stretched her fingers toward the paper again. Finally, she got hold of the edge of the test instructions and pulled them toward her.

"Bye, darlin'," Lillian said. The phone clicked into its hook. In a few seconds, her footsteps sounded as she passed back toward the front door. The screen door slapped closed behind her.

Olivia supposed she would have to figure out something for dinner tonight. Her mother was definitely acting weird. She dismissed Miriam from her mind and focused on the instructions. The whole thing was simple: pee on the stick, wait three minutes, and boom, you know whether or not your whole life will change. *No big deal, right?*

She stared at the test stick where it lay beside her cell phone, debating whether to call Amy *during* the process of doing the test. Maybe it would be better to wait and call *after* it was done. Why hadn't they talked about this possibility before she flew across the country to Virginia?

Screw it. She set her cell phone aside, took a deep breath, and sat down on the toilet.

She stuffed the bag containing the evidence of the pregnancy test into her backpack. She didn't want Lillian to find that particular item in the trash can—or Miriam, for that matter. She sat down on the side of the bed and stared at the picture she was about to text to Amy. She made it larger with her thumb and index finger. Yep, there were definitely two lines.

Her phone buzzed within three minutes of sending the text. "Holy cow..." Amy was breathless. "Are you... are we?"

"I think so." The initial numbness wore off and her heart beat faster. "I can't believe it either. I really didn't expect it to be positive."

"Do you need me? Should I come there?" Already protectiveness in Amy's voice. "I could hop on a plane tomorrow. I can tell the office it's an emergency. Maybe work on my cases from there?"

Olivia considered this. As much as she missed Amy, what could she do if she were here? Besides, it somehow seemed right to face her mother and grandmother alone. A butterfly of a thought: maybe this was about getting better at the adulting thing. "No, I'm okay." She managed a calm, collected voice. "I know you've got a trial starting next week, plus there's Maggie..."

"I know, but—"

"No, really. I'm good. And I need to deal with Gran and Mom on my own right now."

"Are you going to tell them?"

"I'm not sure." Olivia pushed away the mental picture of Miriam's face when she revealed she'd gotten pregnant using a sperm bank. "Nope, not ready to tell Mom yet. Maybe Gran." The rest of the conversation was short; they took turns being shocked and ecstatic. In the end, they agreed to talk more later, after Lillian had gone to bed and the news had soaked in a bit.

Olivia opened the screen door and was surprised to find her grandmother's rocker empty. She hurried back inside and down the hall to the kitchen. Lillian wasn't there either. A stab of anxiety. "Gran," she called. She peeked into her bedroom, into the open bathroom. No response. Then it occurred to her:

the river.

With an unexpected jolt of fear, she rushed down the front porch steps and headed across the front lawn, calling out as she ran, "Gran?"

"I'm here." Lillian's fragile voice drifted toward her. She spied her grandmother at the riverbank and blew out her breath in relief. Lillian sat on the big hemlock root—the one that served as her bench to watch the river from. Rumbling river water, birdsong, and the rustle of hemlock needles and oak leaves overhead filled Olivia's ears.

"There you are." She tried not to sound as panicked as she felt.

"Yes, I was missing my friends." Lillian looked up and gestured around her at the birds and trees. "Did you have a good nap?"

"Yeah, it was fine," she lied. She scooched in beside Lillian, pressing her hands against the exposed root of the massive tree, silky smooth against her palms. She was a little girl again. Playing in the shade of the nurturing tree towering over them. Pretending fairies inhabited the web of roots that reached for the slowly moving river.

Would she bring her baby here? Would Lillian teach him or her about the trees and plants along the river's bank, about the best places to find tadpoles, or where the eddies swirled in the shallow places and tickled your legs when you stepped into the middle of them?

She stole a glance at her grandmother. Wrinkled face serene, gaze cast outward toward the water. A wave of emotion seized Olivia. If Miriam had her way, Lillian wouldn't be living in the farmhouse when the baby was born. She had waited too long to get pregnant. Her baby would not have a chance to share this part of her childhood. An overwhelming sense of loss gripped her. A ragged sigh escaped her lips before she could hold it back.

"What's this?" Lillian reached over and pushed a strand of hair away from Olivia's face.

Olivia avoided looking up and scrubbed away the unexpected tears. "Oh, nothing." She tried to smile. "Just a little emotional today, I guess."

Lillian nodded. "I've cried many a tear right here with this river as my only company."

Olivia watched a fallen branch drift by, carried by the river's current. Her grandmother must be thinking of losing Grandpa so long ago. Olivia thought of the stories she'd heard of a grandfather she'd never known. Another stab of loss threatened more tears. "Do you still miss Grandpa?" The word—Grandpa—felt odd on her tongue. Her grandfather was an abstraction, pieced together from stories and tidbits picked up over her lifetime. Grandpa, Dad, and the sperm donor were *ideas* of men. Unlike the fully formed real men in her life— Uncle Walt and Uncle Dennis.

"I miss him every day," Lillian said quietly. She reached and put a bony arm around Olivia's shoulders. "I wish you could have known him."

She leaned in closer and put her head in her grandmother's lap, allowing herself a moment of being a little girl again. "Gran?"

"Yes, dear?" Lillian smoothed Olivia's hair away from her face with spidery fingers.

"I need to tell you something," she whispered. *Am I really about to say this?*

"You do."

That was not a question. Her heart sped up. Lillian knew and was waiting until she was ready. "I'm pregnant."

"Ah." Her grandmother breathed out slowly. Her hand rested behind Olivia's head. "So, you are."

Olivia sat up so abruptly Lillian reached back to steady herself. "What do you mean, 'so you are'? Did you know?"

Lillian smiled. That same knowing smile she always had. "I suspected."

"But, but... how? Why?" Olivia stumbled to say.

"Oh, little things. A look in your eyes, the way you hold yourself. Remember, I was a midwife back before your mama came along. I've seen lots of women in the family way in my time." Her grandmother looked into her eyes. Such love. And something else? Something Olivia could not name.

"I'm not quite ready to tell Mom yet." Olivia turned to stare at the river. A pair of wood ducks flapped out from under the tree cover and landed on the water, swirling and bobbing with the current.

"Is that so?" Lillian asked. "And why is that?"

Olivia remained silent for several seconds, watching the duck pair. The colorful male and the somber brown female. Why was it, exactly, she was so afraid of telling her mother? If she had the guts to get pregnant, she had to have the guts to tell her own mother. But, what if? She felt Lillian's gaze turn toward her. "You know Mom." Olivia tried to sound light as she glanced at her grandmother. "She has her own ideas about how everything should be done." She picked up a stick and scratched in the dirt at their feet, drawing a continuous spiral.

"Yes, she does at that." They sat for several more seconds of silence. "Song sparrow." Lillian tilted her face upward toward the sound. Olivia marveled at how Lillian could distinguish each bird's call. "Well, if you don't mind me asking..." Her grandmother continued to watch the trees. "I don't rightly know how to ask this... but, last year... well, there was that sweet young woman, Amy... and it was my understanding that you and she were..."

Olivia's heart lightened. She met Lillian's eyes and smiled. A rush of joy. "Right. That was Amy, my partner. We're doing this together." Dropping her hand to her belly seemed automatic. But Lillian looked more confused than ever.

Her grandmother's lips pursed into a question and then
back to a straight line, and then a question again. "I might be
a poor woman from the holler, child, but last time I checked,
you had to have a man to make a baby."

It could have been the expression on Lillian's face, or the
relief from the anxiety of keeping the pregnancy secret, or
maybe the general giddiness of the weird emotional high she
felt. Whatever it was, she collapsed into laughter. Lillian
chuckled deep in her chest as well. For several minutes they
laughed until they both stopped to catch their breath.

"There's no man, Gran, believe it or not." Olivia said, as
she wiped her eyes with the tail of her t-shirt. For the next
half-hour, she explained how the whole thing worked. Lillian
listened attentively, stopping her every so often to ask a question.

"Well, I declare," Lillian said, finally. "What will they come
up with next?" Olivia watched her grandmother's expression
intently, fully expecting a caution or a disapproval. But when
Lillian spoke, Olivia realized she should have known better. "I
think that's fine, Livy." Her eyes shone. "Just fine." Lillian put
her arm around her and squeezed tightly. "A great-grandbaby.
Isn't that something?"

As they walked arm-in-arm back up the grassy slope to the
house, Olivia thought again of how she might break the news
to her mother. And then it occurred to her all the other times
she was going to have to break the same news. Over and over
again. Would there be the same question each time—who is
the father?

"Jo will be beside herself," Lillian said as they reached the
porch. Scrap rose stiffly from his lookout position on the top
step. His old tail wagged slowly in greeting. "No one loves babies like your Aunt Jo." She reached out to pet a nuzzling
Scrap. "Although I'm not sure you need to tell her all of that
business about the freezing and all. Maybe we'd better tell her

you had yourself a little fling." Lillian gave her a sly smile and a wink.

Olivia laughed and pictured Aunt Jo cuddling her baby. A comforting thought. "Gran?" She stood behind her grandmother with a hand on her bony back as she ascended the steps.

"Yes?"

"Why was it you decided to have only one child? Did you ever want more than one?"

Lillian's back stiffened as she reached for the door. Odd. Several seconds passed and Lillian didn't respond. Maybe she hadn't heard. Or worse, maybe Olivia had overstepped into her grandmother's private world somehow.

They made their way to the little sitting room off the kitchen. Lillian positioned herself in her favorite armchair in front of a television that must be at least twenty years old. "Thank you, dear." Lillian reached for the remote. "I'm going to turn on my program."

Olivia pulled her cell phone from the back pocket of her jeans and glanced at the time. "You must be starved. I'll fix us something to eat." Olivia turned toward the kitchen.

"And Livy?"

"Yes?" She twisted to meet Lillian's eyes.

"Your grandfather and I were pleased as punch when your mama came along. We didn't need any more babies. Just the one." Lillian's tone didn't invite more conversation.

Olivia nodded. She replayed all the times she'd heard her mother quote James Redfield: "you should never take responsibility for more children than you can give attention to."

Lillian clicked on the television and immersed herself immediately in Andy Griffith. Olivia wandered into the kitchen, contemplating what to make for dinner. Would she continue the Stewart women's tradition and have only one child?

CHAPTER 16

Miriam

CHARLOTTESVILLE
MAY 26, 2010

Miriam settled into the sculpted seat of her favorite hickory rocking chair on Walt and Dennis's screened porch. The screen door hinges creaked behind her. Walt appeared from the kitchen bearing a tray loaded with Kalamata olives, a variety of cheeses, two crusty baguettes, butter, and his homemade fig jam. "I thought we'd start with this." He set the tray on the antique wicker table positioned in front of hers and three other rocking chairs, forming a semi-circle.

So many times she'd sat on this porch with one, or both, of these men. All those years ago when she and Dennis survived on ramen and rented from Miss Pettiworth—him an apartment in the house, her, the cottage—who could have dreamed they'd end up here, in their sixties, still trying to figure life out? *Well, I am anyway.* Dennis seemed so sure of himself these days.

Through Olivia's first year, Dennis had been Miriam's rock. Although Rachel had helped her find a nanny—once she'd gotten past tsk, tsking about Miriam going back to work so soon—it had been Dennis who stepped in when she had to work late. Dennis who kept her company during the long nights of terrifying childhood illnesses. When he'd fallen in love with Walt, she'd been so happy for him. Actually... truth? She'd been terrified of losing Dennis. She'd worried she and Olivia would not fit into his new life as part of a couple.

She couldn't have been more wrong. By the time Olivia turned two, Walt had fired the nanny and taken over Olivia's care. She sighed as her thoughts moved through Olivia's childhood. The toddler years and frantically childproofing not one, but two old houses. Olivia playing in the garden, fascinated by the koi in Walt's little pond. The school-age years, when she'd climb up to the crook of the sprawling maple that stretched its limbs between their adjoining back yards and read. The teenage years when she wanted nothing to do with any of them. All of it a blur of juggling career and parenting. They had made it work. Yet... When she was with Walt and Dennis, she *still* felt the emptiness of no fourth person—*her* person. The idea of growing old with a man to fill the fourth rocking chair seemed to have passed her by. It was that damned letter from Hugh stirring these thoughts again.

She caught the woody scent of Walt's Armani cologne as he pulled a rocker closer to hers and sat down. He reached for one of the small china plates on the tray and handed it to her. "Here you go, Mimi, dig in. It sounds like you've had a hard day." Walt's deep voice was comforting. He was the only person she allowed to call her Mimi. His lean, tanned face crinkled into a million little lines of concern as he looked into her eyes. She internally squirmed at his kindness and reached for the crusty baguette, tore off a large chunk, slathered it in butter, and popped it into her mouth, moaning with pleasure.

"I bought the last two baguettes at Albemarle Bakery today." Walt tapped her hand with his fingers and pursed his full lips into a sly smile.

"Now Walt..." Dennis slammed through the screen door.

He had changed from his professional clothes to perfectly creased khaki shorts, a sky-blue polo, and Birkenstocks. "Do not pamper her. She has *much* explaining to do."

Dennis carried a tray that held a cocktail shaker and all the components for his famous whiskey sours. He set the tray on the table and, as carefully as a chemist, poured bourbon, simple syrup, and fresh-squeezed lemon juice into the shaker. "I have something here that should loosen your tongue." He looked pointedly at Miriam over his round black glasses.

Raising and lowering his arms to shake the drinks, he reminded her of a sixties go-go dancer. His years of experience and well-practiced rhythm would result in perfectly chilled whiskey sours. While Dennis shook the drinks, she and Walt sampled the olives and bite-size chunks of mellow Havarti cheese.

"I need to check on dinner." Walt stood. "I'm doing lasagna tonight." He passed behind her and reached over the back of her rocker to squeeze her shoulders. "By the way, Dennis told me that Hugh might be back in the picture." His voice was breathy.

She groaned. Of course, they'd already been discussing her problems.

Dennis stopped mid-shake as Walt proceeded toward the kitchen. "Drinks are ready."

Walt paused in the doorway. "Go ahead and pour mine. And do *not* say a word until I get back."

Miriam smiled. They could always lift her out of a morose mood.

"I *mean* it," Walt shouted as Miriam and Dennis watched him disappear into the kitchen.

With a flourish, Dennis poured the topaz liquid into the waiting highball glasses, which he'd already garnished with orange slices. He plopped in a Jack Rudy bourbon-soaked cocktail cherry, handed one of the icy cold concoctions to her, and took one for himself. She savored the sweetness of the bourbon on her tongue.

"That's our Walt." Dennis pierced an olive with an appetizer fork. "Ever the romantic when it comes to Hugh." He sat back, picked up the newspaper Walt had left in the chair next to him, paged through until he found what he sought, and folded the paper neatly. The obituaries. His obsessive daily habit.

"Oh, my goodness," Dennis said quietly.

"Who is it this time?" Miriam expected to hear that one of his former patients had died.

"Your college professor. You know. The one you always said was the reason you went to med school?" Dennis thrust the folded paper toward her and pointed to a column of print with a photo above it.

"Dr. Whitaker?" Miriam took the paper and looked at where he pointed. Instantly, she recognized the 1970s faculty photograph of Dr. Elizabeth Whitaker. "Oh, how sad," Miriam murmured. "I completely lost touch with her." She felt diminished somehow—as if a part of her youth had died along with her mentor from all those years ago. Images of her undergrad self—finally free of Hazel Hollow, so excited, so passionate about science—flitted across her consciousness. The vibrant Dr. Whitaker—a PhD in Chemistry—so unusual for a woman at that time.

The faculty of Mary Baldwin College, which was then an all-female institution, was committed, at least on paper, to developing young women's talents. But most of them did not challenge the social expectation of what the well-educated Virginia woman was preparing herself to do. A career until marriage, but not *during*. Rachel had fit the bill completely for the ideal Mary Baldwin Bluestocking. Except she'd never worked. Ever.

Dr. Whitaker was gloriously different from the other

female faculty members. She held off-campus get-togethers at her century-old four-square style house overlooking Gypsy Hill Park. With Doc Whit, as they'd tagged her, Miriam smoked cigarettes, drank cheap beer, and talked about taboo subjects such as women's lib, sex, and birth control. Rachel had been horrified. Miriam had never felt freer.

Doc Whit was the first woman Miriam had known who lived her life free of commitments other than her work. No husband, no children, and a lover rumored to be a professor at UVA. Doc Whit had even figured out a way to obtain black-market birth control pills.

Dr. Whitaker had seen something in Miriam. "Don't waste your gifts on becoming a science teacher," she counseled. "There's no reason you can't become a doctor. You could come back here and make a difference for women."

"I can't believe she's gone." Miriam handed the paper back to Dennis. He took it, holding the corners of his mouth down in sympathy. She reached for more bread, buttered it, and continued to rock gently as she chewed. According to the obituary, Dr. Whitaker had died single and childless. Miriam wondered if she had ever regretted that.

They sat in silence. Miriam sipped her drink. As Dennis read about death, she ruminated on the three men in her life. Walt, who had always labeled her decades-long, on-again-off-again relationship with Hugh as the *essence* of romance. Dennis, who—more than anyone—knew how vulnerable Hugh made her feel. Only Dennis knew how crazy she'd gotten during those few months so long ago when Hugh had seemed to be a reason to give up everything she'd worked for.

FALL, 1979

"But... how?" Dennis's perplexed face irritated her.

She growled in frustration, clenched her jaw, and glared

at him. "I was getting migraines from the pill, so I went off it."
She groaned, hearing the whine in her own voice. She covered
her face with her hands then pushed her hair back so tightly
her eyes became slits. "I was planning on getting an IUD..."
She threw the pillow she clutched violently across the room.
"Dammit."

"So, what now?" Dennis asked gently.

"I don't want to be pregnant." Her voice had reached a
wail, as she threw her arms out and paced the tiny living room
of the cottage. "What am I going to do?"

Dennis grasped her by the shoulders and guided her over
to the two dilapidated chairs pulled close to the gas heater. He
gently pushed her down into one chair and collapsed into the
other. He threw her a blanket and pulled another around his
thin shoulders. An October cold front had brought an unexpected flurry of snow to Charlottesville and the cottage was
freezing.

"What does Hugh say?" Dennis asked.

She pulled the blanket over her face. Her response was
muffled. "He doesn't know."

"Oh, come on, Miriam." Impatience edged his voice.
"You're kidding, right?"

"I know, I know." She dropped the blanket from her face.
"I'm a total female cliché. First, an accidental pregnancy. Then,
I don't even realize that I'm pregnant until I'm too far gone to
do anything about it. And now, I'm not going to tell the guy
because I don't want to burden him with my screw-up." She
flung her head against the back of the chair and closed her
eyes. She was too ashamed to even look at Dennis.

"He deserves to know." Dennis sounded, as usual, so certain. "Have you told Rachel?"

"Yep." Miriam stared into the heater's tiny flame.

"And?"

"I think you can probably guess." She poked out her

bottom lip and turned down the corners of her mouth, her voice higher, more Southern—mimicking Rachel. "She was all excited, like I've finally joined the *real* women's club. Her very first, *very* first question was—" Miriam held up her forefinger and stabbed the air, "'when are you and Hugh getting married?' Not, oh my god, Miriam. How are you? Or, what will this do to your career? Or maybe even do you want to be a mother? None of that." She blinked, trying to bring Dennis's face into focus, realizing she'd been on a bit of a tirade. "And when I tell her we're not. What does she say?" Dennis shook his head slowly, mouth clamped tight, lips pressed together.

"'But, Miriam...'" Miriam dropped her voice into a secretive, breathy tone. "'What about your reputation?'"

Dennis lifted his eyebrows.

Miriam took the cue. "I said, what reputation is that, Rachel?" Miriam fell silent, brought her knees up to her chest, and propped her chin on them.

"Don't keep me in suspense," Dennis urged. "What did she say?"

Miriam turned to look into Dennis's warm eyes. She rested her ear on her knee and was frustrated when a tear slipped out and dripped down her leg. Her voice dropped to a whisper as she relayed Rachel's words, "She said, 'I just thought—you being a doctor and all—a gynecologist, no less—you'd want to set an example for your patients.'"

After several seconds, during which the only sounds were the pop and hiss of the gas heater, Dennis rose from his chair and folded his long frame onto the floor next to her feet. He didn't say anything, he simply leaned against her legs. And with that simple gesture, decisions dropped into place. She'd have the baby. She'd figure out how to practice medicine *and* be a mother. Screw Rachel and her antiquated notions about motherhood. Dennis would never desert her. What she *didn't* know was how to manage Hugh.

After she'd written to him to let him know she was pregnant, he'd called. "Job is really demanding... can't leave right away... are you sure you want to keep it? ...whatever you decide..."

"I'm keeping the baby and I don't expect anything," she had said. "I just thought you should know."

CHAPTER 17

Miriam

CHARLOTTESVILLE
MAY 26, 2010

The mouth-watering scent of garlic and tomatoes drifted from the kitchen, tearing her thoughts from Hugh. Walt rejoined them, wearing the white apron Olivia had given him several years ago for Christmas. *Real Men Bake* in black lettering blazed across his chest. The apron covered a floral designer button-down shirt; sleeves neatly rolled to his elbows. "So, where shall we start?" He sat down and crossed his legs, a flip-flop dangling from his toe as he swung his leg.

She sighed loudly and looked from one to the other of them. She opened her mouth to speak, but words of explanation scuttled out of her brain as if she'd had a stroke.

Dennis had mercy on her. Sort of. "How about we start with the least surprising news?" He folded the newspaper and set it on the table, took a sip of his drink, set it down, and reached for the baguette with one hand, and the fig jam with the other. She and Walt waited. "The neeewwss..." He stretched out the word. "...that Hugh has inserted himself into the picture again." He looked directly at her. Dennis's lack of affection for Hugh was not a revelation to either of them.

Walt raised the corners of his pursed mouth at Dennis's tone. "Someone sounds a bit skeptical."

"Okay," Miriam countered. "You're right, of course." She set her drink on the table and aggressively ripped off another chunk of baguette. "To be skeptical, that is." She continued in a sing-song voice, relaying the contents of Hugh's letter. "He's getting ready to leave Africa. I'm on his mind, Olivia is on his mind. It's time for a change, yada, yada, yada." She stuffed the bread into her mouth, chewing forcefully.

"Hold the phone." Walt leaned forward. "Time for a change? What *kind* of change?"

Miriam glanced at Dennis. The wariness in his eyes echoed her own. For so many years, Hugh had come and gone. She'd grown accustomed to his restlessness. It had actually worked for her. So why should this letter feel different? But it did, and she wasn't sure Dennis would understand how. She didn't understand it herself.

She tried to swallow the bread, which seemed to expand. She reached for her drink and took a sip. "He's stepping down from his position at Relief International. Says he wants to hike the Appalachian trail, maybe write a book. Something about the journey home." She tried to keep the sarcasm from her voice. It was a defense.

"He's coming back to Virginia?" Dennis was incapable of keeping the incredulous—and protective—tone from his voice. "To stay?"

"It sounds like it." She stared at her drink as she swirled it. "He's asked to spend some time with me." In her peripheral vision she saw Dennis and Walt exchange glances.

Walt was the first to ask. "And what did you say?"

"I haven't said anything. I'm sort of busy right now with my mother, and... other things..." She crossed and uncrossed her legs, shifted in her chair. "And he didn't actually ask for an answer. He's usually more about declaration than interrogation." She waved her hand dismissively. "We all know how he is. It might happen and it might not."

They sat in companionable silence for a few minutes, rocking and looking out over Dennis and Walt's lovely back garden. Paths lined with blousy yellow and pink peonies wandered toward a charming gazebo. Tall purple allium and bearded iris surrounded a wide koi pond, in the middle of which a soothing upward spray of water spattered over the pond's surface.

She tried to let the peacefulness of their home settle over her, along with the pleasant haze caused by the whiskey sour. She was grateful when Dennis changed the subject.

"I suppose we will just have to see what happens with Hugh. Nothing new there, right?" He flipped his wrist as if to swat away an unwanted pest. Without waiting for an answer, he glanced sideways at Walt and said, "What I want to know is how you plan to force Lillian Stewart to move to Charlottesville, and whether Walt and I are going to be granduncles?"

Walt, who had leaned forward to skewer an olive, stopped mid-reach. He turned to her, eyes wide, mouth agape. He looked from her to Dennis and back again. "Obviously, I have been left out of the loop." He turned a prickly gaze toward Dennis. "Since my darling partner neglected to mention either of these two *life-changing* events." His deep voice rose to a higher pitch.

"Sorry, hon." Dennis poured another round of drinks. "I didn't have a chance to tell you quite everything your little Mimi dropped on me today."

As she was about to launch into her dilemma with Lillian, Walt's cell phone alarm jangled, signaling the lasagna was ready. "Drink up, kids." He downed his whiskey sour in one swallow. "I need to be in my kitchen to hear this story."

Miriam and Dennis followed Walt, carrying the glasses and trays. She took up her usual position at the wide Carrara marble central island, the cutting board Walt had laid out waiting. She pulled a knife from the countertop block to cut the salad vegetables. Dennis appraised the collection of red wines in the iron rack sitting on an oak sideboard in the nearby dining area. Walt pulled the delicious smelling lasagna from the oven and set it on the waiting trivets to rest.

"Well?" Walt pushed.

She looked down at the carrot she chopped. "I told Dennis today I think it's time I moved Lillian to Charlottesville to live with me." She glanced up.

"Mm hm," Walt murmured. He held her eyes. "And what makes you think she will agree?"

Before Miriam could answer, Dennis jumped in. "Miriam thinks she's going to ensconce Lillian in the cottage. She's kicking Nate out."

"What? Oh, our little Nate." Walt's expression was dreamy. "I will miss Nate... But wait. Lillian is not going to agree to live in the city of Charlottesville—no matter how small and pedestrian it happens to be."

"I'm hoping I can convince her to at least try it." Miriam frowned at the carrot pieces. How had they turned from sliced to minced? "I'm thinking of a trial run. Couple weeks in the cottage." The more she talked about this, the less she believed in her plan.

"Are you planning on bringing the river with you? And what about her dog... what was his name?"

"Scrap. Yes, she'll have to bring Scrap along too. He may have a harder time than she will..." Miriam mused. "Or...maybe he could stay with Jo for a while."

Over dinner, they tossed around the pros and cons of up-rooting Lillian from her home and at the end of it, Miriam still felt a sense of dread. The conversation was so consumed with her making the right decision, she began to hope they had for-gotten all about Olivia's news. But. It was not to be.

They were watching Walt slice his first key-lime pie of the season. "Mimi?"

"Yes, Walt."

"This little issue Dennis mentioned... Granduncles? I do love the sound of that."

They carried dessert to the screened porch. Darkness had fallen. Crickets chirped and the sweet smell of honeysuckle filled the air. "You know, I always knew Livy would want a baby." Walt's voice was tender.

"Really?" Miriam and Dennis asked simultaneously.

So typical of Walt. He sat back in his rocker and slowly sipped a scotch. He looked at them indulgently in the flickering light of the hurricane candles. "Of course, I did. But then, until I came along, you two were raising her as if you were conducting a scientific experiment in gender-neutral childhood." Walt laughed at their bewildered looks. "Oh, don't tell me you don't remember?" He laid a long slender hand on his chest. "When Uncle Walt came into that child's life, her only toys were a microscope and a spirograph. I mean, really? What two-year-old plays with a microscope?"

Miriam and Dennis looked at each other and nodded. No matter how many books Miriam had read in her attempt to parent correctly, Walt was right. He had always been the maternal force among them. "You bought her a Cabbage Patch doll." She released a wistful sigh.

"And Pound Puppies," Dennis added with a sheepish smile.

"And she adored them. We played dolls and puppies every day." Walt took a deep breath and let out a sigh. "I always had the sense that she would want children... Well, come to think of it, maybe I wasn't sure anymore when she became such a little feminist. Like her mother." He dipped his chin and looked pointedly at Miriam. "Mimi, is our baby really going to have a baby?"

Miriam didn't answer. No surprise, Walt melting into

sentimentality, wiping tears from his eyes. Dennis, as usual, was the more practical of the two. "How, exactly, is she planning to do this?" he asked. Miriam's chest tightened. Another situation she had no control over.

Miriam took a deep breath and enthusiastically described the potential donors she'd identified for Olivia. Her plan was airtight. One of these fantastic guys would be a great genetic combination with Olivia. "Actually, it's working out well with her being here and all..." She got up and stood near the porch screen, staring out at the garden as she schemed. She registered Walt's and Dennis's occasional "Mm hms." Maybe they were a little *too* quiet. She turned to look at them. Faces blank and solemn, they rocked, drinks poised in mid-air. "Well? Are you going to say anything? Or are you just going to sit there, sipping scotch, and judging me?"

Walt looked at Dennis, who shrugged and held up his hands in resignation. Walt's voice was gentle as he looked at her with that exasperating 'bless your heart' expression of his. "Mimi, honey, we're not judging you." He glanced at Dennis again. "It's just that—"

"Just what? She doesn't want her mother to interfere?" Miriam's hackles rose. *Couldn't they see that this was too important to leave to chance?*

"I think the sperm banks are pretty reliable these days," Dennis ventured carefully.

"Really, Dennis? After what I went through with a simple DNA test?" Out of the corner of her eye, she caught Walt's puzzled look, but chose to ignore it. "If a lab can't do that right, what makes you think some random sperm bank is not going to mix up sperm? Or fail to test it thoroughly? Or... I don't know... All kinds of things could happen." She set her glass on the table much harder than she intended. Walt and Dennis both jumped. She dropped back into her chair.

"I think you might be catastrophizing a touch, hon," Walt

said.

"That's what Olivia implied." Stubbornness stiffened her back.

"Maybe she *wants* the anonymity," Dennis offered. "Did you think about that?"

"*Yes*, I thought about that," Miriam spat back. "But that's so silly when all she would need to do is have a legally binding contract—"

"Oh, Mimi."

"What?"

"I think there's more to the anonymity issue than a contract saying he won't claim his rights as a father." Walt's voice was calm. Knowing.

She considered this idea. What more could there be? It began to dawn on her. The notion of an involved father was not quite in her wheelhouse. Well... except for her own father. They all fell silent and sipped their drinks. She sneaked glances at them. Walt chewed the end of his thumb and stared straight ahead. Dennis watched Walt. Dennis's eyes had gone soft and his mouth was tilted up slightly. Walt was the emotional barometer among the three of them, but his perspective on things often felt a bit illogical to her.

The doves began their evening cooing. Finally, Walt spoke into the stillness. "I think there's probably something about looking into the eyes of the person who will... not be the *father* per se, but even just... provide the sperm." Walt swirled his scotch. "When you've met a person, and talked to them... well, you sort of *know* them a little bit, right?" His eyes found hers, then Dennis's. He had a point. "Anyway, maybe our Livy—or maybe Amy—doesn't want a *real* person, a *particular* guy, in her consciousness. He's more than a sperm then, and they don't want a third person in the mix."

Miriam considered this possibility. That nagging feeling of unsettledness and vulnerability gripped her again. Leave it to

Walt to see what was really going on.

Walt shook his head and laughed, trying to lighten the mood. "Livy wants Amy to be the other mother... or parent, without any experience of a father, or donor, or whatever the hell it is they call it. I'm glad it's Livy and Amy doing this and not us." His smile was wistful when he glanced at Dennis. Dennis reached over, clasped Walt's hand, and squeezed it.

A momentary wave of gratitude swept through her. If Dennis had been willing, if times had been different, he and Walt might have adopted a child. Instead, she and Olivia had received all the benefits of their love and support. She couldn't have been a mother without them.

In a sudden change of mood, Walt sipped his scotch, a wicked gleam in his eye. "I know," he mock-whispered, leaning forward. "What about Nate? He's such a darling—smart, absolutely adorable, kind... and that body..." His expression was swoony as he pretended to fan himself. "Who wouldn't want to fall into bed with Nate?"

Dennis reached over and patted Walt's knee. "Down boy." He looked over his glasses. "Olivia is a lesbian, if you will recall."

"I know, I know." Walt pushed his hand away.

Miriam laughed at the ridiculous thought. "Walt, you are a character."

"I thought maybe just the one time she could make an exception," Walt said with a sly grin. "After all, she had that cute boyfriend for a while at UVA."

Dennis slowly shook his head. "I'm not sure Amy would approve."

The weariness of the long day settled on Miriam. "Besides..." She yawned. "Nate is leaving for DC soon." Why hadn't she listed Nate as a potential donor? *Oh god. Enough pondering for one day.* She planted her feet wearily and prepared to push herself out of the rocker. "I have to go home.

I'm exhausted."

"Not yet, you don't." Dennis pointed his index finger toward her. "You still haven't told me why you think your DNA results are bogus."

CHAPTER 18

Lillian

HAZEL HOLLOW
MAY 26, 2010

Lillian lay awake, eyes closed, listening to the rhythmic sound of the first summer katydids drifting through her open bedroom window. *Katy did, Katy didn't.* And always, behind that sound, the reassuring flow of the river.

She smiled. Her suspicion had been accurate. Olivia was indeed pregnant. Although, the way it happened was certainly something she never thought she'd live to see. Nothing short of a miracle. Young women these days could order up a man's seed from some sort of *online catalog*, Olivia had called it. Never have to go to bed with a man. Why, the only thing she'd ever gotten from a catalog was a pair of shoes. Sears and Roebuck, when she was eight years old.

She had been so proud of those shoes.

Lillian reached with her good hand to pull the quilt a little higher under her chin. She would never have traded her nights under this quilt, wrapped in Elijah Stewart's strong arms, for a man's seed that came in a jar in the mail. A twinge of the old pain squeezed her heart. She hoped Olivia and Amy's love was like hers and Elijah's had been. She'd accepted long ago her granddaughter was the kind of woman who loved other women. Good for her. Takes all sorts to make the world go around. In her day, you didn't talk about such things. The few women who were rumored to be *that way* lived together and got labeled old-maid spinsters. No one asked or cared, what they did in private. Except maybe a few of the Bible-thumpers. Those women didn't have the choice of getting a baby from a catalog.

Yes, the world had changed while she'd grown old in this holler. But her world here suited her well. Hadn't she found happiness over the years, even after she'd lost Elijah? She had her home and the river; she had Scrap and Jo, her garden and her chickens. She was accustomed to being alone. Looking back on it now, those years with Elijah in this bed beside her had gone by so quickly. And Miriam's childhood had too. Sadness heavier than the quilt sank into her bones. Sadness so old she could scarcely remember a time before it. Of course, talk of babies always pricked at her like a needle pricking a boil.

She'd been taken aback by Olivia's question earlier today: whether she'd ever wanted more children. She opened her eyes and turned to watch the curtains gently moving in the night breeze. All she'd *ever* wanted as a young girl was to have babies and raise them. She too had been an only child. She'd longed for brothers and sisters.

Funny. Miriam had once asked the same question as Olivia asked today. She'd been about twelve years old. They were hanging sheets on the clothesline at the time. "Did you ever want more kids?" Miriam had stooped to pull a shirt from the clothes basket. Lillian paused, held the wooden clothespin on the edge of a sheet, gripped with worry. How to answer? Miriam was always a smart girl. She spent most of her time with her nose in a book. The child didn't seem to make friends very easily. Maybe she was lonely.

Lillian turned on her side and eased the cast onto the

pillow. She tried to breathe through the dull throbbing in her wrist the way she had taught her laboring women to breathe through their pains. Her answer to Miriam, then, was the same as her answer to Olivia today. She felt a bit disgusted with herself. To think she'd been lying for so long, it came as easily today as it had then. *Wonder what they'd think if they knew the truth.* Huffing, she tried to turn on her other side but wasn't sure what to do with the cast.

Knowing what had happened would not help anyone. Too shameful to talk about. The most important truth was this: every child should believe they're wanted. "No, sugar," she had said to Miriam that day. "The Lord blessed us with you and that was enough." She tried to remember Miriam's expression, but couldn't. Like Olivia, Miriam hadn't asked any more questions.

She reached to turn on the lamp. Maybe a drink of water and some of that Tylenol Miriam had brought would help. She swung her legs off the bed and sat on the side. Awkwardly, she held the medicine bottle with her casted hand and twisted off the lid with the other. After taking two of the pills, she reached into the drawer of the bedside table and brought out the envelope she'd retrieved from her jacket pocket this afternoon. She pulled out the folded piece of newspaper that had been included with the letter. The Staunton News Leader had printed an obituary for Evelyn.

Evelyn Preston, daughter of Albert and Alva Preston of Staunton, Virginia, passed away on Friday at the age of 87. She is survived by her brother, Albert "Buddy" Preston, Jr. and her niece, Rachel Preston Howell...

Lillian could not put Evelyn and death together in the same thought. Evelyn leapt into life the same way Lillian had jumped off the rock outcropping over the deep part of the river as a child. Feet first, eyes open. She rose from her bed and opened the closet. She reached up and pulled the string for the overhead bulb. Her knees creaked as she lowered herself to the floor. She stretched her hand toward the back of the closet, careful to hold the cumbersome cast out of the way. Her fingers moved beyond her two pairs of shoes and the pair of Elijah's boots she couldn't seem to get rid of, to touch the cigar box. She grasped the box and pulled it toward her.

She carried the box to the armchair and eased down, cradling it in her lap. Lifting the lid brought a smile as her nose caught the faint scent of Elijah's favorite Stratford cigars. The postcards from Evelyn lay in two neat stacks. She pushed the postcards aside—too painful now—and lifted the yellowed photograph, taken by the newspaper photographer so long ago. She'd been freckled and gangly, braids hanging to her shoulders, her hands in the pockets of her overalls. Evelyn, in those wide-legged pants she'd convinced Mavis to sew for her. Bicycle balanced against her hip, short curly dark hair tucked behind her ears, a wide smile on her lovely face. Lillian wept again for the fearless girls they'd been. After a while, she pulled a tissue from the box on the table, blew her nose, and sighed. She dropped the letter and obituary into the box, returned the box to the closet, and crawled back into bed.

After Mama died and everything changed, Lillian had thought she'd never see Evelyn again. And then, six years—but what seemed like a lifetime—later, there she was.

STAUNTON, VIRGINIA
SUMMER, 1944

Elijah's twentieth birthday had been Friday. Lillian had wanted the weekend to never end. But it did. Now it was Monday afternoon, and she was delivering him to the Staunton bus station.

Lillian felt duty-bound to say her goodbyes alongside the

other wives and children, mothers and fathers, and the generally curious. As the long red and white bus pulled into the station, she couldn't bear to look at any of the others for fear seeing their grief might cause her to lose her own composure. She kept her focus on Elijah and made sure not to blubber like some of the other women—mostly the mothers. Keeping her chin up, she held Elijah close, breathing in his soap-clean scent and silently willing him to come back to her and to their home in the holler.

"I'll send my paychecks home to you, Lil," he murmured in her ear. "It's going to be over soon. Ain't no Kraut can outshoot me." He rested his chin on the top of her head.

Then he brought his lips to hers and kissed her long and slow. When he released her, he took a deep breath and squared his shoulders. She watched him board the bus, the words *Fort Lee* posted across the front. Within seconds, his head appeared from a rear window. He brought his hand up for a wave. In a cloud of fumes, the bus and Elijah were gone. Lillian waited until the bus rounded the corner and disappeared before turning toward the truck to head for the safety of the holler.

And there stood Evelyn Preston.

Lillian hadn't laid eyes on her since the day she'd watched her bicycling away from Western State Hospital. The day everything in Lillian's world had changed. She felt again the unexplainable shame. She'd never wanted to see Evelyn again. Yet, here she stood, grown up. As beautiful as ever. Evelyn lowered the arm raised in a wave toward the bus and turned. Her green eyes shone when she caught sight of Lillian.

"Lily? Is that you?" She hurried toward Lillian and reached out both hands. She pulled her into a tight hug. Lillian's heart melted. She needed to get control.

"I thought I'd never see you again." Evelyn released her and looked into her eyes. "I thought you had left... Oh, Lily, I don't know what I thought. I missed you so..." She stepped back.

"Evelyn." Lillian acknowledged her old friend with a nod. A confusing mix of sorrow watching Elijah leave and a pang of longing for the girl she had been that summer six years ago fought inside her. The nod was all she could manage.

"Who are you seeing off?" Evelyn asked, glancing toward the road where the bus had been.

"Elijah."

"Elijah Stewart? The boy you talked about that summer?" Evelyn grinned.

"The same." She swallowed hard. She did not want to cry now, not in front of Evelyn. "We married four years ago. He's been counting the days until he could enlist." Lillian brushed her hair away from her eyes.

Evelyn reached again toward her, but dropped her hand before touching her. "I'm so happy for you, Lillian. To have the man and the life you always wanted."

Lillian thought about this. She supposed she did. She smiled at Evelyn. "And you?"

Evelyn looked down at the white leather handbag she clutched. "I was here to say goodbye to some of the boys from town." She looked up and met Lillian's eyes. Her expression was not sad or heartbroken like the other women. No, Evelyn looked annoyed.

"Mother and Daddy are convinced I should marry Lawrence Wilson and...well... he left today."

"And what do *you* think about that?" From Evelyn's irritated tone, Lillian had a feeling about what the answer would be. She was right.

Evelyn drew closer and leaned toward Lillian. "To tell you the truth, I don't want to marry anyone. What I really want," she said, lowering her voice, "is to join the Women's Army Corp."

Lillian had read about the WACs in the newspaper. A smile reached her lips. "That sounds about right, from the Evelyn I knew."

Evelyn laughed. The infectious sound caused a lightness in Lillian's chest she hadn't felt in days. For a few seconds, the distance between her life and Evelyn's fell away, and they were the innocent young girls they'd been, dreaming of completely different futures. "If I recall correctly, you were going to see the world and break men's hearts...or something like that. Sounds like you still want the same thing. So, the Women's Army Corp is about seeing the world, I gather?" Lillian watched Evelyn's expressive face light up.

"Yes," Evelyn said, glowing with enthusiasm. "I want to register now, but my parents won't sign for me. But as soon as I turn twenty-one—in just a few months—I'm going. Whether they like it or not. I have a friend from Richmond who joined, and they sent her to England. Can you imagine, Lillian? England?" Evelyn's expression was dreamy—as if England didn't have trees and rivers just like here.

Lillian couldn't imagine wanting to be anywhere but the holler. However, she didn't want to put a damper on Evelyn's eagerness. "What about the part of your plan to break men's hearts?" She thought of the young men rolling away on the bus to an unknown future. Had Evelyn implanted herself into one of their hearts? This fellow, Lawrence? Most likely, she had.

Evelyn smiled and her cheeks pinkened slightly. Something about the smile defied Lillian to judge her. "Men can be so..." Evelyn seemed to search for a word. "Traditional," she finished. "They want all of these promises about marriage and babies, and making a home."

"And you don't want that?" Evelyn was never one to conform to what other people expected. Seems that hadn't changed.

"No, Lily." Frustration and excitement mixed in her voice. "I don't want to be tied down. I want to see the world. I want to *do* things in the world." She glanced down, a smile playing around the corners of her mouth. "But I *have* discovered something important."

"What's that?" Lillian half-listened, still preoccupied with whether something was wrong with her for wanting exactly what she had with Elijah. Plus babies, of course.

"Well...I have figured out that I like sex."

Lillian's mouth dropped open, and she closed it quickly, lest she look like a fish on a stringer. That was the thing about Evelyn. How could she have forgotten? Evelyn *said* things other women didn't. And, apparently, she *did* things other women didn't do. Or, at least didn't talk about.

Lillian's years of not sharing her private thoughts with anyone but Elijah or the river had taken their toll. She couldn't think of a response, other than a wide-eyed nod, as she looked down. She too liked sex—with Elijah. Very much. Although she preferred to think of it as lovemaking. She'd never known another woman who actually talked about it. Well, there was Mama, but that had been the...mechanics of it. Lillian finally found her voice. "With this Lawrence fellow?" she asked, glancing up.

Evelyn averted her eyes. "It's complicated," she said in a rush. "Lawrence wants to marry me, and I felt so sorry for him... Last night was his final night at home before... before who knows what? But there's also someone *else*."

Who knows what? Lillian thought of how she'd pulled Elijah close to her last night, not wanting to separate her body from his. Evelyn meant that they might never see Elijah or Lawrence again. How could she bear it? She admitted to herself that she had hoped last night, as she always did after they made love, he'd left her pregnant. How did Evelyn keep from getting pregnant? There were rubber condoms or that new thing she'd heard about... some sort of womb veil. But Evelyn would have to be married to get one of those. She scolded herself. None of her business.

Before she could ask anything else, Evelyn looked past her and waved. "Coming," she called. She turned back to Lillian and said, "I've got to go. Mother has me acting as a social hostess for the USO." She walked backward as she hurried away. "I want to talk some more. Why don't you come to the USO dance? You can help me serve punch." Evelyn turned and glanced toward her mother and then back at Lillian, dropping her voice and winking. "I'll tell you about my plan."

Mrs. Preston glared at Lillian from the passenger window of a long black automobile, looking her over head-to-toe, probably judging her plain printed dress and scuffed leather shoes. Lillian glanced away, self-consciously smoothing her hair. She hadn't bothered with a hat. Elijah thought they were silly unless you were trying to keep your head warm. She tended to think the same. When she risked another look, Evelyn turned and waved once. As Lillian raised her hand, the driver pulled away and, once again, Evelyn Preston was gone.

———

Lillian finally began to drift toward sleep, weary in body and soul. So many memories flooded her thoughts these days. Those days of the past were more real to her than the ones she was living right now. But her last thoughts before sleep were of Miriam and of Olivia.

The three of them—she, Miriam, and Olivia—were *all* only children. Strange how that had happened. She reckoned Miriam could have had as many babies as she pleased. But Miriam's work had come before everything else in her life. Mothering had never really interested Miriam. She'd thrown herself into helping her patients make a deliberate decision about being a mother. Pride filled Lillian as she took a deep breath.

Good work her daughter did. Miriam's reach had been long and wide in the community. Retirement couldn't be easy for her.

Now—especially since her accident—the pressure of being Miriam's focus was stifling. Miriam was not going to let the idea of her moving to Charlottesville go. She was determined to get her way. Lillian wasn't sure she had the energy to fight her anymore. Finally, she slept and dreamed of Elijah Stewart's strong hands holding Miriam's tiny body wrapped in a yellow blanket. So long ago.

CHAPTER 19

Miriam

"What's this about a DNA test?" Walt glared at Dennis. "More news I haven't heard?" Dennis sipped his drink and rocked, avoiding eye contact.

Miriam waved a hand with a much more casual air than she felt and leaned forward to pick up her drink. "Oh, it's definitely incorrect. If *Ancestry.com* had their way, I'd be forty percent American Indian."

"Wow." Dennis threw his head against the back of the chair, looking up.

"What?" Walt's mouth dropped open, his eyes glittering. "That's *so* exciting." He put his hand to his mouth, then lowered it. "You might be related to some of the original Virginians. I always knew those cheekbones weren't from Lillian."

Miriam released an exasperated huff to cover the twinge. Walt had an uncanny ability to peek right into her thoughts. A fleeting picture of the night she'd read the DNA results for the first time crossed her mind. She had examined her face in the mirror over Lillian's bathroom sink, searching for clues. None. Her eyes were the same shape as her mother's, green instead of blue. She had her father's smile—or so Lillian had always said. She had always assumed her cheekbones were probably from her Irish grandfather's side—there were no photographs available of him or his people.

"I don't think there were any American Indians on the boat from Ireland or Scotland when my great-grandparents emigrated." Miriam held up her hands. "It's a mistake. Plain and simple. They've mixed up my test with someone else's." She looked at Walt. "That's why Dennis is redoing the test for me, and *probably* why he didn't mention it to you."

"Would it be so shocking? I mean, if somewhere in your family history there was a Native American?" asked Walt.

"Interesting." Dennis rubbed his chin.

"It's not about the shock... it just so improbable." Miriam threw her arms over the chair's arms and leaned back, dropping her head toward Dennis. "What are you thinking?" She recognized the expression Dennis assumed when he was mentally sorting.

Dennis peered up at the ceiling fan, his mouth drawn down. "There was, of course, plenty of mixing between the Native American people of this area and immigrants from Europe. So that wouldn't necessarily be all that surprising in and of itself."

"Okay, I can understand that." Miriam sat up, defaulting to her objective, scientific comfort zone. "It's just that the genetic links between my parents and Ireland and Scotland are so *recent* in the grand scheme of things. My grandmother, Mary O'Toole, emigrated from Ireland near the turn of the century."

"What about Lillian's father—your grandfather?" Dennis brightened. For him, this discussion was an interesting genealogical puzzle.

"Well..." Miriam shifted in her chair and sipped her drink. "...according to Mother, he was an Irish traveling saddle maker. He's the one we know the least about. Mother said my grandmother never talked about him, other than to say he was a good man, but not a staying-put kind of man."

"Hmm," Walt murmured. "Sounds like someone else I know." He dipped his head to the side and raised his eyebrows, peering at her.

Miriam frowned at his obvious reference to Hugh. "I happen to come from a long line of independent, decisive women," she snapped. "We don't necessarily need men to make our lives complete." She hid her frustration as she reached to pour more scotch. In her peripheral vision, she saw Dennis's and Walt's amused expressions. "Anyway...back to my family. That's Lillian's side. Then, you have my father's parents—Jane and Jack Stewart. They settled in this area after *their* parents emigrated from Scotland. So, my point is, how could this be?"

"Unless, of course—" Walt glanced at her and then stopped mid-sentence, returning his gaze to his drink.

"Unless what?" she asked.

"No, no." He cast his eyes up, trying to appear humble. "I've been chastised enough."

"You have to say it now, Walt," Miriam insisted. She and Dennis both turned to Walt and waited.

"Nothing. It's silly." Walt waved his hand, as if he could erase his comment.

"Walt?" Her jaw tightened. "What were you going to say?"

"I was going to say unless-Lillian-had-an-affair-with-a-Native-American-man-and-got-pregnant-and-Elijah-never-knew-it." Walt looked at them meekly. "I told you it was silly."

"Dear god, Walt." The possibility was so incomprehensible that, for a moment, Miriam couldn't respond further. After a few seconds, she blurted, "You know my mother, right?"

"Yes, of course I do." Walt looked a little peevish.

"Can you picture Lillian Stewart having an affair with *anyone*?"

"Good point." Dennis sighed, sat back, and put his hands behind his head. "Elijah Stewart was the love of her life."

"I know, I know," Walt stared at his scotch, slowly shifting the amber liquid.

Miriam was even more unmoored than before. Accidental pregnancy did not fit anything she believed about her mother. She had always seen herself as a *choice* Lillian and Elijah made together. They had thrown their complete support into raising her and helping her be who she was now. No, this alternative story did not fit.

"I don't have an issue with being part Native American, if that were the case." Miriam crossed her legs and jiggled her foot, working hard to stay objective. "It's just so *completely* unexpected and doesn't fit the family story I've sort of, well... based my identity on. My parents were devoted to each other."

"I've always admired Lillian and Elijah's love." Walt dabbed at his eyes with his cuff.

Miriam continued. "And it's not just that..." The jolt of anger rattled her. "It's... well, it's my legacy... what my whole career has been about." An unexpected clarity dawned. Why hadn't she seen it before? Her grandmother and mother had both been midwives, but she had extended their work—brought women more choices. She motioned toward Dennis with an upheld hand. "You, of all people know how important this work has been to me."

Dennis obliged her with a knowing nod.

She sighed in frustration. "Maybe it's the retirement thing. Maybe I'm too old to completely rearrange who I believe I am."

"I get it. This really has you shaken." Dennis laid a warm hand on her shoulder.

"But Mimi..." Walt also reached over and laid his hand on hers. "This doesn't change who you are and everything you've worked for."

"I know. You're right... I guess." Exhaustion crept in,

threatening her resolve. "Maybe I should let it go. The only reason I ordered the DNA test in the first place was because of you." She glared at Walt.

Walt raised his hand to his chest. "Me?"

"You're the one who said that a genealogy project would be fun."

"I did, didn't I?" Walt nodded.

She sipped the last of her drink. "You know, I keep coming back to what Walt said about Lillian."

"How so?" Dennis asked.

"If the results are correct, then you tell *me*, Dennis." She turned to look at him. "*You're* the geneticist. Isn't it true that the higher the percentage of a particular genetic make-up, the more recent the mixture of the DNA?"

Dennis thought about this for a minute. "It *is* true that if you start with the loose idea that you inherit fifty percent of your DNA from each parent and work backward mathematically, that by the time you've reached your great-grandparents, you would have around 12.5 percent of their DNA. But of course, all of that is based on averages. You inherit DNA in chunks. You could receive all of a chunk, or none of a chunk."

"But if the test is correct, a full forty percent of my DNA is American Indian." She voiced the most uncomfortable thought all of this speculation had caused. "It's like Walt said. Could my mother have gotten pregnant by another man?"

Dennis and Walt were silent. The question hung in the night air already thick with humidity.

"I really do have to go." Miriam stood abruptly and reached to hug each of them. She couldn't keep herself together for another moment. She craved the safety of her home and her own silent space. "Thank you for dinner and the company, as always."

"Of course." Walt held her arm. "You know we love you, Mimi."

"Yes," Dennis agreed, putting an arm around her shoulders. "We will run interference if Hugh shows up, we will interview potential sperm donors—" This prompted an "oo" from Walt— "We will help you haul poor Lillian out of Hazel Hollow, and I will personally re-run your DNA test," Dennis finished with a flourish.

Miriam smiled weakly as Walt planted a kiss on her cheek. "Good night, hon. Don't worry. It's all going to work out as it should."

Easy for him to say.

CHAPTER 20

Miriam

CHARLOTTESVILLE
MAY 27, 2010

Miriam balanced a travel mug of coffee in one hand and yawned as she tossed her tote into the back seat of the Volvo with the other. All this traveling back and forth between Lillian's and home was exhausting. As she pulled out of the alley behind her house and onto the street, her cell phone rang. She glanced at the screen and didn't recognize the number. Frowning, she pulled over into the parking lane and answered. "Hello?"

"Dr. Stewart, it's Allison Pridmore with UVA Research & Development. How are you this morning?"

The young grant-writer's cheerful voice brought Miriam instantly awake. "I'm doing well. How can I help you?" Miriam slipped effortlessly into her most familiar role—the doctor.

"I have some excellent news."

Miriam's pulse quickened. "You do?"

"Yes. You've been awarded a grant from the Preston Foundation."

The Preston name immediately riveted her thoughts to Rachel. She sat on the board and assisted her father with the

Preston Foundation. Had she influenced the Board to give the award to Miriam? Rachel had her own philanthropic interests as well. Just last month, Miriam had contributed to yet another of Rachel's fundraisers. This one was something about books for underprivileged kids. Miriam had dutifully attended the gala, dragging Walt along. Dennis had the nerve to be out of town. Over cocktails, Rachel had nagged Miriam, once again, to speak at the annual Junior League *Women's Issues* luncheon. Once again, she'd put her off. She wasn't sure the Junior Leaguers, including Rachel, would want to hear what she had to say about *women's issues*.

The Prestons had been woven into her life, one way or another, for so long, this phone call seemed like some kind of karmic event. Silly thought. But there *was* her college scholarship, sponsored by Rachel's grandparents. *And* the illogical, but ever-present, *Rachelness* in her life—the way she'd come to think of her oldest friend. And now this?

"Hello? Dr. Stewart? Are you there?"

"Yes, yes, sorry about that. We must have lost connection," Miriam lied. "I know the Prestons. I went to high school with Rachel Preston—actually, it's Rachel Preston Howell now."

"Yes, she mentioned your history. The family had nothing but praise for your work. They are so excited to see your project come to fruition." Allison paused. "Here's the best news of all. Are you ready?"

"Yes." Miriam glanced at her watch. "Allison, I'm putting you on speaker. I need to get on the road."

"No problem."

Miriam tapped the speaker button, laid the phone on the car seat beside her, checked for cars, and pulled into the street.

"The award is five million."

"What?" Miriam spluttered. She must have slammed on the brakes. The car behind her honked and swerved around her. The driver flipped her off as he passed. Miriam decided she'd better pull over again.

Allison's voice was full of awe. "It's the most they've ever funded for a project. Congratulations, Dr. Stewart. Your contraception center is going to be a reality."

Miriam pulled herself together. "This is amazing, Allison. Thank you." She tried to take in what this meant. "So... what's the next step?"

"First, there will be a black-tie awards ceremony. But there's a catch."

Miriam's heart sank. "A catch?"

"Yes. Apparently, Dr. Preston is not in very good health, so they don't want to delay any longer than necessary. The Board of Trustees was already holding their annual black-tie dinner on Saturday night, so they want to award the grant then. I'm sorry it's such short notice."

Miriam took a deep breath. Today was Thursday. How could she possibly...? She set her jaw and pushed aside her worries about all of them: Lillian, Olivia, Hugh. This was her dream. An opportunity she'd move mountains to have. "I'll make it work."

"Great, I'll email you the details. And congratulations again, Dr. Stewart. I'm so excited to work with you on this project."

Miriam thanked Allison for the great news and signed off. For several minutes she sat, staring out the windshield at the shady street ahead. This certainly put a new perspective on what she would do with her retirement years. This new role of consultant and not day-to-day practice would require her to shift from doer to delegator. Oh well, no time to fret over it now. She needed a plan. She pulled into the street and tapped Olivia's number as she drove.

"Hi, Mom."

"Good morning."

"Good morning to you. You sound better."

"I'm doing great. I'm just leaving Charlottesville, but I had to call you. I just got some wonderful news."

"Oh? What?"

"I've been awarded a five-million-dollar grant from the Preston Foundation."

"Oh my god, Mom. That's so exciting. Is this for the contraceptive center?"

"Yes. Apparently, it's the most they've ever funded for a project." She couldn't help a surge of pride.

"Wait... Preston? Is that the same Preston as the science building at Mary Baldwin is named after?

"Yes. Albert Preston's son, Buddy, established the Foundation. I think sort of as an homage to his father. He took over his father's practice in Staunton when I was in high school. His daughter, Rachel, was my best friend in high school and we went to Mary Baldwin together."

"Oh, I remember you talking about a Rachel Howell."

"Right, same person. Married name. We sort of parted ways after college. Rachel married a local attorney. She's, um... how should I say it? ...one of those women whose whole life revolves around her husband, her kids, Junior League..."

"Mm, I get it. Not much in common, huh?"

Miriam released a short humph. "Not really. When we were young, her father didn't think very highly of women with careers. Part of the reason I'm so shocked."

"Congratulations. I know how long you've wanted this." Olivia's voice was warm. Miriam felt an unexpected closeness to her daughter.

"It's all down to this great group of young grant-writers I connected with once I started teaching at UVA. Amazing. I'm still reeling."

"So, what happens next?"

"That's the tricky part. They want to award the grant at their annual board dinner. They hold it in the UVA Rotunda.

Quite a fancy to-do. Black tie."

"Mm. We know how you love those."

"You know me too well. But I'll figure out something to wear. I'm sure Walt will help me. The bigger problem is that the dinner is Saturday night."

"*This* Saturday night?"

"Yep. So, here's what I need you to do."

CHAPTER 21

Olivia

HAZEL HOLLOW
MAY 27, 2010

Olivia followed Lillian and Aunt Jo as they made their way around to the back of Lillian's barn. There, they contemplated a wide area of dark brown dirt. "Um, Gran, if you're sure you don't need me, I'm gonna run up to the house and call Amy."

"Why sure, you go ahead. We have this under control." Lillian turned back to the smelly pile of what Olivia deduced was composted chicken shit. Aunt Jo thrust the shovel she carried into the pile and turned over a generous heap. Neither of them gave her a second glance. She couldn't decide whether to be offended or relieved.

"I think it's ready, Lil." Aunt Jo's voice sounded behind her as she walked away. "It'll be great for the tomatoes."

As she neared the farmhouse, she tapped in Amy's number. They chatted about Amy's work, Lillian's manure pile, her mother's exodus to Charlottesville. Olivia complained that nothing tasted right, especially coffee.

"Oh, babe, I'm sorry. I know that first cup is your, like, favorite thing." Amy's voice was soothing.

Olivia lowered herself to the top porch step, balancing her

coffee in one hand, cell phone in the other. She had to admit to herself, she loved that Amy was being so... *present*. "I miss you."

"Me too," Amy sighed. "What are you doing?"

"I'm headed back to the house from the barn. I'm on a mission to find Gran's suitcase and help her pack."

"Already?"

"Yes. Mom just called with some terrific news, actually. She's been awarded a five-million-dollar grant to start her contraceptive center. She's over the moon. However, the award dinner is this Saturday night, so we need to get back to Charlotteville tomorrow." They chatted a bit longer. Amy needed to get to a meeting with a client, so they said goodbye.

Olivia traipsed through the cool, high-ceilinged farmhouse to Lillian's bedroom.

Opening the closet, she checked the floor. No suitcase. There were two upper shelves. She felt along the top one and finally located a hard edge in the dark back corner. She scooched the case toward her and lifted it down. Surprisingly heavy. She laid it on Lillian's bed, finagled the stubborn old-fashioned clasps open, and flipped the top back.

A worn leather-bound book and a thin stack of what looked like old files filled the space. Not what she expected. Files? A book? The book cover read, *Textbook of Gynecology*. Must be from Lillian's midwife days. Curious. Why would her grandmother store a book and files in a suitcase? She picked up the files and laid them on the bed beside the suitcase. *Western State Hospital Confidential* jumped out in faded red letters across the front. Strange. What was Lillian doing with hospital records? A replay of Aunt Jo's odd comment yesterday when they drove past Western State. "That's the loony bin. Where they'll lock you up and keep you for your *whole life*."

She glanced at the door. No sounds came from the hallway. She peeked out the window and caught sight of Aunt Jo disappearing into the barn. Hopefully, Gran was with her. A stab of guilt at invading her grandmother's privacy pricked at her conscience. But the curiosity was overwhelming. She opened the top file, labeled *O'Toole, Lillian*. Gran's maiden name. As quickly as she opened it, she closed the file again when Lillian's voice sounded from the back door. "Livy, could you help us, please?" *Damn.* Gran must have been walking toward the house.

"Coming," she called. Without allowing herself to think about what she was doing, she slipped the files under her arm and hurried to her room. Quickly, she shoved the files into her tote, dropped it beside her other things, and hurried outside.

———

A car rumbled on the road below the farmhouse. Olivia looked out the front screen door. Miriam's Volvo approached. Her mother parked the car and emerged with a determined look on her face.

"Morning." Olivia forced a smile and rode out the little wave of nausea that seemed to grab her whenever she moved quickly. "How was Charlottesville?" A ripple of jitteriness. *Could Mom tell? Was it as obvious to Mom as it had been to Gran?* She'd have to figure out a way to tell her mother soon. After all, Miriam was a gynecologist. *And*, she was already overly interested in *Project Motherhood.*

"Good. Dennis is redoing my DNA test." Miriam pulled her bags from the back seat.

"Oh, that's good."

"Dennis and Walt send their love."

Did Mom tell them about my pregnancy plan? The three of them talked about everything. Oh well. Now was definitely not the time to bring it up. Her mother seemed really preoccupied. She took the bag her mother handed her, then pecked Miriam's cheek as she walked past.

"How's your grandmother?" Miriam asked. "Is she packed yet?" She looked hesitant to go into the house. Strange. The DNA thing must still have her rattled. It could also be the prospect of taking Lillian away from her safe place. The thought of safe places flitted through her mind. Her grandmother was a safe place for Olivia. Amy was safe. Her mother? She wasn't so sure.

"She had a little trouble sleeping last night, but other than that, she seems to be doing okay. She and Aunt Jo are getting ready to plant tomatoes." Olivia dropped the bag beside her feet, picked up her undrunk coffee, and tossed the black liquid into the bushes beside the porch steps.

"Coffee not good? It's from your favorite roaster in Charlottesville." Miriam frowned, creasing the deep lines between her eyes.

Olivia froze, but only for a second. She hoped her mother didn't notice. "Oh, you know...weak. Gran doesn't like it very strong."

Miriam smiled, but her eyes look distracted. "That's true. Now that I'm here, we'll have to make a separate pot for us."

Olivia was surprised when her mother reached to circle her waist and gave her a gentle squeeze. The unexpected affection sent a mix of wariness and longing through her. She stood very still, not wanting the moment to end.

"I talked to Nate on the drive from Charlottesville. He's finished with the cottage interior and exterior painting. Almost had the pond up and running until he realized he had to order a part for the pump." Her mother was chatty today. She scarcely took a breath before she rattled on. But there was an edge to her voice, sort of panicked. Cheerfulness forced. "Anyway, thank heavens for Walt. He's going over today to fluff up the place a bit—you know, some new linens, a coffee pot. He's even going to bring over a rocking chair. She'll love that. Don't you think?" Miriam finished, a little breathless, and stopped to look at Olivia.

Olivia nodded and opened her mouth to speak, but before she could respond, Miriam continued. "Dennis said he would help finish up with the pond, since Nate is due to leave on Saturday."

Olivia fought another wave of nausea as she put her arm around her mother's narrow shoulders. "Mom?" Her mother released her and stepped toward the front door.

"Yes?" Miriam stopped, her hand on the screen door handle.

"I was wondering..." Olivia took a deep breath. "What's your plan if Gran refuses to move to Charlottesville permanently? Because..." Here was the hard part, but for her grandmother's sake, Olivia had to say it. Her heart hammered. "I don't think she's crazy about the idea of leaving here—even for a visit. She doesn't understand why she needs to go *there* when you and I are *here* and she'd rather be here, and, well... I don't either." Ugh. She'd made a mess of that. But it felt wrong to stand by and watch her grandmother be railroaded.

Miriam released the door handle, dropped her tote, walked over, and sank into one of the rocking chairs. Olivia braced herself for her mother's arguments, but for several seconds, Miriam said nothing. She leaned back and rocked slowly back and forth. After the pause, she looked up. Once again, Olivia caught a brief glimpse of vulnerability, of uncertainty, so uncharacteristic of her mother. Then, Miriam set her mouth and the usual stubbornness took over her face. "Livy, you know as well as I do that she can't stay out here in the middle of nowhere forever. What if the next time is something life-threatening?" Her voice rose loudly. Olivia glanced through the screen into the house, wondering if Gran and Aunt Jo were still out back.

Miriam caught herself and lowered her voice. "I can't live out here. My life is in Charlottesville. I'm not ready to give that up. Maybe it sounds selfish, but I need her to be where I can see her, check on her, be there immediately if anything happens." Miriam sat back in the chair and let out a long sigh.

Sudden anger warmed Olivia's cheeks. "But what about what *she* wants? She's still strong and independent. And she has Aunt Jo. How can you take her life away from her because it's not convenient for yours?"

The ravaged look on her mother's face made her wish she could take back her words. But, as she watched, Miriam masked her hurt with a cold, matter-of-fact distance. "You're too young to understand this situation." Miriam's jaw tightened. "When one ages, one has to make decisions. Sometimes, those decisions have unpleasant consequences. I'm sure I'll have to do the same someday."

The last part caught Olivia off-guard. The thought of moving her mother into hers and Amy's home was so ridiculous she almost laughed. It all seemed hopeless. She was stretched between the three poles of their competing needs.

"Not to change the subject," Miriam continued, "but aren't *you* looking forward to going to Charlottesville?" Olivia could tell she was trying to be light. "You'll have the full resources of the UVA library at your disposal. *And*, you can interview Larry and Tom—the students I told you about." Her mother's gaze pierced her. "You're still thinking about getting pregnant, right?"

Olivia nodded, paralyzed with uncertainty. *Is this the right time to tell her?* Before she could think about it anymore, she began, "Mom, I..."

At the same time, Miriam blurted, "And your father's coming."

"What? Dad? When... where... Coming here?"

"Yes. Well, no. To Charlottesville." Her mother's energy around the issue of Dad was even more difficult to read than how she felt about Lillian. She seemed to be working hard to remain matter-of-fact. "Tomorrow evening."

Olivia reeled among her swirling thoughts and tried to figure out how to respond to her mother. Gran and Aunt Jo appeared from around the side of the house.

"Please don't mention Hugh's coming to your grandmother," Miriam whispered quickly. "You know how she is about him."

Olivia nodded, and the two of them turned to greet Aunt Jo and Lillian.

"Time to plant." Aunt Jo brandished her shovel. "Moon was between first quarter and full last night."

Olivia looked over at her mother. Miriam watched Gran and Aunt Jo with a faraway expression, as if she'd stepped back in time. Lillian opened the creaky gate into the fenced vegetable plot. Aunt Jo rolled in the wheelbarrow full of seedlings in black nursery pots. When Miriam spoke, her voice was surprisingly sentimental. "The two of them have been doing this for as long as I can remember." Lillian instructed Aunt Jo how to line up the pots in rows. Miriam's laugh was short and soft. "I remember, as a kid, how excited I was to learn about chlorophyll and the whole process of photosynthesis. I sat right over there..." Her mother pointed to a large flat mossy rock near the edge of the garden. "I read to them from my science textbook."

Olivia smiled at the thought of a nerdy young Miriam reading to her mother and aunt about photosynthesis. "What did they do?"

Miriam turned and met her gaze, tenderness in her eyes. "Mother nodded and smiled and said, 'Isn't that good to know? Jo, did you hear that? *Photosynthesis.*'"

Olivia and Miriam turned toward the sound of Lillian's laughter as Aunt Jo proudly picked up each tomato plant and turned it for inspection. Miriam cleared her throat, a catch in her voice. "She always listened to what I thought was important." Olivia remained quiet. Miriam started down the steps toward the garden and turned back to Olivia with a wry smile. "And then, she'd say, 'Miriam, honey, this garden is not going to plant itself.'"

———

The morning mist burned off and the sun was deliciously hot on Olivia's back as she pushed a wheelbarrow loaded with what Aunt Jo called "yellow gold." Shovels, chicken manure, tomato cages, and the water hose all procured, Aunt Jo declared them ready to plant. Lillian happily supervised the planting of each tomato from her lawn chair stationed inside the fenced-in vegetable plot. With each thrust of Aunt Jo's shovel, Olivia reveled in the smell of fresh earth.

The remainder of the morning raced by as they all—even Miriam—pitched in. Once each plant was tucked into place, caged, and watered, Miriam offered to make lunch and left Olivia with her grandmother and Aunt Jo to finish cleaning up. Olivia was relieved. It seemed she and her mother had silently declared a temporary truce around what would happen to Lillian. She couldn't help but wonder if Lillian would see her vegetable garden grow to maturity this year. As she worked, she considered the news about her dad's visit. Now she was going to have to tell them *both* about the baby. *Focus on right here, right now, on this glorious May morning in this place Gran loves so much.*

"Done," Aunt Jo declared. She leaned on her shovel and proudly surveyed the neat rows.

"Let's eat." Lillian pushed out of her chair and motioned toward the house.

After stuffing themselves with Miriam's famous chicken salad and fresh bread from the Albemarle Bakery, Aunt Jo left for home and Lillian settled into her chair for her afternoon television program. In the kitchen, Olivia handed Miriam a plate to rinse and realized she had absolutely no desire to bring up any of the topics she and her mother probably *should* be discussing. She had a strong feeling Miriam didn't either. Her mother's award. Definitely a safe topic. "Congratulations again, Mom, on your grant. That's awesome."

"Thanks, honey. I still can't quite believe it." Miriam smiled as she placed a plate in the cabinet.

"So, your college friend is the granddaughter of Dr. Albert Preston, whom the Foundation is named for?"

"That's right. High school *and* college, actually."

"But you're not in touch with her anymore?"

"I am. Just not very often." Mom stopped, a plate in her hands. "Here's another small-town thing I was thinking about this morning. Dr. Albert Preston, Rachel's grandfather, and his wife are the reason I went to college."

"What? Really?" Olivia was thrilled. The windows into her mother's past didn't open very often.

Miriam wiped the plate, a far-away look in her eyes. "Yes, I was a senior in high school and I had just found out I was valedictorian..."

CHAPTER 22

Miriam

Valedictorian. Miriam couldn't wait to tell her parents. As the school bus bumped over the dirt roads into the holler, she stared out the open window at the budding dogwoods and planned how she'd tell them. A sudden pang of guilt caught at her happiness. She'd need to downplay how desperate she was to leave. How much the idea of college, a career, a bigger life than theirs meant to her.

When she topped the rise on her walk from the school bus stop, there they were. On the porch; same as every day. Daddy smoking his pipe; Mother sewing. "Ain't that just the thing." Elijah looked at Lillian. Their eyes shone at her news. "What does that mean, exactly? Valedic..." her father asked. She dropped her school books and sat at Lillian's feet, facing him. As she explained, they listened intently, side-by-side in their porch rockers.

Lillian reached to pat her cheek, tears in her eyes. "You always were a smart girl. We are so proud of you." From the pocket of her apron, she pulled out a handkerchief. "I can't wait to tell Jo. She'll be tickled pink." The smile faded from her mother's lips. "What's the matter, sugar?"

"It's... I want to..." Miriam plucked up her courage. "I want to go to college."

"College." Lillian rocked slowly and cast her eyes toward the river. Her expression shifted from thoughtful to sad.

As if he read Lillian's mind, Elijah leaned forward. "Baby girl, we would love to send you to college." He leaned over and placed his hand over Lillian's. Her mother grasped her father's hand as if she needed to hold on to him. "But college costs money." He shook his head sadly. "Money we don't have."

And there it was. She'd known all along the nagging thing she chose to ignore—the constriction in her heart that she could never leave. She was stuck. Her only choices: a job in Staunton, or marriage and children.

She dragged herself to school the next day. Her chance to escape the holler was gone. This place her parents loved so much had defeated her. She dropped into her desk, early as always, and opened her science textbook. She listlessly flipped to the assigned chapter. The tingle of excitement over the current unit—*The Building Blocks of Life*—had all but disappeared. When her favorite teacher, Mr. Busby, stepped into the room, she kept her head down, avoiding his eyes. "Morning," she murmured in return to his greeting.

The scratch of chalk on the board. The increasing volume of laughing students' voices outside the classroom window. Even her favorite smell, the one that drifted from the new textbook she'd been lucky enough to get this year. None of it soothed her today. School was her favorite place in the entire world. In three weeks, her life would be over.

Her classmates tumbled into the room. Beau, Rachel's boyfriend, and Gabe, her boyfriend, smelled of the cigarettes they'd been sneaking. Rachel slipped into the desk beside her, the scent of her Aquanet hairspray lingering. Miriam listened distractedly as Rachel gushed on about her prom dress and whether or not Beau would propose before he left for college. And, then, it happened.

Mr. Busby tapped on his desk. "All right. Let's settle down." The chatter died down to a soft shuffle of books, feet, and papers. Mr. Busby leaned against his desk, adjusted his blue tie, and shoved his hands into his trouser pockets. "Today, I want to talk to y'all about college..."

Miriam's heart leapt. Then sank. Rachel groaned and rolled her eyes. Her parents could afford college and she had no interest. Other girls whispered and glanced around at the boys.

Some of the boys looked bored; others perked up—particularly Walter Fitzner. He'd been a close second for valedictorian. She caught his eye. His chin tilted up in an arrogant sneer. He turned his gaze back to Mr. Busby. Walter was the bank manager's son. He would go to college—probably UVA. The University of Virginia didn't accept women. But it didn't matter anyway. She wasn't going. She was so lost in self-pity, she almost missed Mr. Busby's next words. The ones that changed her life. "For those of you interested in college, but in need of... financial resources..." Mr. Busby looked directly at her. A shiver ran down her spine. "I want you to make an appointment with Miss Pratt. She can guide you toward available scholarships."

Miriam stayed after school, even though it meant a long walk home. Miss Pratt—the guidance counselor, who doubled as the home economics teacher—stood over a sewing machine, a small vial of oil in her hand when Miriam eased open the door of the home economics lab. "Yes?" She peered at Miriam over her cat-eye glasses. Miriam clasped her shaking hands behind her back. Rumor had it, the prim Miss Pratt was of the opinion college was simply to prepare young ladies to make suitable marriages.

Miriam took a deep breath and pushed Rachel's words out

of her mind. "Boys don't like smart girls."

"Hello, Miss Pratt. I'm Miriam Stewart."

Miss Pratt set down the sewing machine oil and crossed her arms. "Yes, I know who you are, dear. Our first female valedictorian."

Miriam felt heat rise in her cheeks. "I'd like to find out about scholarships for Mary Baldwin." She swallowed hard. "I want to major in science and live at college...in a dormitory."

"Hm. Have a seat, Miriam." Miriam sat in the wooden chair in front of the broad, heavy desk. Miss Pratt moved to the nearby metal filing cabinet, opened the top drawer, and shuffled through the files. She pulled out Miriam's school record, then perched on the edge of her desk chair, shirtwaist dress tucked neatly around her thighs, ankles crossed. She opened the file. After what seemed like an eternity, she spoke. "As for your *stated intention...*" Her face looked like she'd been eating a lemon when she pushed her glasses up and looked at Miriam. "Most of the available scholarships will only cover the tuition, not the expense of living in the dormitory."

Her heart fell into her stomach. Essential to her dream was to be able to leave the holler and actually *live* in Staunton at Mary Baldwin.

"However..."

Miriam hung on the word. She scooted to the edge of the chair and leaned forward.

"There might be another possibility. We have a particular donor, Dr. Albert Preston, who is very interested in supporting educational endeavors in the sciences."

Miriam's breath caught. Rachel's grandfather. Why hadn't Rachel mentioned—?

Miss Pratt continued, "Usually this scholarship is awarded to young men." Her thin mouth formed a line; she was physically incapable of hiding her disapproval. She opened a drawer, reached in, and retrieved a thin stack of paper. She slid it slowly toward Miriam. Miriam restrained herself from snatching it, reaching for the papers in what she hoped was a dignified manner. The heading on the top page read: *Application for the Albert and Alva Preston Scholarship for Scientific Higher Education in Virginia.*

And that was how it had happened. She earned a scholarship for tuition and funding for living expenses—including the dormitory. The feeling of freedom was intoxicating.

MAY 27, 2010

Olivia seemed delighted to hear her mimic the prim Miss Pratt. Miriam had never shared her gut-wrenching despair over believing she was trapped in Hazel Hollow. Or the rush of relief and joy when her dream of college came true. She wondered how to stay in this closer space with her daughter, to somehow keep from slipping back to her more serious, controlled self.

"So, that's what I know about Dr. Albert Preston." Miriam closed the cabinet and hung the dishcloth on the side of the drainer.

"Gran doesn't seem to think much of him," Olivia said. "And Aunt Jo was all bent out of shape when his name came up. And then Gran shushed her as if there was some secret about him that I shouldn't know."

"Really? That's strange." Miriam reached for the coffee pot and turned on the tap to fill it. "You know, now that you mention it, I had to go to a reception every year for the Preston scholarship recipients. Your grandmother never attended a single one. I thought it was maybe because she didn't care much for Alva Preston, his wife." Miriam smiled wryly. "Alva and her circle were the closest thing Staunton had to high society. And we know how Lillian Stewart feels about that."

CHAPTER 23

Lillian

HAZEL HOLLOW
MAY 27, 2010

Lillian watched Miriam place neat stacks of clothing, separated by category, on her bed. "This will last you through at least a week." Miriam placed her arm across her waist, propped the other one on it, and rubbed her chin. "Of course, we can do laundry anytime." Miriam gave a quick affirmative nod. "Yes, this will do." In that moment, Miriam reminded Lillian so much of her Mama—the take-charge Mary O'Toole—she felt a shiver down her back.

"All right, then." Lillian was resigned. It was very important to Miriam that they all go back to Charlottesville right away before her awards ceremony tomorrow. She'd decided to go along with the plan. Not make a fuss. When Miriam had explained about the big grant and her vision for a center for women with lots of satellite clinics scattered through the mountains and the Shenandoah Valley, Lillian had felt a swell of pride. About time some of that Preston money was put to good use. Still, any mention of the Prestons put a sour taste in her mouth.

Miriam might not know it yet, but this trip to

Charlottesville was only a visit. Surely Miriam wasn't still thinking she'd agree to move. As far as she was concerned, she'd been clear as glass. She was not about to leave the holler. Irritating, being ignored. Probably one of the worst things about getting old.

She frowned at the clothes. She could have handled packing on her own. Her mind was still good. Might be a little slower and, admittedly, she *had* taken a slight tumble on the riverbank. But she was not ready now—nor would she ever be—to pull up stakes and move in with Miriam. And why on earth would Miriam want that? Her daughter was as accustomed to living alone as she was.

Miriam emerged from another trip to the closet as Olivia slouched into the room, an open bag of pretzels in her hand. "How's it going? Need any help?" She was wearing the get-up she wore to run. Said running was her favorite exercise. Pants looked like a second skin.

"Hi, Liv. How was your run?" Miriam stared at Lillian's clothing as she spoke. Lillian had a feeling her mind was elsewhere.

"Good." Olivia grinned at Lillian and held out the pretzel bag.

Lillian smiled at the sight of her granddaughter's bright young face. She reached for a pretzel. "No, I think your mama has everything under control." She gave Olivia a conspiratorial wink.

Olivia giggled and plopped down beside her. Lillian smelled the outdoors in Olivia's curls and felt the warmth of her young body. The memory of yesterday's conversation struck her like a sudden crack of thunder. *My little Livy is carrying a baby.* The old familiar thrill at the thought of a newborn baby tiptoed through her. Interesting how the intensity of those feelings had never changed.

They munched companionably on the pretzels until

Miriam stopped arranging and re-arranging everything. "Okay, well... if you're satisfied with these clothes, then I guess we can get them packed."

Lillian stood, reached for the stack of underclothes, and placed them in the corner of the case. Miriam hovered and Olivia snacked. Lillian felt Miriam's gaze. Hard to resist the urge to tell her to leave. If she kept focused on the job at hand, Miriam would see that she had it under control.

"I'll go and start dinner," Miriam finally said, after pacing back and forth a few times.

"That sounds good, Mom." Olivia sounded as eager as she was for Miriam to focus on something else. "I'll help Gran."

After Miriam left the room, Lillian paused. She held a folded cardigan against her bony chest and observed Olivia carefully wrapping a pair of house shoes in a plastic bag. "You told your mama yet about the baby?"

Olivia picked up her pretzel bag and sorted through it. She was hedging. She looked quite pale today. And tired. "Not yet." Olivia didn't take her eyes from the pretzels. "She has a lot going on with, you know, the news about the award and getting ready for you..." She looked up, her cheeks pink. "Not that you're any trouble or anything... it's just that, with Dad also showing up—"

"Well, *that's* news to me." Lillian felt a wave of exasperation with Miriam, who must think this particular news wouldn't matter to her. It did in fact matter. Very much.

"Oh my gosh, Gran. I thought Mom told you." Olivia flushed bright pink.

"No." She waited.

"I think he's supposed to arrive in Charlottesville some time tomorrow."

"Mm." Oh, how she wanted to stay home. She didn't have the energy for any more people. The screen door slammed. She recognized Jo's voice drifting down the hall from the kitchen.

"Anyway," Olivia continued quickly. "Maybe I'll wait and tell both of them together. You know, two birds and all."

Lillian nodded again. Olivia had to manage the news about this baby in her own way. As Miriam would manage whatever it was kept her holding on to Hugh. She closed the suitcase. "I think that does it. I'll add my toothbrush in the morning."

"Okey dokey." Olivia lifted the case from the bed and set it on the floor by the chair. "I'm going to help Mom with dinner. Do you need anything else?"

She shook her head and sat back down on the bed, feeling heaviness in her chest again at the thought of leaving home.

"You coming?" Olivia asked from the doorway, worry in her eyes.

She couldn't hide much from this one. "I'll be there shortly. I'm going to sit here for a minute."

Olivia left, her pretty face in a frown. Lillian breathed deeper, relieved to be alone with her thoughts. *So, Hugh was in the picture again.* She had never quite understood Miriam and Hugh's relationship. The on-again, off-again way they had done things over the years.

Lillian had blossomed in the day-to-day solidness of Elijah's presence. She remembered the way his eyes rested on her as she made his breakfast every morning. Working beside him during the day. His arm around her shoulders as they watched the river together in the evenings. The way she turned her body into the curve of his at night. She smiled, remembering the joy of Elijah's naked body against hers. She wouldn't trade a minute of the life she'd had with him. Steady and abiding, his love for her.

The love Miriam and Hugh shared seemed so different from hers and Elijah's. Yet, each time she'd seen Miriam and Hugh together over the years, Miriam had a lightness about her. A sort-of electricity seemed to crackle through her. That kind of spark between two people can't be hidden.

Her thoughts were interrupted by Jo barreling into the room, followed by Scrap, excitedly wagging his tail. "Did you decide yet, Lil? Can Scrap stay with me while you're gone?" Jo's eyes were pleading with excitement. As always, her heart melted at the pure, joyous way Jo embraced life.

"I reckon you'll take good care of him." Lillian laid her hand on Scrap's head as he planted it firmly on her lap.

"I will, and Fanny too." Jo knelt down to put her arm around Scrap's portly body. "Miriam said tell you supper's ready."

Lillian sighed. Didn't have much of an appetite, but certainly didn't want to give Miriam any more reason to think she was getting feeble. "Let's go have some supper." She headed for the kitchen trailed by the most constant beings in her life, Jo and Scrap.

CHAPTER 24

Lillian

CHARLOTTESVILLE
MAY 28, 2010

Already late morning the next day, and drizzling rain, when the three of them pulled into Miriam's driveway in Charlottesville. Lillian had tried to enjoy the drive, but the unsettled feeling she always had when she left home interfered. Jo would take care of everything at home. It wasn't that. She couldn't shake the sense that Miriam saw her as another problem to deal with. Didn't care for being someone's problem.

She had looked out over the fields as they drove. New green shoots glowed against the gray sky. She'd tried to enjoy the rain-soaked wildflowers along the roadsides. If she had to stay in town, at least it was Charlottesville, not Staunton. The memories she'd made in Miriam's town—how she always thought of Charlottesville—were good ones.

Miriam was usually the one to travel to visit in the holler, especially after Olivia was born. She was respectful, even if she didn't agree with Lillian's need to be home. As a matter of fact, Miriam wasn't too fond of leaving her home, either. But she had genuinely wanted Olivia to spend part of her childhood in the holler. And, in turn, she'd convinced Lillian to visit

Charlottesville a few times over the years. Usually, it was just for the day.

The last time she'd been here to stay overnight was Olivia's college graduation. She had felt as proud of Olivia that day she graduated from UVA as she had so many years before when Miriam graduated from Mary Baldwin. Learning was the best way for a woman to make her own way in the world.

Come to think of it, Olivia's father had been in Charlottesville for her graduation. Lillian and Hugh hadn't had much to say to each other. He was always polite, but she couldn't help but wonder what he was holding back. Never quite seemed comfortable around her. She wasn't sure why. Maybe he thought she was passing judgment about his and Miriam's relationship? Lord knows, she was in no place to do that.

Lillian was relieved now that they'd made it to Miriam's. Miriam had seemed tense the whole trip. Had even asked Olivia to drive. From the back seat, Lillian noticed Miriam kept checking her phone. Maybe she was anxious about the award ceremony. Maybe it was the prospect of Hugh's visit. Right before they'd gotten to her house, Miriam had twisted around and peered over the seat. "So, Mother, I meant to tell you last night, but it slipped my mind..." Her voice was a little higher than usual. "I've heard from Hugh. He's planning to visit this week."

Miriam was trying to sound much more casual than her pinched expression looked. Lillian could see it in the way she got twitchy. Best not to comment. "That's nice," she said.

"I wasn't sure how you'd feel about Hugh being around..." Miriam seemed to be struggling. "Anyway, I could have him stay with Dennis and Walt. But I have also had Nate fix up the—Do you remember Nate?" Miriam stopped, turned back to her phone, then twisted again toward the back.

Lillian was a bit confused now. *Why are we talking about Nate?* "Yes, I remember Nate." She smiled. "He's that nice young man who rents your cottage."

"Yes, that's right." Miriam looked relieved.

Olivia turned to glance at her mother. Then she looked into the rearview mirror and caught Lillian's eye. Olivia looked worried. *What were Miriam and Olivia conspiring over?*

"Anyway, Nate graduated. So, he's moved out. I thought you might enjoy trying out the cottage. You know, have your own space?" Miriam's enthusiasm seemed excessive. Nervous.

Lillian nodded and smiled, "Mm hm."

"So, if Hugh does end up staying at the house, you'd be less likely to have to deal with him."

Lillian kept her expression neutral. *Deal with him?* She would rather not *deal* with any of them, truth be told. She was not of a mind to argue either way with her daughter. Miriam needed to do what was best to work this out. Simmering fear mixed with annoyance at the possibility Miriam was fixing up that cottage for her. *I am not about to spend my last years in a house the size of a chicken coop in your backyard.* She set aside the trapped feeling as Olivia opened the car door and helped her out. Miriam walked ahead of them and pushed open the gate. Lillian planted her feet securely on the gravel drive and took Olivia's arm.

Miriam's anxious voice drifted toward them. "Nate? What are you—? What's happened?"

Even though she and Olivia were several yards away, Miriam's tone told her something had gone wrong.

"Wonder what that's all about." Olivia's support was solid under her arm.

"I have no idea, but your mother doesn't look too happy." They reached the gate and the young man, Nate, turned toward them with a shrug and an apologetic wave.

An edge of frustration sharpened Miriam's voice as she turned toward Olivia and Lillian. "Nate's going to grab the suitcases. We've had a slight change of plans."

CHAPTER 25

Miriam

Miriam closed the bedroom door, walked into her bathroom, and turned on the bathtub tap. Exhausted. A bath seemed the best thing right now—hot water to soothe her frazzled nerves. She wished she'd brought a glass of wine upstairs with her, but she was not about to go back downstairs now. Space and solitude would nudge her back on an even keel.

The unraveling of her well-organized life had her so unsettled she trembled a bit as she stripped off her sweater and capris and kicked her sandals into the corner. She peeked at her reflection, then averted her eyes from the large mirror over the sink as she removed her bra and panties. The glimpse of her aging body brought up thoughts of Hugh. His eyes on her. A tickle of desire fluttered between her legs. Then sadness immediately tamped it down. The loss of her younger self was too present these days.

She thought of Rachel fussing over her. Post-Olivia, but still young. Late thirties, maybe? "All I'm saying is there's more to life than your career." Rachel had looked her up and down. "Do you even run anymore?"

Miriam had prickled. "Occasionally."

She tried now to remember the last time she'd been running. It used to be such a joy. Running early in the morning through the quiet, shady streets of Charlottesville. Stopping at the reservoir to stretch. Over the years, her running habit had powered down to an occasional walk in the park, and then further to walking down the hospital corridor, or from her Volvo to the clinic door. What happened? Maybe she should get a dog.

She sighed and pulled open the top drawer in the vanity. Searched in vain for a lighter for the candles. *Everything is out of place.*

Nate had been profuse with his apologies this morning. "Doc, I'm so sorry, but the whole internship was rescheduled. And I was hoping you'd give me a couple more nights. I'll find somewhere else to stay, I promise. And if you can't, I understand." His dark eyes met hers before he looked down at his feet.

"But what about Walt's work on the cottage? The quilt, the rocking chair?" Miriam had blurted, before she could manage to wrap her mind around what was happening. Her plans to surprise her mother crashed down around her. She slammed the drawer closed and continued her search for the lighter in the next one.

"I was about to leave," Nate explained. "Walt was here." He gestured toward the cottage. "Then I got the message about the changes in my travel plans and he decided to wait. I was going to call your cell, but he said you were probably over halfway here already."

Walt had called just after she got the news from Nate. "Hi, Mimi." His voice was cautious. "Change of plans?"

She had mumbled something. Now, she couldn't remember what. She slammed another drawer shut.

"Just wanted to let you know our guest room is always

available." Walt had tried his best to comfort her. "You can send Nate over here, or Hugh. Or even Lillian or Olivia. Hell, leave them all at your house, and *you* come stay over here."

The lighter was on the edge of the tub. In plain sight. She silently shook her head at her scatteredness and reached to light the candles. Walt had made her smile in spite of the anxiety that rose in her chest. As she'd been talking on her cell to Walt, she had watched Nate. He had turned immediately to help Lillian navigate the path toward the house. Of course, she wasn't going to kick Nate out. She stepped into the tub and lay back against the smooth porcelain.

"I've worked it out." She'd been testier with Walt than she'd intended. "Mother can stay in the guestroom, and I'll make up the sofa in my office for Olivia."

Lillian had been gracious and settled into the guest room. She seemed flat... resigned. Olivia had been accommodating. "No worries, Mom. I'm comfortable in here." She had dropped her backpack, tote, and suitcase on the sofa of Miriam's small office. Her energy seemed low. She was pale and her eyes seemed a bit dull. She might be rattled at the prospect of her father's visit.

"You okay?" Miriam had asked.

"I'm good, just a little tired." Olivia had responded with an apologetic smile.

"I'll ask Walt and Dennis if your dad can stay with them until Nate figures things out." She watched Olivia closely for a response.

Olivia's face remained impassive. "Okay, Mom, whatever you think."

Miriam turned off the water and reached for the bar of lavender soap. Absently, she pushed it back and forth across her upper arms and shoulders. The relaxing scent infused the steam rising from the tub. She took deep breaths. *Everything will work out.* But would it? Bringing the disparate people in her life together always put her nerves on a knife-edge. And now, there was the awards ceremony to prepare for. What would she wear?

She tried to focus on why this simple change in plans had her so upended. Was it because there was now no room in her house for Hugh? She ran her hands over her arms, pulled the water over her body, and tried to push away the unexpected disappointment. According to his last text, he'd arrive in Richmond at four this afternoon. He planned to rent a car for the seventy-five-mile drive to Charlottesville. She glanced at the clock on the marble counter. Three-thirty. She'd invited him for dinner, but when he arrived, she'd have to let him know he wouldn't be staying here.

You are sixty-five years old and it is time you let go of trying to control everything. She reached to add more hot water. Every time Hugh returned, she briefly turned back into the young woman who had fallen so deeply in love and lost all sense of herself. And, always, she worried what her mother would think, how Olivia would react to seeing her father. What Dennis might say to Hugh. But... she never worried about Walt. Her face softened into a smile. God love him, he'd offered to make dinner for everyone. He always knew when she needed him most.

Finally, the warm water and the lavender, paired with the gentle late afternoon light filtering through the high windows over the tub, began to take effect. Her shoulders dropped into a more relaxed position. She would manage this. Nate would reschedule his internship. Hugh would be close by at Dennis and Walt's, but far enough away not to run into Lillian at the kitchen table every morning. Lillian could settle into the cottage within a couple days after Nate left. She would get this incredible award that would jumpstart her retirement into something meaningful.

She admitted to herself, she was distracted by the

possibility of time with Hugh. She slid down to let the water cover her body. She rested her hands on her stomach. It was still flat—at least when she was lying down. The undeniable thing about Hugh was... he was such a terrific lover. He knew how to touch, where to touch, how to move. When to talk. When to shut up. Sex just *worked* with him. She'd admitted to herself long ago that she was fatally attracted to the inaccessible. Maybe they were each inaccessible in their own ways. Damn, if it hadn't created a spark.

Before Hugh, she compared every man to her father. None measured up. Gabe, her high school boyfriend, talked big about taking over his father's farm, but wanted a wife and babies. During her college years, there was Joe, who went to UVA. They'd run around together with Rachel and Beau. But when she'd gotten into med school and he'd said, "Marry me. You can do med school. I'll take care of you," she couldn't do it.

Med school had mostly been about random encounters. Guys who were safe, would never demand anything of her. By the time she was willing to consider the idea of marriage, all the men who were possibilities were already attached. And her female med school friends were killing themselves combining medical practices with motherhood. That didn't look too appealing, either.

Then she'd met Hugh. A strong, passionate man who respected her strength. The ultimate turn-on. She blew out her breath so forcefully the candles flickered. Hugh was the love of her life. But when she'd become pregnant accidentally, it had been completely impossible to cohabitate or co-parent with him. She was never able to replace what she felt for him in the men she dated occasionally after he left for Africa. There were times sex felt powerful, times it felt empty, times downright pathetic. And then there was the fact that Hugh dropped in and out of her life every few years. Nowadays, she was happier with a glass of wine, a fantasy, and her vibrator. Problem was, the fantasy was always about Hugh.

She ran her hands over her breasts, sagging more on her thin chest than even five years ago. Could she allow herself all those feelings again? Or had too much time passed?

Reluctantly, she stepped out of the tub and scrubbed herself dry with a fluffy white towel. Her worries all seemed so absurd. She was in the middle of this whirlwind of family: biological and chosen. Her family probably wouldn't make sense to anyone if she tried to explain it. Her ex, who really wasn't an ex, but knew less about being a parent than she did. Her best friends, who were more co-parents than friends. Her fiercely independent mother. Her tender-hearted, vulnerable daughter, who naively approached motherhood as some kind of sacred gift.

Maybe Olivia was right not to involve yet another person in this mish-mash of personalities and needs. Maybe an anonymous donor was less complicated. How much did DNA really matter when it came to making family? Maybe she'd gotten the Mother Gene thing all wrong. A clinch in her stomach. She had almost forgotten about the DNA test she'd asked Dennis to redo. Dennis had put a rush on the test, so the results could be back any day now. Another thing to worry about.

She forced herself to focus on the warmth of her body and the tingly feeling of her scrubbed skin. She had this situation in hand. She was strong, still attractive. She'd had a great career and now, she'd have the center as her legacy. She'd done her best to be a good daughter.

But... The pieces of herself she'd tried for so many years to keep separate were colliding. Her mother self, her professional self, her daughter self, and her lover self, demanding her to show up, simultaneously. Breathing in slowly through her nose, then out, she addressed her reflection in the mirror, while smoothing cream over her face. All her identities thrown

together left her off-kilter—a one-woman play. A new character and costume for every scene.

She dropped her shoulders and stared into her own eyes,
digging deep for the determination she counted on. *Get yourself under control, Miriam Stewart.*

CHAPTER 26

Olivia

CHARLOTTESVILLE
MAY 28, 2010

Olivia collapsed on the sofa in her mother's study. She couldn't move. Not at all. She looked at her open bag and considered the idea of changing before dinner at Uncle Dennis and Walt's, but the effort stopped her. She'd read most women experienced fatigue during the first few months of pregnancy, but this was ridiculous.

Maybe part of her mood was the guilt of helping bring Lillian to Mom's house. Her heart had ached for her grandmother, who carefully arranged her wrinkled face into appreciation when Miriam ushered her into the guest room. Lillian's resistance was palpable, but she'd been so polite. Her mother had been too preoccupied with the prospect of Dad's arrival to notice.

Dear old drop-in Dad. He *would* choose *now*, of all times, to show up. Her mother was already as prickly as a cactus. On top of that, whenever her dad was about to show up, her mother became this other person. Unrecognizable. For years, Olivia had resented him for it. How dare he show up and expect to be part of their lives? Finally, tired of the internal battle, she had resigned herself to the facts. This was simply how her family worked.

She had followed her mother's lead. Allowed Dad to drop in and out of her life, even tried to embrace it. What was the alternative? It occurred to her that she and her mother had never had a conversation about on again, off again, Dad. The story? Her father was away doing his thing in one foreign country after another. Nothing was going to change that. Not a little girl's desire, nor a grown woman's needs. When she occasionally envied other kids their day-to-day dads, she had never complained to her mother. Her mother's complete acceptance of Dad's role in their lives had always been a wall Olivia had never tried to climb over. And besides, whether she voiced her *daddy dreams* or not, Uncle Dennis and Uncle Walt always seemed to step in at just the right time.

Olivia wondered what their reaction would be when she announced her pregnancy at dinner tonight. Uncle Walt would probably melt into a puddle of sentimentality. She sort-of counted on him for that. Uncle Dennis would be happy in his subdued, intellectual way—ask about the process and the sperm donor's background. Mom would fume. Gran already knew, so she was at least a solid foundation of support. Dad was a wildcard. A stab of uncertainty. Then she settled into her usual feeling about her father—a neutral zone in her emotional landscape.

Miriam was another matter. The prospect of her mother's reaction brought a tightness to her chest as she imagined Miriam's pursed lips, her expression of surprise and disapproval. *Is it wrong I want to protect myself by telling Mom along with everyone else?*

She startled at a knock on the study door. Sitting up straighter, she noticed a dull cramping deep in her abdomen. "Come in." She tried not to sound as drained as she felt.

The door opened and Miriam stood before her looking like

a J Jill model. She wore one of her white linen shirts, cuffs turned up crisply and symmetrically. Creased navy capris and ballerina flats completed her outfit. She'd swept her silver hair up in a tortoise shell clip and silver hoop earrings sparkled in the afternoon light filtering through the study window. So beautiful. A tiny bit of envy crept through. Today, especially, her pregnant body felt thick and sluggish in contrast to her mother's lithe frame.

"Just checking on you." Miriam's brightness seemed a little bit forced. "Your grandmother says she wants to walk over to Walt and Dennis's, so I thought we'd leave here about..." she glanced down at the large-faced leather watch on her wrist, "five o'clock? Walt's going to have cocktails, of course." Miriam smiled. She seemed to be trying hard to be relaxed. "He's making your favorite Amaretto Sours."

"Great." Olivia forced a smile. How she'd miss Uncle Walt's signature cocktails for the next nine months. "Have you heard from Dad?" She rummaged through her bag for a clean t-shirt. Glancing down at her jeans, she decided they would do for tonight.

"Not yet. He said he'd let me know when he was leaving the airport. We won't wait dinner on him."

"Okay." She mustered her remaining energy. "I'm going to grab a quick shower and I'll meet you downstairs."

"Sounds good." Miriam glanced at the t-shirt in Olivia's hands and pressed her lips together. Good. No questions about her wardrobe choices. That was a relief, at least. "I'll check on Mother and see if she needs anything." Miriam turned toward the door and as she left, she threw over her shoulder, "Oh, and I asked Nate to join us for dinner. Poor guy is feeling really out of sorts."

"Cool," Olivia replied as Miriam closed the door. *Great. One more person to deal with.* But Nate was an easy-going enough guy. Besides, he'd been around their family long enough to have a sense of the dynamics. She vaguely wondered what Nate would think of hers and Amy's decision about donor insemination. She really didn't know Nate very well.

She took off her clothes, dropped them on the bathroom floor, and stepped into the shower, savoring the feeling of the hot water flowing over her body. She placed her hands on her crampy abdomen and imagined the baby growing there. A boy or a girl? She wondered when it would move inside her. She reached down and ran her fingers over her legs. Three-days-worth of unshaven nubs. Annoyed she had forgotten her razor, she stepped out of the shower onto the rug and reached for her toiletry bag.

Razor in hand, she turned toward the shower. A bright red trickle ran down the inside of her leg. The water from the shower sat beaded on her skin, but the red stream flowed steadily, making its way toward her ankle. A vice-like cramp seized her lower abdomen. The intensity took her breath.

Gasping with the pain, she instantly knew what was happening. *No. No. No.* Women spotted early in pregnancy. Something she'd read about, right? She wildly flipped through her mental rolodex of early pregnancy symptoms, pleading with an unnamed force. *Please don't let me lose my baby.* The blood pooled on the rug at her feet. She had to save her baby. The next cramp brought her to her knees. She curled in on herself. Maybe she could hold the baby inside her somehow. Maybe if she was very still.

But the squeezing grip of pain came in waves. With each assault, her desperation increased. She ignored the still-running shower, crawled to the bathroom door, and reached for the knob.

CHAPTER 27

Lillian

From Miriam's guest room, Lillian heard Olivia cry out. Cursing her stiff joints, she pushed herself up and hurried down the hallway. Olivia lay on the floor in the open doorway of the bathroom. One glance and Lillian knew immediately what was happening. She collapsed onto her knees beside Olivia. The old familiar need to take action mixed with uncertainty. Decades had passed since she laid her hands on a pregnant woman. "Miriam. Help," she called out with all the strength she could muster.

Seconds later, although it seemed ages, Miriam rushed up the stairs. Lillian managed to pull herself up off the floor and stood back, out of the way. When their eyes met, Lillian felt a memory pass between them of a night so long ago. The dead of night. A knock on the farmhouse door. Elijah rose from their bed. "I'll go."

She had jumped up that night at the sound of Miriam's frantic voice. "Daddy, please get Mother." A low keening groan. Not Miriam. Who? Lillian had rushed into the hall. She'd taken one look at the young woman clutching her belly as she held onto Miriam. Rachel. Buddy Preston's daughter.

Lillian shook away the memories fogging her mind. "How can I help?"

"Towel." Miriam pointed to the towel rack; her tone completely calm. Lillian grabbed a towel from the rack and handed it to her daughter. Miriam wrapped it around Olivia's naked, shaking body. She quickly took in the trail of blood from the shower to the rug and only asked the necessary questions. "Olivia, what's happened?"

"I'm pregnant, Mom." Olivia wailed through a rush of tears. "I'm sorry I didn't tell you. My baby," she sobbed. "I don't want to lose my baby." Olivia clutched at Miriam, weeping uncontrollably.

Miriam took control in a quiet, firm way. "Olivia." She took her daughter's face in her hands and forced her to look into her eyes. "How far along are you?"

Olivia hiccupped with small sobs, finally able to manage, "I think about seven weeks." She grabbed at her mother's hands, pleading with her, "Mom, please save my baby. Please."

Lillian simply could not bear it. The pain in both their faces broke her heart. To make herself useful, she slowly worked her way over to the shower, reached in, and turned it off. She wanted so much to help ease her granddaughter's pain, to hold her close, but Miriam should be the one.

Olivia began to shiver. Lillian walked as quickly as she could back to the guest room and pulled a blanket from the end of the bed. She returned to the bathroom and quietly handed the blanket to Miriam. "Thanks." Miriam met her eyes. For a moment she saw in her daughter's expression that familiar misery a mother feels when she knows she can't shield her child from hurt. They shared the unspoken knowledge. Olivia's baby could not be saved. Just as Rachel's couldn't all those years ago.

Miriam dropped to her knees and wrapped the blanket

around Olivia, doubled up again on the floor with another spasm. "Mother." Miriam's voice had only the slightest quiver, but it was there. Lillian wanted so much to be useful. "In the bottom right drawer of my desk in the study is a medical bag. Could you bring that to me, please?"

"Of course." Lillian hurried down the hall and retrieved the bag. She returned and held it out to Miriam, who took it with a nod of thanks.

"Olivia." Miriam opened the bag and took out a pair of gloves. "I going to check your cervix. I need for you to turn on your back."

Lillian turned away from the bloody sight. Though decades had passed, it was still achingly familiar. She busied herself picking up Olivia's clothing and folding it. The feeling of help-lessness deepened. She was all too familiar with what Miriam would find. Olivia groaned with the discomfort every woman feels when fingers probe her cervix.

"Your cervix is wide open." Loss, resignation, sadness all in Miriam's voice.

Olivia raised her head briefly and looked at her mother, anguish on her pale face. "What does that mean?"

"I'm so sorry, Livy." Miriam moved behind Olivia and took her head in her lap. "It means your body has expelled the baby. And I can tell from the amount of blood and...well... other things, that you've had a miscarriage." Olivia turned and sobbed into her mother's lap.

"I'm so sorry..." Miriam stroked Olivia's hair.

There was such torment in Miriam's face, Lillian felt the heaviness in her own chest—so many memories of when "I'm sorry" was the only thing to say.

———

Later on, as she sat alone at Miriam's table, a knock on the back door interrupted Lillian's thoughts. Relieved with the distraction, she rose, walked slowly through the kitchen, and peered through the mullioned window of the door. Nate's nervous smile greeted her. He brought his hand up in a subdued wave. Lillian was a bit surprised, but pleased, to see his handsome young face. A little company would be welcome.

"Um... Hi, Mrs. Stewart." Nate rocked back and forth slightly; his thumbs hooked in the belt loops of his jeans. "Doc Stewart called from the hospital. She asked me to check on you... I, um... are you doing okay?" He was so earnest, with his wide brown eyes and worried young face.

She pushed a weak smile onto her lips, reached out, and took his arm. "Come on in here, Nate. I'm glad of your company." Good to lean a bit on his young strength. "Did Miriam give you any news?"

"Not much. She did say Olivia is resting now. Walt and Dennis are on their way back."

Lillian nodded as they sat down together at the table.

"Doc Stewart said they'd fill us in on everything." Nate fidgeted in his chair. He looked over his shoulder into the kitchen. "Would you like some coffee, or hot tea, or something?"

"Yes." She tried to shake off the cobwebs of memory that kept clouding her mind. "Coffee would be good."

"All right, then." Nate appeared relieved to have a job. He rose and fiddled with Miriam's coffeemaker. One of those with more buttons and dials than was necessary. He carried the pot to the sink to fill it. The back door opened with a bang and they both jumped.

"We're back." Walt teetered into the kitchen, balancing two casserole dishes and another plate wrapped in aluminum foil. Dennis followed close behind with two bottles of wine. A salad bowl covered in plastic wrap tucked under his arm.

Nate rushed to help them. Lillian rose from her chair, surprised at how relieved she was to see the two of them. She had always enjoyed their company over the years. But now, she'd hear the real story, unfiltered by Miriam, about what was going on.

"You two must be starving," Walt called from behind the kitchen counter. "I told Dennis, we *must* go by our house and pack up dinner. I was just taking this pork roast out of the oven when we got the call." He pulled back the aluminum foil and looked at the delicious smelling meat. "I hope it's not too dry."

After setting the dishes on the kitchen counter, Walt stepped lightly over to her and wrapped her in a warm hug. How easy it was to let him make a fuss. He was the only person she'd ever seen Miriam allow to do that. The man was an expert. "How are you, darling?" He stepped back and looked into her eyes. "You must be worried sick. Here, sit back down. Dennis is going to fill you in on everything while I get dinner ready."

Lillian sat down obediently while Walt bustled back to the kitchen. "Nate, open one of those bottles of wine. I'd say we all need a drink after this day." Walt pulled wine glasses from a cabinet.

Lillian and Nate locked eyes. He seemed to be asking her approval. Nice of him. She smiled and nodded. Nate began to dig around in the kitchen drawers.

"The corkscrew is in that drawer," Walt said, pointing.

Dennis turned a chair to face her and folded his lanky frame into it. He reached for her hands. "Good to see you, Lillian." His smile was warm. So kind.

Calm descended over her. "So, how is she?"

Dennis was about to speak when Walt appeared with two glasses of red wine. "Here you go. Don't you worry, Miss Lillian, your granddaughter is in good hands. Miriam made sure of that. Our Livy had some kind of AC/DC procedure and she was asleep when we left." He moved to stand beside

Dennis and put his arm around his shoulders. "You're not going to believe who showed up at the hospital," he whispered. He glanced over his shoulder at Nate, who was pulling silverware out of a drawer, then returned his gaze, wide-eyed, to Lillian. She was fairly certain of the answer, but knew Walt wanted to tell her. "Hugh." Walt pursed his lips and widened his eyes. "Of course, he *had* to step in and try to take over. He and Miriam started arguing, and well..." He raised his hand to his chest and shook his head. "I'm glad Dennis was there to referee. It could have gotten ugly."

Dennis reached up and squeezed the hand Walt had rested on his shoulder. "Hon, how about you work on dinner, and I'll fill Lillian in on what happened at the hospital?" Walt looked a bit sheepish, but nodded, walked back into the kitchen, and started giving Nate instructions.

"Now..." Dennis released her hands and sat back in his chair. "Miriam brought in one of her colleagues and together they decided that a D&C would be the best route to take for Olivia." Dennis was matter-of-fact.

Lillian sensed him studying her for understanding, so she nodded. She didn't really know what he meant by D&C. She did know that sometimes, when a woman miscarried, part of the placenta could be left in the womb and cause problems. How little these young people knew about who she had been and what she had done. Her own fault. Too late to tell those stories now. His next words confirmed her suspicions.

"A D&C is when they go in and clean out the uterus to make sure there aren't any retained fragments from the pregnancy."

"Did Miriam do the operation?" Lillian tried to imagine how Miriam would have felt, operating on her own daughter.

"Oh, no," Dennis replied quickly. "She had one of the doctors in her former practice do it. I think that was a good idea."

"Yes, so do I."

"So, they'll keep Olivia overnight. She'll probably sleep most of the time she's there—at least that's what we hope." Such sadness in his eyes. "Walt and I, of course, had no idea that she'd gone ahead and inseminated and was pregnant. Did you know?"

A flash of uncertainty. Should she reveal Olivia had shared her news? As quickly as it came, the uncertainty dissipated. This was Dennis. He was a man to trust. Reminded her so much of Elijah. "Yes, I did. She told me last week." She sighed. "I think she might have been planning to tell you all tonight... together." She watched Dennis to see if he understood her meaning.

He tilted his head back and dropped the sides of his mouth. "Oh, I see," he nodded. "Safety in numbers." He smiled knowingly at her.

"So, how did Hugh come to show up at the hospital?" Lillian was curious to hear about that turn of events.

Dennis puffed out his cheeks and blew his breath out in a whistle. Lillian and Dennis had shared a similar distrust of Hugh over the years. They'd never discussed it, but each of them seemed to read the other's thoughts. "That was interesting." A wry grimace. "Apparently, Miriam must have texted him about what happened. His plane arrived later than expected, so he drove straight from the airport to the hospital. Of course, he rushed in all worked up and firing off opinions..." Dennis waved his arms in the air. Made her chuckle. "It was all 'We should do this' and 'We should do that.' And you know your daughter, she would have *none* of it. Unfortunately, the two of them were standing in the middle of the Emergency Department, getting progressively louder." Dennis rubbed his hand over his bald head as he shook it slowly.

"Oh, my." Lillian winced, imagining the scene. "And you stepped in?"

"Yes, I had to, Lillian." Dennis paused and looked away.

When he turned back to Lillian, his eyes glittered with anger. "Did he think he could waltz in and start directing everyone around?" Dennis counted off on his fingers. "A, he hasn't been around in... What? Eight years? B, he doesn't know the hospital or the medical staff. And C, has he forgotten that this is Miriam's specialty? Not to mention the most obvious fact—he's *not* a doctor." Dennis pulled his hand over his mouth in exasperation. "The man is a piece of work."

"He is that," Lillian agreed. "Did you get it all sorted?"

"Yes, finally." Dennis shifted to let Walt pass by with plates and napkins.

"He was amazing," Walt threw over his shoulder. "He calmed that man right down—Hugh's so passionate, you know. And he really does love his little girl."

Lillian glanced at Dennis and caught him rolling his eyes. Walt came to stand beside Dennis and folded his arms across his chest. "Dennis took him by the arm and *very* quietly, he said, 'Hugh, how about you and I let Miriam handle this? Let's go and get a cup of coffee and then you can peek in on Olivia before she goes to the OR. What do you say?' I'm telling you, Lillian, Hugh was putty in Dennis's hands." Lillian and Dennis exchanged looks. Her heart warmed. What a pair these two were.

CHAPTER 28

Miriam

CHARLOTTESVILLE
MAY 29, 2010

Miriam eased her aching body into a chair close to the sofa, near Olivia. The tension in her neck would probably take days to release. The least of her worries right now. Her priority had been to get Olivia back home this morning.

"I don't want to be in the bedroom alone," Olivia announced when they returned from the hospital. So, they'd parked her on the sofa and covered her with a blanket. Her daughter's listless expression turned to a weak smile when Walt and Dennis tiptoed in.

Lillian, who was keeping vigil in the other chair, greeted the men. "Mornin."

"How's our girl?" Walt dropped onto the edge of the sofa and caressed Olivia's face. Tears coursed again down Olivia's cheeks. Walt leaned over and kissed Olivia's forehead. "Livy, we are so sorry about the baby," he murmured.

Dennis squatted next to him. "Is there anything we can do?"

"No." Olivia sniffed and reached for a tissue. "I'm glad you're here. I'm sort of a mess." She wiped her eyes and gave them a pitiful look.

"Of course you are." Walt patted her arm. "And every reason to be."

Miriam sat back and allowed herself a moment of relief, comforted by Walt and Dennis's presence. When she looked over at Lillian, she saw her own sadness reflected in her mother's eyes.

Walt and Dennis chatted quietly with Olivia for a few more minutes, then excused themselves to the kitchen to make coffee and breakfast. Dennis would soon leave for work. Nate had gone to the airport to pick up Amy. Hugh was over at Walt and Dennis's. She was still irritated with him after last night's unexpected altercation. Hopefully, he would not show up any time soon. Lillian rose to follow the men to the kitchen in search of coffee, and she was left alone with Olivia.

Miriam was relieved when Olivia dozed. She could study her daughter without interruption. Her porcelain skin was such a contrast to the dark leather sofa; the sleeping-baby innocence of her face so young. Miriam vividly remembered those few weeks just after her birth.

Olivia's birth had brought everything between her and Hugh into sharp relief. For a while, they pretended it could work. He spoke of leaving Relief International. He'd find a position in the States with the Red Cross. They would marry. He would move into her house. In a moment of insanity, she had even considered bringing Olivia along to Africa. She'd be the young female doctor who brought *salvation to the masses.* How different hers and Olivia's lives would have been if she'd chosen that path.

She released a long sigh and closed her eyes. It would never have worked—a traditional relationship with Hugh. His constant restlessness. His longing to be back in the fray. She had become frustrated with his inability to understand her methodical, scientific approach to her work. And after Olivia?

She had struggled to trust—or even tolerate—his constant suggestions.

The exasperating thing about Hugh—as last night's experience proved—was his definite opinions about literally everything. Didn't matter if he knew anything about a subject. For him, scientific research was a mere excuse for taking too long to make a decision.

Miriam's eyes jerked open in response to the sound of the coffee grinder. The soothing smell of freshly ground coffee beans filled the air. Olivia's eyes were still closed. Miriam's breath caught as she struggled to dismiss the memory of her daughter, bloodied and sobbing, on the bathroom floor. She shifted to the fact Olivia had chosen to use a sperm donor bank and had kept it from her. A surge of anger flared. *Why wouldn't Olivia want her own mother, a gynecologist, whose specialty was this very thing, involved?* She could have helped.

But underneath the anger, Miriam had a sinking notion her response was about control. Not being in control would *never* be easy for her. Maybe Walt was right. Olivia needed it to be her and Amy's choice.

She stirred from her thoughts when Olivia mumbled, through closed eyes, "Mom?"

"Yes?"

"Did you really *want* me? I mean... when you found out you were pregnant... were you *sure* you wanted me?" Olivia slowly opened her eyes, peeked at her, then closed them again.

Miriam was completely caught off guard by the question. Her heart hammered in her chest. Words fell out of her mouth without thought. "What kind of silly question is that? Of course, I wanted you." *How to answer honestly?* She hoped Olivia would drop this uncomfortable topic.

Olivia opened her eyes and pushed up higher on her pillows. "I'm sorry I didn't tell you, Mom... that I was pregnant." Her dark eyes filled with misery.

Miriam inwardly cursed the fragile vulnerability this beautiful child brought out in her. Their mother-daughter relationship made a mess of her composure. She wasn't sure if she'd ever recover from the images of last night. Olivia crying out in pain. The need to examine her own daughter in a way she'd never expected to. The sad, sick feeling when her fingers touched the objective sign—felt so many times, in so many women—an open and bleeding cervix. The small round opening in a woman's body could bring such shattering emotional and physical loss. But this was not just any woman. This was Olivia—her own flesh—and Miriam hadn't even had a clue she was pregnant. How could she not have known? She turned her focus to Olivia. "I...I think I understand why you weren't ready to tell me."

Olivia sighed. "You know, I've been thinking about how getting pregnant was such a process—choosing a donor, ordering the sperm, inseminating... I mean...we never thought about it really happening, you know?"

Miriam nodded in support when Olivia raised her eyes. She ignored the scientific part of her brain that seemed to never turn off. The logical calculation of probabilities—*you're young, healthy, and ovulating. Introduce sperm and...shouldn't the results be obvious?*

Fortunately, as she searched for how to respond, Olivia continued. "But when it did happen so quickly, I realized I had been so focused on the *getting* pregnant part, that I hadn't even thought about the *being* pregnant part. And, Mom, honestly, I was so overwhelmed with doubt... so much doubt." She reached for another tissue. "Dammit. I can't seem to stop crying."

Miriam hated the helpless feeling. She moved from her chair to the end of the sofa and took Olivia's feet into her lap. This particular kind of physical closeness had always worked for the two of them. It seemed silly, but she was comfortable holding her daughter's feet. She turned toward Olivia and a surge of love made her feel as if her heart might burst. The longing to take away Olivia's hurt was overwhelming.

Olivia blew her nose and tossed the tissue into the pile forming beside the sofa. "But now? Now, I *know* I *really, really* want a baby. Now I know I'm ready. Does that make any sense, Mom?"

Miriam nodded and swallowed hard. She tried desperately to understand, terrified at how low her defenses were right now. Thoughts of her own struggle with pregnancy marched back into her consciousness, unbidden. Hugh and the youthful passion they had shared. Passion that tempered and changed over the years. Their argument last night at the hospital. "Hugh, you cannot drop into our lives every few years and expect to take over. I have this under control." She had been so frustrated with him her whole body trembled with anger, on top of an already deep level of anxiety.

"You don't have to be so damned hardheaded. I thought you might appreciate the support," he'd said.

"I have plenty of support." She'd been steely cold with resentment at his arrogance.

He'd gone silent then. And Dennis had stepped in, or she might have embarrassed herself. Retired or not, in front of her former hospital colleagues was *not* the place for her and Hugh to air their private grievances.

Miriam gently massaged Olivia's feet. "I understand the doubt part. For me..." She bit her lip and looked down at her aging hands holding Olivia's soft feet. "...as you have probably guessed... getting pregnant was not planned."

Olivia's mouth turned down. "Yeah, I've kind of always thought I was an accident." She scratched her nose. "But we've never talked about it."

"No, I guess we haven't." After several seconds, Miriam took a deep breath. Her cheeks felt warm as she blurted,

"Okay, I admit it. You're probably having a hard time believing this... but I completely lost myself in your father for a short time." She stared at Olivia's lovely long feet. So similar to Hugh's. After all these years, she still puzzled over what happened to her logical, practical self during those few weeks right after she'd met Hugh. "I was just getting my practice going." She glanced at Olivia. "Your dad and I met at an international women's health conference at UVA. He was one of the presenters." Miriam paused, remembering the tall, passionate man whose international work in women's health was so impressive. She'd made it her mission to seek him out. He stirred something inside of her she couldn't name.

Thinking back on it now, that something had a name. Lust. But then? She was still naïve enough to think it was some kind of fairy-tale love story. On the other hand, from the moment they met he was unattainable, committed to the work that took him all over the world. Had she wanted to hold on to a part of him? She shook herself. What a silly thought. She'd simply been young and foolish—at the exact wrong time.

Miriam turned to look at Olivia. "The last thing on my mind during that time your dad and I shared together was birth control...which is ironic, considering that was a main topic of the conference."

Olivia ogled her with disbelief. "I'm sorry." Her voice was incredulous. "But I can't imagine that side of you, Mom."

"Well..." Miriam didn't have an answer. She too was having a hard time lately, recapturing the young, fearless woman she had been.

"So..." Olivia was hesitant. "How did you feel about being pregnant?"

Miriam sat back and sighed. She looked across the room through the opening to the dining room and beyond, to the kitchen. Walt and Dennis moved around the island, chatting quietly. Lillian sat on a stool at the counter, watching them cook. Walt handed Lillian a cup of coffee. Something about feeling the solidness of their presence made her feel stronger. Maybe the openness she expected from Olivia had to go both ways. She took a deep breath. As she spoke, she had a sudden sense of knowing something she hadn't realized before.

"At first, I blamed myself for creating an anchor to your father. One that I wasn't—and he certainly wasn't—ready for." Olivia's pained expression caused her to hurry to explain. "You have to remember my generation, too, honey. Even with all my feminist aspirations, I still thought, at first, I had to choose between being a mother and being a doctor. *But*... it was never a choice to have you or not have you."

Olivia nodded slowly as she contemplated this idea.

"For me..." Miriam placed a hand on her chest and gestured with the other, searching Olivia's eyes for understanding. "The choice was what kind of mother I would be *because* I was a doctor...does that make sense?" She was dizzy with conflicting emotions. The struggle to express herself.

"So, you knew you wanted both."

"I did." Miriam brightened at the click of connectedness. "But I also knew I needed help because, obviously..." She lowered her chin and raised her eyebrows. "I am a bit ill-equipped when it comes to the whole nurturing thing."

Olivia smirked, "Ya think?"

Miriam was surprised at the sense of relief that washed over her as they laughed together.

Why had this been so hard to admit to herself?

"Breakfast," Walt called from the kitchen. "Olivia, we will bring you a plate. Don't you move. Mimi, honey, you have to come serve yourself."

Miriam and Olivia looked at each other and smiled. A sense of rightness settled over Miriam. She had chosen a family that balanced her, allowed her to follow her own path. She had always worried Olivia had not gotten enough of her time or energy. Today, for the first time, she started to see that *enough* wasn't just about her. "I was lucky to have those two incredible men in there." She nodded toward the kitchen and swallowed the intensity that threatened tears. "They have done as much, or maybe more, mothering than I have." She gently moved Olivia's feet, stood, and planted her own feet firmly on the floor. She shook off the vulnerability. "What would you like to drink?"

Olivia sat up and reached for her hand. "Mom?"

"Yes?" She sat down, snuggled in close, and placed her arms on either side of her daughter. And she let go—of fear, of control, of being an inadequate mother. Instead, she *saw* the young woman before her. An adult, struggling with a choice Miriam herself had never consciously made.

"This might be kind of weird to say..." An odd longing filled Olivia's eyes. "But I'll never have that experience of getting pregnant in an act of passion like you did."

Miriam's breath caught. She opened her mouth to speak. "Oh, Livy..."

"No, listen..." Olivia interrupted, leaning in. "There's something...I don't know...mystical about... the whole love-child thing."

Miriam pulled back and rolled her eyes toward the ceiling. Couldn't help it. Mystical? Love-child? Really? Shades of that old Diana Ross song floated through her mind. All she could do was smile at Olivia's naiveté. Olivia frowned. "What, Mom? It's true." Miriam's smile turned to a chuckle, which made Olivia laugh. Then they both collapsed into repeating cycles of breathless laughter and sloppy tears.

Walt appeared with a plate. "What are you girls giggling about over here?" He pulled up a tray and set down a delicious smelling plate of eggs, bacon, and fruit. "Mimi, come and eat. It's getting cold." He laid his hand on her shoulder.

"I'm coming." She squeezed Olivia's hand. "I happen to

think the way you and Amy are going about this is perfect for you." She absorbed the newfound truth of her words. "And your baby will be every bit as much a love-child to you as you were to me."

"Do you really think so, Mom?"

"I do."

CHAPTER 29

Olivia

CHARLOTTESVILLE
MAY 29, 2010

Olivia woke up to find Amy curled in the chair at the end of the day-bed in Mom's study, her feet tucked under her, laptop balanced on the chair arm. She kept her eyes semi-closed and watched Amy for several seconds, so intently focused on her work. She'd dropped everything to fly to Charlottesville last night. The loss of their baby weighted Olivia's heart. Everything that had happened yesterday seemed like a blur now. One thing was absolutely certain, she had never felt more loved than she had through this horrific process. Everyone had rallied around her and Amy. Even Dad. Which was mostly a strange coincidence.

"Hey," she said softly. Amy looked up immediately from the screen and smiled. She set the laptop aside and moved over to sit on the side of the bed.

"Hey there, sleepyhead. How ya feeling?"

Olivia sat up, rubbed her hands over her face, and pulled her hair back with the ponytail holder from her wrist. "Better. No more cramping."

"That's good to hear." Amy leaned forward and kissed her

gently. "Tell me what you need."

Olivia sighed. "I don't really know. It's just so weird, you know? One moment we're going to have a baby and then next... no more baby." She sniffed as Amy reached up and wiped tears from her cheeks. "It's so sad." Amy crawled into bed beside her and held her while she cried.

After the tears finally subsided, Amy took her chin and tipped her face up to gaze into her eyes. "You know we can try again, right?"

"I do..."

"When the time is right." Amy was being so strong for her. She loved her all the more.

"Yeah." Olivia took in a deep breath and released it. She looked out the window and realized how late it had gotten. "I must have slept a long time. What's everybody doing? Did I miss any drama?"

Amy laughed. "Not really. You were the main drama, my love." Amy got up and stretched. "Let's see... Your mom and Dennis just left for her shindig at UVA."

"I'm glad she decided to go. I didn't want her to miss it for me."

Amy laughed. "I think your grandmother finally put her foot down. Said she thought four adults might be able to manage the situation."

Olivia grinned. "That sounds like Gran."

"Um... Lillian and Walt are making dinner, I think." Amy plopped into the chair and threw her leg over the chair arm. "And... last time I was downstairs to grab some coffee, Nate and your dad were deep in conversation about Africa." Amy picked up her coffee and took a sip. "There's a rumor about a spades game after dinner. You in?"

Olivia shook her head. "Ugh. I don't think I can face everyone right now."

"I get that. You can stay up here as long as you need to."

Amy opened her laptop. "I'm just going to finish up this brief and maybe we could watch a movie?"

"Sounds good." Olivia leaned back against the pillows. Maybe she could at least read or something. She spied her tote bag leaning against Miriam's desk. "Ames, could you hand me that bag, please?" She pointed and Amy reached for the bag and placed it on the bed beside her.

"Thanks." She opened the bag, planning to start reading one of the articles she'd collected for her dissertation literature review. But instead of the stack of black and white printed articles, she spied the dull gold color of old medical files. She gasped.

"What's wrong?" Amy popped up so quickly she almost dropped her laptop.

"I'm fine. I'm fine." Olivia reached into the bag and pulled out the file labeled Lillian O'Toole. "With everything that happened, I forgot about this."

"What is it?" Amy frowned.

"I'm not sure, but I think it's my grandmother's medical file."

Amy wrinkled her face in confusion. "How... why?"

"It was the day Mom called when we were still at the farmhouse. She was all excited. She'd gotten the award and said that we needed to come back to Charlottesville. She asked me to help Gran pack. So, I went into her closet, fished around on the shelf, and pulled her ancient suitcase out. I opened it and this was in there. I thought maybe she'd forgotten about it or something..." Olivia looked down at the file in her hands. "You know how I told you Mom had gotten the DNA results and had asked Uncle Dennis to re-run the test?"

"Yeah?" Amy was looking at her now with suspicion in her eyes.

Olivia continued. Her voice came out sounding whiny in her ears. "I don't know. I just thought there might be a clue in here." She held out the file and met Amy's eyes long enough to see the surprise. Amy didn't take it. She looked down again. "So, I put it in my tote. I thought I'd ask Gran about it later." She squeezed her face into a grimace. "Do you think I shouldn't look?"

Wrong person to ask *that* question. Amy crossed her arms and sat back. "Jesus, Livy. What were you thinking?"

"Oh, come on, Amy. She probably doesn't even remember the file was in there."

"So... what? You're just going to say, 'Oh, Gran, by the way, I accidentally found this medical record from—'" Amy peered at the file. "'—Western State Hospital—'" Amy stopped abruptly and frowned. "Wait a minute." She turned to her laptop and typed in something. "Isn't that the place your Aunt Jo called the loony bin?"

"Yeah..." Olivia got up and looked over Amy's shoulder, scanning the page Amy had brought up about the history of Western State.

"Look at this." Amy pointed to a line on the screen. Olivia read the line: Dr. Albert Preston, Sr., Superintendent 1920 to 1959. "Isn't he the guy the foundation is named after? The one giving your mom the grant?"

Olivia nodded absently. She was still reading. She clamped her hand over her mouth. "Oh no," she murmured.

"What?" Amy asked urgently.

Olivia picked up the file and opened it. Slowly, she leafed through the sparse, yellowed pages.

"What are you doing? Shouldn't you ask your grandmother's permiss—"

Olivia wasn't listening. She set the file on the bed and grabbed her tennis shoes.

"Livy?"

"I can't explain now, but I need you to take me to UVA. I've got to see Mom before that award ceremony."

CHAPTER 30

Miriam

UNIVERSITY OF VIRGINIA, CHARLOTTESVILLE
MAY 29, 2010

Miriam's breath came in short bursts as she mounted the curved staircase to the Dome Room of the UVA Rotunda. At the top, she stopped to take in the sight. Flickering candles graced fifteen white linen-covered tables. The elegantly dressed guests laughed and chatted as they found their places. Her usual appreciation for the beauty of the historic space was lost. She kept picturing Olivia's pale face, the fury in her eyes. "What are you going to do?" she'd asked. Miriam hadn't stopped to answer. She clutched the file as she approached the small group preparing to take their seats around the table nearest the central dais. Dennis looked up as she drew near. "Miriam, there you are. I was just—"

Ignoring Dennis's perplexed expression, she quickly moved to stand before Buddy Preston. "Before you sit down, Buddy, I'd like to speak to you in private, please." She held the file at her side and attempted to still the trembling that threatened her resolve.

Buddy bestowed his usual charm on her. "Why, Miriam, dear, can it wait? They're just about to serve dinner." He pulled out his chair.

Rachel and Beau turned from their conversation with another couple. "What's wrong?" Rachel asked, coming to stand near her father.

"No. It can't wait. I need to speak to you now." Miriam glared into his eyes and motioned toward an area outside the Dome Room. "Please."

"Well, then, let's not keep the lady waiting," Buddy said with a patronizing smile. Slowly and deliberately, he moved away from the table, leaning heavily on his gold-handled cane.

Rachel huffed and glanced around the room. In a low voice, she said, "Really, Miriam? Now?"

Miriam ignored her and turned toward Dennis. She met his gaze with an unspoken plea. He hurried past her, through the towering white columns surrounding the Dome Room. Looking around, he spied an empty study room and opened the door. Miriam followed him. Behind her, she heard Beau ask Rachel, "What's going on?"

They gathered in the small room. Dennis closed the door. Buddy lowered himself into one of the leather chairs, his cane held between his knees, hands crossed on top. Rachel and Beau assumed positions on either side of him. Dennis moved to hover somewhere near her elbow. The shock of what she'd read only moments ago threatened to silence her. Miriam took a deep breath and held up the file. "This is my mother, Lillian's, medical record." Her voice caught. She paused and looked down, swallowing against the rage building inside.

Buddy let out a short humph and a wheezy cough. He looked from Beau to Rachel and back to her, smiling. "Now is hardly the time to discuss your mother's health. But, you can certainly schedule—"

"From Western State Hospital," Miriam interrupted. "1938."

Buddy looked at her in confusion. "1938? What has this

got to do with me?" He started to stand.

Miriam took a step toward him and pushed the record close to his face. He jerked his head back. "This record documents Lillian O'Toole's bilateral tubal ligation. The surgeon? Dr. Albert Preston." Miriam waited for her words to sink in. Buddy looked confused. "Your father sterilized my mother." Miriam stared into Buddy's watery eyes as he dropped back into his chair. As if from a distance, she heard Rachel gasp. She felt the file leave her hands as Dennis took it. In her peripheral vision she saw him open it. "She was only fourteen years old." Miriam could no longer keep the grief at bay. She gritted her teeth against the tears.

"Now, Miriam..." Buddy addressed her as if she were a child. He pushed himself up to stand at his full height. "I'm not sure what you have there, but my daddy—

"He also sterilized my father, two of his brothers, and his sister... Why?" The horror of the injustice rolled over Miriam again, threatening to flatten her.

"Hold on a minute, young lady." Buddy had the gall to sound insulted. She couldn't believe it. "My father was an upstanding member of this community. He did important work for Western State Hospital."

"Did you *know* about these operations?" Miriam could scarcely take this in.

"I... I was... I knew there was a surgical aspect to his practice," Buddy sputtered. "I am absolutely certain that every single operation he performed was entirely legal with proper consent. He was making things better, don't you see?"

"Better? For whom?" She was so incredulous, she almost laughed at the absurdity.

"The community. He was building a stronger, healthier community." Buddy puffed up his chest and looked at Rachel for reassurance. She stepped closer to him and took his arm.

"By sterilizing children?" Miriam did not try to keep the

disgust from her voice.

Rachel's eyes widened. "Miriam, stop this. This has nothing to do with my father. That was a long time ago. Things were different then." She patted her father's arm. Buddy was breathing heavily, his lean cheeks flushed. "Here, Daddy. Sit back down. You know it's not good for your heart to get upset like this."

Buddy slowly lowered himself into the chair. The room was silent for several seconds. Miriam was at a complete loss. Words left her. She was vaguely aware of the sounds from the Dome Room—low voices, the clink of silver on china.

Buddy's resonant voice broke the silence. "Come now, Miriam. Let's be reasonable here." Miriam met his gaze. His eyes were clear, confident. "My father's work and yours are actually very similar. Your contraceptive center will carry on his legacy. You'll be doing your part, just like my father did, to keep the unfit from reproducing."

Rachel piped up, her voice coaxing, flattering. "It's true, Miriam. Your work is so important. You and I both know there are people who should not have children. First of all, children deserve a mother and a father who are married—that's how God meant it to be."

Miriam almost choked on the bile rising in her throat. Rachel's pretty face shifted and twisted as memories came flooding back. Rachel screaming in pain. Lillian's strong hands, soothing words. "You're going to be all right. The pains will pass soon." Holding Rachel as she wept over the loss of the pregnancy, Miriam was sworn not to tell anyone about—especially Rachel's parents. "They'll disown me." Her shock when Rachel sobbed, "What if Beau won't marry me now?"

Miriam shook herself. Rachel was still talking. "Plus, these people take such a toll on the taxpayer—living on entitlement programs. No desire to work. They let their children run wild while they're taking drugs. It's shameful." Rachel looked at her father, who nodded his agreement. "And... you have to admit, Miriam, your Aunt Jo could never have handled children."

"How do you know that? She was twelve years old, Rachel."

"And besides, there must be some mistake." Rachel was unphased. She paused. Miriam froze. "Your mother and daddy had *you*, didn't they?" Rachel came closer and touched her arm. Miriam flinched. "What say we put off this conversation until tomorrow? We'll talk when we have more time... and we're calmer. Why, this is probably a big fuss over nothing."

Miriam felt Dennis's hand slip into hers. She could not speak. Buddy and Rachel's faces blurred before her. She forced herself to breathe. Dennis tightened his grip. She jumped at a knock on the door. Rachel rushed over and opened it.

"Um, excuse me sir." The young server stepped cautiously into the room and addressed Buddy. "They wanted me to tell you that the awards ceremony begins in five minutes."

"Thank you, young man." Buddy turned to Miriam as the waiter hurried out of the room. "Now, Miriam, I'm about to go into that Dome Room and award you five million dollars. All you have to do is accept the money and we will forget all about this unfortunate conversation. You can carry on with your work. Our full support will be behind you."

CHAPTER 31

Olivia

Uncle Walt was pulling a pan of brownies from the oven when Olivia slumped into the kitchen of her mother's house. Amy followed close behind. A rich, comforting, chocolatey smell filled the air. "Here they are," Uncle Walt said. Dad and Nate rose awkwardly from where they sat at the kitchen bar, half-full wine glasses in front of them.

Weariness gripped Olivia. The dull ache that had returned low in her abdomen was hard to ignore. She quickly scanned the dining room and through to the den. Lillian was nowhere in sight. "Where's Gran?"

"She's gone to bed." Uncle Walt plunked the dish on the counter and ripped off his hot mitts. "What happened? Why did you girls rush out like that?" He took one look at Olivia and enfolded her in his arms. As she buried her head against his chest, relief over not having to face her grandmother yet washed over her, followed by a tumble of confusion.

Olivia couldn't speak. What had she just done? Miriam had gone pale when she'd opened the file. She scanned it for only a few seconds, then she'd barely looked up. "I will see you back at home." And her mother had turned around and walked away.

Amy jumped in, her voice uncertain, but steady. "Liv found some... old documents... um... about Lillian. She thought her mom should see them right away—"

Uncle Walt released Olivia and stepped back, crossing his arms. "*Before* the awards ceremony? But why?" Walt's voice was incredulous.

Olivia glanced at her dad and Nate. Should they know about any of this? Nate sat down and sipped his wine, looking like he wanted to disappear. As if Dad had read her mind, he moved around the counter and kissed the top of her hair. He held her shoulders gently and dipped his head to look into her eyes. "Whatever this is about, you and your mom and Lillian are going to work it out." She bobbed her head and dropped her gaze. Dad stepped back, reached to gently tip her chin up, and smiled. "You Stewart women are strong like bull." He raised and curled his arms, making his biceps bulge. She laughed in spite of herself.

Dad strode over to Uncle Walt and clapped him on the back. "Walt, my man, thank you for a delicious dinner. I'm going to make my exit now, perhaps take advantage of that fabulous hot tub of yours."

Uncle Walt grinned. "Enjoy." He pointed to Dad's wine glass. "Take that with you. Do you want a brownie to go?"

"Better not." Dad slid his hands across his abdomen, sucking in and giving it a slap. He turned to Nate. "Join me? I have another story about a smallpox outbreak I haven't told you yet."

"Sure." Nate jumped up and followed Dad. Olivia was certain he was relieved to escape. He looked back and forth between Olivia and Amy. "Sorry again... about your baby." Olivia glanced at Amy. Now they were both close to tears.

"Thanks, Nate." Amy reached to hug him. Olivia had been

surprised at how quickly Amy had warmed to Nate.

Nate looked down awkwardly. He raised a hand to Walt. "G'night. Thanks for dinner."

The door closed behind them. Uncle Walt began transferring the brownies to a platter. Olivia collapsed into a dining chair. Amy sat sideways in the chair beside her, looking worried. "Babe, maybe you should get some sleep."

"Are you kidding? When Uncle Walt's brownies are still warm from the oven?" She tried to smile. Her mouth didn't cooperate.

"What'll it be, ladies? Wine or cold milk?"

"Wine," they said in unison.

Uncle Walt set plates of warm brownies and glasses of Pinot Noir before them. Olivia put the first delicious fudgy bite into her mouth. Amy started to explain to a confused Uncle Walt what they had found in Lillian's medical record. With a whoosh, the back door opened, bringing the scents of Uncle Dennis's cologne and Miriam's ginger lotion. She, Amy, and Uncle Walt all looked up as Uncle Dennis stepped back for Miriam to enter.

"I really gotta pee." Everyone watched, speechless, as Miriam dropped her evening bag on the table. Her heels clicked across the pine kitchen floorboards, a swish of chiffon as she disappeared through the kitchen door to the front hallway.

Uncle Dennis pulled the elegant silk evening scarf from around his neck and dropped it on the table. "Well family," he said, his gaze traveling across each of their faces, "Miriam Stewart has just walked away from 5 million dollars."

CHAPTER 32

Miriam

CHARLOTTESVILLE
MAY 29, 2010

Everyone was moving back toward the dining table when Miriam returned from the bathroom, still shaken, still feeling as if she'd just awakened from a bad dream. Walt silently held up the wine bottle. Miriam shook her head. "Just water, please." She needed all available wits about her right now. Imprinted in her mind was the way Buddy's expression had changed from smug to shocked at her two simple words, "No, thank you." Somehow—thank god for Dennis—she had turned, found the door, and walked out. Gotten back home. She dropped into the chair at the end of the table.

Olivia and Amy sat next to each other on her left. Walt turned off the kitchen light and picked up two scotches in one hand and water in the other. He set scotch at his and Dennis's places, water in front of her, and took a seat across from Olivia and Amy on her right. Only a small light on the sideboard illuminated the space. Even in the soft light, Miriam spotted the dark circles under Olivia's eyes. She really should be in bed. Another snap of the guilt rubber-band. Tonight, Miriam felt like a failure at Every. Damn. Thing.

Dennis removed his tuxedo jacket, hung it on a hook by the back door, and folded himself into a chair at the opposite end of the table from her. Miriam met his gaze. Warm, dependable... worried. Sadness and anger tightened her chest again. His voice was gentle, but clear. "Do you want to talk about it?" She breathed in deeply and let it out. Dennis removed his cuff links and rolled up his sleeves.

Slowly, she took in each of their worried faces. Her eyelids fluttered up and back down. "What is there to talk about? It's got to have been some horrible mistake—" No matter how she tried, she could not make any sense of what had happened to her mother and father. Her uncles. Aunt Jo.

"They called it Eugenics." Dennis's voice was the only sound other than the ticking of the grandfather clock in the front hall. Miriam looked again at Walt, Olivia, and Amy. They all stared at Dennis, looking as puzzled as she felt.

"Eugenics?" Olivia asked.

Miriam placed her hands flat on the table, one on either side of her water glass. The world was tilting.

Dennis removed his glasses, set them on the table, crossed his legs, and leaned back. "Eugenics was a pseudo-science, based on a lot of really bad data. Had its hay-day in the U.S. from the early twentieth century right up until World War II. As a matter of fact, the Nazis borrowed ideas from American eugenic scientists." Dennis took in a long, deep breath and released it. "The eugenicists believed that poverty, mental illness, developmental disabilities, alcoholism, and generally being what they called a *degenerate* were all genetically inherited traits. So, they wanted to cultivate a pure race of people they considered fit to breed."

"Oh my god." Walt put his hand over his mouth.

"Right," Dennis said. He was in teaching mode. "They had two ways of doing it." He held up an index finger as he spoke. "The first was positive eugenics—encouraging the people considered fit to have lots of kids. They even went so far as to have these competitions called *Fitter Family Contests.*" He grew more animated, set down his drink, and rested his elbows and upper arms on the table. "The 'fit' families were white, of western European descent—not just any old white immigrant would do—they needed to be educated, heterosexual, healthy, and at least middle class—"

"Are you sure this has gone out of fashion?" Walt kept his expression blank.

Dennis smiled wryly. "Good point."

Miriam was still too sick inside to smile. Buddy's words of less than an hour ago filled her mind. *My father's work and yours are actually very similar...* She jerked her head up when Olivia's voice broke the brief silence.

"And the second approach?" Olivia had looked at her with such pride when she'd come back into the kitchen from the bathroom. Apparently, Dennis had revealed her big exit from the award ceremony. She wasn't sure she deserved anyone's admiration. She couldn't get past Buddy comparing her work to his father's. Everything. *Every single solid thing* about herself puddled around her like melting ice.

Dennis held up his hand again and added his raised third finger to the other one. "The second approach was negative eugenics—anyone considered unfit was sterilized and/or institutionalized. They used so-called intelligence tests to classify people. The intelligence test was in its infancy then. The questions were arbitrary and extremely biased toward middle to upper class cultural knowledge. Poor, uneducated country people were classified as morons, imbeciles, or idiots and therefore, were sterilized to keep them from producing more unfit people."

The words from her mother's medical record were seared into Miriam's mind. *Assessed from appearance and history to be at Moron level of intelligence.* Those words did not fit the mother she had known for sixty-five years. "But... but..." she blurted. "Buddy said all those operations were with consent. Surely, Mother didn't agree to this?" Miriam's voice sounded louder than she intended.

A vague impression of a tennis match as Amy's, Olivia's, and Walt's eyes turned back to Dennis. He dropped his chin with sadness. "No, I don't think any of them knew what was happening at the time. When I found out about your DNA results, I suspected, but I didn't want to mention it."

"Why not?" Miriam asked. Frustration tumbled over helplessness. "If you *knew* about this... eu... eugenics thing?"

"You were so sure the test was wrong. I really believed we should give it the benefit of the doubt." Dennis's expression was resigned as he tapped his index finger on the file in front of him. "No need for DNA now. This medical record proves it. The Stewart children and your mother were part of a mountain sweep."

"A mountain sweep? What the hell is that?" Amy asked. A cold chill ran down Miriam's spine.

Dennis glanced at the file, then looked around the table. He sighed. "In 1927, the Supreme Court upheld Virginia's Eugenical Sterilization Act of 1924. The Act said people who were genetically unfit could be sterilized without their consent. They used the term 'feeblemindedness.' The Eugenics Society had this righteous zeal to cleanse the population.

"So, by the 1930s, county officials—usually the sheriff and his deputies—were driving up into the mountains and picking up young people from poor families considered to be unfit. They used the guise of bringing them in for health testing. Loaded them up and drove them to one of the state institutions, like Western State Hospital. There, they'd either be sterilized or retained—if they refused the surgery—through their childbearing years. Many of them didn't know they'd been sterilized until much later on after they'd spent years trying to have children and never could either father a child, or get pregnant."

"I think we need another brownie." Walt pushed his chair back and stepped into the kitchen to retrieve the platter. He set it in the middle of the table. Miriam had no appetite. No one else reached for one either.

"Maybe I *will* have a glass of wine," Miriam sighed.

"Let me open another bottle." Walt started to rise from his chair.

"I'll get it." Dennis, looking like some elegantly dressed sommelier, stood and walked over to the pitifully stocked wine rack Miriam kept on the kitchen counter. "Oh, Miriam. I keep telling you to let me pick out some good wine for you." Miriam frowned when Amy and Olivia sniggered. After pulling out and returning two bottles, he finally settled on a third and picked up the corkscrew. The grandfather clock struck ten.

Miriam tried to sort her random thoughts as she accepted the glass from Dennis. Her automatic go-to strategy, the one that always served her well, was logic. Safe. Predictable. "So, this was 1938. My grandmother, Mary, died in 1938. Then, Lillian lived on her own until she married Daddy..." Miriam reached up and scratched absently where the itchy dress rubbed at her collarbone. "Did she somehow get picked up along with the Stewart kids?" Crushing pain ripped through her chest thinking of her fourteen-year-old mother, who was probably looking out for Aunt Jo the whole time.

She nodded to herself, grasping to line up the facts. "So, she and my father were both sterilized. Then, in 1942, they got married..." She looked up from her musing to find four sets of eyes staring at her. She looked at Dennis, grounding herself in his solid gaze. "I always thought she got pregnant when he was home on leave... that she'd already had me by the time he came home." Tears filled her eyes. "There was the story about him, after his discharge, walking down the road toward the cabin..." Again, the world tilted. She leaned forward, rested her elbows on the table, and dropped her face into her hands.

"Mom?" Olivia's hand was cool on her arm.

She raised her face, but couldn't look at any of them. She looked beyond their anxious faces, through the dining room window, into the black branches of the maple tree in the garden beyond. "Where did I come from?"

CHAPTER 33

Lillian

CHARLOTTESVILLE
SUNDAY, MAY 30, 2010

Lillian sipped her coffee, enjoying the first taste of the new day. Such a pleasure. Her wrist felt much better now, except for the itchiness of the cast. Miriam set a placemat in front of her on the polished dining room table. "What would you like to eat, Mother? I have eggs, toast, yogurt, oatmeal..." She must have named six more things. Lillian settled on eggs and toast. Couldn't remember all the others. Miriam insisted she stay put. "You just enjoy your coffee. I can handle breakfast."

Lillian missed the comfort of her own kitchen and the beaten-up old table where she had sat for so many years. But she reminded herself, Miriam's dining room was sunny and warm, with lots of those hard-to-kill kinds of houseplants by the window. It was nice. Not home, but comfortable.

Amy and Olivia's footsteps sounded on the stairs, and they popped into the kitchen. Olivia looked better today—still a little pale—but brighter. They each wore those baggy pants and t-shirts young women liked. They went straight to the coffee pot. Amy poured two cups and handed one to Olivia.

"Mornin, Mom. Mornin Gran," Olivia called. Olivia walked

over and leaned over to kiss Miriam.

"Good morning." Miriam turned her cheek up to Olivia, her hands busy cracking eggs into a white bowl. Miriam seemed a little jumpy this morning too. Maybe she was tired. Lillian hadn't heard them come in last night. Could have been late.

Both girls came through from the kitchen to the dining room. Each sat on the edge of a chair. Olivia looked from her mother to Lillian. "We're headed over to Uncle Walt and Uncle Dennis's to have breakfast with them and Dad and Nate." From Miriam's expression, this was not a surprise to her. Lillian reckoned it would just be the two of them for breakfast.

"We will be back in a little while." Olivia rose, moved in front of Lillian, and bent down to give her a quick squeeze. Amy gave Lillian one of her sweet smiles. Amy reminded her of herself a bit as a young woman—stick-straight hair, all angles and bones, strong body. Lillian hugged Olivia as best she could from a sitting position.

"Bye girls." After the back door closed behind them, Lillian rose from her chair, walked into the kitchen, and refilled her coffee cup. She leaned against the counter and watched Miriam scoop strawberry jam from a jar onto each of their plates. "How was your award ceremony last night?"

Lillian was curious about how it had gone. Miriam didn't care much for fancy events. Had always complained when she had to go to them. Even the ones during her college years. The sound of the Preston name—when she'd heard the award was from the Preston Foundation—had set her teeth on edge, but none of that was Miriam's fault. All in the past. No need for it to stand in the way of Miriam's future and the center she wanted to build.

"Fine. It was fine..." Miriam stiffened. The spoon she was using clattered to the floor, sending strawberry jam flying. "Shit." She grabbed a paper towel from the holder on the counter, stepped to the sink to wet it, and stooped to wipe the floor.

"Can I help you, honey?" Lillian took a step toward her daughter.

"No, no. I got it." She held up a hand. After cleaning the floor, she stood, tossed the paper towel in the trash under the sink, and leaned against the counter, head hung. Her chest moved like she was breathing hard. When Miriam looked up, Lillian felt her chest grip. She had not seen this kind of look on Miriam's face since her daddy died.

"What's the matter?" Lillian asked. She took a step toward Miriam. This was more than a spill of jam. "Is this about Olivia? You worried about her?"

"I'm okay," Miriam answered instantly. Didn't appear okay. Looked worried and sad. Miriam drew away. "Okay, well maybe not... I... I wish..." Her voice dropped to a whisper, even though they were the only ones in the house. "Seeing Olivia like that the other night..." She rubbed her hands across her face, smoothed back her hair. "Even though I've seen it so many times..." Miriam looked at Lillian with a faint, resigned smile. "I guess I'm not as objective as I've always thought I was."

Lillian nodded her understanding. "Do you think she'll try again?" Lillian asked.

"Yes, I think she will. Dr. Larch says there's no reason why she shouldn't." Miriam turned on the gas burner, set a skillet on it, dumped in the eggs, and pushed them around with a wooden spoon. "From what Olivia told me this morning, this miscarriage clarified for her—she definitely wants a baby."

Lillian listened quietly. A flash of memory of her younger self. She shook off those particular cobwebs. When Miriam glanced her way, she kept her expression blank. *My sweet Miriam.* So smart. So capable. Painful to watch her cope with something she had no control over—like Olivia's miscarriage.

Lillian had always believed it was seeing her friend Rachel miscarry all those years ago that set Miriam on the path to being a doctor for women—giving her patients some say over whether or not they got pregnant.

They ate breakfast mostly in silence. Miriam opened the newspaper out on the table. Made occasional comments about articles. When they'd finished, Miriam jumped up to clear the plates. "How about we take a cup of coffee outside and sit by the koi pond? I haven't really gotten a chance to look at it since Nate and Walt got it going again."

"Sounds nice," Lillian said.

They made their way down the back steps and out into the garden. They stopped to admire the fresh coat of yellow paint and the white trim on the little cottage. The gravel path led past a great big white oak shading the whole yard. Two comfortable wooden chairs were placed near the little pond. There was even a deep pink water lily floating on the surface. The air had that fresh summer morning smell. Different from home—earthier, mossier here. Probably all the shade. Lillian sat down, shivering a little in the coolness.

"I'll be right back with our coffee." Miriam turned and started for the house.

"Bring me one of those blankets from the sofa, won't you, dear?"

"Sure will."

Wasn't long before Miriam was back balancing two mugs of coffee, a blanket thrown over her shoulder. Miriam set the mugs on the little tiled table between them. She pulled the blanket from her shoulder and handed it to Lillian, who gratefully spread it across her lap and over her knees. The warmth felt good. As Miriam sat down, she pulled something from under her arm. Looked like a file of some kind.

Lillian's gaze riveted on the file folder as Miriam tucked it quickly under her leg, as if she was trying to hide it. Why did it look so familiar? Then, a flash of memory. Lillian knew. That medical file and the book to explain it were the only things she'd asked of Evelyn that day in 1944, when she'd shown up at the cabin. But why did Miriam have it? Her hands felt cold and she started to tremble. Her heart raced. The suitcase. She'd left the hateful file in her old suitcase, along with the medical book. Evelyn had stolen both from her father's office all those years ago. Why hadn't she gotten rid of them?

CHAPTER 34

Lillian

HAZEL HOLLOW
FALL, 1944

Invigorated from her morning walk along the river, Lillian sat on the front porch, sipping coffee and contemplating the chill in the air. She worried over whether or not she had enough wood stacked for winter. With Elijah gone, she had to go back to the old, familiar way of living on her own. All thoughts of winter, wood, anything else left her mind when Evelyn Preston appeared. She trudged up the dirt track to the cabin, dusty and breathing hard. How had she gotten from Staunton up to the holler? She set the question aside and nodded at Evelyn, raising a hand in greeting.

"Hello, Lily," Evelyn called. "I got a lift on the milk truck with Mavis's husband. I hope you don't mind some company."

Lillian hid her surprise as she struggled with a mish-mash of feelings: excitement at the possibility of renewed friendship, suspicion of Evelyn's motives, and complete bewilderment at the strangeness of the situation all at once. "Of course. Can I fetch you some coffee?" All she could think to ask. Evelyn leaned against the porch rail, breathing hard.

"No thanks. But I could use some water." Evelyn seemed a

bit tamped down today. Looked like a *Ladies Home Journal* model posed against a country backdrop in her brown dungarees rolled above her ankles, starched white shirt with upturned collar, and saddle shoes. The dirt path at her feet, the sweeping meadow that ran green and gold down to the river behind her, and the shadowed rolling mountains that rose above her. The expression on Evelyn's face was not the sassy, rebellious girl from town. Lillian tried to read Evelyn's emotions and could not.

Two victory rolls framed her pale oval face, held in the back by a crocheted snood. She wore red lipstick. When she swept a stray hair out of her eye, Lillian caught the matching nail polish. There was a fullness to Evelyn's face that Lillian hadn't noticed before. Her pinched mouth and the furrow between her brows made her look as worried as an old crone. Certainly not the carefree girl Lillian had watched walk away at the bus station. Lillian invited her into the cabin kitchen where they took seats at the table. Lillian handed her a glass of water.

"Thank you for having me." Evelyn sounded formal as she reached to take the glass. Took a long drink, set the glass down, and stared at her hands as she twisted her fingers together in her lap. She glanced up, "I have something to tell you... and to ask you." She met Lillian's gaze.

This time Lilian was surprised to see stubbornness in Evelyn's eyes. *There's the old Evelyn.* "All right then, ask me."

Evelyn placed her elbows on the table and leaned forward. Lillian waited several seconds while Evelyn stared at the kitchen table, tracing the grain of the wood with her long, slender finger. A tear fell onto the table and Lillian knew. No longer able to stand the suspense, she blurted, "Are you pregnant?"

Evelyn looked up with an incredulous expression. "How did you know?" She brought her hands to her face. "Yes, I'm pregnant," she wailed. "I'm six months already and I'm afraid it's starting to show." She dropped her hands to her waist.

Lillian followed Evelyn's hands and sized up her belly. She could scarcely see any change, but this was a first baby and Evelyn was a slender girl. "Who is the father?" Wasn't that always the obvious next question?

"I don't know." Evelyn would not look up.

Lillian's mind screamed *What do you mean you don't know?* She wasn't naïve enough to believe this didn't happen. Women had sex with more than one man. But the women she'd known in the holler who'd gotten pregnant and weren't sure who the father was hadn't done so by choice.

For a moment, Lillian was aware of a stab of resentment. She desperately wanted to be pregnant with Elijah's baby and still, he had left her here, childless. "Oh?" was all she could manage.

"It's complicated..."

"Not really." Lillian realized she was much angrier than she should be. This was not her problem, after all. "You have relations without protection, there's a good chance you'll get pregnant."

"I know *that*, Lillian." Evelyn's voice was cold.

They sat in silence for several seconds. Then Evelyn let out a growl of frustration, stood, and began pacing the floor. "I think I told you about the USO dance and Lawrence leaving the next day... and well, I..."

"I remember. So, you'll marry him then?" Lillian asked. This seemed the obvious choice. Wouldn't she want to be with the baby's daddy?

Evelyn glared at her, green eyes luminous in her pale face. A doe, standing stock-still in the woods, staring. "No... I don't want to get married..." She collapsed into a chair and dropped her head onto her arms on the table. "I'm such an idiot. How could I have let this happen?" She choked out the words through her tears.

"Do your folks know?" Lillian wondered what she was about to get herself into the middle of. Once again, the resentment surfaced. *It's all well and good to like having sex until you get yourself pregnant.*

Evelyn picked her head up from the table and took the handkerchief Lillian held out to her. She wiped her eyes and nose and sniffed loudly, then wadded the handkerchief into her hand and took a deep breath. "My father, the good Dr. Preston..." Disdain dripped from her voice, "must never know about this baby."

At the sound of Dr. Preston's name, Lillian cringed inwardly. She had worked very hard to forget that name. She felt the wide gap between herself and the woman sitting at her kitchen table. Life had shown each of them different sides of itself.

"What about your mama?" Lillian thought of the cold, aloof woman she'd seen the day Mama died. "Does she suspect?"

"I think so," Evelyn said. "She looks at me strangely, you know?"

Lillian nodded. "Mothers have a way of knowing these things." She got up from the table to pour herself a cup of coffee.

"Could I have a cup of that coffee now?" Evelyn sniffed.

Lillian reached for another cup. After pouring, she returned to the table and watched as Evelyn dipped two large spoonfuls of sugar into her cup and stirred. "What is it that you want from me?" Lillian asked.

Evelyn stopped stirring, pulled her leg underneath her in the chair, and looked into Lillian's eyes. "Our housekeeper—you remember Mavis, don't you?"

Lillian nodded. She hadn't seen Mavis much over the years. Old Mrs. McDonald—Mavis's mother and Mama's best friend—had died the year after Mama. Lillian had read the obituary in the paper.

Evelyn was still talking. "Mavis told me the mountain people say you're the best midwife in the holler," Evelyn said.

Lillian snorted, embarrassed to feel flattered. "I'm the *only* midwife in this holler."

Evelyn smiled with admiration. Lillian flashed back on her younger self with Evelyn, newly borrowed books in hand, climbing into a twisted old oak tree to read and while away a summer afternoon. "I had no idea you'd followed in your mama's footsteps," Evelyn said. "You disappeared for so long, Lillian. Where did you go?"

"I've been here. In my home." Her chest felt heavy with loss. First Mama's death, now Elijah gone to war. She remembered the time she'd sworn to never leave the holler. "After Mama died, folks around here started calling on me, and well... here I am." Lillian took a sip of coffee, swallowed hard, and asked the question she could no longer ignore. "Is that what you want from me? To deliver your baby?"

"I was hoping you would consider it." Evelyn's eyes were intense, searching.

Lillian tried to sort the situation. "I'm not following your thinking." She took a sip of her coffee and set the mug on the table. "You haven't told your parents. You're about to start to show. What are you planning to do until the baby is born?"

"Well... that's the other thing," Evelyn said. This time her expression was definitely pleading. "I was hoping I could stay up here in the holler with you."

Lillian struggled to take in Evelyn's request. "What will you tell your parents?"

Evelyn sighed. There were shadows under her eyes, a droop to her mouth. "That's the point. I can't tell them anything." Her eyes flared with anger. "I won't be forced into their box for me. If I tell them about the baby, they'll insist I stay and marry Lawrence—even though..." She seemed to think better of what she was about to say. "Anyway, I turn twenty-one in a few months and they won't have any say over me. Maybe I'll take the baby and move to California. I don't know," Evelyn's voice rose, and she clasped her face in her hands, pulling at her cheeks. "I can't stay here. That's for sure. Maybe I'll write to them someday and explain—when I'm far, far away."

Lillian couldn't decide whether to feel honored or used.

"It will give me time to figure out what to do. Please, Lillian, you're my only hope."

Lillian knew in her gut that she would say yes, but why? Why should she complicate her own life this way?

"Could I use your restroom, please?" Evelyn asked.

"Of course." Lillian pointed toward the door. "Just in there."

Evelyn rose and ran her hands over her stomach to smooth the front of her dungarees. Lillian could see only the slightest bump. However, Evelyn could not hide this much longer. She must be feeling desperate.

Maybe the right thing to do was to shelter Evelyn, help in her time of need. They were friends, after all. But what about the peaceful life she'd made here in the holler? Resigning herself to wait for Elijah to come home. With a tinge of self-doubt, she faced the fact that recently she had begun to drift back into the withdrawn, lonely existence she'd experienced during the years between Mama's death and her marriage. The thought of Elijah stirred the familiar longing for him. What would he say about Evelyn's dilemma?

Perhaps taking Evelyn in would ease her loss a bit; give her a sense of purpose. But Evelyn was a town girl and Lillian could not see how Evelyn could be satisfied with living in such a small space as this cabin—even with the indoor plumbing and bathroom Elijah had insisted on installing, and the electricity from the TVA, which still felt like luxuries.

When she looked up from her musing, Evelyn had returned from the bathroom and was examining the cabin as if she were picturing herself in the space. Lillian suppressed a small niggling feeling of embarrassment at the simplicity of her home, and brought her chin up higher. "You wouldn't have the luxuries here that you have in Staunton at your parents' house."

She was surprised when Evelyn's face flushed with relief. She glowed as she dropped into a chair. "You mean you'll consider it?" She reached over and grasped Lillian's hands. "I can't begin to thank you."

"Hold on a minute. I haven't said yes... yet." Lillian pulled her hands away. "I have questions."

CHAPTER 35

Lillian

HAZEL HOLLOW
FALL, 1944

"Ask me." Evelyn's voice was clear and determined.

Lillian took a deep breath. The strong feeling of stepping into the middle of something unknown set her nerves on edge. "How do you propose to manage this? Are you planning to tell anyone where you are?" Lillian leaned forward and propped her elbows on the table. "You must have already told Mavis."

Evelyn nodded, refusing to look up.

"What if she tells your daddy and he comes running up here to fetch you?"

Clearly, from the look on her face, Evelyn had not considered these questions.

Heartless, but she pushed on. "And what about the baby's daddy? Are you going to tell him? What will you do when he comes back from the war and wants to marry you? Are you going to disappear from your life? Are you willing to do that to your baby?"

Evelyn stared at the table. Lillian wasn't even sure if she heard. "How about you go back and you tell them?" Lillian was gentler. Maybe Evelyn's people would care enough for her to take her back, to help her through this pregnancy. Surely she could see that this baby needed its family.

Evelyn dropped her hands from her face and stared, open-mouthed, at Lillian. "I hate them." Evelyn lowered her voice. Lillian heard the rage. "All they want to do is control me and make me marry Lawrence Wilson." Evelyn reached into her handbag and pulled out a package of cigarettes. "Do you have a light?"

"Um... no... I..." Lillian remembered the matches on the back of the stove and pointed.

Evelyn got up, walked over to the stove, selected a match from the box, and struck it, puffing her cigarette into flame. She inhaled deeply and blew the smoke out the side of her mouth. "Lawrence's daddy owns the bank and they have a load of money." She waved the cigarette in the air.

What a strange creature this girl is. Like watching a para-keet in the hen house. Lillian got up from her chair and pulled open a drawer searching for one of Elijah's ash trays. Finding it, she set it on the table and pushed it toward Evelyn.

"I showed them," Evelyn whispered loudly, as if they shared a girlish secret. She winked and smiled bitterly as she tapped her ashes on the ashtray.

"What do you mean you showed them?"

Evelyn's face flushed. "I am not a cow to be auctioned off to the highest bidder for breeding." The words came out clipped "I am my own woman and I will have sex with whom-ever I please."

Lillian tried not to look shocked. She'd never heard a woman talk this way before and she noticed a deep discomfort followed by an undeniable curiosity. "Is that what you've been doing? Having sex with whomever you please?" Lillian tried out using Evelyn's straightforward terms and found the word *sex* strange on her tongue, but very liberating. She'd never considered having sex with a man other than Elijah.

"Yes, as a matter of fact, I have." Evelyn thrust her chin forward. Lillian's face must have betrayed her. "Oh, don't look so shocked, Lillian. There were really only two. I was curious, you know?"

"Curious?"

"What it would be like." Evelyn's eyes rested on her red fingernails, looking for chips. "I'm a modern woman. I believe women have a right to have sex without having to be in love and engaged to be married. That's what men do." She regarded Lillian as if this were the most practical advice ever dispensed.

Lillian wasn't conscious that she'd drawn back until Evelyn looked stubbornly at her, "Well, they do."

Lillian couldn't quite imagine having sex just for the pleasure, without the love. "You obviously don't believe in using protection, either." She immediately felt a blush warm her cheeks.

Evelyn laughed harshly. "That's the bad part. Unfortunately, I miscalculated. You see, I learned all about the rhythm method from Daddy's doctor books." She sighed. "And I was all set for the right timing, then... one of my...boyfriends... had to ship out a week early... and well... I decided to take a chance. Anyway, now I'm pregnant and I've ruined my life and all my plans. It's my own stupid fault." Evelyn's voice was bitter. Lillian knew the rhythm method well. How often it didn't work.

"If I tell my parents, I know exactly what will happen." Evelyn swiped tears and glared at Lillian. "Daddy can't have his precious little girl possibly getting bred by the wrong stock. I'm certain he'll try to force me to marry Lawrence. Daddy has to preserve his image. Having an unwed mother for a daughter would not fit into his and Mother's plans."

Lillian pulled her head back. What father thought of his daughter as breeding stock? There was going to be a baby.

Wouldn't that change their minds?

Evelyn continued, an ominous tone in her voice. "My daddy is not just anybody. He's the President of the Eugenics Society. Me having a baby on my own would cause him to completely lose face. His professional reputation would be ruined."

"What is the Eu... what kind of society?" Lillian had no idea what she was talking about.

"The Eugenics Society," Evelyn spat out the words with disgust. "It's this group of men, all doctors and scientists, who think that there should be a master race made up of the right people."

"Oh?" Lillian considered this. *The right people?*

"And that's not all." Evelyn reached into her pocket for a handkerchief and blew her nose. "I've read the stuff that Daddy leaves in his office. They intend to breed this all-white race by encouraging only certain people to have lots of babies. Do you know they even have a *Fitter Families Contest* going on in Staunton right now? Daddy fully intends for me to enter that contest someday."

At hearing the words "Fitter Families," a cold shiver ran down Lillian's spine. A greenish, sick feeling settled into her belly. Her mind filled with the image of two women, a blue hat with a yellow feather, a yellow-flowered dress... "Mrs. Stewart, we are members of the Fit Families Society." The words from long ago echoed in her mind.

"What kinds of people are *supposed* to have babies?" Lillian asked. Even though she didn't want to hear the response, she couldn't seem to stop herself.

"Only people who are from the right families and have a certain level of intelligence, go to church, have good-paying jobs, and live in town in nice houses." Evelyn's eyes glittered with anger.

Lillian harrumphed. "Well, I reckon I won't be entering the

Fitter Families Contest." She tried desperately to make light of this horrifying conversation.

"And it gets worse," Evelyn pushed on, so absorbed in her tirade, she was oblivious to Lillian. She creased the handkerchief and stuffed it again into her pocket. "The operations have slacked off now with the War and all. But, for a while the sheriff and his deputies would go out and round up boys and girls from up in the hollers and bring them to the hospital. My daddy operated on them so they couldn't have babies."

A sickening wave of icy darkness washed over Lillian. A flash of people swathed in white. Masks, gloves. Cold, hard steel under her back.

Her fingers, which were wound tightly together in her lap, reflexively loosened and spread across her belly. She took a deep breath to calm herself.

Was Evelyn babbling on because she was angry with her folks for keeping her cooped up? Could it be that the real reason Evelyn was having sex was to get back at her high-brow parents? Surely Evelyn was being dramatic, trying to get a rise out of her. "What are you talking about?" Lillian asked, trying desperately to escape the feeling of doom.

"At the lunatic asylum," Evelyn said. "You know, Western State?" Evelyn looked into Lillian's eyes, searching for recognition.

In the dark back room of Lillian's mind, something that had been pushed into a corner and covered over with a blanket, out of sight, out of reach, started to move. To stretch and unfold like a sleeping cat. Lillian willed it back to sleep. Lillian kept her expression blank. "Yes, I know it."

"Daddy does operations. He's done thousands of them. He has a chart in his office like some kind of score card." Evelyn held up her arms, spreading them wide.

"But why?" Lillian asked.

"The Eugenics Society says that mountain people are not

fit to reproduce—" Evelyn reached for Lillian's hands. "Oh, Lily, I'm so sorry. Of course, this isn't you or your mama. You mustn't think that." She carried on. "The eugenicists believe poor, ignorant people breed sick, ignorant children. They operate on them so they can't have babies. Or they keep them at the hospital until they're too old to have babies."

The floor under Lillian was going to give way. She would sink down into the ground and be covered over with black dirt. Whatever stirred in the far reaches of her mind crawled from beneath the blanket. An evil, ugly creature opened its jaws wide. She swallowed hard to stave off the wretched blackness. She forced herself to speak. "But those operations; they're to take out appendixes... so they won't become a problem later on..." She trailed off. The wall of her denial melted like ice on the river in spring.

Evelyn was so caught up in her own disgust, she did not seem to notice. She snorted. "That's what they tell the people up here..." Evelyn stopped. "Lily?"

Lillian's heart raced. Her thoughts blurred. *Could it be?* She pictured her fourteen-year-old self sitting in the back seat of the deputy's car, trying to assure Jo they were safe. Watching as Elijah, Daniel, and Ephraim climbed into the back of the Sheriff's car, punching each other and trying to act tough.

"Lillian, what's wrong?" Evelyn's voice was very far away.

Several minutes passed before Lillian could compose a thought or could allow herself to speak. She rose abruptly, leaving Evelyn sitting at the table, and moved quickly around the kitchen. She washed and dried her breakfast plate. She opened the cabinet to put the plate away, only to realize that she was staring into the icebox.

The memories of what had happened six years ago threatened to reduce her to a shameful heap. Drawing in her breath, she decided she did not believe it; not any of it. She would do *nothing* for this woman who had come into her home and rewritten in five minutes the story she had been telling herself for six years. What proof was there that Dr. Preston had taken away her ability to have babies? None at all. Ridiculous.

Then, as if her thoughts were an eddy in the river that abruptly stopped swirling, her mind cleared. "Evelyn, if I let you stay here, I want something from you."

Evelyn frowned and sat back in her chair. "I'll do anything."

CHAPTER 36

Miriam

CHARLOTTESVILLE
MAY 30, 2010

Miriam pulled the medical file from under her leg and laid it on the table between them. "When Olivia got your suitcase out of the closet on the day we were helping you pack, she found old medical files inside. This one is yours. She... um...we... looked at it."

Lillian glanced at the file briefly, but did not reach for it. Her mouth flattened into a line. She turned to gaze at the pond. Her tone was cold when she spoke. "You all shouldn't be prying into my private papers."

Miriam swallowed. Guilt threatened to stop her. "I know. We didn't mean to pry, but... I'm sorry."

"Sorry for looking at those records or sorry for what you found out?"

"Both."

Lillian frowned. She still would not look at Miriam. "Long time ago. No need to dig it all back up now."

Miriam fought down irrational anger with her mother. Did she honestly not understand that everything Miriam had known had been ripped out from under her? Was she really not going to talk about what happened? She forced herself to slow her breathing, to try to see the situation through her mother's eyes. This was uncharted territory between them. Her heart beat hard in her chest. "Mother, I know."

"What is it that you know, Miriam?"

Was it shame causing her mother's coldness? Embarrassment? Miriam fished for the right words. Not accusing words or hurtful words. But what was left? "I know that you're not my biological mother." There it was. Those words. Miriam felt a knot forming between her shoulder blades.

Lillian's mouth opened and closed. She frowned. Her eyes flicked around the ground as if chasing a laser light bouncing on a screen. A flash of something Miriam had so rarely seen. Anger? Quickly replaced with a closed mouth and set jaw. After a long gaze at the pond, Lillian turned to face her. Miriam's heart ached with the pain she saw in those blue eyes. Maybe she should have left it alone. But it was too late now. She was in it. She hurried on before she lost her nerve. "I think I understand how it happened...your operation." Lillian flinched as if the word stung her. "You and Daddy, his brothers, and Aunt Jo must have been caught up in some twisted, horrible campaign to sterilize poor children without their knowledge... or consent—" Miriam stopped to breathe. She shook with anger. "Why didn't you tell me?"

Lillian sat back in her chair and seemed to be staring into her memories. Miriam's heart ached for her. When she finally spoke, her voice was so quiet, Miriam had to lean forward to hear her. "I reckon I've been asking myself that question for sixty-five years, Miriam." She pulled the blanket up toward her waist and fussed with it, tugging and tucking. Her voice was ragged when she said, "It was a shameful thing. After I found out myself, all I wanted to do was put it behind me." When she looked into Miriam's eyes, her own were full of tears. "But then, I got to be your mama. And well... it was my second chance. I never looked back."

Miriam's heart rate quickened again. This was the part she wanted desperately to know, but was equally afraid to hear. "How?" She gazed into her mother's eyes, so full of pain and love. "How did you get me? I mean... where did I come from?"

A series of expressions crossed Lillian's wrinkled face. Her eyebrows rose, then lowered as she frowned. She set her mouth into a line and brought up her lower lip. Looked resolved. Miriam's chest tightened. She'd been holding her breath.

"Miriam, I have a story to tell you." Mother's voice was clear now, determined.

"I'm listening."

Mother took a deep breath, reached into her pocket for a tissue, and dabbed at her nose. She looked straight into Miriam's eyes and gave her the same wise, loving smile as always—the one that crinkled the corners of her blue eyes and brought out the dimple in her cheek. The same smile that had reassured Miriam her whole life. All would be well. But, for the first time she could remember, Miriam doubted.

Just as Lillian was about to speak, the gate between Miriam's yard and Dennis and Walt's creaked. "Hello," Dennis called softly. "We thought we'd check on you two." He crept toward them; Walt close on his heels.

"Bad time?" Walt asked, cringing. He and Dennis stopped and waited expectantly.

Miriam looked at her mother. Lillian inclined her head toward Miriam. "Up to you, darling. I reckon these boys would want to hear this too."

Miriam motioned them forward. "Mother was just about to tell me how she... um... how she and Daddy came to be my parents."

Walt gasped and clapped his hand over his mouth. He dropped his hand. "Miss Lillian, can you wait just one second?" He turned to Dennis. "Hold this." He handed Dennis the Mimosa in a champagne flute he held and rushed off toward Miriam's porch. He returned a few moments later with two of the folding lawn chairs she kept stored there. He opened the chairs, frowned at the dust covering them, but must have decided to ignore it as he pulled the chairs close, sat in one, and waved Dennis into the other. He leaned forward. "This is so exciting." His eyes gleamed. She tried to smile, tried to see the mystery of it all through Walt's eyes, but it wasn't working. Dennis, whose chair was beside hers, placed his arm across the back of her chair.

Lillian looked around at each of them, her face solemn. "As you already know..." She glanced at the file on the table, then back up to meet Miriam's eyes. "...Elijah and I couldn't have babies of our own."

CHAPTER 37

Lillian

HAZEL HOLLOW
FEBRUARY, 1945

Lillian's breath was a white cloud and ice crystals formed in her nose as she made her way to the barn. This winter had been especially cold. She had grown accustomed to wearing extra clothes because Evelyn could no longer bear to have the cabin too warm. Evelyn had reached that stage of lumbering heaviness in this last month of her pregnancy. Evelyn complained of being hot, yet she wouldn't budge from her chair by the fire, absently running her hands over her swollen belly and staring into the flames. Their conversations had slowed to minimal interactions.

Lillian was pondering Evelyn's condition when she startled from her reverie at the sound of Jo's shout. Jo marched across the pasture toward Lillian. "Mornin." Jo waved a mittened hand.

The fog had lifted somewhat and Lillian returned Jo's wave through a flurry of sleet. Lillian pulled open the barn door and breathed in the warmth of the animals. Pearl, who had long since been put to pasture, snuffled at the hay mow in the corner of her stall, and the cow, Bonnie, bawled loudly.

"Morning all." Lillian spoke softly into the warm stillness of the darkened barn. Leaving the door slightly ajar for Jo, she approached Bonnie's stall and retrieved the milking stool from where it hung on a nearby hook. Oh, to hold on to this peaceful feeling—the simple days of taking care of only herself seemed so long ago now.

The barn door opened and Jo stepped in, stomping her feet and bringing with her a whoosh of frigid air. "It's starting to turn to snow now," Jo said merrily. Snowfall brought out an innocent joy in Jo that was a thing of wonder. Lillian, who wasn't too fond of being cold, could pass hours watching Jo frolic in the snow.

"Best get the milking done quick then," Lillian said.

"You reckon Miss Evelyn's going to have that baby soon?" Jo asked.

"Not sure, but I *am* sure that she's ready." Lillian lowered herself onto the stool and patted Bonnie's rounded belly. Jo let herself into the winter chicken coop and hummed while she gathered eggs.

Lillian pressed her face into Bonnie's warm flank and reached for a teat. She pulled and squeezed. The only sounds in the barn were Jo's humming and clucking to the chickens and the tinny sound of Bonnie's milk hitting the bottom of the bucket. A powerful feeling of sadness descended over Lillian. She tried to shake it, but it caught in her throat. Like last summer when she had swallowed a tiny bone from a bream she'd caught from the river.

"I'm going to walk up and meet Pete at the mailbox." Jo set her egg basket at her feet and pulled on her gloves. "I'll drop the eggs off at the house."

"All right." Lillian kept her face turned toward Bonnie so Jo couldn't see her reddened eyes. "I'll be up to the house shortly."

Jo pulled her hat down over her eyes and left the barn.

Lillian finished up her chores and made her way through the thickening snow to the back door of the cabin. She shed her coat, boots, and hat, and hurried into the kitchen to put the coffee on.

As Lillian was setting the coffee pot on the stove, Evelyn burst from the door of the bedroom. Lillian looked up in surprise. Evelyn's countenance had shifted from that of a swollen-faced, sullen, burdened victim to bright-eyed excitement.

"Lillian, I found that bloody show you told me about in my underpants."

Lillian grinned and threw her arms around Evelyn. "Good. That's good." She matched Evelyn's excitement. "That means it won't be long now." Lillian reached down to Evelyn's huge belly. "Are you having any pains yet?"

Evelyn's hand was propped in its usual place on the small of her back. She shook her head slowly. "No, not ..." Evelyn's expression changed mid-sentence. She frowned, her mouth formed into an O, and she grasped underneath her belly, plopping down hard in a kitchen chair. "Oh, dear," she winced, squeezing out the words. "I think they're starting."

Lillian placed her hands on either side of Evelyn's belly and nodded. "Yes, they are. I can feel it. That was a pretty good one." She pulled up a chair in front of Evelyn and took her hands. "You ready for this?"

"I thought I'd be ready. It seemed like it was never going to happen. But now?" Evelyn squeezed Lillian's hands hard. "Oh, shit, Lillian. Do you think I can do this? What if I can't do this?"

Lillian laughed. Relief at the wonderful feeling a pending delivery always brought—of being outside of herself—washed over her. "I reckon you don't have much choice now." She reached into her pocket for the gold pocket watch that had been her mother's. "Take this." She thrust it toward Evelyn. "Time how long before your feel another pain."

The coffee pot started its burbling perk. Lillian methodically gathered her birthing supplies, taking comfort in the warm fire and the smell of strong coffee. Clean towels from the bathroom shelf. Her delivery bag, where she kept the strips of cloth to tie off the cord and her scissors to cut it.

This would be the first time she had delivered a baby in her own home. She had always pictured herself lying down in the bed she was preparing now. She had pictured Elijah on the porch, pacing. She probably would have called on a midwife from over in the next holler to attend her—just to help out a bit. But she would know exactly what to do. The best ways to make the baby come. The best positions for different kinds of labor—back labor, labor with a breech, labor that was too fast, too slow.

But now? Now, it would not be her having Elijah's baby. It would not be her gasping with the pains. Finally feeling the relief of the slippery baby emerging from her body. It would not be her seeing Elijah's beaming face as she handed him their child bundled into the soft blanket she was even now collecting from the drawer in the bedroom. Her chest tightened. She swallowed hard as she heard Evelyn's low keening when a second contraction seized her. She rushed into the kitchen, trying to breathe, reminding herself that this was not her body.

"Another one." Evelyn released a deep, guttural moan. "I don't think I can do this."

"Stop that," Lillian said irritably as she poured coffee for herself, and returned Evelyn's cup to the shelf. Perhaps some herbal tea in a little while for her. "Yes, you can." Lillian had to get ahold of herself. She was the midwife. Her job was to deliver the baby and support the mother. And for today, she had to think of Evelyn as just another mother in a long line of deliveries. "How long since the last one?"

"About twelve minutes." Evelyn started to breathe

normally.

"Good." Lillian nodded. "It could be a long day, Evelyn." She ducked her head to peer out the kitchen window at the snow. "The weather's going to make sure we stay in today."

Evelyn stood, still clutching her belly, and padded in her sock feet over to the window. "It's so beautiful," she said, a look of wonder in her eyes. "Do you think it'll get deep enough for a snowman?"

"Hello in the house." Jo barreled in, dropping snow from the jacket she jostled off as she walked toward them.

"Jo," Lillian scolded. "Take your coat off at the door." She reached for the coat and took it back to shake the snow onto the rug.

"Sorry, Lil." Jo looked sheepish. "Got the mail." She held out the bundle of letters she had stowed inside her jacket.

"I'm going to sit by the fire." Evelyn sounded discouraged.

"What's wrong with her?" Jo whispered in her not-so-quiet voice.

"Well, for starters, she's in the early stages of labor. Meaning... the baby is coming."

Jo dropped the mail onto the table with a thump. "You mean now?" Her eyes widened.

"Yep, that's what I mean." As much as Jo adored babies, she did not want to be anywhere near a birthing room.

"You think I'd best be heading home now?" Jo's expression said *please say yes*.

Lillian pulled Jo into a hug. She smelled fresh—pine trees and snow. She tousled Jo's cap of straight brown hair. "You go on home now. Come back and check on us in the morning."

———

Lillian reassured herself it was not unusual for a first baby to come slowly.

"Dear God almighty, how long is this going to take?"

Evelyn wailed. She writhed in pain with each contraction.

Each time Lillian patiently coaxed her to breathe. She imagined the little one making sure it was safe to come out into the world. Each time she checked Evelyn's progress throughout the long, cold day, she repeated this to herself. The snow made deep drifts outside the cabin as the afternoon light faded. By nightfall, the snow stopped and the stars came out. There was no moon, but the brilliant white of the snow created an eerie glow in the meadow across from the cabin.

When Lillian next checked the exhausted Evelyn, she was so relieved to feel the top of a hairy little head she sank back on the end of the bed and laughed for joy. "The baby's crowning." She gave Evelyn a wide smile. "That means it won't be long now." She grasped Evelyn's hot hands. "You can do this."

On the next contraction, Lillian readied herself for the last stage of the delivery. "The head's coming now, Evelyn." She raised her voice above Evelyn's angry groan.

"Dammit, Lillian," Evelyn yelled. "I'm never going to have sex again."

Lillian chuckled. "I doubt that's true. Now, one push. Just one. Then go back to your breathing like a hot old hound dog under the porch."

In spite of herself, Evelyn smiled, then, growling, she panted.

"A headful of black hair." Lillian grinned. She lifted her gaze from the baby's head she held between Evelyn's legs into Evelyn's tired eyes. "Are you ready? The next pain and you'll push her out."

"Her?" Evelyn said through gritted teeth.

Lillian could see the contraction was coming on fast. She'd had a feeling all along that this child would be a girl. But, for now, she ignored Evelyn's question. Evelyn moaned again and Lillian matched her volume with a loud, "Push, Evelyn, push."

The baby charged into the world from Evelyn's body,

bluish pink, covered in cheesy fluid, with a headful of black hair. Lillian tore her eyes momentarily from the baby to look up into Evelyn's exhausted face. She propped on her elbows, looking down at Lillian and the baby.

"You have a girl, Evelyn," Lillian said softly. "And she's a healthy-looking little thing, too." Evelyn smiled weakly at Lillian, then glanced at the baby and frowned.

"She's so small." Evelyn's expression was odd. Not the joy Lillian expected, not even happy relief. It occurred to Lillian she looked sad. Silly, she told herself, she's just tired.

"You lie back now while I cut the cord, then I'll hand her to you."

Evelyn collapsed back onto the bed with a heavy sigh as Lillian laid the baby on her rounded, softened belly. Evelyn did not reach for the baby, as Lillian expected, but once again, Lillian chalked it up to exhaustion.

The baby wailed softly. *Why, she's already raging at the world.* Lillian smiled. This child would be a fighter. She tied off the cord and clipped it, then, after expertly swaddling the baby in a blanket, she handed the small bundle to Evelyn.

"You go ahead and put her to your breast," Lillian laid out newspapers to hold the afterbirth when it was delivered. "That way the afterbirth will come sooner." She had a few minutes before Evelyn's placenta came. Her arms ached to cradle the baby girl. She moved up to stand beside Evelyn, who held the baby limply as the tiny mouth searched for her swollen nipple. Lillian felt an odd tingling sensation in her own breasts.

"You take her." Evelyn released an exhausted sigh. "I'm just too tired."

When Lillian took the baby, Evelyn closed her eyes and frowned. Lillian assumed the final pains of the afterbirth were starting. She nestled the baby close against her chest, noticing an unfamiliar feeling of tender fullness in her breasts. As she admired the perfect little round face and cupid's-bow mouth, she heard the cabin door burst open. She peeked through the open bedroom door. Jo stomped her feet, bringing in a rush of cold air and a flurry of snow from the cap she yanked off her head.

"Lil, the road's plowed," Jo yelled from the doorway. "And Pete delivered the mail."

"Shut the door, Jo," Lillian called. "You're going to freeze the baby."

"Baby?" Jo said incredulously, as if she'd completely forgotten Evelyn was in labor. "Can I see it?" She shut the door and hurried in sock feet toward the bedroom.

"Just a peek," Lillian said. "You're too cold to handle her now. Bring in some more wood for the fire and warm yourself up. I'm going to need you to hold her in a bit."

"It's a girl, then?" Jo stood on tip-toe and peered shyly over Lillian's shoulder.

"That's right," Lillian couldn't tear her eyes from the midnight-blue wide-eyed stare of the funny little face surrounded by a hat of dark straight hair beginning to poke out in every direction. Gently, she laid the baby on the top of the bureau in the nest of soft blankets she had made. She took a square of cotton, dusted the cord with burnt flour, and laid the cotton square over the stump of the cord. She picked up the scale and checked her weight. Seven pounds, six ounces. The baby wailed as Lillian put the preventive drops in her eyes. Once the drops were in, she stopped crying and opened her eyes wide.

"She's funny looking." Jo's smile was dopey. Completely smitten.

"All brand-new babies are funny looking, Jo." Lillian pushed her elbow out toward Jo. "Now go. Get yourself washed up and warmed up, and get ready to hold this baby for me."

"She's mighty little, Lil." Jo scratched her head and frowned.

"That's why you need to help keep her warm. Now, get."

Evelyn let out a soft moan. Lillian's cue that the afterbirth contractions had started.

Lillian stood in the doorway holding the baby. She kept one eye on Evelyn and the other on Jo, who did as she was told. She stoked the fire, washed her hands at the kitchen sink, sat down in the rocker, and scooted it closer to the fire. "I'm ready," she called.

Lillian brought the baby and settled her into Jo's waiting arms.

"What'm I gonna do if she cries?" Jo asked as Lillian hurried toward the bedroom.

"Sing to her," Lillian threw over her shoulder, chuckling. An awareness caught her—a deep joy at this new little presence in their lives.

The delivery of the afterbirth happened smoothly. Lillian placed fresh towels underneath Evelyn, who turned to her side and pulled her knees up. Lillian gently placed one of the new-fangled maternity pads Evelyn had insisted on between her legs to absorb the remaining blood from her womb. She covered Evelyn with the heaviest quilt she had.

"You sleep now." No need for this instruction. From the sound of Evelyn's breathing, she'd already fallen into a deep slumber.

From the other room, a small whimper. Jo launched softly into a selection from her repertoire of mountain songs. "Keep on the sunny side..." Jo sang, trying to replicate the Carter Sisters' Kentucky twang. Lillian smiled as she walked over to Jo's chair and once again felt the ache in her arms and breasts to feel the baby against her body. She reached for the baby and Jo stood, tenderly transferring her to Lillian's waiting arms.

A deep breath and renewed energy filled Lillian's body. Whatever Evelyn was thinking in refusing to feed the baby, Lillian could not control, but what she *could* do was make sure the little girl she held in her arms had the best crack at life any child could have.

"Jo," she said. Jo's eyes filled with relief at the sound of Lillian's take-charge voice. "In the pantry there are a couple cans of Carnation milk and a bottle of Karo syrup. Now listen carefully, because we might need to feed this little one, so we're going to mix up some milk for her."

Jo started for the kitchen and Lillian followed, shifting the baby to her shoulder and making soothing sounds. Jo found the Carnation milk, shook it, and popped the top. "What's next?" she asked.

"Light the stove, and pour the milk into a saucepan and put it on the burner on low. Add two tablespoons of Karo and about half a cup of water." Jo hurried to follow her instructions. Lillian found the box of extra supplies and stopped Jo in her process of heating the milk to pull the box down for her and set it on the table. She rummaged through the box and found two glass baby bottles and the nipples she had stored there. Most mothers she delivered breastfed their babies, but occasionally a baby would have trouble latching on and it could take a few days for the mama and the baby to work things out. For those times, Lillian kept a bottle or two in case the family couldn't afford to buy one.

She had Jo add another pan of water to the stove and placed the bottles and nipples in the water. "Turn that one up high," she directed. "We need to boil the bottles and nipples before we use them."

"Right." Jo stooped to peer at the flame under each pot.

The baby cried out and without thinking, Lillian opened her dress and brought out her small breast. She clasped her nipple between two fingers and lightly brushed the baby's cheek. Instinctively, the baby turned toward her nipple and opened her tiny mouth. Hungrily, she shaped her mouth around the nipple and began to suck. Lillian felt the sensation pulse through her body to her groin. She thought of Elijah again, and how his lips on her nipple caused her body to feel like this. But his lips created desire—a longing for him to be inside her, as deep as he could be. *This* was different. *So different.*

Feeling this baby sucking at her breast created an all-too-familiar longing, longing for all that was lost to her; all that she would never have. And while the milk for the baby warmed and the bottles and nipples boiled, she allowed herself to have this moment, giving herself and the part of her that was capable of succor to this baby girl. Jo knew better than to speak into the stillness. The only sounds were the bottles rattling in the boiling water, the fire crackling, and the sucking noises of the baby.

Lillian watched the baby and did not realize she was weeping until her tears splashed on the baby's forehead. She struggled to rid herself of the images she had held so close for so many years—the soft blanket of her dreams. Her with a baby at her breast. Elijah with their toddler on his knee. Her with the children in the vegetable patch. Him showing a boy how to use a new hunting rifle. Then, on to their old age and grown children. Grandchildren. She had played it out so many times it was as if she had a repeating movie reel in her mind. Time for those thoughts to stop. Soon, Evelyn and the baby would be gone and she would have to figure out a new reason to live.

————

Before the sun set the day the baby came, Lilian sent Jo home to take care of her animals and to check on her daddy. After Jo wrapped up in her coat, hat, and gloves, Lillian held her close, taking comfort in the warmth of Jo's strong, capable body. "I'm so glad you were here." Lillian gently pushed Jo by the shoulders out in front of her.

Jo dipped her head and scuffed her boot on the step. After

a pause, she looked at Lillian, fierceness in her eyes. "You done good, Lil. You done good by Evelyn. Can't nobody ever say otherwise."

Lillian attempted a smile. "You go on home now."

All through the long cold night, Lillian slept fitfully in the chair between rising to feed the baby her bottle and checking on Evelyn. She startled awake at one point and quickly got up to look at the baby in her cradle near the fire. She watched her little chest, counting breaths. Brought a finger near the tip of her nose. She smiled at her fearfulness. She'd done exactly what all mothers did in those first nights, worrying the baby might not be breathing.

Ignoring the sense of gloom descending over her, she threw on her coat and tramped out through the snow to the woodshed for more firewood. Halfway back, she was seized with panic. She had left the baby too long. She rushed back into the house, hastily dumped the armful of wood she carried onto the hearth, and ran to the cradle.

The baby slept peacefully; her tiny hands balled into fists and her little round mouth making sucking motions in her sleep. Lillian brushed her cheek with the back of a finger, and continued across the thick dark hair that sprang from her head like wild onions in the spring.

She yanked off her coat and dropped it on the floor. The baby began to stir, whimpering softly. Gently, Lillian lifted her from the cradle and sat down in the rocker. Bittersweet longing filled her whole body. Slowly, she pushed away the pain and allowed herself these stolen moments with Evelyn's baby girl.

CHAPTER 38

Lillian

HAZEL HOLLOW
FEBRUARY, 1945

The morning dawned with blinding sun reflecting off the snow tucked in around the cabin like a white blanket. Lillian felt punished by the beauty of it. Her feelings were as raw and tender as the yellow crocus trying to push through the snow.

She forced herself to stand and fill the coffee pot. She spooned coffee into the basket, lit the burner and placed the pot on the stove. Slowly, as if she watched chunks of ice drift by on the current of the river, she watched scenes in her mind.

Evelyn sitting close as Lillian poured over Dr. Preston's medical book and finally understood what had happened to her. Evelyn laughing as Jo tried in vain to teach her to fish. Her own hands gripping Evelyn's growing belly, feeling the strong movements of the little girl who now lay in the cradle. The excitement in Evelyn's eyes when the labor began. The fear and pain as she labored so many hours. All the intensity of the past few weeks would soon end with Evelyn and the baby's departure.

Lillian opened the bedroom door, the baby in her arms, just as Evelyn woke up. Lillian smiled, hoping Evelyn might show some interest in nursing the baby. "Here she is." She spoke softly and edged toward Evelyn, watching her eyes for interest. "This little girl is going to need a name. Any thoughts about that?" Lillian sat down on the side of the bed, her hip pressing into Evelyn's.

Evelyn sat up and gingerly propped herself against the pillows. She didn't reach for the baby as Lillian had hoped. "I want you to keep the baby," Evelyn blurted, her jaws tight.

Lillian instinctively pulled the baby closer and stood up, staring at Evelyn, unable to formulate a response. *Where was this coming from?* After several seconds, she shook her head at the impossibility of taking another woman's baby. "No. I can't do that." Lillian choked out the words.

Evelyn reached for Lillian's hand and pulled her back down toward the bed. "Why not, Lillian? It's perfect, can't you see?"

Lillian sat down, refusing to make eye contact. The panic inside her chest quickened her breathing. Evelyn put her hand on Lillian's shoulder. Lillian looked down at the baby girl's little face and felt such a spasm of fear she thrust the baby into Evelyn's arms and walked out of the room. "I'm going to pour a cup of coffee," she threw over her shoulder. "You want any?"

"Yes, please." Evelyn rose slowly and followed her into the kitchen, gingerly holding the baby.

Lillian snatched the pot from the stove, yanked open the cabinet door, and plunked the cups on the counter, hard. She picked up the coffee pot, watched the steaming liquid flow into the cups, and tried to sort through the muddle of her thoughts. None of them fit into the right places.

She'd just started to make a new picture of herself and Elijah *without* children. Maybe their love for each other would deepen. Maybe they would even leave the holler when he got back from the war. Become town people. The thought was far-fetched, but everything seemed so different now. Even though she had tried, no particular plan had ever become clear in her thoughts. Life without babies was a haze of possibilities, and they were all sad. So sad. But it was anger that pushed out her next words.

"Perfect?" Lillian couldn't look at Evelyn when she uttered the useless word. "To raise someone else's child? To never be able to carry a baby in my own body? To look at a child and see someone else and not myself or Elijah?" Lillian's anger closed her throat. Her breath came short. She choked out the words as she pushed a cup toward Evelyn. "You think that's perfect? How can you give away your own baby?" She managed to look into Evelyn's eyes.

"Yes, Lily. As a matter of fact, I do. I think it's a perfect solution for both of us."

What Lillian saw in Evelyn's expression at that moment confused her even more. There was no anguish. There was no fear, guilt, or even sadness. It was several seconds before her mind sorted what she saw in those green eyes.

Hope.

Something inside Lillian shifted. The picture in her mind came into focus like the bottom of the riverbed after the water settled. A baby girl in her arms. A tiny hand reaching up to touch her face. Elijah smiling as he took her from Lillian and gently carried her out to the porch, where he rocked her to sleep as he watched the sun set. She saw herself inside the cabin, making supper, and pausing from her work to look through the screen door at the pair of them.

Lillian clamped the flow of those thoughts as if she were clamping an umbilical cord. There was no such thing as perfect. And yet...

Was there still such a thing as hope? Hers had been crushed. The possibility for a baby had been taken from her body without her knowledge. She had wrestled with despair in the few months since she'd learned the truth about what happened. And now, a second chance to be a mother was standing before her in the person of Evelyn, this puzzling woman she had come to love, but could never quite understand.

Did she dare to choose this chance to be a mother? She needed to convince herself Evelyn could give away her baby because she didn't *want* to be a mother. Lillian could not fathom that. The very thing Evelyn didn't want, she needed like air.

"Aren't you going to want to see her? Be part of her life?" Lillian couldn't stop herself from being practical about how this might work. Maybe she would be like the nursemaids she'd read about in English novels. Raise the baby for Evelyn, a glorified nanny. Could she make peace with such an arrangement for the chance to give this baby a mother? She steeled herself, preparing for Evelyn's response.

"No." Evelyn's expression had changed. There was a resolute set to her mouth, a determination in her eyes.

Lillian thought of so many arguments. You will miss her terribly. You'll wonder constantly who she has become. You might change your mind. Lillian didn't know if she could live with these possibilities. But, on the other hand, could she live with herself if she didn't take this chance?

"I want her to be yours and Elijah's in every way." Evelyn looked into Lillian's eyes. "No one knows about her except you, me, Jo, and Mavis. Think about it. Because you're a midwife, you can fill out her birth certificate with yours and Elijah's names. I want you to be her mother, Lily. I promise you that."

Lillian sank into a chair and stared out the window. Evelyn did the same, holding the baby stiffly. The baby made soft grunting noises in her sleep.

Lillian looked again at Evelyn, trying to understand how she could do this.

"There is one thing." Evelyn leaned forward, her mouth a

straight line.

Lillian's small glimmer of hopefulness faded. Here was the catch.

"I want to stay in touch with *you*. I need your friendship. You are like a sister to me."

The baby wriggled and whimpered. Lillian's arms were reaching out before she could form another thought. Evelyn didn't hesitate to nestle the baby into Lillian's waiting arms.

Lillian was unable to speak for several seconds as she took in what Evelyn had said. Friendship. She struggled against the thought of not deserving this baby. How could she continue to be Evelyn's friend *and* take her baby? If she didn't allow herself both, how could she ever bear losing either? She could choose to remain as she was and not risk her heart. She could take a chance on what life had put in front of her.

Lillian held the baby close in the crook of her arm and reached for Evelyn's hand with her free one, pulling it toward her. Both their hands rested on the baby girl swaddled beneath the blanket.

"Friendship."

"Sisters," Evelyn said.

"Sisters."

———

Not quite forty-eight hours after the delivery, Evelyn emerged from the bedroom wearing her best fitted blue suit, a smart new gray hat, stockings, and pumps. Her hair was done, her skin glowed with health. "How do I look?" she asked, turning with her arms out, finishing with a flash of her green eyes and a shy smile.

"You look ready to take on the world." Lillian admired Evelyn from where she sat in the rocking chair, holding the baby. No one would ever know Evelyn had a baby two days ago. Even Evelyn's figure cooperated with her plans. A marvel. She picked up the small suitcase, packed Lillian knew, with just enough clothing for the journey. Two days on the train to Fort Des Moines, Iowa. The WAC training center.

"The War is almost over, but if I get there now, I have a chance of getting stationed somewhere exciting." Evelyn pulled a compact out of her handbag and checked her lipstick. "I have to take this chance."

Lillian nodded, still trying to comprehend that the baby in her arms was to be *her* daughter. Still trying to understand how Evelyn could leave, that she didn't want to be a mother.

"And Lily?"

"Yes?"

"I won't be back, you know?"

"I know."

———

Lillian watched out the window as the milk truck rolled away, taking Evelyn to the station. She turned and slowly walked to the baby's cradle. She cupped one hand under the baby's little bottom, the other under her head, and picked up the sleeping little girl. Tenderly, she kissed the wrinkled forehead and in her deepest, most secret places of longing, she claimed this baby as her own.

"We must give you a name, little one," she whispered, gazing into the baby girl's dark eyes.

Thoughts of a Bible story told by the traveling preacher floated through her mind. A baby named Moses, left in a basket in the river. The Pharaoh's daughter spotted the basket while she was bathing and plucked it out of the water. The baby's sister, Miriam, who hid nearby, offered their mother as a nursemaid for her own baby. A child given away to keep him safe. The sister who made sure he was protected. Lillian hadn't paid much attention as the itinerant preacher held forth about God preparing Moses for greatness. She'd been struck with the brave sister who made sure that baby got the mothering he needed. As Lillian held the baby in front of her and gazed at her peaceful face, she pondered the story. Finally, she bent and kissed the baby girl's velvety cheek. "I'm going to call you Miriam."

CHAPTER 39

Miriam

Miriam sank into the story of the young Evelyn Preston. For a moment, as she processed the revelation that her biological mother was Buddy Preston's sister, the aunt Rachel spoke of who had recently died. She lost track, momentarily, of what Lillian was saying. Miriam's oldest, if not closest, friend, Rachel, was actually her first cousin. She refused to let herself interrupt her mother's melodic voice, even though questions tumbled into her mind one after the other. Lillian had been tender as she described the months in Hazel Hollow during the war, when Evelyn hid away from the prying eyes of her parents and the community. Pregnant, unwilling to name—or perhaps uncertain of—the father. Miriam's father.

As much as Lillian seemed to try to soften the blow with her own joy at getting to raise Miriam, the fact remained. Evelyn didn't want her. Miriam was surprised that it felt like a knife to her heart. Near the end of her story, Lillian's voice weakened—from emotion or fatigue, Miriam couldn't tell. Finally, her mother fell silent; she seemed exhausted.

The sun had moved higher overhead, dappling the pond

and garden with warm light. Birds twittered and the air smelled sweet. Miriam tried to reconcile the beauty of the day with the roiling mix of emotions. Her biological mother had made a practical decision. One that gave her the future she wanted. So why did Miriam feel like the earth was falling away beneath her?

Dennis leaned forward and rested his elbows on his knees. "May I ask a question?"

Lillian looked from him to Miriam. "Of course."

"Is it possible that one of Evelyn's..." Dennis seemed to be searching for the right word.

Walt jumped in. "Suitors?"

"Yes, thanks." Dennis pinkened. "One of Evelyn's suitors was Native American?"

All eyes turned to Lillian. She frowned, looking puzzled. "Do you mean Indian?"

"Yes."

Miriam was momentarily relieved to have a more practical topic to hold on to. She turned to her mother. "I recently had a DNA test done," she said, dipping her chin to nod at Walt. "Walt and I were going to do this genealogy project together after I retired. You know, the whole family tree thing—"

Walt jumped in. "I thought it would be fun if we knew about our DNA."

Lillian nodded. "Mm hm." She smiled apologetically. "Sorry, but I don't rightly know what DNA is."

Miriam looked at Dennis. "Help," she squeaked.

Dennis patiently, and simply, explained. "We can examine DNA by looking at cells from our hair, or our sputum. DNA holds a sort of code for our bodies—physical appearance, personality... It reveals our ancestry... the people we've come from."

Lillian turned toward Miriam, curiosity in her eyes, "And you've gotten the results of this DNA test?"

"I have. My DNA shows I am forty percent Native American. That's why Dennis was asking about the men Evelyn had sex with." Miriam knew it sounded harsh. She didn't care.

Mother broke eye contact and turned to stare out across the garden. After a few seconds, she smiled and pulled her lips inward. She nodded slowly, as if some puzzle piece had just settled into place. "That explains it." She spoke to no one in particular.

"Explains what?" Miriam tried to contain her impatience.

"I thought Mavis was just spreading gossip," Lillian said.

"Gossip?" Miriam managed.

"One Saturday, just a few days after Evelyn had come to stay with me, Mavis's husband was down with the flu. He always brought Evelyn's mail up to the holler on the milk truck. But this time, Mavis had to step in and run his route. I met her at the mailbox and we chatted for a few minutes. I asked after her mother and she asked after Elijah and Jo—and Evelyn, of course. I invited her in for coffee. But then we agreed. Evelyn wouldn't want to see anyone."

Miriam crossed her legs and jiggled her foot.

"We got talking about the war and so many young men in the community either lost or still overseas. Mavis said how her husband had to break up a fight at the USO dance a few months before. Said he'd just recently remembered to tell her about it. Mavis said 'you know how men are. They forget the most important details.'" Lillian chuckled at the memory.

"So true." Walt glanced sideways at Dennis.

"And so... there was a fight..." Miriam urged. She glared at Walt.

"Yes. Between Lawrence Wilson and a Monacan Indian man by the name of John Beverly. Both of them had just joined the Army and were getting ready to leave for basic training camp."

Hearing the words "Indian man," Miriam felt a frisson of

anticipation.

"Now that I think of it, Evelyn told me about being sweet on an Indian boy when we were younger. But she lost touch with him when his family sent him to Hampton for more schooling. Called it a doomed love affair. She was always so dramatic, you know." Lillian looked around the group and smiled. "Not many of the old Indian families were left in the holler after they made them register as colored. John's family was one of the few holdouts. I knew the family. Went with Mama to deliver a couple of their babies. They seemed to have all but disappeared by the time the war broke out."

Dennis nodded. "The Racial Integrity Act of 1924. It's where the *one drop rule* originated. If a person was thought to have *any* Native American or African American family members anywhere in their heritage, they were forced to fill in colored on their birth certificates."

Lillian continued. "That's right. Mama was angry as a wet hen about her birth certificates getting changed." She paused, picked up her coffee, and took a sip. "Back to Mavis's gossip. Turned out this John Beverly must have been the same boy Evelyn had known all those years before. He had kept at it, just like Evelyn said he planned to do, until the courts agreed to let him register for military service as Indian, not Colored. That night, he showed up at the white USO, instead of the colored USO across the street. Lawrence Wilson, one of Evelyn's beaus, took it upon himself to show John the door. Not too gently, according to Mavis. That's when the scuffle started. Evelyn was serving punch that night. According to Mavis's husband, she stepped right between those two men, pushed Lawrence away, and left the dance with John. Acted like they knew each other."

Lillian looked at each of them. Her eyes came to rest on Miriam. There was a faint sparkle in her eyes. "I remember thinking, when Mavis told me the story, maybe he was

Evelyn's other fellow. But I put it out of my mind when Evelyn started getting letters from Lawrence. And—as you know—Evelyn never would say."

"You're right, Lillian," Dennis slapped his knee. "That explains the results."

Miriam was marooned on a raft in an ocean of disconnectedness. Did she feel less for Lillian, with the knowledge a different woman conceived her, carried her, gave birth to her? Then there was the fact—she still couldn't take it in—Lillian knew nothing about the man who was apparently her biological father. Had Evelyn loved him? Had she been trying to protect him?

She couldn't speak. She couldn't move. Through a fog she watched Walt rise from his chair and walk over to Lillian. He placed his hands on her shoulders and lowered his cheek to the top of her head. Lillian raised her uncasted hand across her body to cover his. "Dear, dear Lillian," he murmured. "Such a story. You are an amazing woman." Dennis nodded in agreement.

Tears welled in Miriam's eyes. The people in front of her were the only family she'd ever known. But what about Evelyn Preston ... and John Beverly? How was she supposed to factor them into who she was? She didn't know where to begin.

CHAPTER 40

Lillian

CHARLOTTESVILLE
MAY 30, 2010

Lillian took Dennis's arm as he helped her out of the car. Held on to him as they navigated the shady flagstone pathway lined with hostas and impatiens. When they reached the stone steps leading to the heavy oak door of Buddy Preston's residence, he paused. "Are you sure you want to do this, Lillian?" After all of the years of doubt and uncertainty, she'd never felt surer of anything. Especially after learning that Miriam had refused five million dollars because of what had happened to her.

"Yes, there are things that need to be said," Lillian replied as she squeezed his hand.

"All right, then. I'll wait for you in the car." They mounted the steps. Dennis released her arm, rang the doorbell, and gave her shoulders a light squeeze. "Good luck." While Lillian waited for someone to answer the door, he returned to his car parked in the circular drive. The car door closed. Dennis's presence was a comfort. She pressed the doorbell again. The deep gonging sound seemed to echo through the house looming over her. It wasn't long before the door opened and Rachel Howell appeared, a surprised look on her perfectly made-up face.

"Mrs.... Stewart?"

"That's right, Rachel. How're you doing?"

The child stuttered around, saying she was fine. Then she glanced over her shoulder. "Look, if this is about my grandfather..." She looked nervous. "Miriam has made it perfectly clear she doesn't want anything to do with the Preston Foundation." She stepped forward, closed the door behind her, crossed her arms, and fixed her eyes on Lillian. "And Daddy is sick. The doctor says it's his heart. And we've recently gotten news about the death of his sister... my Aunt Evelyn. They were estranged, you see. She left home when she was in her twenties and never returned. He's... well, he's just crushed. I really don't want him disturbed. So, if you'll excuse me—" She turned and placed her hand on the door knob.

"Wait." Rachel dropped her hand, recrossed her arms, and looked at Lillian, impatience in her eyes. Lillian's chest had tightened at the mention of her dear Evelyn's name. Buddy Stewart didn't even know her. He had no idea who she had become, how she'd lived her life, or why she'd chosen to never return to Virginia.

She pushed on. Had to get this girl's attention. "Rachel, I remember waking up one night—let me see—must have been more than forty years ago now. There was a commotion downstairs. My husband, Elijah, answered the door that night." Rachel blanched and looked down. "Do you remember that night, Rachel?"

"Yes, ma'am, I do." Rachel glanced nervously behind Lillian toward where Dennis sat waiting in the car. When her eyes came back to Lillian's, they were so sad, Lillian almost stopped. But certain things had to be said.

"Now, I never told a soul about you losing that baby. Never thought it was any of my business that you were pregnant before you and Beau married."

"Mrs. Stewart, you saved my life. You know how grateful I have always been."

"And I appreciate that. Now, I need to ask something of you. I need to see your daddy. There are things he needs to know."

"What things?"

"It's best if I talk to him."

Rachel sighed, opened the door, and motioned for Lillian to enter. "Come in." Lillian stepped into the marble-tiled foyer of the grand old house. A wide staircase with a polished oak banister swept in a graceful curve toward the upper floor. "This way," Rachel said as she opened a door off the foyer into a darkened room. Lillian's eyes adjusted to the dimness. The walls were lined with books. Behind a heavy wooden desk, Buddy Preston sat, poring over a document under the weak light of a green-shaded lamp. He looked up as they entered, his eyes rheumy. His wheezing caught Lillian's attention from across the room.

Rachel approached the desk. "Daddy, this is Mrs. Lillian Stewart. She's Miriam Stewart's mother." She motioned with her hand toward her father. "Mrs. Stewart, this is my father, Doctor Buddy Preston." Interesting how the child referred to her father as "doctor."

Preston raised his head, frowned, and pulled his glasses off, slowly lowering them to the desk as he glared at Lillian. "Stewart, you say?"

Rachel moved over to the windows and pushed back the heavy curtain. "Daddy, why do you always have it so dark in here?" She turned to Lillian. "Please, Mrs. Stewart, have a seat."

"Dr. Preston." Lillian dipped her head in greeting as she lowered herself into one of the soft wingback chairs facing the desk. Chair was so low, she prayed she'd be able to get herself out of it when the time came.

Buddy cleared his throat and coughed. Chest sounded rattly. "Now, if you're here to speak on behalf of your daughter, then I have to tell you, she has flatly turned down our money. Walked away and didn't look back."

Lillian took a deep breath and sat forward in her chair. "And she explained her reasons?"

Preston looked away. His hands trembled as he opened a cigar box and closed it again. Probably wasn't supposed to smoke any more. "Yes. Your girl made some mighty audacious accusations about my father." The effort to talk seemed to exhaust him.

Lillian did not relent. "All of which are true."

"Now, if you're here to start with more of the same kind of talk, I'll have my daughter show you out right now—"

"No, I don't think you will, Buddy," Lillian interrupted. "Not until you hear what I have to say."

His mouth dropped open. But he closed it again and remained silent.

"We were children when the sheriff and his deputies came to the holler for us. Elijah and I were fourteen. His sister, Josephine, was only twelve. Twelve, Buddy." Her heart raced and heat crept up her neck. "What right did he have to do what he did? Who made him God to decide none of us got to have children of our own?

Buddy reached into his pocket, pulled out a white handkerchief, and mopped his brow. "He was doing what he thought was right, Mrs. Stewart."

"Well, it wasn't right. It was dead wrong."

Buddy glanced up. A flash of something akin to pain or guilt crossed his face. Replaced quickly by a mask of denial. "I'm sorry you feel that way. I'll tell you like I told Miriam. There must be some mistake. After all, you and your husband... what was his name?" Buddy pushed papers around on his desk, adjusted the light, and generally kept his eyes downcast, refusing to meet her gaze.

"Elijah Stewart."

"Yes, Elijah. Seems that the two of you had your daughter, Miriam. And here she is all grown up and a brilliant doctor. Stubborn, but a smart girl."

Lillian waited quietly until he finally met her eyes. "That's where you've got it wrong, Buddy. Your father sterilized both Elijah and me. We weren't able to have any children."

"Then... what...? You adopted?"

"You might say that." Lillian swallowed hard. Now that it was time to tell the story, she wasn't sure she could. But she'd be damned if her Miriam would suffer from this man's ignorance.

"Look, Mrs. Stewart, I'm sure this is important to you all, but, frankly, I don't have the energy for this today. I've just found out that I lost my dear sister, Evelyn. And I'm grieving. So, if you don't mind—"

This was the moment. *Courage, Lillian.* "Yes, I know Evelyn is gone. Your sister is the reason I got to be a mother."

"What?" Buddy choked out the word. Another fit of wet coughing seized him.

Lillian waited until he caught his breath. Chose her words carefully. "Furthermore, Miriam Stewart, the woman you insulted by comparing her work to your father's, is Evelyn's daughter."

Buddy stood up so quickly he swayed. Lillian sat forward, thinking she might have to call someone to pick him up. He pressed his hands flat onto the desk surface and bent forward. His face flushed with the effort to breathe. "What are you talking about, woman?"

"Sit down, Buddy. I have a story to tell you."

CHAPTER 41

Olivia

"I think I'm going to have to give up my favorite jeans," Olivia sighed. She met Amy's eyes. "Are you laughing at me?"

Amy feigned a cough. "Of course not."

She bit her bottom lip, grimaced, and pulled the two sides of the denim waistband toward each other. Nope. Buttoning them was impossible. Time to give in to the baby bump.

She reached into the tiny closet—temporarily stuffed with hers and Amy's clothes—and pulled out her baggiest flannel shirt. She coaxed the shirt together over her swollen breasts. A frustrated growl. "Nothing fits anymore." *This is what you wanted, so why is it so frustrating?*

Amy stepped behind her. Lean, muscular arms encircled her belly. "We will buy you some of those cute preggo pants with the panel in the front." She nuzzled Olivia's ear.

Olivia jerked away and twisted to face Amy. "We most certainly will *not*." Horrifying image. Amy's sarcastic grin. "You're such a jerk." She pushed Amy aside. "Where are my yoga pants?"

"They're probably with the other laundry up at your

mom's house." Amy was distracted by a text message on her cell phone.

"What's up?" Olivia asked. Amy frowned at the screen, thumbs flying as she typed a response. She finished the text and looked up, staring into space. Olivia waited expectantly, trying to read Amy's expression. Her face was so... blank. "Ames?" Olivia stepped toward her. *Please, not another rejection.* Amy had been through so many interviews—and an equal number of rejections—since they'd moved to Charlottesville. Amy opened her mouth to speak, then closed it again and held up one finger, signaling for Olivia to wait.

"Oh, no." Soft-voiced, she stepped beside Amy and encircled her with an arm. "Is it bad news?" Each time Amy got another rejection, a sting of guilt. After all, it had been her crazy, impulsive idea to move back to Virginia. Pregnant again—after losing their baby last summer—coming back was the most certain she'd ever felt about *anything.* But... they'd uprooted their life together in Boulder—home, jobs, friends. It was a lot to ask of Amy.

Amy scooted away from Olivia and turned toward her, face animated. "It's actually good news." Her mouth went slack, slightly open. "I can't believe it." In slow-motion, she sat down in the chair next to the tiny cottage fireplace.

Olivia plopped on the end of the bed across from her. Curiosity itched at her brain. *Give her time.*

"Do you remember the staff job at Legal Aid?"

"Yes. The one they had just filled?"

"Yeah..." Amy looked down at her phone. Then, eyes up, she stared past Olivia's shoulder. Finally, she spoke. "The attorney they hired had a family emergency and had to turn down the job. And, well..." Amy grinned. Her heart leapt.

"And they offered you the job?"

"They did. They want me to start next week."

———

Skyline Drive in the fall was even more beautiful than Olivia had remembered. Hiking gear on, Amy at the wheel. Her celebratory mood made the day even more special. Red, gold, and orange leaves danced from the trees and eddied on the road before them. How differently things had turned out than she had expected.

First, there was her grandmother's shocking... sad... happy—how to think of it? —story. Then, the decision to move back and the chance to be close to her family again—in a whole new way. And also the unexpected opportunity to at least *start* to get to know Dad. Something within her had shifted. For one thing, Lillian's story crystallized her dissertation topic. With Uncle Dennis's help accessing the Western State records, she'd thrown herself into the work with renewed passion. There were so many people like Lillian, who had their choice to have children taken away. She wanted to tell their stories.

Amy clicked the blinker on and broke into her thoughts. "How are things between your mom and dad?"

"As far as I know they're going well." Dad. Such an enigma. Surprisingly, she felt a little more open to him these days. He could never replace Uncle Walt or Uncle Dennis. But... he was interesting, sort-of socially awkward. That is, until he began telling stories about his experiences around the world. His stories were...endearing. Strange feeling. "Funny, Mom asked me the other day if I thought I had *daddy issues*." She gestured quotation marks.

"What does that even *mean*?" Amy pulled the car off the road into the trailhead parking area.

"I'm not sure." Olivia turned and reached into the back seat for her CamelBak. "I guess she wants to know how messed up I am from the way she and dad chose to do their relationship."

Amy laughed. "Wow. Perfect opportunity to blame someone else for your problems, if you ask me."

"Right?" She grinned, then brought up her bottom lip. Turned down the corners of her mouth. "But you know... I don't think I do." She rolled the idea around. "It's like I told Mom, maybe I *should* have—if you ask a therapist—but I honestly don't think I do." The beauty of Amy's profile, eyes turned to stare out over the mountain ridge, caught at her heart.

Amy turned toward her and reached for her hand. "Or... Maybe it's because your mom was always honest with you. I mean... she made it clear your dad wasn't the kind of man to be around very much, right?"

"She did. So, when it came to feeling like I needed someone dad-like, I always had Uncle Walt and Uncle Dennis—well, more Uncle Dennis." She dropped her free hand to her belly, marveling at the little flutter of movement. It always caught her by surprise.

"Speaking of dad-like..." Amy ran a hand down the side of Olivia's face, tucked a curl behind her ear. "I heard from Nate. He's going to make it to the party."

"Good." She breathed out slowly. It all felt so... right.

CHAPTER 42

Miriam

CHARLOTTESVILLE
NOVEMBER, 2010

"Tell me again why we're having this party?" Dennis asked distractedly. He pulled a bottle of red wine from his monthly wine club subscription box.

"It's called a *gender reveal* party." Miriam was just as clueless, but trying to be supportive of Walt's idea. "Amy and Livy are going to find out the sex of the baby."

"So, can't they just tell us?" Dennis held up the bottle of wine to examine the label more closely. He pushed his glasses up on his bald head and turned to stare at her, eyes narrowed, mouth formed into a wincing expression.

"Apparently, they don't know yet either." Miriam dutifully spooned olives into the dish Walt pushed toward her. "They want us all to find out together."

"Oh, honey." Walt tapped Dennis's shoulder as he walked past him to the refrigerator. He pulled out a tray of shrimp. "It's exciting. It's something young people do now. Try to go with it." Walt had orchestrated the whole thing. He was looking rather smug.

"Okay, okay." Dennis picked up the small pamphlet to read

about his wine selection.

Miriam sorted the olives by color. A smile played around her lips. If anyone was more practical than she, it was Dennis. They'd both resigned themselves to the silliness of the gender of the baby as an *occasion*. When Walt turned away, they looked at each other and rolled their eyes.

As the three of them worked in companionable silence on the party preparations, Miriam thought back over the past six months. Surreal, it had only been a little more than four months since Olivia and Amy announced—at Dennis and Walt's Fourth of July party—Nate would be the sperm donor for their baby. Not one single person in this patchwork quilt of a family had been more surprised than she had.

She'd endured the Fourth of July party in emotional chaos, while trying to smile supportively. She had finally gotten a moment alone with Olivia. They gathered in McIntire Park, waiting for the fireworks, and she'd gently pulled Olivia aside. Her chance, but then she couldn't seem to formulate the question. "What... why...why the change of heart about knowing the donor?" she finally asked. "And why Nate?" she threw in.

"I don't know exactly." Olivia's face was relaxed, luminous in the evening summer light.

Miriam had been surprised by the ache of longing for a time so long ago, when her own life was new and opening up. "It just seemed right." Olivia sighed contentedly. "We both really connected with him. Amy was worried, at first, that it would be confusing if we knew the donor. But, Nate... Somehow, knowing Nate felt different. And, he's good with the idea..." She was distracted when a woman walked by with an infant in her arms.

"And does he want to be... *involved*?" Miriam had felt uncertain about how to approach the topic. *Wasn't the whole issue in the first place that the donor be someone they would never know personally, or even meet?*

Olivia met her eyes and squinted, pursing her lips. "Maybe, but not on a regular basis—you know, he wouldn't be like a dad or anything."

The irony of Olivia's reference to how a "dad" would be had not been lost on Miriam. She had opened her mouth to point it out, but, in the end, had simply nodded. Life was strange... so strange.

"Mimi, could you grab the puff pastry from the freezer, please?" She jerked back to the present at Walt's voice. As she reached into the freezer, she envisioned Nate. Tears stung her eyes. She wiped them quickly with the back of her hand and glanced at Walt to be sure he hadn't seen. Nate had been so excited when he left for his training in Africa. Thanks to Hugh's help, he had secured a staff job with a relief organization in Mozambique.

She missed Nate. *How strange.* Why had she never realized before how much he had become a part of her day-to-day life? Over his four years in her cottage, he'd become family— but father to her grandchild? *Uh oh.* She wasn't supposed to think of him as a father. This was all so complicated.

In her misguided attempt to find donors for Olivia from among her medical students, she had chosen the top academics, the most organized. Each of them had a plan, definite goals, and never veered. She'd never have considered someone like Nate. So... was it... ordinary? No, that wasn't it. Nate was far from ordinary; he was smart, handsome, spontaneous, passionate...

"Mimi?" Walt's insistent voice pierced her musing. "You look a million miles away."

"She's dreaming of being a grandmother." Dennis threw the sarcasm over his shoulder as he carried trays of shrimp cocktail through the swinging door to the dining room.

She tried to focus on Walt's familiar face. She'd just had a small epiphany. And she didn't want to lose it. "Walt?" She held the puff pastry in one hand, her other hand rested on the marble counter.

"Yes?" He glanced up from the stove.

"Do you think Nate is like Hugh?"

Walt stopped stirring, laid his wooden spoon on the spoon rest, and turned to look at her. His expression was grave. He stepped close to her and glanced toward the door where Dennis had exited. "Honey, does that worry you?" His voice was soft.

"So, the answer is yes... you *do* think Nate is like Hugh?"

"Well, of course he is." Walt's face opened in a wide smile. "Why do you think Livy and Amy chose him?"

"Believe it or not... Never occurred to me before now." Miriam stared at the box she held, marveling at how blind she could be. She set the puff pastry down and laid both her hands on the counter. She liked the solidness of the marble.

Walt circled her with his arms, and pulled her in for a hug. His clean, spicy scent mixed with the savory notes of his tortilla soup comforted her. "Oh, Mimi, Mimi," he sighed, "so slow to figure these things out." He held both her arms in his hands. "It has all worked out like it's supposed to."

She nodded. It did take her a while to see things clearly. Walt released her arms, and turned back to the stove. Dennis came through from the dining room, whistling. Miriam was relieved to see that Dennis's curmudgeon cloud had lifted. She began arranging the cheese board.

Looking up from the cheese she was slicing, she tilted her head. She pushed her glasses up on her nose with the back of her hand. "So, Walt, tell us how it all works—this gender reveal thing."

"Yes, what will happen?" Dennis asked.

"It's so exciting," Walt breathed, his eyes bright. The man loved any reason for a party. Even this. "There were lots of options: balloons, colored confetti. I even saw a gender reveal idea on Pinterest that used Silly String." Walt laid his hand on Dennis's arm. "Wouldn't that be fun?"

Dennis stared at him. "Wait... you've been looking at gender reveal ideas on Pinterest?" Walt looked down sheepishly and Dennis groaned.

"Thank god you're not doing any of that." Miriam focused on the smoked gouda. "What *are* you doing?"

Walt looked a bit peeved with them. "I had a cake made."

"A cake?" Dennis stopped transferring rolls to a basket.

Walt chuckled. "When they cut into it, it will either be pink or blue."

"Oh," Dennis smirked. "Okay, then." Miriam shook her head.

All three of them looked up when the doorbell rang. Walt glanced at the clock hanging above the kitchen sink. "Now, who could that be?" he mused. "The girls aren't due back from hiking for another two hours. I haven't even picked up the cake yet." Walt wiped his hands on the towel hanging from the pocket of his apron and left the kitchen.

Dennis paused with a knife poised over an apple. Miriam stopped midway between the refrigerator and the kitchen island. Walt's footsteps echoed in the entry hall. The front door opened. The distinct sound of Hugh's laughter rang out. "Look who I found at the airport."

Walt's gasp. "Good gracious, Nate. You're supposed to be in Africa. We didn't think you'd make it." Muffled voices drifted toward the kitchen.

"Is it too early for a drink?" Dennis dropped his knife, wiped his hands on a towel, and opened the cabinet for a glass.

She tensed. Dennis was her dearest friend. The last thing she wanted was to lose her closeness with him because of Hugh. She longed to plead. *Hugh is different now, more settled, less restless.* Maybe she had to convince herself first. That was going to take time. But how much time did she have left, really? "Make me one too?" She winked at Dennis. A frisson of relief at his familiar comrade-in-arms smile.

Walt burst through the door with Nate on his heels, Hugh bringing up the rear. "Look who's here." Walt waved his dish-towel in fanfare. "Fresh from saving the world."

"I don't know about that, Walt." Nate blushed as Miriam hugged him.

"Nate's a bit overwhelmed *literally* with the weight of the world right now." Hugh put his arm around Miriam and pulled her in close beside him. Walt smiled indulgently, but when Miriam glanced at Dennis, the smile drawn across his handsome face was tense.

"Drinks, everyone?" Dennis's voice was chipper as they all fell silent.

"Yes, definitely," Walt answered. "And, Nate, we want to hear all about your training before everyone gets here for the *big reveal* and we're all caught up with your... their..." He stopped abruptly and huffed in frustration. "How the hell are we supposed to refer to you, dear boy?"

She joined the others as they all turned to Nate. Walt had asked a very good question. She couldn't wait to hear Nate's response. He dropped his shoulders and looked down at the counter. His wavy brown hair was pulled into a neat ponytail. His ears were pink. "How about Nate?" He looked around the room shyly, then directly at her. Such intensity in his search-ing brown eyes. "I'm not pretending like I'm going to be a dad or anything like that. I mean... I love the idea of helping Olivia and Amy have a baby. And I'm sure I'll love him..."

"Or her," Walt chimed. He hurried into the dining room. In seconds, he returned with a bottle of whiskey.

"Or her..." Nate continued, looking flustered. "But they have to decide how they will... um... factor me in... so to speak."

Dennis focused on the whiskey sours. Walt returned to the stove. Miriam busied herself with folding napkins. When

Hugh chuckled, she glared at him. She struggled to see the humor in this. Dennis pushed the whiskey sours across the counter toward everyone. Hugh was the first to raise his glass. "A toast to biological fathers, *and...*" Hugh paused, waiting for their attention. They all looked at each other. And? "An even bigger toast to those who do the *real* work." Hugh thrust his glass toward Dennis first. Miriam's jaw relaxed and her face softened. The two most important men in her life clinked their glasses together. She fought back tears when one side of Dennis's mouth lifted in his lopsided smile.

They dropped onto bar stools around the island and sipped their drinks. The men chattered about Nate's first assignment. She lost herself in the comfort of their voices until a glance at her watch brought her to her feet. "I have to get Mother and Aunt Jo." She hurried over to the back door and pulled her coat from the hook. "The time got away from me."

"Don't rush." Walt squeezed her and whispered in her ear. "Lillian and Jo will be waiting for you. Everything here will be fine. Don't you worry."

CHAPTER 43

Miriam

ON THE ROAD TO HAZEL HOLLOW
NOVEMBER, 2010

Miriam was relieved to have an excuse to leave as she prepared for the drive to Hazel Hollow. She'd come to treasure the weekly solitary travel to the farmhouse to fetch her mother for weekend visits—their compromise. Last summer's revelations had shaken her out of her stubborn resolve. She'd admitted to herself that moving Lillian to Charlottesville was more harmful to her mother's well-being than any extension of life gained by her being close-by. Even more important, she'd begun to treasure Lillian as a whole person—not simply a mother to be enshrined. Lillian had loved, lied, kept secrets, worried, and made a life-time of decisions, big and small.

So often, in the months since she'd asked the simple question, "Where did I come from?" she had contemplated the past Lillian slowly revealed. Like a sculptor chipping away at a block of marble. The truth about Miriam's birth seemed to free her to share many other stories—there was so much Miriam had never known.

She turned on the car stereo and tapped the steering wheel to the rhythm of soft jazz. Her thoughts turned to the shock

last May when she'd found out about her mother's sterilization; the subsequent shift in her perspective when she began
to learn about her biological mother. Mothering is messy. No
formula for *how* to do it, *who* should do it. No guarantee of
what the outcome would be. Buddy's words that night at the
awards ceremony still haunted her. "You'll be doing your part,
just like my father did, to keep the unfit from reproducing."

———

On a hot summer afternoon in June, a month after the awful
scene at the Rotunda, she and Lillian sat on Lillian's porch,
sipping iced tea. Miriam shared with her mother what Buddy
had said about her work. Lillian rocked, nodded, listened.
Didn't act in the least surprised. With a long sigh, Miriam said,
"I always saw my work as giving women choices, you know?
A way to take control of their lives, their bodies—*not* me trying
to control who had children."

After a few seconds of silence, Lillian asked, "And now you
doubt that?"

Miriam stared out at the trees along the river, pondering
the question. Did she doubt? When she spoke, she felt as if she
was giving voice to something deep, something she hadn't
known before. "What he said, especially on the heels of finding
out what happened to you... shook me to my core." She looked
into Lillian's eyes and saw the empathy there. "But it pushed
me to realize something important. Maybe the most important
thing about my medical career." She snorted with a small
laugh. "Too bad it took me until retirement to figure it out."

"What's that, sugar?"

"You can't *give* a woman a choice, like you *give* her an in-
jection. She has to recognize she *has* choices—that she is a
chooser. You can only show her the possibilities." She picked
up her glass, met Lillian's gaze. She saw in her mother's eyes
complete understanding. Lillian Stewart knew all about choices.

———

She exited the highway onto the two-lane road up into the hollow. Lillian's words rang in her mind. "Sometimes—so you don't get eaten up inside with anger or guilt—you have to forgive other people for their choices. Sometimes, you have to forgive yourself for yours."

She'd questioned that notion of forgiveness. Seemed too soft. There should be consequences. But she'd learned that Lillian Stewart's form of forgiveness was not about being a victim. She'd never justified what happened to her, Jo, Elijah, and the brothers. What forgiveness had done was free her up to love more, to accept people where they were. Miriam had been the recipient of that love.

She gazed out the windshield at a cloudless blue sky, sharpened by the dry November air. She had struggled with being pregnant. Even more, with being a mother. Always torn between her responsibilities to Olivia and to her patients. Maybe—if there was a genetic test—she would be one of the ones *without* the Mother Gene. *Warning: Don't Reproduce.* But then, Olivia's lovely face, kind eyes, and earnest heart floated into her consciousness. She couldn't imagine life without her daughter. She wondered... had she done okay as a mother?

Who knew? Maybe it was *the mother choice*, not *the mother gene*. Most days now, she forgave Evelyn for making the choice she had. And, she celebrated Evelyn for having the courage to give her baby to a woman who wanted, and instinctively knew how, to mother. Miriam forgave herself for not being Lillian. Maybe, just maybe, she was more like Evelyn than she knew.

She considered Evelyn Preston; the woman who had reluctantly carried her for nine months. The woman who had maintained a lifelong friendship with Lillian. After their return to the farmhouse, her mother had shown her the only photograph she had of Evelyn—the one taken of the two of them in 1938, to commemorate the opening of the new library in Staunton.

Miriam had held the yellowed, sepia-toned photograph in trembling hands. She scrutinized Evelyn's confident smile, the bicycle she held against her hip, the basket full of books, her shiny short curls, the wide-legged pants and saddle shoes. She searched for something familiar in Evelyn. Relief muddled with defeat. She could not find herself in Evelyn. Then she examined the young Lillian. Lillian stared solemnly into the camera, clutching a stack of books lovingly to her chest. Her freckled face was framed by long braids. She wore faded overalls and scuffed shoes. In young Lillian, Miriam saw her mother.

From beneath the photograph, Lillian had pulled a stack of postcards; all from Evelyn. The oldest from the WAC training center in Des Moines, Iowa, dated March, 1945. Then postcards from England through the end of the war. Afterward, into the 1960s, Miriam counted at least ten different countries where Evelyn had traveled. A memory seized Miriam then. She was eight years old. She had run up the back steps and wandered through the house, calling out, "Mother... where are you?" She found Lillian on the porch, reading a postcard. "Who is it from?" Miriam admired the exotic picture of an elephant, palm trees, colorful flowers.

"A dear friend." Her mother had a far-away look on her face. "You go on in and get your homework done, now." She smiled and dabbed at her cheek with a handkerchief. "I made us a special treat for supper." Thinking back on it, Miriam remembered flopping onto her bed and opening her science book. She'd thought then how odd that her mother—who never wanted to leave home—had a friend who traveled all over the world. Time, and preoccupation with her own life, had erased her memory of Lillian's delight in those postcards.

There were only a few red and gold leaves clinging to the trees as she wove her way on the curvy road toward the farmhouse. Soon, another winter would arrive. Along with it, so many changes. Continuing to sort out this retirement thing, becoming a grandmother, Hugh's renewed presence in her life. She contemplated her reaction that day her mother had shown her the postcards.

"I'm just not sure how I feel about *not being wanted.*" Miriam struggled with the muddle of feelings still so new to her. She held her breath and hoped Lillian would argue differently. But she didn't. She simply nodded. Which only confirmed her suspicion. Not wanted. She was irritable, edgy with emotions she couldn't reconcile.

After several seconds of silence, Lillian looked into her eyes, her gaze serene. She reached out and caressed Miriam's cheek with a cool, soft hand. "My sweet Miriam, you were so *very* wanted. I wanted you more than you can imagine. Watching Evelyn go through those last weeks of her pregnancy was one of the hardest things I've ever done. Do you know why?" Lillian's eyebrows lifted as she cocked her head to one side.

"Because you knew you couldn't have a baby." Miriam's gut wrenched. Was it torture for her mother, watching Evelyn's pregnancy, knowing she would never have the experience?

"Yes." A flicker of pain in Lillian's eyes. "And while I was trying *not* to want you, Evelyn—I truly believe—was trying to *want* to be a mother."

"But, she didn't." Miriam contemplated this idea.

"No, darling, she didn't. I know how hard it is to understand. It took me a long time to take it in. But I finally had to step out of my own way of seeing things. I looked at the world through Evelyn's eyes. Me being your mother truly *was* the perfect solution—just as Evelyn said the day she told me she wanted me to keep you." Lillian paused and looked down. After several seconds, she looked up, her eyes searching. "Do you think you can live with that?"

No ready answer came. Evelyn had been able to fulfill her dreams; join the WACS, meet a man in Paris who loved her and wanted to be... how had Evelyn phrased it on her postcard? The line was so painful when Miriam first read it. "He wants to be free too, Lily. Life with Charlie is such an adventure, and I'm so happy."

Miriam remembered finding out she was pregnant with Olivia. The turmoil. Wondering if she could follow her own dream to practice medicine and be a mother at the same time. Yes, in 1980, she had that choice. In 1945, she wouldn't have.

She had reached for her mother and enfolded her into a hug. She soaked in Lillian's strength, allowed herself to experience how much she was loved and wanted by this woman who had willingly, joyfully been the solid ground she could always return to. "Yes. I can live with that."

She allowed herself the deep contentment of knowing she had *exactly* the right mother. She also gave in to the searing pain of how short the time left with Lillian would be. She vowed she'd make the most of the years they had left together... on Lillian's terms.

As Miriam made the last turn toward the farmhouse, she wondered what her life might have been like had she been born into—or brought up by—the Preston family. Buddy Preston had died of heart failure in August. She'd decided not to attend the funeral, even though she now knew he was her uncle and Rachel, her first cousin. Her sense of loyalty to Lillian, along with her unresolved anger, had held her back. One of the biggest shocks of her life was the day in September when Rachel had called.

———

Miriam was making her bed when the call came in. She was surprised to see Rachel Howell's name pop up on her cell phone screen. She tapped to answer. "Hello?"

After an awkward greeting, Rachel said, "We've just come from the reading of Daddy's will. I wanted you to know Daddy left you the money."

"What money?"

Rachel's voice was tense. "The five million for your contraceptive center."

She sank to the floor, her back against the bed. "But... but, I thought I was clear, Rachel. I can't take your father's money. Not after what happened with my mother and father."

"I think you'll see this differently when you hear what the will says."

She agreed to meet Rachel for lunch at The Nook at the pedestrian mall in Charlottesville. Rachel arrived looking as gorgeous as the September day, dressed in russet-colored slacks and a vibrant gold jacket, her blond hair falling softly around her shoulders. Miriam's heart ached. Could they ever recover the friendship they'd once shared?

They ordered burgers and fries. "Remember how we'd drive all the way from Staunton back in the day to meet the guys here for burgers?" Rachel's voice was wistful.

"Yeah, I remember. Those were good times." Miriam thought of the young women they'd been; the women they'd become. Connecting in the same way with Rachel again seemed hopeless.

Their food arrived and they busied themselves preparing to eat. Rachel took a bite of her burger, then set it on the plate, and reached into her purse. She slid a folded piece of paper across the table toward Miriam. "Here's a copy of the part of the will that involves you."

Miriam wiped her hands on her napkin and reached for the paper. She unfolded it and read the brief paragraph, focusing on the words: *Miriam Stewart is free to use the money in any way she sees fit without expectation of attribution to the*

Preston name. She met Rachel's eyes. "So, what does this mean, exactly?"

"It means Daddy had a change of heart. You can build your center, if you still want to. There's no expectation that it be named after the Prestons."

Miriam was speechless. She tried to gather her thoughts. "But... why?"

"Lillian." Rachel dropped her mother's name into the space between them and sipped her Coke. She stared at Miriam as if waiting for her to comprehend.

"My mother?"

Rachel nodded slowly, a smile playing around her lips. "Apparently, it was quite a story your mother told about my Aunt Evelyn." She set her drink down and looked into Miriam's eyes. "Cousin."

It had been Olivia's idea to dedicate the contraceptive center to her grandmother. And to have a plaque commemorating the men and women whose choices were taken away during those years when the mass sterilizations occurred. The name of the center would be the Lillian Stewart Contraceptive Choice Center. They'd break ground for the building in the spring. Rachel and Miriam would never completely see eye to eye. But at least they were talking again. Today, Miriam decided to focus on hope.

She pulled the Volvo into the drive and got out of the car, pulling her coat closer against the chill. As she mounted the porch steps, she noticed a small package leaning against the screen door. She picked it up and read the label as she entered the farmhouse. "Mother. I'm here," she called. The postmark on the package was from France. Strange.

"Mornin," Jo called from the kitchen. "We're back here. Wrapping up Lil's apple cake."

Miriam walked into the sunny kitchen. The scent of coffee and the cinnamon, nutmeg, and cloves of Lillian's famous freshly baked apple cake filled the air. Jo grinned with anticipation for the trip to Charlottesville. Lillian smiled and turned her cheek up for a kiss. "What you got there?"

"I don't know. It was leaning against your door." Miriam turned the small package over. It was wrapped in brown paper and taped securely. "It's postmarked from France."

"Open it, Lil," Jo insisted.

"Hold your horses." Lillian pulled a pair of scissors from the drawer. She handed them to Miriam with a trembling hand. Miriam sliced open the wrapping with one side of the scissor blades. Inside was a small box. She handed it to her mother, who opened it and removed a folded note. Silently, Lillian read it and handed it back to her.

"Read it out loud, Miriam," Jo urged.

Miriam glanced at her mother, who nodded. "It says, 'Dear Lily, Evelyn wanted you to have this, since you were the reason she was able to serve.' It's signed Charles."

She and Jo stood on either side of Lillian and peered over her shoulders as she looked at the contents of the box. Against a blanket of dark blue velvet lay a bronze military medal attached to a bright green and gold ribbon. "Women's Army Corps," Lillian read. The inscription encircled the helmeted head of the goddess Athena, depicted against the background of a sword and oak and palm leaves. Lillian reverently touched the medal. "Isn't that something?" Miriam glanced at Jo, who looked at Lillian with adoration in her eyes. As kept happening lately, Miriam was at a loss for words.

Lillian broke the silence as she closed the box and set Evelyn's medal carefully in the middle of the kitchen table. "We best get this cake in the bag and get our coats on, Jo. We've got a party to get to." Her eyes twinkled as she winked at Miriam.

CHAPTER 44

Lillian

CHARLOTTESVILLE
NOVEMBER, 2010

Lillian sat in her new chair and watched the festivities. Walt and Dennis had given her the soft leather recliner for her birthday. "We'll keep it here for when you visit," Walt had said. Such a sweet man, that one. What a good father he'd have made.

"This is a good spot, Lil." Jo grinned in appreciation when Dennis placed a chair for her beside Lillian's. She dug into her cake with enthusiasm.

"Yes, it is." She smiled with contentment. It was good to have Jo here today. They had both been so sad over the past few months, since Scrap died. Although she still didn't much like leaving home, a day or two on the weekend wasn't too much for Miriam to ask.

Her chair was stationed in the corner by one of the floor-to-ceiling windows in the room Dennis called the *great room*. Her favorite spot. She could gaze out the window and watch Walt's garden change as the seasons passed. Even better, to-day, she watched the goings on at the party without being in the middle of everything. She was a little embarrassed her hearing wasn't what it used to be. But truth be told, she'd never been the chatty type, so sitting and looking-on suited her perfectly.

She'd had a good chuckle when Miriam explained the purpose of today's party. *What would they come up with next?* Lillian looked around the room. Olivia had healthy color in her cheeks now. She gestured toward her belly and laughed about some little story she was telling Amy's parents. Nice folks. Flew in all the way from... Wyoming? Someplace that sounded like one of those Westerns Elijah used to love to watch after they'd gotten their first television.

Oh, how she missed Elijah today. So many years without him. Still made her heart ache to think of his crooked smile, those dove-gray eyes. *Lord, I feel old.* Family gatherings always made her long for him. In their early days together, he had loved nothing better than to wrap Miriam up in her blankets and walk over the ridge to gather with his brothers and Jo at the old family cabin. His oldest brother, Kenneth, had married a woman from near Charlottesville and moved off. But he'd bring her and the kids for Thanksgiving. Up until Miriam had come along, Kenneth had been the only one with children—on account of the operations. Elijah was so proud of his baby girl.

She remembered with the clarity that only old-age can bring, the day Elijah came back from the War. March 18, 1945. She was standing at the mailbox. She'd left Miriam in the cabin, asleep in her cradle. The weather had been dry that spring, the air was balmy and scented with the daffodils growing around the mailbox. She'd turned to go back into the cabin when she caught sight of him. Her hand flew to her mouth when she recognized his tall figure on the road. The dust kicked up from his boots as he walked up the road toward their cabin. Still wore his uniform.

He had been shy with her when he finally reached the

cabin. Almost like he wasn't sure of himself, or of her, after so much time apart. Her own heart had pounded in her chest. Felt alive again for the first time since Evelyn left.

She smiled now, remembering what she'd said to him, as he'd stood there, hat in hands, looking around with hungry eyes at their homeplace. "Elijah Stewart, you'd better kiss me before you start thinking about what you're going to do on this farm now you're finally home."

She reached up to brush away a tear as Nate approached. She smiled as he held out a coffee cup toward her. "Just the way you like it, Miss Lillian," he whispered loudly and winked at her.

"Thank you, Nate." He'd put a splash of that Irish crème in it. What a nice little discovery that had been. "Sit with me for a minute." She gestured toward the big floor cushions stacked near the chair, on the other side of where Jo sat, deep in conversation with Walt.

Nate set his bottle of beer on the floor and easily flexed his young body onto the cushion. He stretched his legs out in front of him. He was dressed in a flannel shirt that looked like it had seen quite a bit of wear, loose-fitting jeans and scruffy brown boots. He crossed his ankles and leaned on one arm, his face close to her chair. They surveyed the room together in silence.

Lillian pondered the complicated notion: Nate was the father of her grandchild, but *not* the father—according to Olivia. What was it she had called him? The donor. That was it. But how...

"Nate?"

"Yes, ma'am?"

"Call me a nosy old grandmother, but I was wondering about how things work with what you youngsters are doing. They tell me you're not called the father of the baby... you're the..."

Nate looked up at her and took a sip of his beer. "The

donor. Yes, ma'am?"

"Does that mean that you and Olivia... well, you know what I mean... did you..." She was frustrated with herself now and wished she hadn't asked. After all, it wasn't her business.

Nate look puzzled for a moment and then realization seemed to dawn on him. "Oh..." He blushed as pink as the cake Lillian held in her lap. "You mean, did we..."

Lillian nodded, relieved he knew what she was asking.

"Gosh, no," he said quickly. "Um... not that I wouldn't want to... but, well... anyway, I..." She waited patiently. They were in this conversation now. Might as well finish it. He looked at her, his eyes squinted with embarrassment. "It was in a cup. And then Olivia and Amy... you know."

Oh... now she understood. Sort of. She nodded to reassure Nate he didn't have to say more. He looked relieved and turned to face the party again, ears still glowing pink. She sat back, took a bite of her cake, and marveled at this arrangement. Seemed to suit the three of them. Wonders never ceased.

Interesting to watch each of the couples—Walt and Dennis, Miriam and Hugh, Amy and Olivia, Amy's parents. Connecting and disconnecting, they all visited with each other. Walt left Jo to chat with Hugh, then moved back to Dennis, who was talking to Miriam. Walt pointed to the table and pulled Dennis toward the kitchen. Miriam walked over and put her arm around Amy and said something. They laughed, then Miriam strolled over to Hugh as Amy turned back to her mother. Hugh launched into telling one of his stories to Amy's father. Lillian knew this by the big gestures he was making and the fact that Amy's father began to laugh so hard he pulled a handkerchief from his pocket to wipe his eyes. That Hugh could spin a yarn. When it came to storytelling, he reminded her of Elijah. Elijah could always tell a good story.

She looked at Nate. Handsome young face. The beginnings of a beard. He would look right nice with a beard. She'd loved a beard on Elijah. No matter how she tried to stay focused on the here and now, it seemed everything today made her think of him.

MARCH, 1945

Lillian and Elijah sat at the kitchen table for a long, long time talking on the day Elijah came back. After she told him the truth about what had happened to him, to his brothers, to Jo and to her, he'd simply said, "What's done is done." When Miriam began to cry, he jumped like he'd heard a gunshot. "Lillian?" He half-stood from his chair. "Was that a baby?"

Her stomach weighed heavy with dread. She could no longer put off telling Elijah the whole story. Would he be angry? Would he refuse to raise a child who wasn't his own? She stood quickly and held up her hand to stop him. "You stay here." She forced herself to contain her nervous excitement. This was the moment of truth. "I'll be right back."

She returned with Miriam in her arms. Scarcely a month old; she was beginning to fill out from the shriveled-up little red blotchy thing she'd been. Her black hair could not be tamed, and it stood out in clumps from her head like a Banty rooster's comb. "I need you to meet somebody." She carefully placed Miriam in his arms. He looked from her to Miriam and back, mouth open, eyes searching. "Now, before you speak, I need to tell you something." She pressed on, urgently relayed Evelyn's story and everything that had happened. She scarcely stopped for breath. "And so... I kept her."

He did not look up from Miriam's little face the entire time Lillian spoke. There were a couple times she wondered if he was listening. After several moments of silence, he finally looked into her eyes. All her worry had been silly. "I reckon I'll build us a proper house," he said softly, turning Miriam onto his knees to face him. Lillian laughed with the joy of it. "Now that we have ourselves a little girl to raise and provide for. I reckon we're lucky to have her." And that was all that was ever said.

————

Now, there would be another Stewart girl. Lillian took another small bite of the cake she had watched Amy and Olivia cut into a little while ago. She never thought she'd live to see her own granddaughter—or any woman for that matter—mail order a baby. Because, as best as she could understand it, that was what Olivia had done the first time she tried to get pregnant. She heard again Olivia's sobs as she miscarried the first baby. The darkness of the thought shaded her mood. But Olivia had rallied. She and Amy had made a new decision for themselves. Certainly, none of it was the way folks usually did things. But the *usual* way was not always the *only* way, or even necessarily the *best* way.

Her gaze turned to her daughter. Still so beautiful. Miriam's eyes were full of...was that love? ... as she listened to Hugh. She was softer these days. More apt to laugh. Lillian loved her daughter's laugh. Miriam reached out to touch Hugh's arm every now and then. As if she wanted to make sure he was still there. Lillian had a little burst of hope and smiled at her silliness. Everyone knew Miriam and Hugh had been satisfied with their separate lives over the years. But now... well, it would be good to see Miriam have that steady, day-to-day love.

Had she been a good mother to Miriam? Miriam had certainly been angry when she first told her the truth. She had planned to take the secret to her grave, but she supposed it wasn't meant to be. Oh, how Miriam had raged against those people like Dr. Preston who took away so much from so many folks. "Mother, why haven't you ever done anything about this?" she had demanded. "The state of Virginia should compensate you for this."

But Lillian didn't want compensation. What was she going to do with the money? And how would that change anything? No. What had changed her life was being Miriam's mother.

Funny old thing, this life. During Miriam's angry stage, Lillian had spent a lot of time listening to her daughter work through things. One particular day, toward the end of the summer, Miriam had slammed her hand down on the table. "They had no right, Mother." Her eyes blazed. "They took away your choice."

The words of the nurse so long ago had echoed through Lillian's mind. "Lillian, you can cooperate with the operation, or you can live with us here at the hospital."

Miriam and Olivia were chatting now. Her heart filled when they both looked her way and smiled. She *had* made a choice. And it had been the right one.

She hoped she lived long enough to meet the new baby. She was pleased with her decision to leave the farmhouse with Olivia, Amy, and their baby girl. A good place for the three of them to make their family. Just as it had been for her and Elijah and Miriam.

ACKNOWLEDGMENTS

Many thanks to the team of experts at Atmosphere Press for your support of my work: Alex Kale, Managing Editor; Matthew Fielder, Cover Designer; Erin Larson, Production Manager; Cameron Finch, Book Publicity Director; and especially Asata Radcliffe, Developmental Editor, for your insightful guidance.

Tremendous thanks and love to my dear friends, critique partners, and fellow writers, Gina Edwards and Rhett DeVane. You gently pointed out my persistent writing errors. Will I ever learn? You made me laugh when I wanted to cry. Most of all, you comforted me through the necessary loneliness of writing a novel.

To Tricia Harris, much love and gratitude. We have shared this mothering journey since the time baby Claire threw up on my grandmother's handmade quilt. You are everything *chosen family* means to me.

To Honey Lea Gaydos, for your willingness to shift roles at any moment from cherished friend to stand-in therapist. I count on you for a kick-in-the-ass when I'm wallowing or tamping down. As James Hillman says in *The Soul's Code,* "...we seek friends that we may be seen, and blessed." You have truly seen me—warts and all—and blessed me with your friendship. Thank you.

To my grown-up children, Lindsay, Josh, and Haley. Thank you for letting me try this mothering experiment. I know there are times I get it right and other times I am ill-equipped. But that's why we have our Sue, right? To my granddaughter, Olivia, thank you for giving me a chance to work on the fun parts. And finally, eternal gratitude and love to my wife, Sue, for your extraordinarily loving heart, sustaining confidence in my work, and for having the mother gene when I don't. You are my rock.

BOOK CLUB
Discussion Questions

1. *The Mother Gene* introduces lots of types of women and mothers. Which one do you relate to the most, and why?

2. Do you remember a fictional, movie, or television mother who influenced you as a child or young woman? What was it about her that you wanted to emulate?

3. *The Mother Gene* includes several different types of mother/daughter relationships. How did you respond to the relationships between Lillian and Miriam, Miriam and Olivia, Mary O'Toole and Lillian, or Alva Preston and Evelyn?

4. What are your thoughts about women's choices when it comes to being a mother?

5. Do you believe certain people should *not* be allowed to have children? If so, which people and why?

6. What are your thoughts about *chosen* family in contrast to biological family?

7. Miriam dreams of a mother gene—a scientific predictor of predisposition for mothering. What are your thoughts about this idea?

ABOUT ATMOSPHERE PRESS

Atmosphere Press is an independent, full-service publisher for excellent books in all genres and for all audiences. Learn more about what we do at atmospherepress.com.

We encourage you to check out some of Atmosphere's latest releases, which are available at Amazon.com and via order from your local bookstore:

Icarus Never Flew 'Round Here, by Matt Edwards

COMFREY, WYOMING: Maiden Voyage, by Daphne Birkmeyer

The Chimera Wolf, by P.A. Power

Umbilical, by Jane Kay

The Two-Blood Lion, by Nick Westfield

Shogun of the Heavens: The Fall of Immortals, by I.D.G. Curry

Hot Air Rising, by Matthew Taylor

30 Summers, by A.S. Randall

Delilah Recovered, by Amelia Estelle Dellos

A Prophecy in Ash, by Julie Zantopoulos

The Killer Half, by JB Blake

Ocean Lessons, by Karen Lethlean

Unrealized Fantasies, by Marilyn Whitehorse

The Mayari Chronicles: Initium, by Karen McClain

Squeeze Plays, by Jeffrey Marshall

JADA: Just Another Dead Animal, by James Morris

Hart Street and Main: Metamorphosis, by Tabitha Sprunger

Karma One, by Colleen Hollis

Ndalla's World, by Beth Franz

Adonai, by Arman Isayan

The Journey, by Khozem Poonawala

Stolen Lives, by Dee Arianne Rockwood

ABOUT THE AUTHOR

Lynne Bryant's forty-plus years as a nurse and nursing academic have prepared her well for creating intimate human stories featuring the unheard voices of ordinary women. Lynne is the author of two previous novels: *Catfish Alley* and *Alligator Lake*. She and her wife share a home with their three dogs—and occasionally their three children—in Manitou Springs, Colorado, where she attempts to grow flowers that deer don't like and writes novels featuring delightfully flawed women in all their complexities. Find Lynne online at www.lynnebryant.com.

Also by Lynne Bryant:

Alligator Lake
Catfish Alley